Law Maker

Susie Tate

G. P. PUTNAM'S SONS
New York

PUTNAM
— EST. 1838 —

G. P. Putnam's Sons
Publishers Since 1838
An imprint of Penguin Random House LLC
1745 Broadway, New York, NY 10019
penguinrandomhouse.com

LIBRARY OF CONGRESS CATALOGING-IN-PUBLICATION DATA
has been applied for.

ISBN 9798217436149 (trade paperback)

This work was originally self-published, in different form, in 2026.

G. P. Putnam's Sons trade paperback edition / August 2026

The authorized representative in the EU for product safety and compliance is Penguin Random House Ireland, Morrison Chambers, 32 Nassau Street, Dublin D02 YH68, Ireland, https://eu-contact.penguin.ie.

156275337

Content Warning

This book features scenes of domestic violence and assault, and mentions of child neglect. Please read at your own discretion.

For the survivors.
Your bravery lights the way for others.

Chapter 1

It was a dick move

Clara

"Hey Ozzie," I said softly as I took one of the tiny chairs at the timeout table.

Ozzie gave me one brief, furious look, then crossed his arms over his little seven-year-old chest and glared out of the window.

I sighed.

Since the beginning of the school year, Oscar Sterling had consistently been the most challenging child in the class. Today, he'd ripped pages out of his reading book and then thrown the book at Margot Harding. At a normal school with normal kids, maybe this wouldn't cause all-out panic, but I didn't work at a normal school. Molton Prep was one of the most exclusive prep schools in London. These were no run-of-the-mill seven-year-olds. Margot was the daughter of Oliver Harding, the Duke of Buckingham, and Oscar was Lord Sterling's son. Both of these men were utterly terrifying.

Luckily, being only a teaching assistant, I didn't have

much direct contact with parents. That had been one of the stipulations I made before accepting this job. It meant I took the lower-paid assistant role, rather than that of form tutor, but that suited me just fine. I was able to keep the lowest profile possible – something I always aspired to – and I didn't have to deal with any Dukes of this or Lords of that on a regular basis. Given my almost crippling shyness when it came to adults, coupled with my unusual… circumstances, which made anonymity of vital importance, even the school agreed that this was for the best.

Lily, the form tutor, was deep in conversation with a furi-ous-looking Margot, whose tiny body was stiff with affronted rage, her small fists clenched at her sides. Lily gave me a very brief "oh shit" look before going back to placating the little girl. We had just over an hour to defuse this situation before parents started to arrive. My mind flashed to Ozzie's dad, and my breath caught in my throat. Lord Sterling was one of the most intimidating men I'd ever seen in my life. Tall, built, dark hair, eyes so blue they were almost otherworldly, deep commanding voice (no doubt inherited from centuries of his ancestors ruling over the lesser mortals of this country). He was super scary, completely fascinating and, given that he was a barrister of all things, about the last man *I* should be obsessing over.

Luckily, someone like him would never notice someone like me. And I should be grateful for that. Lord Rafe Ster-ling was one of the most renowned criminal barristers in the country, and apparently on course to be one of the youngest judges ever appointed in the UK. Clearly not satisfied with the vast Sterling wealth, he was chasing the ultimate promotion.

For me, contact with police, barristers and especially judges was extremely ill-advised given my background. Not that I could have spoken to Lord Sterling anyway. Considering I could barely string two words together when talking to our very kind and motherly headmistress, I doubted a conversation with a man like Lord Sterling would be on the cards.

That didn't mean I couldn't watch him, though.

If there was one thing I was good at, it was watching. Silent observation had been a survival technique for me when I was growing up, and it still served me well. So, every Tuesday morning and afternoon, I would look out of the classroom window, making sure I was out of sight behind some questionable year 3 artwork, to see Lord Sterling drop Ozzie off at school and pick him up at the end of the day. Usually, he was in a three-piece suit. In the colder months, he wore a long, dark coat over his suit, which flew out behind him in the wind and made him look one hundred percent the aristocrat he was. This was one small highlight of my narrow life, one thing I let myself have just for me. I stored up those images of him and revisited them at night when I was alone.

Fantasising about the totally unobtainable Lord Sterling was the closest thing I'd had to a sex life in years.

In my fervent imagination, I wasn't mousy and short, I didn't have to wear glasses to see beyond my fingertips, and I wasn't in woolly jumpers and thick tights (all of which were either black or grey). No, I dressed in the kind of glamorous, attention-grabbing outfits I'd seen the women in his life wear when he took them out (I may have Googled the man a time or hundred).

"Ozzie, love," I said gently again, shifting closer to his stiff little body. "I can see you're having some big feelings. Maybe we could talk about them. You know it's not okay to rip up books, and it's definitely *not* okay to throw them at other children."

"I hate books," he mumbled, still staring out of the window. "And I *hate* Margot."

"Hate's a very strong word, Ozzie. Margot's your friend. I think she'd be really sad if she thought you hated her."

Ozzie shifted on his chair and glanced over at Margot who was still talking to Lily. "She's a know-it-all teacher's pet."

My eyebrows went up at that. "Teacher's pet? Really, Ozzie?" I didn't argue with the know-it-all comment – that one was fairly accurate – but Margot Harding was anything but a teacher's pet. She was a great kid, but submitting to authority was *not* her strong suit. "Hun, she locked Mrs MacGraw in the supply cupboard when she was filling in for me last week."

The corner of Ozzie's mouth lifted in a small smile. "Yeah, that was funny."

I bit my lips to stop myself smiling too. In all honesty, it *was* funny. Mrs MacGraw was a stuck-up bitch. Still, Margot shouldn't have done it. I bumped Ozzie gently with my shoulder.

"Why don't you tell me what made you sad?"

He looked down at his lap and his shoulders slumped. When he spoke, his voice was only just above a whisper, and I had to strain to make out the words.

"I still can't read very good."

I swallowed past the lump in my throat. He sounded so completely defeated. His defiance from earlier evaporated, and insecurity took its place.

"Ozzie, we've talked about this, love," I said softly. "You find reading a little bit tricky, and I think that's because your brain muddles the letters up a bit. But there are lots we're going to do to help. Are you finding the new books easier?"

I had started the assessments for dyslexia with Ozzie two weeks ago. Even this early, I could tell that he was profoundly affected, so I'd gone ahead and bought some resources. The books he was using now had dyslexia-friendly fonts with wider-spaced lines, and some, like the one he'd ripped the pages out of, had coloured paper instead of white, all of which might help Ozzie make better sense of the words.

"Margot asked why my paper was yellow," Ozzie mumbled. "She thinks I'm stupid."

"Did she say that?" I asked in surprise. Margot was a handful, but she wasn't a cruel child.

"No, I guess not," said Ozzie as he scuffed his shoe on the floor.

"Ozzie, do *you* think you're stupid?" I said in a quiet voice. He shrugged and my chest ached again. "Sweetie, we've gone over this as well. Having dyslexia doesn't mean you're stupid. It just means you've got a different type of brain. That can actually be helpful for some things. Some of the most successful people in the world have dyslexia. Thinking differently isn't always a bad thing. Do you think Einstein's stupid?"

Ozzie shrugged again and I decided to go for someone a little more modern. "How about Tom Cruise?"

That got his attention. His little body shifted so he was facing me a little more and he blinked up at me with the startling blue eyes he'd inherited from his father. "Tom Cruise has dyslexia?"

"Yes, and whatever anyone says about the man, nobody thinks he's stupid, do they?"

Ozzie considered this for a minute and then slowly shook his head.

"I happen to think that you're very clever, Ozzie," I told him. "All we have to do is help your brain out a bit with the muddling up the letters thing, and then there'll be nothing stopping you."

"I shouldn't have chucked the book at Margot's head."

"Do you think you should say sorry?"

Ozzie nodded. I looked up at Lily, who was still trying to placate an irate Margot, and gave her a quick nod. Lily smiled and spoke to Margot again, pointing over to where Ozzie and I were sitting. Then Margot marched over to us to stand in front of the desk, planting her feet wide and putting her hands on her hips. She looked like a seven-year-old unexploded bomb of attitude.

"Hey, Margot," I said, "Ozzie has something to say to you."

"Sorry," muttered Ozzie at his lap.

Margot tilted her head to the side. "I'm gonna need more than that, Oscar Sterling," she said with all the sass I had expected.

"I shouldn't've chucked a book at your head," he said a little more clearly, but still not giving her eye contact. "It was a dick move."

"Oscar!" I admonished. "That was a bad word. You know we can't use those words at school."

Okay, so it wasn't ideal that Oscar used the d-word, but at least now Margot was smiling.

"Yeah," she said. "It *was* a dick move."

"Margot!"

"Why'd you do it?" Margot asked, her attitude-laden pose from before relaxing somewhat.

"Dunno," muttered Ozzie.

"Yeah, you do," she countered, scowling down at him.

"My brain works funny, and I was embarrassed," Ozzie said eventually.

"Funny how?" Margot asked, her eyebrows going up and her head tilting to the side.

Ozzie scuffed the floor again with his shoe. "I get my letters mixed up."

"Oh, you mean *dyslexia*," Margot said, and Ozzie blinked at her in surprise.

"Er... yeah," he said. "That's it."

"Well, what's the big bloody deal?" Margot asked and I rolled my eyes again.

"Margot, I am sitting right here, love," I told her. "If you could just *pretend* not to swear, that'd be great."

She grinned at me. "Sorry. Mummy's always telling me off. She blames Daddy." She turned back to Ozzie. "Well, dyslexia's not a big deal. My cousin's got it, and she gets to go to her own special room for exams, which is way cooler than the exam room. She gets snacks and everything cause her exam is longer. Last time, she had a *whole packet* of Jaffa Cakes."

"Snacks?" Ozzie asked, perking up significantly. "Hey, Miss Clara. You never mentioned the snacks!"

"Er... right, yes. Not always the first thing I think of to discuss."

"Well, it should be," Ozzie said in disbelief. "I love snacks. Especially Jaffa Cakes."

I suppressed a smile again. "Right, I'll lead with the snack info in future."

Margot huffed. "Okay, Ozzie, you're forgiven. I've taken you off my list."

Before I could ask her any more about the ominous list, she turned to flounce away.

"Feeling better about it all now?" I asked Ozzie once Margot was out of hearing distance.

"Yeah," he said, managing a small smile.

"Wanna play Awesome Alliterations?"

He perked up even more at that. Ozzie was responding really well to the games I'd started with him last week. The alliteration game helped dyslexics sort out letters and identify sounds. He was getting pretty good. I smiled at him and reached over to grab the stack of cards that we used for this game. Unfortunately, this caused my sleeve to ride up my arm.

"What's that purple blob, Miss Clara?" Ozzie asked, and I quickly pulled my jumper back down over my wrist. I cleared my throat as I kept my eyes focused on the cards I was sorting out.

"Oh, it's nothing, love," I said with a shaky smile.

Ozzie narrowed his too-intelligent eyes at me. "It looked like a big bruise. I got one like that the other day cause that di—" I gave him a sharp look and he rolled his eyes, "that punk, Lucas kicked me in the shin at football. It really hurt." He glanced around to check the coast was clear and lowered his voice. "I even cried it hurt so much, but I pretended that I got a fly in my eye. Daddy covered for me."

"It's okay to cry, love."

Ozzie rolled his eyes. "Not on a football team, it's not. Anyway, my bruise went that colour, but it wasn't even half as bad. Did someone kick you too?"

I opened my mouth and shut it again, struggling to come up with an excuse. I was usually much more adept than this at excuses, to be honest, but having the question come from a child threw me somewhat. "I... fell."

"You fell?"

"Yes, silly of me. I tripped and fell down some stairs. My arm took a big hit. But I'm okay."

Ozzie was still staring at me. It was a little disconcerting. "Is that why you had a puffed up face at the start of term? Did you fall then too?"

"Um... yes. Yes, I... fell into a door then."

"You must be super clumsy, Miss Clara," Ozzie said. When I looked at him he was frowning up at me. That tightness in my chest was back again.

I forced a laugh. "Yes, I've always been a bit flibbertigibbet. They called me Clumsy Clara at school." I lowered my voice then. "To be honest, I'm a bit embarrassed about it, so don't tell anyone, okay?" I winked at him.

"Okay, Miss Clara," he said slowly, and I quickly pulled out the Awesome Alliterations cards to distract him.

I knew you shouldn't lie to children. And I knew you shouldn't ask them to keep secrets. I *knew* that.

But some lies were necessary, and some secrets needed to be kept.

Chapter 2

Like a ghost

Rafe

"Miss Summerfield," I clipped, very close now to losing my fucking patience. What was wrong with these people? Anyone with this level of incompetence would have been fired from my chambers immediately. "Unless your first name is *Clara*, I'm afraid you can't help me."

Miss Summerfield narrowed her eyes at me and stood her ground. I was mildly impressed. Most people did not stand their ground with me; quite the opposite.

"No, Lord Sterling, my first name is not Clara, it's Lily. But I *am* your son's form teacher and, as such, am perfectly capable of answering any questions you may have pertaining to his education here."

I scowled at her and crossed my arms over my chest. I did not have time for this level of fuckwittery. "I need to speak to a *Miss Clara*," I said through gritted teeth for what felt like the hundredth time that morning. Did this Clara woman have the plague or something? Why was it this hard to have a simple conversation with her?

"Miss Clara doesn't deal with parents," Miss Summerfield said, also for what felt like the hundredth time. "She's only a teaching assistant."

"Well, she's the one my son has been talking about for the last month non-stop. And she's the one who told my son his 'brain works differently' yesterday, so I would like to bloody well speak to her *now*."

"Daddy, you can't say swears here," Ozzie said as he tugged on my trouser leg.

I uncrossed my arms to ruffle his hair as I smiled down at him. "Sorry, buddy. I'll do better, okay?"

"Miss Clara's super shy with big people," Ozzie went on to say. "She only talks to Miss Lily. I don't think she'll wanna talk to you. Specially if you're gonna use your *scary voice*."

"I'm not using my scary voice," I lied as I crouched down so I could be eye level with him. "All Daddy wants to do is speak to her, okay? I'm not going to scare her. She's a grown adult and a teacher, Oz. She can handle talking to a parent." Ozzie looked sceptical, and I began to wonder what the fuck was wrong with the mysterious Miss Clara.

"Hello, Lord Sterling." I straightened up at the headmistress's voice. Finally, someone who could make sense of this shitshow.

"Mrs Clayton," I said brusquely, straightening to my full height and towering over both women.

"Lily," Mrs Clayton said. "Why don't you and Oscar go back to class? I'll deal with Lord Sterling."

Lily let out a relieved breath and smiled at Ozzie who took her hand.

"No more swears, Daddy," Ozzie said over his shoulder as he was led away.

"Sure thing, Oz," I called after him. "I'll see you later, buddy. Have a good day."

The smile I'd worn for my son dropped as soon as they were out of sight, and I turned back to the headmistress.

"I'm not sure what sort of show you're running here, Mrs Clayton," I said stiffly. "But if I want to meet with my child's teacher, that request should be accommodated."

Mrs Clayton gave me a shrewd look. My *scary voice* certainly had very little effect on her. But then again, she'd been the headmistress of Molton Prep for twenty years, and before that she'd been *my* form teacher. Not much could scare Mrs Clayton.

"Rafe Sterling," she said in her very own scary voice, "don't you come in here and throw your weight around like I haven't seen you shove Blue Tac up your nose and cry after Molly Anderson pushed you into a puddle."

I felt heat creep up my neck. Bloody hell, she was like a damn elephant. I'd been a scrawny little shit at prep school. It was only after I hit puberty that I'd "hulked out", as my sister liked to put it. That bitch Molly Anderson had been twice my size back then. I shoved a hand through my hair and shifted on my feet just like I was a naughty nine-year-old again.

"Okay, fine, I'm sorry," I muttered, relaxing my stance as I looked toward Ozzie's classroom, then back at Mrs Clayton. "Listen, I'm not trying to throw my weight around. It's just that Oz has been talking non-stop about this *Miss Clara*. And I know she's the one assessing him for dyslexia. I have a right to speak to the person educating my son."

Mrs Clayton tilted her head to the side as she stared up at me. "Are you unhappy with her input?"

"Not exactly," I said carefully. "I mean, Oz definitely seems less frustrated now, but I need to know what's going on. He talks about her all the time, and I'm not sure I agree with all this *brain working differently* chat."

"Oscar's brain *does* work differently, Rafe," Mrs Clayton said gently. "And Miss Clara is the very best at helping children with different needs. I won't have you coming in and bullying her."

My eyebrows went up. "Bullying her? I just want to speak to the woman. I'm not sure what the hell is going on here, but you can't hide employees away from parents who are paying exorbitant fees and, in the case of my family, making significant financial contributions to the school on a regular basis."

"Now see here, young man," Mrs Clayton said in her most stern tone, the same one she used when I painted Molly Anderson's ponytail blue, "I *know* you didn't just try to use your money to get your way. I know this because I expect better from an Old Moltonian."

"Yes, Mrs Clayton," I chanted like I was back in her office as a naughty kid.

She stared at me for a moment, then let out a sigh. "You're not going to let this go, are you, Rafe?"

I stood my ground and shook my head. No, I was not going to give up until I met the elusive Miss Clara. Where the fuck had they been hiding her? I hadn't come across her at any of the school parents' evenings or functions. She was like a ghost.

Mrs Clayton looked away from me for a moment and bit her lip in a highly unusual display of indecision and concern.

"Okay, I'll see if I can set it up."

I huffed out a frustrated breath. "Can't I just see the woman now, for God's sake?"

"Don't take the Lord's name in vain," Mrs Clayton said

distractedly. She still looked like she was struggling with something. Then she focused back on me and gave me a stern glare that would have had me shaking in my plimsolls thirty years ago. "If I agree to this, you've got to promise me not to be so... well... *you*."

"I beg your pardon?"

"Rafe, honestly, you know what I'm saying. You treat every situation and every person in it like you're in your courtroom. I'm immune as I've seen you wee yourself at the school nativity but..."

"That was Ollie Harding!" I snapped. Bloody Ollie. Twenty-seven years later and I was still taking the flak for his lack of bladder control.

"Goodness, it doesn't matter now, dear," Mrs C said in her patented placatory tone. Alright for her – *she* wasn't the one being reminded of shit that went down in prep school. "What I'm saying is that you're intimidating. This girl, Clara, she..." Mrs C trailed off and looked over my shoulder towards the classroom door, her expression troubled. "She's quiet."

"She seems to have plenty to say to my son."

"No, not with the children. She has a natural affinity with the children. It's adults Clara struggles with. Her employment agreement is clear on no contact with parents."

I thought back to all the various ways Ozzie had described Clara. Everything was "Miss Clara this" and "Miss Clara thinks that," "Miss Clara told this joke and I nearly peed myself laughing" – what kind of stunt was this woman trying to pull? Clearly, she just wanted to waltz off with her paycheck and not have to face any of the tricky aspects of teaching, like communicating effectively with the parents who were *providing* her damn paycheck.

It seemed as though she had Mrs Clayton and that form teacher wrapped around her little finger too. She must be some sort of master manipulator. Did I want another manipulative woman around my kid? I'd had enough of that with his mother.

"I'm sorry, but I insist she makes an exception for me," I said firmly. Mrs Clayton stared at me for a long moment and I decided to go in for the kill. "Of course, I could always take my concerns to the governors. Are they aware that there's a teacher at the school declining meetings with parents and only answerable to the pupils? Is that something they'd be happy with?"

Mrs Clayton's face reddened and she narrowed her eyes at me again. "You always were a stubborn little blighter," she said in a low voice, and I suppressed a smile. "Fine. I'll set it up. But I need a chance to talk to her first."

I felt a wave of frustration but tamped it down. I could wait a few more hours. Tuesdays were my day with Ozzie, the one day I never scheduled court. I took him to school and picked him up every week. On my other days with Oz, his nanny did the drop-offs. Officially, I only had fifty percent custody of Ozzie. Unofficially, his mother was always fucking off to Europe and the States, so despite her having made my life hell in the custody battle, she rarely made an effort to be in the country to spend the time with Ozzie that she had fought so hard for. I was determined to give him some stability and be the parent he could rely on. So Tuesdays with Ozzie were sacrosanct, even if it pissed the clerk at chambers off.

"I will arrive here thirty minutes prior to collection time today. I presume I can meet her then?"

Mrs Clayton sighed, that troubled look was back in her

eyes again and for some reason I felt a twinge of unease. But no, I told myself. It is not unreasonable to want to meet the person my son talks about nonstop. She couldn't possibly be that pathologically shy, could she?

Chapter 3

Do you, by any chance,
actually speak?

Clara

"Clara," Mrs Clayton said, and I looked up from the French plait I was redoing in Margot's long hair. Her original plaits had long since fallen victim to her various playground escapades, and all that hair needed to be wrangled out of her face so that she could finish her painting. "He's here early, dear."

My heart felt like it was lodged in my throat at her words as I continued to try and finish the plait with shaking fingers. When Mrs Clayton had approached me earlier to ask if I would meet Lord Sterling, I'd given her a flat no. Then she'd told me that he was threatening to go to the board of governors, that it could put my position in jeopardy, and I realised I'd have to go through with it. I could not risk this job. It was a lifeline for me at the moment.

A wave of resentment swept through me then. People like Lord Sterling had no idea how terrifying any threat to your employment was when you were struggling to get by in London like me. When you *had* to live independently.

17

When going to your family for help was out of the question. I shuddered at the very thought. No, people like him just demanded stuff. They issued commands and expected us lesser mortals to do their bidding.

Work was supposed to be my safe space, one of my *only* safe spaces, and he was ripping that away from me. My bloody contract said I didn't have to meet parents, but I was guessing Lord Sterling didn't care about that as long as he got his way.

"O-o-okay," I stammered and bit my lip as I frantically tried to finish the plait, annoyed with myself that I'd let that speech impediment creep back in. I was usually really good at staying calm and talking normally at school, but of course, most of the time, I was talking to under-tens with no prospect of over-large lords interrogating me. Thankfully, I managed to finish the plait after a few more painful seconds of struggling to control my shakes. But as I was about to stand, Margot grabbed my hand with her tiny one.

"Are you okay, Miss Clara?" she asked, her blue eyes filled with concern as she blinked up at me. For someone who was prepared to lock a supply teacher in a cupboard, Margot had surprisingly well-honed empathy. I forced a smile.

"Of course I am, love. You finish off your lovely painting now, okay, and I'll be back in a jiffy."

"Daddy!" shouted Ozzie, jumping to his feet and sprinting across the room, knocking his chair over in the process. With a sickening lurch, I turned to the doorway to see Ozzie collide with the long legs of the large man filling it. He was all the way across the room, but this was the closest I'd ever been to Lord Sterling, and he seemed even more intimidating than when I spied on him from the first-floor window.

When he looked across at me, I thought I might pass out. His ice-blue eyes stared straight into mine, fixing me in place like I imagined a lion would fix an antelope. His intensity was almost too much for me to cope with. I wanted to run but was frozen to the spot. Thankfully, he looked down at his son, breaking the connection and allowing me to take in some much-needed oxygen.

"Hey buddy," he said in a warm voice which did not match his intense, icy stare from moments ago, as his hands went to his son's hair to ruffle it. Then he did something that, if I didn't already have a raging crush on the man, would have kick-started one in a serious way – he dropped down to crouch in front of Ozzie so that he was at eye level with him and smiled the most glorious smile I'd ever seen in my entire life. I heard Lily mutter, "Jesus, Mary and Joseph," from behind me, so I knew I wasn't the only one affected. Even Mrs C let out a small sigh. "You had a good day, mate?" Lord Sterling asked after giving his son a brief hug.

"Yes!" Ozzie said. "Miss Clara taught me another game which helps my brain sort out the letters, and then she showed me all the actions to the sounds and then—"

"Did she now?" Lord Sterling said, looking over his son's head and straight at me again. Bloody hell. I was not going to survive an actual conversation with this man. There was simply no way I could manage it. Lily gave me a nudge, and I stood up awkwardly from the child-sized chair I'd been perched on, pushing my glasses back up my nose and tucking my hair behind my ears. "Well, I'm going to have a little chat with Miss Clara now before the end of school," Lord Sterling continued, his eyes still fixed on me. His deep voice saying my name gave me the weirdest swooping sensation in the pit of my stomach, almost as though I was free-falling on a rollercoaster.

Ozzie looked between his father and me with a small frown on his face. "Be nice to Miss Clara, Daddy," he bossed, some of his father's tone leaking into his little boy voice. This didn't surprise me. Ozzie was a miniature carbon copy of his dad. Lord Sterling ruffled his son's hair again and smiled down at him. The swooping got worse.

"I'm always nice," he said.

Ozzie laughed at this obvious lie as Lord Sterling looked back over at me and raised an eyebrow. For a moment, I had the most outrageous urge to laugh. It was like we'd gone back in time a couple of centuries, and he was Lord of the Manor expecting a subject to do his bidding in response to a simple facial expression. Lily gave me another shove from behind, and I swallowed down the nervous laugh as I made my way over to him with leaden feet. I stopped about five yards away. Any closer, and I felt like I might self-combust with nerves.

"Miss Clara, I presume?" Lord Sterling said. I had to look away from the intense blue of his eyes, instead focusing on his tie as I nodded. "You are a difficult lady to access." I felt heat spread up my neck at the accusation in his tone. "But if you could spare me a moment of your time, it would be much appreciated. I presume your hair-dressing duties can wait for now?"

Ugh, the condescending prick was taking the piss. Well, Margot's hair was important to her. It made her happy, and making children happy was my jam. Belittling me for doing my job was a *dick move* as Margot and Ozzie would say. But then I was used to men in authority behaving like entitled dicks, so I didn't know why Lord Sterling doing it made me feel so let down. He'd demanded this meeting hadn't he? It may have been because the Lord Sterling I fantasised about wasn't an entitled, condescending prick, so the IRL version was always going to be a disappointment.

I swallowed the lump that had formed in my throat, wishing I could reply like a normal human, but knowing that if I did speak just then it would probably come out more like a small squeak and make me look even more odd. So, I just nodded again, still focusing on his tie.

"Wonderful," he snapped, his tone even more irritated than before. He swept out his arm to the door next to him, saying, "After you," as if he, rather than Mrs Clayton, ran the school.

Lily gave my arm a quick squeeze, whispering, "You'll be fine," in my ear and then giving me yet another gentle shove. I managed to make my feet move towards Lord Sterling, but in order to pass him and go through the door, I had to come within a couple of feet of him, and his proximity was completely overwhelming.

He was absolutely huge up close – well over six feet, with broad shoulders under his tailored suit; he towered over us women and all the kids.

I got a light waft of expensive aftershave and clean male scent that made my heart rate stutter then pick up at double time as I walked out of the room, concentrating on not tripping over my own feet. Lily was talking to Ozzie now and leading him away. Lord Sterling and Mrs Clayton had followed me and I heard the door shut behind us. When it was just the three of us, Mrs Clayton turned to Lord Sterling with a stern expression.

"Remember what we talked about, Rafe," she said in an equally stern voice. I blinked in shock. Had I not witnessed it with my own eyes, I would never have imagined *anyone* would have the guts to address Lord Sterling by his first name and certainly not to speak to him like he was a naughty child.

"Yes, okay, Mrs Clayton," Lord Sterling replied in a resigned tone. "You don't have to give me another lecture."

She gave a sharp nod, then her expression softened as she turned to me. "You can use the Art Room, Clara. Lord Sterling just wants a quick chat about Ozzie. Like we talked about, okay?"

I nodded again, still not able to speak, and she sighed. "Right then. I'll be back soon." This was directed at Rafe and sounded very much like a warning. As she walked away down the corridor, I had the most ridiculous urge to shout after her to come back, which was cowardly in the extreme. I could do this. I could talk to a concerned father like a normal person.

Couldn't I?

"Shall we?" Lord Sterling asked after a few moments of silence. Impatience was creeping into his tone now, and I realised that he didn't actually know where the Art Room was. I needed to start being a functioning human and lead the way, so I nodded again and turned towards the right door, opening it up into the bright space. The Art Room was the best-lit room in the building, with lots of natural light pouring in from the double-aspect windows. I moved next to the teacher's desk and then nearly jumped out of my skin at the sound of the door closing behind us. Not knowing whether to sit down, I just stood on the spot and fiddled with the sleeves of my jumper. I was looking down at the floor when the large feet, clad in expensive Italian leather shoes came into my eyeline. I jumped at that too.

"Miss Clara," Lord Sterling snapped, and my eyes flew to his for a brief moment before going back to the far safer territory of his tie. "Do you, by any chance, actually speak?"

Oh dear. Clearly, I *couldn't* talk to a concerned father like a normal person.

I started nodding again but then closed my eyes in humiliation as I realised my mistake. Right, time to woman up. I cleared my throat in an attempt to loosen up my vocal cords. His expensive, manly smell was surrounding me now, his broad chest filling my entire line of sight.

After swallowing twice, I managed a small, "Yes." I meant to say it at a normal volume but it came out as a hoarse whisper.

"Well, that *is* a relief," he said with an edge to his voice, "I was beginning to become concerned."

"S-sorry," I whispered.

Apologising was a nervous habit for me, along with the stutter I developed when I was stressed.

My brother Freddie's voice filled my head then: *"Every other fucking word out of your mouth is sorry, you useless bitch. Sorry this, sorry that. You're fucking pathetic. I can't believe I'm related to you."*

I felt that heat in my neck creep up to my face. Great, now I was full-on blushing in front of this man. He made a muted sound of impatience, and his feet shifted slightly in front of me.

"I'm not asking for an apology, Clara," he said, his tone softening just slightly. He sighed. "Listen, I just want to discuss Ozzie. He talks about you all the time, and last week he told me you said that his brain works differently."

I nodded again. Ugh, Clara, get it together and actually form words, you mumpty!

"Ozzie's brain *does* work differently," I said after a long pause, relieved that I didn't stutter and that, at least this time, my voice was just above a whisper. Lord Sterling crossed his arms over his broad chest, and I kept my eyes focused on his tie.

"I would appreciate you not filling my child's head with ideas without formally assessing him. Don't you think you're jumping the gun?"

I shook my head, frowning at that. My need to communicate how important this was overriding some of my shyness. "N-n-no," I said, annoyed by my bloody stutter but soldiering on. This was important for Ozzie and his father needed to understand it. "There shouldn't be any waiting. It's super important that Ozzie doesn't fall behind anymore, or his confidence could be affected. I—"

"Exactly what qualifications do you have to diagnose my son with dyslexia, Clara?"

I glanced up at his face for a brief moment but instantly regretted it. He was staring down at me like I was a bug under the microscope that he was vaguely disgusted by. It took all my effort to stop myself from taking a large step back to put some distance between us.

"I-I-I..." I closed my eyes in frustration and gritted my teeth. But he cut me off before I could speak again.

"Because I have not been given a formal report or informed of any additional needs with Ozzie. If I'm honest, based on this conversation – if, in fact, you can call it that – I'm doubting you have it in you to teach full stop, let alone make complicated educational judgements with your limited experience. How old are you anyway? Nineteen?"

Through the thick fog of anxiety, a sudden bolt of anger shot through me. You could criticise me for most other things – I was well aware of my abject failure in other areas – but there were no grounds to criticise the way I did my job. I was damn good at my job. Too many things had been taken away from me over the years, and this arrogant man, who thought he owned the school and everyone in it, wasn't taking this as well. The anger somehow loosened the lump in my throat, and the vague ringing in my ears blocked out my anxious thoughts. When I spoke again, I didn't stutter, and I did maintain eye contact.

"I have a BSc in Chemistry, my PGCE and a Masters in Learning Difficulties. I have been teaching for four years, and I have *never* had any of my assessments questioned or reversed. Not that it's any of your business, but I am not a teenager; I'm twenty-seven years old. When I started with Ozzie two months ago, he had behavioural issues at school, which largely stemmed from his frustration with his undiagnosed dyslexia. No, I have not given you a formal report yet. If you had waited another twenty-four hours, you could have had one. I don't rush into these judgements as it is incredibly important to get it right. The reason I told Ozzie his brain works differently is because it does. He believed he was stupid which is absolutely unacceptable as he's an exceptionally intelligent boy. I had to give him an explanation, and I'm *not* going to apologise for that."

Chapter 4

The mouse and the kitten

Rafe

SHE WAS ANGRY. IT WAS ALMOST FASCINATING TO watch. She'd gone from terrified mouse to bristling, hissing kitten in under a minute. To be honest, up until this point, I had wondered if she could string two words together.

When I came into the classroom earlier, I had trouble believing that the Miss Clara I was presented with could possibly be the one that Ozzie raved about at home. Mouse-brown hair with a heavy fringe which she used to hide underneath, thick-rimmed glasses, small pale face, tiny frame swamped in an over-large jumper, worn trainers that had seen better days. I was shocked that Mrs Clayton allowed such a scruffy individual to work at the school. Then seeing her shuffle after me like she was being led to the gallows and shaking like a leaf in front of me once we were alone, avoiding eye contact and barely managing to get her words out, was all just plain ridiculous.

Well, her chocolate-brown eyes were meeting mine now. For the first time, I could properly see her face and, with her delicate features flushed with anger, I realised that she was actually quite pretty. No, scrap that, with the thick dark lashes framing her eyes, her high cheekbones, lipstick-free light pink lips and delicate jawline set at a stubborn angle, she wasn't just pretty – she was beautiful.

"Ah, so you *can* speak," I said as a slow smile spread across my face. "I haven't been so thoroughly put in my place for a long while."

She blinked up at me a couple of times and swallowed nervously. I watched the angry flush on her cheeks fade until she was almost unnaturally pale. My smile dropped as the shutters came back over her beautiful eyes, and then I clenched my jaw in frustration when she broke eye contact to look back at my goddamn tie. For fuck's sake.

"S-sorry," she whispered, back in mouse mode.

"Apologising when it's unwarranted is a very annoying habit," I snapped. Maybe I could irritate her back into the defiant kitten again? I told myself it was because that version of Miss Clara was capable of communicating about my son, but, in reality, it had more to do with wanting to see her gorgeous features alive with anger again and not shuttered away.

"I know," she said quietly, looking past me towards the door, clearly counting down the seconds until she could get away, which pissed me off as well. The way she said *I know* didn't sit right with me. It was with a strangely resigned tone that had an almost hopeless quality to it.

My hand went up to squeeze the back of my neck – a habit I fell into when I was at a bit of a loss, which was rare. But then I noticed something. Little mouse's gaze followed the path of my arm and then watched my chest expand as I moved. Two small flags of colour appeared high on her cheekbones, and she blinked twice. Maybe she was terrified of me, but that didn't mean she was incapable of finding me attractive.

Desire shot through me so strongly then that I had to shove the hand that wasn't squeezing the back of my neck into my trouser pocket to stop myself reaching for her. I cleared my throat. I needed to get a hold of myself and sort this out. Ozzie was my priority now, and I was not in the habit of allowing my attraction to a woman influence any interaction I had with them.

"Listen," I said, then almost smiled again when her gaze snapped back to my tie. Little mouse had been too distracted to realise she was checking me out. Good. "I'm the one who should apologise."

That got her attention. She blinked in shock and then even managed a very brief bit of eye contact as she frowned up at me in confusion.

"I'm sorry I questioned your teaching ability," I explained. "But I needed to know what was going on. Like you say, Ozzie has struggled over the last few months. I want to make sure his teachers are getting it right this year, and I wasn't convinced that telling him he's different was going to be very helpful."

The mouse and the kitten were grappling for control now. That bit of defiance set her features again, and she met my eyes for a moment before focusing back on my tie.

"It will *help* his confidence to know that his brain works differently." She swallowed and squared her shoulders, clearly working up her courage again. "Different isn't always bad. He needs to understand that, otherwise his confidence will sink even lower. Th-th-th..." She broke off and closed her eyes for a second before she continued. "The games we play and the aids I use at school are helping

Ozzie. Have you noticed a difference at home? With his reading, I mean?"

I rubbed my hand down my face before I spoke again. "Ozzie won't read for me at home," I said quietly. "I've tried everything, so has his nanny, but he just... won't do it."

"Oh, I..." she broke off and bit her lip. "Well, is there anyone at home who...?" She closed her eyes again for a moment and shook her head. "Lord Sterling, is there anyone at home who might have been less than encouraging with him? Anyone who has maybe been somewhat... impatient with him when he's reading?"

I frowned. "Are you accusing me of lacking patience with my son, Clara?" My voice was low and threatening now. It was the same tone I used in court when defendants stepped out of line. Unfortunately, judging by the way Clara was now shaking like a leaf again in front of me, it may have been overkill in this situation.

"N-n-no," she stammered. Bloody hell, I'd brought the stammer back. "I-I didn't necessarily mean you." She swallowed nervously again. "There might be another caregiver who has maybe put him off. It's not always deliberate. Sometimes people think dyslexics are being deliberately lazy or obtuse when they can't see the words or understand how to process things."

I huffed. "I'll talk to Ozzie," I conceded. "But the nanny I employ is highly qualified, I assure you."

Clara made a humming noise, and I raised my eyebrows. "You have an opinion on Ozzie's nanny?" I asked.

"N-n-no, I—"

The shrill noise of the school bell cut off whatever she'd been about to say, and Clara flinched before her shoulders sagged in relief.

"I have to go," she muttered then turned quickly on her heel and literally sprinted out of the room.

Now, rightly or wrongly, with the way I looked, my bank account being the way it was and my reputation, it was incredibly rare for a woman to run in the other direction. I tilted my head to the side as I watched Clara disappear through the classroom door. And for the first time in my life, I had to resist the urge to chase after a woman.

"Oz, you know how you're not keen to read to me at home?"

Ozzie stiffened in his position perched on a stool at the kitchen island. His hand, holding a cookie which was halfway to his mouth, froze.

"Yeah," he mumbled, lowering the cookie and frowning down at his plate.

"Well, why do you think that is, buddy?" I asked gently. This was the first time we'd actually discussed this calmly without it being some sort of battle. Normally, I approached Oz with a book, told him we had to do his school reading, and he lost his shit. He'd shout at me that reading was stupid. It broke my heart, and I just didn't know how to handle it properly.

"Dunno," he mumbled, pushing the cookies around on his plate now, having seemingly lost his appetite. I climbed onto the stool next to him and scrubbed my hand down my face, searching for the right words. Why the hell was this so hard when all day at work I managed complicated legal cases with complete verbal ease?

"Was it something *I* said to you, Oz?" I asked, my heart in my throat. I knew I could be impatient and I had a bit of a temper, but I tried really hard to rein that in with my son. I had thought I'd done a pretty good job up until now. Ozzie only really ever saw me angry about his mum, and even then I made an effort to mask my frustration with her.

I couldn't remember upsetting him when we were reading; just one day, he came home and point-blank refused. Greta, his nanny, told me he wouldn't read with her either. It was weird. It pained me to admit it, but I had to agree with Clara – something was off here.

"Nope. Can I have a sleepover with—?"

"Oz, let's stick with this for the moment, right? I need to get to the bottom of it. You've got to read at home as well, mate. If I'm doing something wrong, then—"

"I'm not stupid, okay?"

I blinked in confusion. "Ozzie, I never said you were stupid. That's the last thing you are. What's going on?"

"S'nothing," he muttered, jumping off the chair. I stood to block his path before he could bolt.

"Please, talk to me, Ozzie," I pleaded. "I can't help sort it if I don't know what's bothering you." I crouched down so that I was eye level with him and put my hands on his small shoulders. "We're a team, right? You and me: we're the best team. Like *The Octonauts*, right?"

He rolled his eyes. "Daddy, I'm not a baby. *The Octonauts* are lame."

I smiled. Ozzie still watched *The Octonauts* all the time, but whatever. "Okay, like *The Avengers*." I softened my voice. "You've got to tell your team members what's going on, right?"

He blinked down at his feet, and then, to my shock, I saw a tear tracking down his cheek.

"Hey," I said gently, pulling him in for a hug. His little arms wrapped around my neck as his body shook with low sobs. I felt like my heart was breaking. "What's all this now?"

"I-I-I..." His breath was hitching too much between sobs to get his words out. I lifted him up in my arms and strode across to the sofa, sitting us down and then stroking his hair back so I could see his little red face.

"Take a few slow breaths, Oz," I said softly. "You can tell me in your own time, okay?"

He looked up at me with his tear-filled eyes. "The thing is, Daddy, I know I actually *am* stupid. I know it." There was a long pause, and I forced myself to wait for him to speak again. "I been told it."

Pure rage shot through me at that, but I tamped it down, making my voice even when I asked, "Ozzie, who told you that?"

Chapter 5

Stick to the plan

Clara

I CLOSED MY EYES, TRYING TO KEEP MY BREATHING steady.

"Zach, I'm not sure it's the best idea for me to come round there again, love," I said into the phone. My brother sniffled on the other end, a telltale sign that he was crying, not that he'd ever admit that to me. "It, um... it didn't go very well last time. And Dad's been on edge since Freddie was arrested. I think he might—"

"Please, Clara," he begged quietly, and my chest felt like it was going to cave in on itself. "I wouldn't ask if it wasn't important, but I've got my mocks next week, and all my revision guides are totally fucked."

"Language, Zach."

"For fuck's sake, Clara," he snapped. "Who gives a fuck? The f-word is probably one of the first words we heard as babies."

"We don't have to be like them, Zach," I said fiercely.

"You're not like them. You never have been. Don't start speaking like them either."

He sighed heavily. "Well, I'm going to end up like them if I can't bloody revise."

"How about that subscription to the online learning platform I bought for you?"

"I need the physical copies, Clara. You know I do. And I..." He cleared his throat. "Look, I know it's a big ask, but I need you to come over and test me as well. If you could bring those flashcards with the questions on, that would really help. I can't learn it all by myself. Not if I want to get a nine."

Zach was doing his GCSE mocks, and he was absolutely determined to do well. His driving desire was to become a vet. He loved animals to the very depths of his soul and had always wanted to look after them, even as a tiny child. He was kind, empathetic, gentle and studious – all qualities that were not held in very high regard within my family. Zach and I were oddballs as far as the Masons were concerned. Aberrations in the matrix, and they hated us for it. I'd felt horrendously guilty when I left home at eighteen. I'd never forget Zach's heartbroken little face when I walked out of the house. I'd wanted to take him with me, but even if, as a broke student, I'd had the means to support him, our family would never have let him go.

They were into possessions, you see, be that material goods, money or people. And they didn't like having their possessions removed from their control. I'd always flown under the radar as a small child, largely avoiding my father and older brothers. My mother had checked out years before I was born, so she wasn't much help. I fended for myself and then Zach after he came along when I was ten. I was always aware that my father and brothers didn't like me and thought I was totally useless, but it was only when I began showing signs of breaking away from the family that things had escalated.

But for now, I shoved all those memories down. If I had to go back to the house for Zach, now was not the time to relive all of that. His little face on the day I left swam into my consciousness again, and I sighed. Guilt would drive me back there again, just like it always did. And I would pay the price, just like I always did.

THE NEXT DAY, I WAITED UNTIL ZACH TEXTED TO SAY the coast was clear and that it was just him and Mum at home. It took Mum a good few minutes to answer the door when I knocked, which felt like an eternity as I glanced nervously up and down the road for any of my dad's cronies who would report back to him. Everyone was terrified of Frank Mason. You couldn't take a shit in this neighbourhood without it being reported back to him in full.

"Oh, it's you," Mum said, her lifeless eyes giving me a once-over as she stepped back from the door.

"Hi, Mum," I said softly. "Can I come in? I've got some stuff for Zach."

She nodded vaguely as she drifted back in the direction of the kitchen, where she was likely nursing her fifth or sixth glass of wine. Life had beaten down Marie Mason so thoroughly that now she was really only a shell of a human being. From the age of seventeen, when my father knocked her up, she'd had her spirit slowly and relentlessly crushed. I sometimes saw a flash of resentment in her eyes when she looked at me, like she was jealous that I'd managed to make it out of that house and away from the family. But Marie knew as well as I did that you could never really escape the Masons. If my family wanted me to be somewhere or do something for them, they would be able to make me do it. I only had as much freedom as it suited them to grant me. If they wanted me on a shorter leash, they could make it happen. But for the moment, I was lucky that they had bigger fish to fry.

I shook my head and turned to the stairs, taking them two at a time to get to Zach's room at the top of the house. The house was large and had over four floors. Dad had decorated it in marble and gold, like the ostentatious new-money wanker that he was. It was cold and desolate, and I hated it. I rolled my eyes when Zach didn't answer his door at my knock and pushed my way in. As expected, he was at his computer with his noise-cancelling headset on, talking to his mates as they marched around a virtual world together.

"Hey, loser," I said as I pulled one side of his head-phones off his ear. He jumped, then grinned up at me, telling his friends he had to go before he leapt to his feet to give me a hug, which squashed the books and stacks of revision cards I had in my arms between us.

"You came," he said with relief onto the top of my head. Zach had long since passed my height. He was six-foot now to my measly five-foot-two, but still skinny and gangly, not being keen on the relentless gym routine that my scary older brothers kept up with. One of the books dropped to the floor between us, and we broke apart to pick it up.

"Of course I came, you wally," I said through my tight throat. That guilt swamped me again, but I pushed it down. "Don't I always come when you ask?"

His expression darkened as he helped me unload the books onto his desk. "It's just..." he paused and swallowed, a flash of fear and apprehension in his expression, "After last time. After what happened, I..." he broke off, dumped the remaining books on his desk and then sat heavily on his bed. "Maybe I shouldn't have asked you to come, Cla-Cla."

When Zach was a baby his Rs had been tricky. He'd always called me Cla-Cla and it stuck. There was a time when he started calling me mummy, probably because I was doing all the things you would expect a mummy to do. But I had to shut that down quickly. Mum hadn't seemed to care, but it annoyed my dad, and anything that annoys Frank Mason is not a good idea. He was happy as long as his wife was immaculately turned out with a full face of make-up and perfect figure. He did not care if she was neglecting her children, but he certainly didn't want other people to know that was the case. Hence we stuck to Cla-Cla.

"Hey," I said, sitting next to a dejected-looking Zach on the bed and laying my hand on his back to rub the small circles that always soothed him as a child. "Don't you worry about that. You needed me and I'm here. Everything's going to be fine. Okay?"

"You were really hurt last time," he whispered. Zach had always done that too. He'd always whispered when he talked about me "getting hurt". One reason was likely because my dad didn't like to overhear us talking about it, but the other was because I think Zach felt like if he said it out loud it made it more real. More scary.

"Hey," I said softly, laying my hand over his on his lap. "I'm fine now. And you're going to kick butt in your mocks with all this junk I've bought you, so cheer up, geek-face."

Zach managed a small smile and turned his hand over to

grip mine. "How's work?" he asked and my smile dropped a little. He frowned in concern. "Shit, sorry, Cla-Cla. I thought talking about work would cheer you up. It always does, normally."

I shrugged. "It's fine. It's just there's this dad..."

I trailed off and felt some heat hit my cheeks. Zach squeezed my hand, and when I looked up at his face, his eyebrows were in his hairline. "You fancy a *dad*?"

"W-what?" I pulled my hand from his and jumped to my feet. "No, of course not! Why would you even say that?"

Zach grinned. "Er... maybe because you're blushing like a tomato, and you wouldn't look me in the eye when you mentioned him."

"Ugh, you're ridiculous," I snapped, putting my hands on my hips to glare at him. "I do *not* fancy this guy. He's just a bleeding nuisance."

For the past week, since my meeting with Lord Sterling, he'd been trying to engineer another meeting with me, and I'd been trying to avoid him – which I'd managed to do on most days. Unfortunately, yesterday, I'd been late leaving and he'd cornered me in the corridor, looking absolutely bloody furious.

"Miss Clara," he'd said through gritted teeth, his big body blocking my way to the exit. "I have attempted to speak with you on a number of occasions regarding Ozzie."

"Hi, Miss Clara," Ozzie said, giving me a small wave from where he stood next to his dad and a gap-toothed grin. "I told Daddy 'bout the new game and 'bout the reading level."

I smiled at him, relieved not to have to look up at his father. "That's great, love. I hope you told your dad how fantastically you did today in the reading circle?"

He nodded, completely oblivious to the waves of frustration coming off his father towards me.

"Yes," Lord Sterling snapped. "I understand Ozzie is doing brilliantly. I'm very proud of him." He ruffled Ozzie's hair and gave him one of those glorious knicker-melting smiles before looking back at me and letting it drop to a glare that made a shiver go down my spine. "And it would be *even better* if the teacher who he achieved these goals with would do me the courtesy of discussing them with me."

"I gave my report to Miss Summerfield and—"

"I'm not talking about the fu—" he broke off and glanced down at his son, then back at me, taking a deep breath before he continued. "I'm not talking about the report. That was, of course, very comprehensive. I wanted to talk to you more about Ozzie and try to—"

"Rafe Sterling," Mrs Clayton said in her firm, no-nonsense voice. "What are you doing here, young man?" God knows where the woman got her courage from. She was even shorter than I was. "You know you're to pick up Ozzie at the gates. Meetings with teachers are by arrangement only."

"Mrs Clayton," Lord Sterling said through gritted teeth, two flags of colour appearing high on his cheekbones, "that is what I'm trying to do. I need to speak to Miss Clara as a matter of urgency."

"You can talk to my secretary and—"

"I don't want to talk to your bloody secretary!" he semi-shouted. "She's standing right there, for God's sake. I want to talk to Clara *now*."

"Daddy," Ozzie said, his tone accusatory. "You gotta use your inside voice in the school. And you can't say the Lord's name in pain."

"That would be vain rather than pain, but otherwise quite right, Oscar," Mrs Clayton said briskly. "Now, Rafe, listen to your son. I'll set up something with Miss Summerfield."

"I don't want to meet with Miss Summerfield. I—"

"Off you go now," Mrs Clayton cut him off, then proceeded to actually shoo him down the corridor. If I wasn't so scared I would have burst out laughing at the ridiculous image of a well-over-six-foot peer of the realm being shooed out of the school like a misbehaving toddler.

"Sorry, dear," she said when she locked the doors after them. "He's becoming a real nuisance. Don't worry, I'll speak to his mother. She'll sort him out. I won't have him harassing my staff members. Bloody cheek."

So Mrs Clayton had put him off for the moment, but she couldn't keep him away forever. I got the impression that Lord Sterling wasn't easily put off when he wanted something.

"Right, enough about me, Zach," I said briskly. "You wanted to do some revision cards? I brought you a new set for chemistry."

Zach's face lit up as he pushed back to sit cross-legged on the bed, just like he had done since he was small, and reached for the cards. I smiled at him and handed them over, taking a seat cross-legged at the other end of the bed. It was a familiar position for us. We'd sat facing each other in this room, trying to ignore the chaos below us countless times.

"You are a massive dweeb," I teased. "I've never seen anyone so excited about revision cards."

"I've got to do well in these exams, Cla-Cla," Zach said, his expression turning serious. "I have to get out of here. I have to build a life separate from *them*."

"I know," I said softly. "And you will, Zach. You're the brightest in your year. All your teachers told me that last parents' evening."

Seeing as it was me who filled in Zach's forms for secondary school, I was the one who received the emails about school, and the one who was invited to his parents' evenings. My parents had very little interest in education, and even if they did turn up to meet the teachers, my dad would scare the absolute shite out of them, which would be counterproductive.

I'd told the school that my dad was busy working and that Mum was "unwell". They didn't seem to mind. It was a busy comprehensive and they likely had more pressing concerns than one skinny kid whose sister attended parents' evening instead of the parents.

A dark look passed over Zach's face. "I have to have the stuff to learn though. How can I do that if Dad's gonna be such a twat?"

"Just stay out of his way," I whispered, and his eyebrows went up.

"I do try to stay out of his way, but that fucker took all my books, revision notes and test cards and binned them when I was at school. I'm gonna have to lug all this lot around with me every day now just to keep it safe."

For some reason, Zach's education rubbed my father up the wrong way. Prior to Freddie's arrest, he'd largely ignored it, but since he'd lost his eldest son – likely for a good long time – Dad had refocused his efforts into putting Zach off school and instead getting him interested in "the family business". This was why Dad had gone off at me a month ago when he caught me tutoring Zach, grabbing my arm and throwing me out of the house. The only injury I'd sustained then was the bruising around my wrist where he'd held on to me too tight, which Ozzie had subsequently spotted, but it was enough to serve as a warning.

"He hasn't..." I paused and swallowed the lump in my throat. "He hasn't hurt you, has he?"

Zach shook his head, and a wave of relief washed over me.

"No, Clara, he reserves that for girls half his size or men he has restrained and kneeling in front of him because he's a fucking coward. You know this."

"I know, but without me to—"

"To use as his fucking punching bag?"

I bit my lip. Zach was looking absolutely furious now. I'd begun to worry over the last six months as he grew into his six-foot frame that all this anger he was carrying would explode out of him and put him in danger. We'd both always tried to stay out of their way, not cause trouble. But it had been easier to convince Zach that this was the right strategy when he was a scared little boy. This large, angry teenager was starting to rebel against that, and his tolerance for the person he loved most in the world being hurt was running low. Plus, I knew the tension in the house had ramped up significantly. If Freddie went down, it would get a whole lot worse.

"Please, stick to the plan, Zachy," I said softly. "Only three more years and you'll be home free. And I'm safe now."

"You weren't safe last month."

I shrugged. The reality was that even when I was at my small flat I wasn't one hundred percent safe. They knew where I lived. It was just a case of out of sight, out of mind. At first, when I left home, they were pissed off that their personal slave wasn't there anymore, but then they'd employed an army of staff and settled into a new way of life.

Their chef was actually much better than me, and Freddie (before he was arrested) got to fuck the new maid, so I knew it suited them better. And they certainly had the money for it.

My family had a *lot* of money.

"It might all be over much sooner, though," I whispered, glancing at Zach's door, then back at him.

"What?" he whispered back. "Because of the..." he paused and swallowed, his face paling as he stared across at me. "Because of the Big Terrible Thing?"

I nodded at him as my heart rate escalated. "If stuff happens soon, then... well, we might be home free in weeks, even before your exams."

"I just don't know how much more I can take," Zach said in a broken voice, his beautiful brown eyes filling with tears. "I can't live here, Clara. Yesterday they..." he paused, blinking rapidly in an attempt to dispel the tears, but one still made it down his cheek. "There was screaming," he whispered, as if someone might overhear us, "Jesus, Cla-Cla, the screaming..."

"Who was it?" I asked in a low voice. "Mum?"

Zach shook his head. "I think it was a bloke who stole part of a shipment from them."

"Did they...?" I swallowed, not able to say the unthinkable out loud.

"I don't think so. But he won't be stealing from them again. I'm not sure if he'll walk again judging by the state of him when he was dragged out. I watched from the window."

"Zach, don't let them catch you watching," I said in a panicked voice. "If something like that happens again, you know the routine."

Zach nodded slowly, his jaw clenching. "Yeah, yeah, lock the door, shut the curtains, headphones on."

I took my glasses off to rub my eyes. "Bloody hell, you'd better pass these exams. You're going to have to pay for *a lot* of therapy for both of us once you're a vet."

Zach smiled at me, and I smiled back.

But then, just as I was about to pick up the cards, Zach's door crashed open.

Chapter 6

Hurt really bad

Rafe

"Where is she?" I stood my ground in the classroom door. I wasn't going anywhere until I had answers. Clara had disappeared off the face of the earth. She hadn't been to work in over a week. Ozzie was back to being reluctant to go to school. The way he pushed his breakfast around his plate this morning was heartbreaking. He missed her, and this was a crucial time for him with the new dyslexia diagnosis.

"Lord Sterling," Miss Summerfield said in a voice edged with impatience. Christ, the outfits this woman wore. Today she was in a yellow dress that was practically neon. She'd teamed this with tights which had, if I wasn't very much mistaken, small pineapples all over them. No sane adult woman would dress this way, surely? "I've told you, Clara is not well. We've provided a perfectly good replacement teaching assistant to support Ozzie."

"Ozzie doesn't want him," I snapped, gesturing towards the classroom at the random bloke who was supervising.

45

Okay, so I hadn't been convinced about Clara's abilities, but compared to that wet lettuce, she was a fucking genius when it came to teaching. "He wants Clara. What could possibly keep her off work for so long? It's been over a week."

A troubled look passed over Miss Summerfield's face as she broke eye contact with me to look out of the window. "Clara will be back as soon as she can," she said eventually, blanking her expression when she looked back at me. "She wouldn't have taken time off if it wasn't strictly necessary. Believe me, she lives for her work."

I snorted. "Fine way of showing it, swanning off for a week and leaving my son in the lurch."

To my surprise, Miss Summerfield's eyes flashed with anger, her face flushing. Even more surprising was how she spoke to me next.

"How dare you?" she said in a low voice. I blinked in shock, for once at a total loss for words. Was this woman suicidal? "You know *nothing* about Clara's circumstances. She's..." I didn't think I could be any more shocked, but then Miss Summerfield's eyes filled with tears. What the fuck was going on? One tear fell down her cheek, and she scrubbed it away in a furious motion. "You've no idea what you're talking about, okay? For you, this is just some inconvenience. People like you are so entitled and selfish, you just—"

"Miss Summerfield," Mrs Clayton's voice sounded from the door, and Miss Summerfield broke off. Her mouth snapped shut and she gave Mrs Clayton a defiant look. "I think it might be best if *I* spoke with Lord Sterling, don't you?" Miss Summerfield gave a stiff nod and then, with jerky movements, grabbed her handbag and stormed out of the classroom.

I turned to Mrs Clayton and threw my hands up. "Did you hear that?"

She sighed. "Yes, Rafe, I heard," she said, walking over to the front of the classroom to sit down heavily in the teacher's chair. At that moment, she looked every one of her sixty-five years. I put my hands on my hips and frowned over at her.

"You think it's acceptable for a teacher to speak to a parent like that?"

"I think that Miss Summerfield is *very* worried, *very* angry and, like me, she feels incredibly helpless."

I frowned. "What are you talking about?"

"Clara will be back at work tomorrow," she said, and the angry energy drained out of me.

"Oh, right," I said, still frowning. "Well, why couldn't Miss Summerfield just tell me that?"

"I only just got off the phone with Clara. Miss Summerfield likely did not think she would be able to return as soon as she is, but Clara insists she's able to work."

I frowned. "You don't agree?"

Mrs Clayton sighed heavily. "Rafe, I'll be honest with you. I don't agree with any of what's happening with Clara. And, no, in my opinion, she's not ready to come back to work."

My eyebrows went up in surprise. "In my experience, if you don't agree with something, you tend to be upfront about it and put it right."

Mrs Clayton shook her head, and her shoulders slumped. The dragon lady I knew from childhood looked utterly defeated. What the fuck was going on?

"Not this time, Rafe," she said in a quiet voice. "Not this time."

"Maybe if you'd explain what the—"

"Just stay away from her when she gets back," Mrs Clayton interrupted me. "God knows the girl needs some peace. At least allow her that."

"Hey, Daddy!" shouted Ozzie as I walked out of the school. He broke away from his aunt to run to me, grabbed my hand and then bounced up and down on the spot. "Did you find out where she is? Are you going to bring her back?" I smiled down at him. He had complete confidence in me and my ability to sort any problem out.

"She's coming back tomorrow," I told him.

"Hurrah!" he shouted, punching the air and then turning to run to my sister. "Hear that, Auntie Poppy? She's back tomorrow!"

"I heard, little man," Poppy said, joining him in his bouncing, the two of them dancing around the pavement like lunatics – Poppy in designer heels, a Louis Vuitton dress paired with the most ridiculous sleeveless fur coat I'd ever seen. My sister dressed like a demented fashionista one hundred percent of the time, even if she was just picking up her nephew from school. "Woohoo!" They were punching the air now. Poppy nearly took out a businessman trying to pass them. I rolled my eyes and steered them both down the road before they caused an accident.

"Come on, you two," I muttered. "Let's get home before we get papped again."

This was the downside of having my famous It-girl sister look after my son. She was constantly followed by paparazzi. It was extremely tedious. But since I'd fired Ozzie's nanny, Pops was my only real option. It was tricky because, as well as running the Sterling charity foundation, Poppy looked after our Granny as well, a formidable ninety-year-old with a stubborn streak as wide as Poppy's. But Ozzie loved Poppy to pieces so we were making it work on a temporary basis. I had a huge workload at the moment in the run-in to being appointed as a judge, and I needed Ozzie to be looked after by someone he loved. Especially after everything that had happened.

After Clara asked me if there was a reason Ozzie wasn't engaging with reading at home, I'd started asking questions – and I found out that not only had Ozzie's nanny called him stupid, but she'd been eroding his confidence for a while. I couldn't get the woman out of my house quickly enough. Unfortunately, although Ozzie was happier now, he still wouldn't read with me at home, and as much as he loved his aunt, he wouldn't read with her either. Poppy had cried when I told her about his dyslexia. She had severe dyslexia herself but it had gone undiagnosed right up until secondary school.

It wasn't that our parents didn't care about Poppy academically. It's just that, back then, the school she attended, whilst astronomically expensive, was fairly backward when it came to special educational needs, and our family's attitude to Poppy since she'd been a tiny toddler was that of rampant indulgence. I think that we Sterlings were just so bowled over by this happy little ball of sunshine being born into a long line of serious, boring aristocrats that we all loved her beyond reason and wanted life to be simple and easy for her. When she struggled academically, my parents just told her it didn't matter, and they never pushed too hard for assessments. When she was finally diagnosed, it was too late to catch up with the rest of her year group. She still had problems reading, especially when she was stressed out, saying that the words all blurred together if she felt under pressure.

I blamed myself somewhat as I was twelve years older, and I should have questioned everyone's assumption that she was *just a bit dim*. But by that stage I'd been off making my own way at law school, then in chambers, and I hadn't had time for my little sister. I hadn't had time for much of anything. Well, I wasn't neglecting my family anymore. With Ozzie, I was determined not to make any of the same mistakes I'd made with Poppy.

"Hey, *I* wanna meet this Miss Clara," said Poppy as we walked to my car. "She sounds like the absolute goat."

I raised one eyebrow at Poppy. "I hesitate to ask, but how on earth do farmyard animals come into the equation, Pops?"

Both Poppy and Ozzie rolled their eyes in unison.

"Greatest Of All Time, old man."

"She is as well!" said Ozzie as he jumped from crack to crack on the pavement. "Miss Clara's the bestest teacher *ever*." The news of Clara's return had seemed to revive him from the listless child I left this morning to his normal chatterbox self. "She can help you with your words too! We play games like Amazing Alliterations and the Alphabet Game. It's super fun."

"That does sound super fun, darling," said Poppy softly when we made it to the car. "You know, you're frightfully lucky. I wish I'd had a teacher like that when I was at school."

"Miss Summerfield says that Miss Clara is really special. She says that she's never met a teacher who is so good with kids whose brains work differently." As Ozzie climbed into the car and I pulled the seatbelt over to plug it in, his smile dropped a little. "She looks really worried about

Miss Clara. And last week, when she was telling us that Miss Clara had an accident, her face got all red, and her voice got all wobbly like mine does when I'm about to cry."

"An accident?" I said with a frown. "I thought she was ill."

Ozzie shrugged. "Miss Summerfield said it was an accident. She said Miss Clara was hurt really bad but they made her all better in the hospital."

"The hospital?" I said in shock. Nobody had mentioned hospitals to me. Ozzie frowned at me.

"Yes, Daddy, of course," he said as if I myself was a bit dim, "that's where people go if they get hurt really bad. I had to go there when I broke my arm after I climbed that tree with Margot, 'member?"

"Right, yeah, okay," I muttered, my hand going to the back of my neck to squeeze the muscles there before I slammed the door shut and rounded the car to get to the driver's side.

"You alright?" Poppy muttered from the passenger seat, and I realised I'd been staring through the windscreen for God knows how long without actually starting the car. I shook my head to clear it.

"Yeah, I'm fine," I said, starting the engine and trying to focus as I pulled out into traffic. "It's just they never mentioned an accident or hospital."

Poppy shrugged. "Maybe they didn't know when they talked to you?"

I felt my expression darken as I gripped the steering wheel harder.

"They knew," I said in a tight voice. "I have a feeling they know a lot more than they're letting on. I just don't know why they would try to hide it from me."

Chapter 7

Not people who are safe

Clara

"Jesus Christ, what happened to your face?" Martin said when he walked into the staff room. Molton Prep's PE teacher was not known for his tact. My hand fluttered up to the still swollen cheek and left eye unconsciously and I felt myself flush.

"Bloody hell, Martin," snapped Lily. "Bull in a china shop as usual. Let Clara eat her lunch."

Martin shrugged. "What? I'm supposed to ignore the fact Clara looks like she's gone a couple of rounds with Muhammad Ali? I'm not supposed to ask what the fuck happened?"

I cleared my throat. "I fell down some stairs."

I'd decided that the *walked into a door* or *tripped over my own feet* excuse wasn't going to cut it this time. I simply had too many visible bruises. Oh, and there was the small issue of my broken wrist.

Martin crossed his arms over his broad chest, and his eyes narrowed. "Hmm, whatever you say, love."

He was clearly not convinced but knew he wasn't going to get any more out of me, so he walked off to the fridge. Lily leaned over to squeeze my hand. She knew that I lived in a ground-floor flat. She knew *way* too much, to be honest.

I felt a twinge of unease as I smiled at her. It wasn't really safe for her to be close to me. I was naturally shy, but I also kept my distance from people for a reason. The same reason I didn't use my real last name at school. But Lily had been one of the only people to relentlessly pursue a friendship with me until she eventually wore me down. After a year of us working together now, I'd thoroughly and completely let her in. It felt so good to have someone on my side that I just couldn't resist. And Lily was my extrovert. She stood up for me, helped me fit in with the other teachers, stopped me looking like a mateless weirdo.

At my last school, I'd barely spoken to anyone other than the kids. Lily had changed that here. The drawback was curiosity, like from Martin this morning. When I glanced over at him, I noticed he was still looking at me with a troubled expression. If a man like Martin had suspicions, he was not going to stay silent. But he didn't understand. He didn't know that there was nothing he or anyone else could do.

Lily understood that now. So did Mrs Clayton.

"Do you think you should have let some of the swelling go down a bit?" whispered Lily, eyeing Martin nervously.

I shrugged. "The bruising will still take ages to fade, and I have to wear this brace for at least another three weeks. I can't be off work for that long." The break hadn't been that bad. It was only a hairline fracture and was stable enough to be supported by a wrist brace.

"Okay, hun," Lily said softly, her voice breaking a little before she got herself together again. I felt bad. Lily had done way too much crying over me in the last week. At first, when she came to pick me up from the hospital, she'd been enraged and started back on at me about going to the police.

"Surely there's something we can do to get those bastards?" she'd cried.

But it wasn't long until that rage faded to bleak acceptance. That's when the crying started. Unfortunately, there really wasn't any other choice. Snitching about this was not an option. I'd known practically from birth what happens to snitches. There weren't many rules in my family's world, but that was one of them. *Snitches get stitches* was one of their favourite sayings. I reached up to my temple to feel the threads of the stitches there. Okay, so sometimes you got stitches even if they didn't think you were a snitch. I didn't want to find out how bad the repercussions could be then. I doubted I would survive it.

Of course, there was still The Big Terrible Thing, but I'd been promised that would never be linked to me.

I was an expert at dealing with the police now. I simply ignored them until they went away. I used to come up with excuses, but I couldn't be bothered with that anymore. The police knew what had happened. What was the point of lying? But if they wanted to nail the Masons, they were going to have to do it without my testimony about assaults on me. Maybe that made me a coward, but I tended to think of it simply as me trying to survive. I wouldn't be much help to Zach if I was at the bottom of the Thames. And anyway, I'd done my part with The Big Terrible Thing. Anything else was asking too much.

Yes, Grant had been pissed off when he rang me last night. He didn't buy my "fell down the stairs" excuse, and he reminded me of my options. But I wasn't leaving London, not while Zach still needed me.

"Clara," Lily's soft voice penetrated through my dark thoughts. "Can you eat something, hun? Just a few bites. I know it's sore with your mouth, but you've got to eat something, okay?"

I nodded and lifted my sandwich, wincing when I chewed around my swollen lip. Unfortunately, I'd lost a fair amount of weight. Apart from the anxiety, which was my constant companion and always put me off eating, there was the split in my lip, which kept reopening. That particular cut hadn't actually required stitches as it was on the inside of my mouth where apparently the mucosa would heal itself. Well, I wished it would bloody well hurry up and get on with it.

As the day wore on, I felt myself relax ever so slightly. I loved my job; I loved the kids, and I loved working out what made them tick and how I could get them excited about learning. Ozzie was sticking to me like glue. He was shocked when he first saw me that morning.

"Wowsers, Miss Clara," he'd breathed. "Those stairs must have been super high."

His little face was full of worry as he stared up at me. The questions continued throughout the day. He wanted to know which bone was broken in my wrist, how long until it healed, if it still hurt, if I could see out of my eye, if my eye just "smushed". I answered all of them and eventually he settled down so that we could get some work done.

By the end of the day, though, I was exhausted and stiff. My arm had started to ache, and I had a headache building. As the kids began to leave, I sat down heavily in Lily's chair and blew out a long breath. Maybe Lily was right. Maybe it was too soon to come back.

"What in *the fuck* happened to you?" I flinched as an

unexpected, low, deep voice filled the classroom, the sudden movement jerking my arm and worsening the pain.

"L-L-Lord Sterling," I stammered, straightening in the chair and wincing again at the strain on my battered body. "What are you doing here?"

He strode into the room like he owned the place, which was how I imagined Lord Sterling entered every room. When he was in front of the desk, just a few feet from me, I had to tilt my head back to look up at him, which intensified my headache. I was suddenly tired. So, so tired. I did a long blink, wishing I could simply teleport to Lily's sofa to watch *Bridgerton* with a jar of Branston Pickle, which was the plan I'd been promised earlier.

I was staying with Lily for the moment. Not only was I too scared to go back to my flat, but with my wrist I wasn't really able to sort out food or do other basic chores. It wasn't ideal as Lily only had one tiny bedroom, but she wouldn't hear of me staying on my own until I had full use of my arm again.

"I came to see *you*," Lord Sterling said, his eyes sweeping from the bruised and swollen side of my face to my wrist. "I wanted to talk to you about Ozzie." He crossed his arms over his chest. "But *now* I want to talk to you about what *the fuck* happened to you?"

I did another long blink and let out a breath. With that breath, I seemed to expel all the fucks I had left to give. I was done. I was too tired to feel fear anymore and, anyway, Lord Sterling might be massive and intimidating, but he wasn't going to hurt me, at least not physically.

"I fell down some stairs," I said by rote. I'd repeated the same story a few times now.

"You fell down some stairs? Jesus Christ, your arm is broken."

I let out a small, humourless laugh. "Oh really? I hadn't noticed."

"Clara, I—"

"Listen, Lord Sterling," I interrupted him as I closed my eyes to shut out his too-handsome, too-intense presence. "I'm tired, I'm in pain, and I'm afraid I simply can't cope with a man like you at the moment."

There was a long silence. I really, really hoped he'd give up and go home, but the man was stubborn. When I cracked an eyelid open, I was disappointed to see him still standing there with his arms crossed over his chest and a grumpy expression. I'm quite sure the great Lord Sterling did not appreciate being ignored.

"Clara," he said slowly and with waning patience, "I find it hard to believe that the injuries you've sustained are merely the result of falling down some stairs. I'm not quite sure what on earth is going on here, but I *do* know my son missed you. An uncomfortable amount. I would very much like to have your assurance that you will not be absent from your post in the future."

I pressed my lips together to prevent the nervous laugh I could feel bubbling up.

He narrowed his eyes at me.

"I'm so sorry that my injuries have inconvenienced you, Lord Sterling," I said, still unable to conjure up the same deference and nervousness he usually inspired in me. Honestly, it was like the tiredness had crept into my very bones. I was starting to realise that I should have followed the hospital's advice and taken longer off work. But the truth was, I simply didn't want to be alone at Lily's whilst she was at work. I felt safer in the school.

The one time I went back to my flat to fetch my things, I'd spotted Skinny Pete loitering around the entrance to the tube. I knew what Dad was trying to do. He was making it clear that I needed to keep my mouth shut. In all likelihood, Skinny Pete and whoever else he'd sent to watch me would leave me alone, but I was too traumatised to completely convince myself of that. "I will, of course, endeavour to remain injury-free for the rest of my tenure at Molton Prep."

There was another long silence. When I glanced up at Lord Sterling he was frowning at me with his head tilted to the side.

"I'm a determined man, Clara," he said. "And right now I'm determined that my son receives the best possible help." His voice dropped lower then with a firm edge to his tone as he went on. "Maybe someone needs to check what the safety precautions are like in your building? *Maybe* someone needs to look into the circumstances of your injuries? And maybe I'm in a perfect position to do that."

At this point, I'd had enough. Someone looking into my building to see if it was safe, someone poking around in my life, trying to see beyond what I presented to the world – that was completely unacceptable to me and extremely dangerous. I took a deep breath in, forgetting that some of my ribs were bruised, and then winced on the exhale.

"Lord Sterling," I said, my quiet voice shaky but firm as I slowly pushed myself up to standing. I somehow needed to set this man straight. "My life is none of your business. I teach your son, and that is it. I've given you my report. There was adequate teaching assistance for your son while I was away. I-I-I don't feel that this requires any further explanation."

Ah bugger. I'd nearly got to the end of that speech without losing it and stammering. I gritted my teeth. At least I'd managed to get out the majority without sounding like a complete weakling.

"What have you got to hide, Clara?" he asked in a softer tone, and I blinked at him. His blue eyes were boring into mine as if he were seeing into the very depths of my soul. My heart rate increased, and my breathing sped up. I could feel the trickle of sweat down my spine as I stared back at him.

"I d-d-don't have anything to hide," I said. This wasn't going the way I wanted it to at all. For some reason, despite his size and muscular frame, up until now I hadn't felt threatened by him. But his current tone sent a shiver of apprehension down my spine. It seemed more dangerous than the irritation from before, and I wasn't very good at distinguishing one danger from another. The air was crackling with tension and I couldn't quite put my finger on why. I broke eye contact with him to glance at the exit. It was rare that I would position myself without clear access to an exit in a room, but for some reason, I'd let my guard down sufficiently to allow it.

Where was Lily? She said she'd only be five minutes. I really, really needed Lily to come back. I cleared my throat and then swallowed against the lump that had formed there.

"If you'll excuse me," I muttered as I started to skirt round him, but he moved fast to block my path with an agility I wouldn't have thought possible for a man of his size. I came to an abrupt stop, my eyes widening in shock. His arms had uncrossed from his chest.

"No," he snapped. "I will not excuse you."

He slashed his hand through the air to make his point, and that's when it happened.

I flinched. And not just a small movement – no, I *really*

fucking flinched. My hands went up to protect my face and I fell into a half crouch, preparing to run.

At my flinch, his angry expression was immediately replaced with shock.

"What the fuck?" he whispered, holding his hands up in surrender as if I were a wild animal he was trying to reassure. "Clara?"

I backed away, shaking my head in jerky movements.

"Clara, I'm sorry," his voice was much softer now. "Did you think I was going to hurt you? Did... did someone hurt you?"

I carried on shaking my head, unable to speak. A panic attack had set in so deeply now that I knew it would take a while to claw my way out. My ears were ringing, and my body had gone into fight-or-flight mode. I hugged my arms around my middle, forgetting about the brace for a moment, then winced in pain when I put pressure on it.

"What the hell is going on here?" Lily snapped from the doorway. Lord Sterling turned to look at her, and, to my absolute shame, I let out a very small whimper. "Lord Sterling, if you wouldn't mind getting out of *my* classroom, a place you have not had permission to enter, and stepping away from *my* teaching assistant, I would very much appreciate it."

Lord Sterling lowered his hands to rest them on his hips as he looked between me and Lily, his too-intelligent eyes narrowing with suspicion. Ignoring Lily, who gave a harumph of disapproval, he turned back to me but, this time, kept his distance.

"Clara?" he said softly, in a much gentler voice than I'd ever heard from him, even with his son. "I'm going to leave now. But I want you to know that I would never hurt you. I also want you to know that I'm not stupid. People don't react the way you just reacted. Not people who are safe. I'm not going to let this go, okay?"

I pressed my lips together and looked down at the floor.

"That's quite enough, Lord Sterling," said Lily. When I glanced up at her, I saw that her face was flushed with anger. "You can leave now," she told him.

He gave me one last long look and then turned to Lily.

"This isn't over," he told her, back to that commanding, firm tone devoid of all the gentleness from before.

Chapter 8

Non-scary voice

Rafe

"You've got to be gentle with Miss Clara," Ozzie said as he stared up at me. "And you can't use your bad words at school, Daddy. It's *really* naughty. Mrs Clayton doesn't let *anyone* use bad words."

"I promise to be gentle, Oz," I said through gritted teeth, "And I promise not to use any of my bad words. Okay, buddy?"

"Hmm," he muttered. "I bet you don't use your bad words at work, Daddy."

I suppressed a grin. Only that morning, I'd called one of the other barristers in my chambers a "fucking incompetent cockwomble". It was an accurate description. The case he was working on as prosecutor would have been better handled by my seven-year-old son, to be honest. The defendant was part of a family that headed up a large crime syndicate in east London. These crime families had a way of spinning things; they had a way of getting to the evidence, and I had a sneaking suspicion that they even had a way of getting to the prosecuting barrister. I really hoped my suspicions were baseless, but that didn't stop me from going off on a rant to my team when I found out how badly the case was being handled.

"Let's just see if she'll even talk to me today first, okay, Oz?" I said in the brightest tone I could muster. In all honesty, I wasn't feeling the least bit bright. I was feeling pissed off.

I was very, *very* used to getting my way, so the situation with Clara was totally foreign to me. But I needed to get a handle on my temper this time. Intimidating the poor girl would get me nowhere and made me feel like a total shit.

It had been two weeks since I scared the crap out of Clara in that classroom. During that time I'd dug up as much as I could about her, which was, sadly, very little. I had an address, which was a tiny flat in a dodgy neighbourhood. But I still couldn't even find out her last name. Her only real friend appeared to be Miss Lily Summerfield, and, apparently, she had no family whatsoever.

Now, I wasn't in the business of scaring women. In fact, I was in the business of making sure large punishments were meted out to men who did intimidate and scare women. As a criminal barrister, this was my bread and butter. So it galled me when Clara had looked at me two weeks ago like I was the problem.

She actually fucking flinched.

I still couldn't quite believe it. And I could not get out of my mind that look on her face. Her expression had gone from utter resignation and abject weariness when I first came into the classroom to total terror in a matter of seconds. The fear emanating from her and filling that room was so strong it felt like you could have cut it with a knife.

So I'd deliberately backed off for the last two weeks,

hoping that would give her time to heal. Hoping that she might forget how badly I'd scared her. But now the two weeks were up, and I needed her help, whether she was still terrified of me or not.

Ozzie still wasn't reading with me; the same went for simple sums or even counting the money in his piggy bank. He simply wouldn't do anything outside school that was vaguely academic. He'd even started refusing to listen when I read him a story at night. I mean, what father couldn't read their own son a goddamn story?

I'd talked to my ex-wife Sophia about it, but talking to Sophia about *anything* was a road to nowhere. The woman was so wrapped up in her own existence that she probably wouldn't notice if her son was in her house or not, let alone reading – and that was when she was even in the country. It had been three weeks since Sophia had actually had Ozzie for any length of time. I wasn't quite clear on where she even was, but when I rang her, she told me Milan. All I got out of her was, "He's fine, Rafe," and, "Stop fussing over every little thing." It was infuriating. The fact our son wouldn't read to either of us was not a *little thing*.

I got a bit further with our joint housekeeper, Martha, who told me that as far as she knew, Sophia wasn't even attempting to read with Oz when she had him. I did not confront Sophia with this nugget of information, merely storing it up for the next custody hearing. Sophia allowed Martha to work as a housekeeper at her house whenever she had Ozzie, as it suited her well and I was paying. If she suspected that Martha reported anything back to me, she very likely wouldn't let her past the threshold. It would never occur to Sophia that I might ask Martha anything. To Sophia, staff were practically invisible.

So, the only person that Ozzie would read with was

Miss Clara. Which meant that Clara was going to *have* to deal with me. I was a man used to getting what he wanted, and I was happy to use whatever means I had at my disposal to achieve that.

That was why Ozzie and I were waiting in our car outside the school, and had been for the last half an hour. We'd wait all evening if we had to. I was not going to miss this opportunity, and I was not going to put this off any longer. I let Ozzie win two more matches of thumb war before I finally saw the small figure emerge from the back door of the school. After the fruitless hour I'd spent in front of the school waiting for her to emerge last week, I had now worked out that this must be the exit Clara used.

I was hoping that having Ozzie in tow would make me less intimidating today. With her scarf wrapped firmly around her neck and her hat pulled down over her ears, I could just about see her eyes and nose. She was darting looks up and down the street like someone would jump out at her at any moment.

"There she is, Oz," I said.

"Remember to use your inside voice, Daddy," Ozzie warned, making it very clear *again* that he didn't want me upsetting or scaring his precious Miss Clara.

Just as she was about to walk past the car, I opened my door, stopping her in her tracks.

"Miss Clara!" Ozzie shouted as he jumped out of the back seat and ran to her. "We've been waiting for you!"

Clara's wide, chocolate-brown eyes went from me to my son. She pulled down her scarf to give him a shaky smile.

"Oh, hi, Ozzie. You okay, love?"

"Daddy's got a pro puzzle," said Ozzie in excitement, and I smiled.

"A pro puzzle?" asked Clara, frowning down at Ozzie, then glancing at me. "I'm not quite sure what—?"

"What Ozzie means to say is that I have a *proposal*, Clara," I said in a smooth voice as I climbed out of the car. As I rose to my full height, Clara took a small step back, sticking close to Ozzie. I didn't think before I slammed the car door shut, and when the sudden noise made her flinch, I cursed inwardly. I needed to be very, very careful here. So I rocked back on my heels as I tucked my hands into my pockets, trying to appear as non-threatening as possible. It wasn't an easy task, seeing as I was over a foot taller than her and nearly twice her weight.

"Er... hi," she whispered.

"You don't have to be scared of Daddy," said Ozzie, perceptive as always.

"No, Clara," I said gently, "you don't have to be scared of me. Really, you don't."

She forced a small laugh but shuffled even further away from me towards Ozzie.

"Of course I'm not scared. Don't be a silly sausage, Oz," she said, attempting a light tone, but the shaky quality of her voice gave her away. She cleared her throat. "Anyway, how can I help you?"

"I need a tutor for Ozzie," I said.

She frowned at me. "A tutor? What has that got to do with...?"

I turned to Ozzie. "Oz, do me a favour, mate, and get in the car, okay? I just need to talk to Clara on my own for a minute."

"Okay, Daddy," Ozzie said warily. "But you remember, you've got to be really, really, *really* kind. Miss Clara makes all of us be kind all the time. And Miss Clara makes sure that we're always gentle and use our inside voices, so no shouting. So you can't use your *scary voice*. Miss Clara's not used to it. *I* know that you give really good night-night hugs, and *I* know that you make the best beans on toast with cheese on top, and *I* know that if I'm sick, you'll get me the special hot chocolate that I like with cream and marshmallows. So I know all these nice, kind things about you, Daddy, but Miss Clara doesn't. And so if you just use your scary voice, Miss Clara will just think that *you're* really scary."

"Okay, thanks, Ozzie," I said. "That's a great character reference for Miss Clara to be going on with. I'll use my non-scary voice, I promise. Okay?"

Ozzie huffed, but he did as I said, closing the door behind him.

When I turned back to Clara, I took a deep breath in and let it out slowly. One of my hands came out of my pockets to go up and squeeze the back of my neck. In all honesty, this treading carefully thing was not my speciality.

"Listen, Clara, I'm sorry if you feel like I'm ambushing you," I said in a soft voice. "I know I scared you the last time we spoke, and I'm sorry about that too."

Her eyes flickered to my chest and arm, and my mouth quirked up at the side. Little mouse was checking me out again. I cleared my throat, and she startled, looking back down at the pavement between us.

I sighed.

"I really need some help with Ozzie," I said. "I know it's a lot to ask, but I also know that teachers aren't well paid And that you shouldn't be living where you're living."

Her troubled brown gaze shot to mine and she frowned.

"You know where I live?" she whispered.

I shifted uncomfortably. "I have a lot of resources, Clara."

Her face shut down at that. She didn't like hearing that for some reason. "Hmm," she hummed quietly. "Resources, okay." She took another step away from me and I huffed out a frustrated breath.

"Listen, we've tried everything with Ozzie. He simply won't read with us. I really need your help. You're the only person who can connect with him. All I want is to read with my son like any other father."

"I'm sorry, Lord Sterling," Clara said, shaking her head.

I'd lost her.

Jesus, this was so frustrating.

For a man who commanded everything and everyone in my work life, to have so little control over a situation and a person crucial for my son's well-being was foreign to me. I needed to make this woman understand I wasn't going to take no for an answer.

"I will pay you extremely well," I told her. She glanced up at me again, something lighting in her eyes before she shut it down.

"I-I-I don't think that I would be of any use to you," she said. "I'm sure that Ozzie would start reading with you if you just..."

"He hasn't read with me in *months*, Clara," I was getting really frustrated now, which was counterproductive. The sharpness of my tone caused her to take another small step back, and I gritted my teeth. "I'm sorry, but this is not going to improve on its own. I need your help. I need you to be his tutor, and I need it every night that I have him at home, Sunday through to Wednesday officially. Although, in reality, most weeks I have him every day."

She looked to the side and then back at me again.

"How much money?" she whispered.

Ah, we're getting somewhere, I thought. Clearly she

doesn't really care about Ozzie, but she does care about *money*. I swallowed down a snap of anger. So much for the beleaguered teacher just out for the welfare of their students. Well, everyone had a price, and disappointingly, Clara had hers.

"The pay is a hundred pounds an hour," I told her. "You'd be working from three-thirty until seven every night for at least four nights a week. So that is one thousand, four hundred pounds a week; five thousand, six hundred pounds a month. Does that sound reasonable to you?"

Clara's mouth fell open, and she gave me some rare, brief eye contact before she dropped her gaze down to my tie again. "Five thousand a month? Are you serious?"

I raised one eyebrow. "It's five thousand, six hundred, and I'm rarely anything but serious, Clara," I told her.

What I didn't tell her is that if she pushed me, I'd offer her five times that amount.

"Look," I said into the silence, "why don't you just come with me and Ozzie tonight? We'll talk about it. I'll explain the possible terms of your employment while I drive you home, and then you can make a decision. I'd need to know by tomorrow. I want you to start working for me as soon as possible. Is that clear?"

She shook her head in small movements.

"I'm not getting in your car," she whispered. "I can't. I—"

It was then something caught her attention behind me. The little colour in her already pale face drained completely away and, before I knew what was happening, she'd wrenched open the door that Ozzie had gone through into the back seat of my car and jumped in after him, slamming it behind her.

"What the fuck?" I muttered, looking at the door. I

could just about see through the tinted windows that she was chatting to Ozzie now, whose wide smile told me that he was thrilled that I'd managed to talk Clara around.

I turned to look down the road to see an elderly couple across the street and a skinny kid walking along with his hands shoved in his pockets. Nothing untoward or out of place. I frowned, pulled my car door open and slid into the front seat. When I turned to Clara and Ozzie, they were smiling at each other in the back.

"Clara," I said, "I appreciate that you are willing to talk to me about this, but if we are going to speak about your terms of employment, it might be better if you sat in the front seat of the car rather than—"

"Right," she said in a small voice. She glanced out of the window but didn't move. I cleared my throat.

"Clara, that will require you to actually disembark the car in order to move to the front seat."

"Yes, yes, totally," she said, her gaze still fixed on the outside. I waited another full minute before she finally got out of the car to transfer to the front.

As I pulled away from the curb, she was glancing back behind her still. Once we turned off that road, she sank back into her chair and blew out a relieved breath. She'd pulled off her hat now, and her light brown hair was muzzed from the wool. I snuck glances at her while I was driving. There were dark circles under her eyes behind her thick glasses. Her cheekbones were more prominent than a few weeks ago, as if she'd lost quite a bit of weight, which, to be honest, I didn't think she could afford to lose. The bruises on her face had all faded significantly, and she no longer wore her brace, but it was clear that her wrist was still bothering her. She cradled it in her lap as if to protect it from the bumping motion as we went over potholes.

"How long would you need me to tutor Ozzie for?" she asked quietly.

"Yay!" Ozzie shouted from the back. "You're gonna do it, Miss Clara? I knew you would. I knew you'd do it. I told Daddy you would. I *told* him I don't want any new nannies if Auntie Poppy's busy. I want *you* to be my new nanny. And I know you can because you told me you don't have any small people of your own at home. You said the only thing you've got at home is George the Goldfish. And George the Goldfish is fine. He can come too. You can bring him to my house."

Clara turned in her seat and smiled back at my son, and my breath caught in my throat. When she smiled, a genuine smile like just now, her tired expression faded, and she was so beautiful it was almost blinding.

Chapter 9

Close Protection

Clara

SKINNY PETE WAS WATCHING ME AGAIN. THIS WAS A huge problem, seeing as I was taking Ozzie home today, and I had absolutely no doubt that Skinny Pete would watch that too.

I sighed and rubbed my wrist absently. The ache there was an ever-present reminder of what was at stake. But I was becoming so, so tired of being afraid. People were starting to notice how it affected me. I jumped at the slightest noise – yesterday, I shrieked when Lily dropped a wooden box of crayons, and Margot felt the need to hold my hand and tell me that everything was okay. A seven-year-old child reassuring a twenty-seven-year-old woman that a loud noise wasn't going to hurt her? It was ridiculous. *I* was becoming ridiculous.

In all honesty, I knew I needed to move away from London and the constant fear. Maybe even accept Grant's offer. But I couldn't do it without Zach. I couldn't just take off without him like that.

Unfortunately, my living situation was becoming completely untenable. Lily cared about me enough not to say anything, but there was only so long that two people could share a one-bedroom flat that had the square footage of most people's bathrooms without being seriously uncomfortable – and we were coming up to the one-month mark now. If I wasn't going to leave London, I needed to woman up and move back to my own flat.

I knew my family were watching me whilst I was at Lily's anyway. I'd spotted Skinny Pete lurking behind the newsagent on her road only yesterday. Staying with Lily wouldn't put them off the scent. They'd want to keep a close eye on me wherever I was. My father wouldn't trust me to keep my mouth shut about what happened without keeping a serious handle on my whereabouts and being relatively obvious about it as a constant reminder to me not to snitch.

It was all about control with my family. Control, power, money and greed were all everyone cared about – everyone except for Zach, of course. My beautiful, caring, kind, funny, intelligent Zach, whom my family viewed as weak like me, but also as another asset to exploit due to his natural intelligence. It made my blood boil, but I was stuck. I was stuck in a halfway life where I was terrified all the time, where loud noises made me jump and where I was a shadow of the person I wanted to be.

"You okay, Miss Clara?" Ozzie asked, giving my skirt a couple of sharp tugs. I forced a smile as I looked down at him and ruffled his hair.

"Of course I am, Ozzie. Just doing a little bit of lolly-gagging."

He nodded solemnly. "Ah, I know *all* about lollygagging, Miss Clara," he said. "Miss Summerfield tells me I'm a *world expert* at lollygagging."

I pressed my lips together to hold back laughter. Ozzie had staring out of the window down to a fine art now, which was great if you're thinking up stories as he invariably did, but not so great if your teacher needed you to learn your times tables.

I turned back to where Skinny Pete had been standing, but, as was his way, he'd already faded into the shadows.

"Righty-ho," I said in a fake bright tone, smiling down at Ozzie again. "Let's get a wriggle on, shall we? Your dad texted me your address, and it's only a couple of bus rides aways so we——"

"The bus?" Ozzie interrupted in a bemused voice. "I don't get the *bus*."

"Um... well, how do you...? It's too far to walk, love."

Ozzie laughed. "No silly. Dave takes me."

I blinked down at him but followed him out of the classroom towards the school exit, waving goodbye to Lily on our way. I was ashamed to say that the only days I consistently watched the kids leaving were the ones where I was guaranteed to get my ya-yas looking at Lord Sterling from a safe distance, so I wasn't too sure how Ozzie got home on the other days. I had seen his famous aunt pick him up before, though. Everyone within a mile radius would have noticed Poppy Sterling sweeping in through the school gates with a cloud of glamour and disruption. Her laugh alone could probably be heard clear across London. But from my cowardly vantage point in the window, I couldn't see the road, so I had no idea how the Sterlings made their way home on the school run.

As we walked through the school gates, a huge black car pulled up in front of us. Then, a grey-haired man in an immaculate suit sprang out of the front seat and grinned across at Ozzie.

"Hey, Davo!" Ozzie cried, running over to him.

"Hey, little lord," Dave said through his smile, clapping Ozzie on the back and then ruffling his hair. "Good day with the other posh kids?"

Ozzie rolled his eyes dramatically and turned back to me as I approached the car with a hell of a lot more caution than my seven-year-old friend. "Dave thinks he's *so* funny," he complained.

"I'm bloody hilarious," Dave said and then reached out his hand to me. "You must be the famous Miss Clara?"

"Yes, I, um..." I trailed off, not quite sure what to say or who this man was. I did manage to lift my hand though for a brief handshake.

"This one keeping you busy?" Dave put in as he pulled open the door to the backseat for Ozzie and me to climb in. I couldn't actually remember the last time anyone had opened a car door for me. He shut the door after us and slid into the driver's seat.

"I'm Miss Clara's star pupil," said Ozzie proudly, some of his father's arrogance leaking into his tone. To be honest, this was pretty true. Ozzie was coming on in leaps and bounds now. His natural intelligence was finally shining through the mist of the dyslexia.

"Is that so?" Dave asked, catching my eye in the rearview mirror and giving me a warm look. I cleared my throat.

"Of course you're a star, Oz," I said, and Dave smiled. "Mr... um..."

"I'm Mr Parker, but you can call me Dave, love."

"Dave. I'm sorry. Lord Sterling didn't give me the

specifics and I didn't quite catch who you are in relation to Ozzie?"

"Dave drives me places, Miss Clara," Ozzie told me, as if a seven-year-old having his own chauffeur was completely normal and to be expected. "He's also a soldier." The last was said in a breathy, seriously impressed tone.

"Oh really?" I said, feeling a little confused.

"I'm not a soldier now, little lord," Dave corrected.

"I know that," said Ozzie. "But you could be if you wanted to be. Daddy said that you could protect me from anything."

Dave chuckled. "I can be pretty handy when it comes down to it," he said. "But remember the first rule, little lord?"

"Ugh, you're so boring," grumped Ozzie. "Dave teaches me to fight, but he says the first rule is to run away."

"That's right," Dave said firmly. "It's always better to get away from an unsafe situation, ex-soldier or no."

"Um, are there many circumstances when you might need to er... run away?" I asked.

Dave caught my eye in the rearview mirror again. My expression must have been more than a little apprehensive.

"Nothing to worry about, Miss Clara," he told me. "I'm a close protection officer, but it's overkill, really. There are no active threats against the Sterling family. It's just a precaution."

"Oh, right," I said weakly, settling back into the soft leather of the car. "That's good to know."

Ozzie tapped on the glass of the tinted window and grinned at me again.

"And this glass is *bulletproof*," he said with that breathless excitement. "Isn't that cool? And we've got jets on the back of the car just like Batman if we need to get away from someone, and we can shoot them with missiles from our wheels if we need to take them out. Right, Davo?"

Dave chuckled from the front of the car. "Well, the glass bit is true enough, Oz. But don't let any of this freak you out, Miss Clara," Dave put in quickly. "As I said, no active risk, okay?"

Dave must have misinterpreted my shocked expression for concern when the opposite was true. There may not have been an active risk against the Sterling family, but there certainly was an active risk against *me*. As I settled back against the leather again, I felt my resting heart rate slow to a level it hadn't been at for over a month. A feeling of calm and peace settled over me. I was safe in this car. I had an ex-soldier, bullet-proof glass and tinted windows you couldn't see in through. This was maybe the safest I'd ever been in my entire life.

And that feeling of safety only increased when we got to the Sterlings' house. It was a huge mansion in Putney. There were electric gates on the outside, an extremely complicated alarm system: it was practically a fortress.

I absolutely loved it.

Chapter 10

Emotional Safety

Clara

THE STERLING HOUSE WAS VAST, BUT SOMEHOW... COSY. I was surprised. Rafe Sterling didn't look like the kind of man to choose large, squishy sofas and velvety fabric for his living room. The kitchen was far more what I would consider up his street with its ultra-modern, minimalist vibe, but the subtle sparkle running through the vast acres of granite worktops didn't quite jibe with what I expected to be Lord Sterling's taste either. Maybe his ex-wife chose everything?

Ozzie ran straight to the biscuit tin.

"Right," I said. "Shall I make a start on dinner?"

Ozzie tilted his head to the side as he stuffed a cookie into his mouth.

"Start dinner?" he asked around his full mouth. "Whad'ya mean?"

"I mean, make dinner, Oz. You know that meal we all eat at the end of the day?"

Ozzie laughed. "You're not cooking dinner. Dinner's in

the fridge, like always." I opened up the fridge, revealing a huge homemade lasagne sitting on one of the shelves and a big bowl of salad next to it. "Martha makes lasagne on Mondays," Ozzie told me. "It's my favourite."

"Okay," I said, glancing between Ozzie and the lasagne. "Is Martha daddy's... friend?"

Ozzie frowned. "Er, I guess. She cooks all our meals," he said as if it was perfectly natural to have your own personal chef. At least, I *hoped* Martha was a personal chef and not an over-enthusiastic girlfriend. Gah! Wait! What business did I have hoping that Lord Sterling didn't have a girlfriend who made perfect lasagnes? I knew he was divorced. His ex-wife never came to the school – she must have been even more of a workaholic than him. Poor Ozzie.

"Right, where do you want to read, Ozzie?" I said, having put the lasagne in the oven. The helpful instructions written by the chef/girlfriend said forty-five minutes, so we had time.

Ozzie bit his lip and shuffled his feet. "I don't really read at home, Miss Clara. I only read at school. With you."

I crouched down in front of him so that we were at eye level. "Why only at school, Oz?" I asked softly. "I bet Daddy would love to hear you reading."

Ozzie shuffled his feet again, his face settling into an unhappy expression. "Daddy's really clever," he whispered. "Really, really clever. Everyone always says how clever my daddy is and how lucky I am to have such a clever daddy. I don't want to make Daddy sad. I don't want him to know how badly I muddle up my letters and numbers." He paused for a moment, twisting his lips to the side before he spoke again. This time his whisper was so quiet I had to strain to hear it. "I'm stupid."

"Who told you that, Ozzie?" I said, trying to keep my

voice steady despite how my chest tightened with anger. Who would tell this precious boy that he was stupid? Pigeonholing children and putting them down like this was one of the things that made me angriest when it came to teaching. "Whoever told you that you were stupid, they were wrong – very, *very* wrong. And I won't stand for it," I said. Ozzie looked at me in surprise, not used to hearing my voice sharp with anger. But the more I thought about it, the more furious I became. "Would you tell me who said that to you?"

He shook his head in sharp, jerky movements. I decided to let it lie for the moment.

"Okay, well, you know that *I* don't think you're stupid, Ozzie. So let's do some Amazing Alliterations and then we can read from your new reading book. Okay?"

It took quite a bit of coaxing and a tiny bit of bribery from the secret stash of Fruit Pastilles I kept in my handbag. But Ozzie finally caved.

IT WAS PAST SEVEN WHEN I HEARD THE BEEPING OF THE alarm system. Ozzie was curled into my side on the sofa, and we were watching *Britain's Amazing Hedgerows*. Ozzie loved hedgehogs. Apparently, there was a group called the Hedgerow Warriors, which had a monthly newsletter and was run by somebody Ozzie called Hedgehog Vicky, who sounded a special kind of eccentric. Ozzie saved all his newsletters under his bed, and we'd actually worked on reading one of those tonight after we'd tackled his reading book.

After a few moments, I heard the heavy footsteps down the corridor, and then Lord Sterling appeared, filling the room with his ultra-masculine, almost electrically charged presence.

Rafe Sterling was an absolute force of nature. In his three-piece suit, his hair slightly damp from the rain, and his jaw darkened with stubble, he was almost too beautiful to be real. For a moment, my mind blanked. I just sat there staring up at him with my mouth open and Ozzie still tucked into my side, completely under this magnetic man's spell.

"Daddy!" shouted Ozzie, jumping up from the sofa and running to his father, who lifted him up in a big hug. "I've gone up another reading level! We read a whole book tonight and one of The Warrior's newsletters. Miss Clara says I can get up to the next level by the end of term if I carry on like this. She told me I'm amazing."

Lord Sterling smiled at his son. It was the first time I'd seen the man smile close up and my breath caught in my throat. It was so bright, so white, so glamorous that it almost hurt to look at him. My belly whooshed and my heart rate, which had settled whilst feeling so safe in the house, sped up again.

"That's fantastic, buddy," Lord Sterling said as he lowered his son to the ground. "Maybe you and I could—?"

"Gotta go brush my teeth, Daddy," Ozzie put in quickly, backing away from his father. I could feel the frustration rolling off Lord Sterling as his son darted out of the room. Clearly, Ozzie knew where the conversation was headed, and he didn't want to read in front of his dad.

I felt my anger spike again from my earlier conversation with Ozzie and I jumped to my feet.

"Can I have a word?" I snapped in a voice that I didn't even recognise as my own. Lord Sterling's eyebrows went up as he looked at me. I suspected that he was not a man used to *anyone* snapping at him, least of all the meek, scaredy-cat teaching assistant who he was employing at vast expense to tutor his son.

When I stood up from the sofa, though, I lost my nerve. The height difference between us, the fact that I was in his house, the fact that he was paying me an extortionate amount to look after his son – not to mention how in all my years of being beaten down it had never been safe for me to stand up for myself – all resulted in me lowering my gaze from his, my shoulders dropping.

But then a vision of Ozzie's little face, swamped with sadness as he told me he was stupid flashed into my mind and I forced myself to look up, straight into that piercing blue gaze.

"It's really important that Ozzie f-feels safe at home," I managed to force out. Yes, there was a small stammer, but other than that my voice was still firm.

"Yes," Lord Sterling said slowly. "Of course, I thoroughly agree. That is why I have a highly trained personal protection officer in place for Ozzie and why my house has a very advanced security system."

I shook my head, dislodging my glasses, so that I had to push them back up my nose again. "I'm not talking about physical safety, Lord Sterling. I'm... well, I'm talking about *emotional* safety."

Lord Sterling's eyebrows went up. "Are you suggesting my son isn't *emotionally* safe in his own home, Miss Clara?" His tone was deceptively calm, but I could sense that subtle undercurrent of threat there. This was not a man who took criticism well. I would have normally shrank back and retreated from that sort of tone automatically, but it was the condescending way he was looking at me that triggered another snap of anger.

"Someone—" I said, my voice breaking before I swallowed past the lump in my throat to get the rest of my words out, "Someone told Ozzie that he's stupid. I asked you before if anything like that could be happening and you told me no, but Ozzie isn't lying."

Lord Sterling's defensive posture relaxed then, which only made me angrier. He knew about this? Would *he* have told his son that he was stupid? Why did that cause a huge wave of disappointment to crash over me?

"Dyslexia has nothing to do with stupidity," I said, my voice shaking with fury now. It wasn't just about Ozzie; it was all the kids overlooked and belittled for something beyond their control. How dare he make his kind, intelligent son feel less than he was? "Ozzie is very intelligent, actually," I went on. "But what he lacks is confidence. Putting him down and telling him he's stupid is absolutely counterproductive. Even if your aim is only academic success, knocking his confidence will not help, and is the absolute worst thing you should do if you care at all about his emotional well-being. I-I won't stand for it, okay?"

Lord Sterling was actually smirking now. He had the temerity to quirk one side of his mouth up as he stared down at me and crossed his arms over his chest.

"You'll not stand for it, will you?" he said, his voice sounding amused rather than angry.

"N-n-no, I won't," I said, my arms straight down by my sides and my hands clenched into tight fists. "You can't treat him like that. It's not fair. Y-y-you can't..."

To my absolute horror, I could feel the back of my eyes start to sting. Oh my God, this was probably the most unprofessional moment of my career. But I was telling this man his son wasn't emotionally safe, and he was smirking at me like it was some kind of joke.

I often felt powerless, and this was just another situation weighted against me. I didn't *really* have any say here. Ozzie wasn't *my* son. I was just an employee. Lord Sterling didn't have to take what I was saying seriously. He didn't have to change his treatment of his son. There was literally nothing I could do.

"He just doesn't deserve to be treated that way," I said, my voice small. Back to weak, pathetic Clara. A wave of self-disgust hit me then. Ozzie was just another kid that I couldn't protect, that I would fail.

"Clara?" Lord Sterling's voice was soft now, the amusement from before completely gone. When I looked up at him, I saw he had uncrossed his arms, and he wasn't smirking anymore. "Clara, hey. I'm sorry."

I blinked in shock. *I'm sorry* was not what I was expecting to hear.

"I absolutely take my son's emotional well-being seriously. Ozzie's last nanny was a fucking bitch. I didn't know what she was saying to Ozzie for a long time and he was too embarrassed to tell me. It was actually you who prompted me to look into it. When I found out, I sacked her. No one speaks to my son that way, Clara. I promise you that I kept him safe."

A wave of relief shot through me, and my tense stance relaxed. But as the adrenaline faded, the pounding in my ears changed to a low ringing, and a wave of nausea swept over me. I started to feel a bit faint.

Oh bugger.

When had I last eaten?

Whilst I was staying with Lily, I couldn't make sandwiches at her flat, so I had to pop out to get lunch every day now. But this lunchtime, when I'd spotted Skinny Pete hovering around the newsagents, I simply didn't have the courage to go out and buy anything. Lily had made me take half of her tuna roll, but I was so worked up after seeing Skinny Pete that I couldn't manage more than a couple of bites. And I didn't feel comfortable eating any of the Sterlings' food. I didn't know if it was my place. My vision narrowed as I swayed on my feet.

"Clara?" Lord Sterling snapped, panic in his tone as he stepped closer to me. Then his large hands enclosed my upper arms to hold me upright which was enough of a trigger for another adrenaline surge. This close, I could smell his expensive aftershave mixed with his own clean, woodsy, masculine scent. His broad shoulders filled my field of vision completely, his muscular frame straining under the confines of his suit jacket.

It was all too much.

I wrenched away out of his grip.

"Shit," he muttered under his breath. "It's okay, Clara."

He was holding his hands palms up now like he had the last time he scared me. It wasn't fear of him hurting me that drove me away this time, though, more fear of what I would do with him that close. A wave of embarrassment hit me then, and I moved back to sit down heavily on the sofa behind me.

Bloody hell, I thought, *this man must think I'm completely off my rocker.*

"Clara, I'm sorry," he said in that soft tone again. "I shouldn't have put my hands on you, but it looked like you were going to pass out."

"No, it, it's fine, I'm fine", I told him. "Sorry, I... er... I skipped lunch, so I'm just a bit off."

I tucked my hair behind my ears and swiped away the tear I could feel on my cheek. What I really wanted to do was put my head between my knees to help this lightheadedness settle, but I didn't want to appear even weaker in front of this man.

Then something bizarre and almost wonderful happened. Lord Sterling walked over to me and sat on the coffee table in front of me so that he was at my level. It was a manoeuvre I would never believe possible from a man like him if I hadn't seen it with my own eyes.

"I appreciate you looking out for my son, Clara," he said, and at his sincere tone I managed to raise my eyes from the carpet to meet his intense blue gaze. "I'm really fucking pleased that you'd protect him even against me, and if you ever have *any* more concerns I want you to know you can tell me. Understood?"

I nodded woodenly, not trusting myself to speak.

"Now that we've got that out of the way, I want to know why the fuck you haven't eaten lunch and what the fuck you're playing at not eating with Ozzie?"

Chapter 11

This was a command, not a request

Rafe

Okay, so I was spoilt. You could blame my parents who worshipped the ground I walked on, or my sister who thought of me as her all-knowing big brother, or my secondary school who never liked to stand up to me seeing as my family had paid for their science building... but whatever the cause, I was definitely *way* too used to getting my own way.

Now, with Clara over the last month that she'd been working for me, I certainly had *not* been getting my own way.

Since that first day when she'd confronted me about my son's emotional safety, brave, quietly furious Clara had disappeared to be replaced by shy, scaredy-cat Clara who avoided me like the plague and barely spoke two words to me.

It didn't help that I'd been allocated another new case which was proving to be extremely time-consuming. The barrister I'd called a cockwomble had proven his incompetence again and actually dropped the entire case out of the blue, which was almost unheard of so far into the proceedings. The Crown Prosecution Service had then allocated it to me. They needed an experienced barrister – not due to the complexity of the case itself (some thug who was being done for GBH), but because of the wider case that it was linked to. The thug's family – a fucked-up crime syndicate with a penchant for violence – was the target of a much bigger police sting operation which had been in the offing for months. The guy at the top was evil personified. He had some sort of God complex, loved to make people kneel in front of him before he beat them to shit. The police had been trying to take down the entire family for years and had only recently had a breakthrough. Someone from within the organisation had given them the access code to the dark web messaging system they used, which contained a motherlode of evidence against them.

The trial for the first case – against the thug – would be in a couple of months. The arrests for the second case hadn't even been made yet as the police still had the family under covert surveillance, gathering as much evidence as they could with which to nail the fuckers and bring down the entire organisation.

So I'd had no choice but to take on both cases, hence an even higher workload, meaning that I often arrived home after seven, which was when Clara officially finished. Most days, by the time I walked through the door, she was already up on her feet with her bag over her shoulder, prepared to leave. She would give me the very briefest of handovers about Ozzie, muttered directly to my tie, and then scurry out of the door like the hounds of hell were on her heels. With anyone else, I would have simply blocked their path, forcing them to interact with me. But I'd already scared

Clara twice, and I wasn't about to make the same mistake again.

The entire situation was extremely frustrating. Most things in my life I could control, most *people* in my life acquiesced to me without complaint, but Clara was totally aberrant. It was ironic that this tiny mouse of a woman was the first person to stand up to me properly in well over two decades (the last had been Mrs Clayton who never stood for "my nonsense" as she put it).

One thing that could be said for Clara was that she was stubborn. It took a week of clipped commands when I had the chance as she was scurrying out the door, and angry emails and texts from me to her before she started eating the goddamn food with Ozzie. I was happy that she looked slightly less emaciated than she had when she first came to my house, but she was still underweight. I knew some women went on weird fad diets, and I had briefly wondered if that was the case with Clara. But actually, once she did start eating, she seemed to put away a fair amount and didn't seem to shy away from carbs, so I doubted that she was starving herself deliberately. I considered the food consumption situation a small win, but I still wanted to actually speak to the woman.

She seemed to have no problem speaking to my bloody sister. Although Clara had taken over from Poppy with childcare duties, my sister still regularly made herself at home in my house. I'd arrived back last week to the three of them playing a spirited game of Uno at the kitchen table. Clara had been laughing when I walked in. A glorious sound that abruptly shut off when she realised I was in the room.

"Oh balls!" Poppy had cried dramatically. "Fun Sponge is home."

I ignored her, focusing instead on a flustered Clara who had abandoned her cards to scrabble around and collect her stuff.

"Hey, Clara!" Poppy said when she realised Clara was leaving. "You can't leave us hanging. I'm about to smash your butt!"

Clara smiled at Poppy which elicited the weirdest snap of anger in me. Clara *never* smiled at me. Poppy and Clara were total opposites. My sister was a frivolous, posh, fun-loving explosion of a person with bright blonde hair and even brighter clothing (that day she'd opted for some sort of neon romper suit, which was honestly toned down for Poppy), and Clara was shy, quiet, reserved, with a soft London accent and dark, baggy jumpers. I was surprised they got on so well but then again Poppy was so social she could bring literally anyone out of their shell. But having Clara play a game with her and bloody well smile at her was galling when I couldn't even keep the woman in the same room as me for more than a few seconds.

Well, at the end of last week, I'd finally wrapped up my previous caseload, leaving me free to concentrate solely on the new ones I'd been allocated. Therefore I was now able to execute my leave-Clara-with-no-choice-but-to speak-to-me plan. So, on this particular Monday, it was five o'clock rather than my usual seven o'clock when I pushed into the house and reset the alarm system.

My eyebrows went up in surprise when I heard the music blasting from down the corridor. I followed the noise and stopped dead at the doorway to the kitchen. Ozzie and Clara had their backs to me, and they were doing some sort of bizarre dance routine which involved much flailing of arms and bouncing on the spot. When they both dropped down to the floor on their arses and spun around to face me, Clara froze.

Her normally pale face was flushed, she was grinning, her light brown hair was up in a high ponytail, she wasn't wearing her glasses, and her fringe was slightly damp with sweat. She'd also ditched her normal oversized jumper, leaving her in a skin-tight tank top, which I was quite sure she had not meant for anyone but Ozzie to see. My mouth went dry. Yes, she was too scrawny for my usual taste, but clearly the woman did have some curves under all those baggy clothes. I watched, spellbound as she stumbled to her feet. Her top moulded to her small breasts, then down to reveal a slither of flat stomach where the material had ridden up. Her jeans sat low on her hips which flared out slightly from her tiny waist.

"Daddy!" Ozzie shouted as he jumped to his feet and ran to me, colliding full force with my legs and throwing his arms around them. I smiled and squatted down to give him a hug. "Clara's helping me practise for the play!" he shouted right into my ear, likely blowing straight through my eardrum. I pulled back to look at his excited face and save myself from permanent deafness.

"Is that right?" I said, my gaze going from his to over his head where Clara was standing. She blinked a couple of times in our direction before moving towards the kitchen table with her arms outstretched. I frowned when she started feeling the surface of the table, then I saw her glasses in among a load of other clutter and realised that she was struggling to find them. So I patted Ozzie on the shoulder a couple of times and pushed up to standing, striding to the table and grabbing the glasses just before her fingers were about to close over them. When her hand brushed mine, she pulled back fast as if I'd given her an electric shock. I picked up her glasses and then moved so that I was standing directly in front of her. Once I'd opened the arms, I lifted them up and slid them onto her nose. Her hands came up to cover mine at her ears briefly before she leapt back.

"I-I-I didn't realise that you'd be home so early," she said. "I can... I'll just..." She reached for her jumper and threw it over her head, dislodging her glasses and her high ponytail. Once her jumper was on, she pushed her glasses back up her nose and tucked her hair behind her ears, shooting me another nervous glance. "Well, if there's nothing else, I probably should go. But, um, I might have..." She cleared her throat and risked a small moment of eye contact before looking back at my tie. "I might have made dinner tonight. It's just meatballs, but Ozzie said that he, um, he really wanted that today, so... I picked up some ingredients at lunchtime and made it for him. I hope you don't mind." Why the fuck would I mind her buying food and cooking for my son? "So I'll just be going, okay?"

She practically ran for the door then but it was Ozzie that blocked her way this time, his small body bristling in outrage as he put his hands on his hips and scowled up at her.

"Miss Clara, you've got to stay. You told me you would do the *whole dance* with me, and you still haven't eaten your supper. Daddy says it's super important I make you eat supper."

I smiled. Ozzie was sounding more and more like me every day.

Clara gave Ozzie a strained smile. "Um, well, Oz. Your dad's home now, so I should probably get going. You won't want me hanging around."

"Clara," I said in a soft but firm tone that got her attention immediately. Both Clara and Ozzie turned to me. "I believe that I am paying you until seven this evening. That's not for two hours."

She blinked. "Uh... okay, well, you can maybe just, uh... dock my wages? I don't want to intrude on you and Ozzie and—"

"Clara," I interrupted her stuttering. "You're staying." There could be no confusion about my tone. This was a command, not a request.

She snapped her mouth shut. Her gaze flicked to the exit and then back to me. I could tell that she wanted to run. I could tell that she wanted to tell me where to shove the two hours I was insisting on. But, disappointingly, that fire in her eyes settled into defeat, and she swallowed before she spoke again.

"Right," she said in a small voice, and I frowned.

Ugh, tell me I'm a bossy prick, why don't you? Tell me to fuck off. Don't just give in without a fight. I opened my mouth to speak again, maybe even to take back my words and let her go home, but just then the pasta boiled over, the lid clattering on the metal.

"Crap," Clara squeaked before she jogged over to the stove, giving me a wide berth on her way there. Clearly flustered and not quite thinking properly, once she'd taken the saucepan over to the sink, her hand closed over the lid handle, and she jerked back, wincing in pain. "Shit," she said under her breath and then gave me a worried look. "Sorry, sorry. I don't usually swear in front of Ozzie, I promise."

I shook my head. Why was she worried about swear words when she'd burnt her hand?

She started backing away from the sink, and I'd had enough. Did this woman have no common sense? How was she in charge of children? Before she could back away any further, I strode over to her, covering the distance in only a few long strides and took her hand in both of mine. She sucked in a shocked breath as I stared down at the red burn marks forming on her fingers. Her hand looked tiny in mine. Without wasting time, I crowded her back over to the sink, turned on the cold water and then held her hand underneath the spray, both my arms around her and her back to my front, my body completely enclosing hers. She stiffened in fear and stopped breathing altogether.

"Breathe, Clara," I murmured low, just above her ear. I didn't want her nearly passing out again. At my instruction, she took a deep shuddering breath in and let it out slowly.

"It's fine, I'm fine," she said, attempting to pull her hand away from mine and away from the cold water.

"Keep still," I told her, my voice hoarse now as her small body moved against mine. Fucking hell, I needed to get a hold of myself and not get hard for my son's goddamn nanny. This close, I could smell the lavender and citrus scent of her hair, and a wave of desire stronger than I'd felt in a long time shot through me.

Why couldn't I have felt this way on my date last weekend? Ever since I'd met this small, shy, weirdly nervous woman, I didn't seem to work properly in the libido department. Being close to other women felt strangely incorrect.

"I-I-I can do it," she whispered.

"You don't have the best track record of self-care, Clara," I told her. A small blister was forming on the skin of her hand now. "This has to stay under running cold water for at least ten minutes."

"Yes, listen to Daddy," Ozzie said from beside us. He was peering around me, trying to see Clara's hand. "He always knows what to do when I get hurt."

"Everyone should always listen to me, Oz," I said. Clara

huffed, and I smiled. That little huff was the most backbone she'd shown me in a while.

"The p-pasta needs draining," she said, attempting to pull her hand from mine again.

"Can I trust you to keep your hand under the water?" I asked.

She nodded, and I moved back, taking the pasta to the other sink to drain.

So that was how Clara was stuck by the tap whilst Ozzie and I got the rest of the meal ready. I retrieved the meatballs from the oven; Ozzie grated the cheese.

"Oh, I can sort that now," Clara said when I started to get the plates out. I gave her a pointed look when she took her hand out from under the cold water, and she was sensible enough to put it back again. I only let her come away after a full ten minutes.

"Okay, let's see," I told her when she backed away from the sink.

"It's fine," she muttered, flexing her fingers and then hiding her hand behind her back. I gave her a narrow look but let it go and ushered her to the table.

"I can wait in the other room while you eat," Clara said, darting me a nervous glance as I pulled out a chair for her.

I tilted my head to the side in confusion. "Why would you wait in the other room?"

"Yeah, that's weird, Miss Clara," said Ozzie. "Anyway, Granny says I'm not allowed to eat in the living room, not after the *chocolate pudding incident.*"

Clara smiled at Ozzie. "Uh, right, okay, it's just I..." She looked to the side and then back at me.

"Clara," I called in a soft but firm voice, "You will be staying here until your designated work hours are finished.

That is not for another one hour and forty minutes. Have I made myself clear?"

She frowned and pressed her lips together but gave a sharp nod. Oh, there was that little spark of anger again. I smiled to myself. If behaving like a condescending bastard was going to bring out a tiny bit of fire in her, then that was what I was going to do.

"Daddy, you'll never guess what," said Ozzie once we all started eating. Clara winced in pain when she grasped her fork but covered it when I looked over at her. "Margot Harding slit my throat today. It. Was. Amazing."

I had just taken a sip of water when he made this pronouncement, and I choked when it went down the wrong way. When I'd managed to clear my throat, I put my fork down and looked straight at Ozzie.

"What was that, Oz?" I said in a hoarse voice.

"Margot, she slit my throat. It was awesome." Ozzie paused for a moment and frowned. "There needs to be waaaaay more blood, though. But Miss Summerfield pinky-promised that in the real thing there'll be a *ton* of blood. Maybe even some guts and gore and stuff."

Clara cleared her throat, and I glanced over at her. Her lips were pressed together with just the corners turned up as she suppressed a smile, and her eyes were twinkling behind her glasses. It was the first time I'd seen her genuinely amused, and she looked so uncommonly pretty that I almost started choking again.

"What Oz is trying to say is that they're rehearsing for *Sweeney Todd* at school," she said in a soft voice. My eyebrows went up in surprise.

"*Sweeney Todd*? As in, *The Demon Barber of Fleet Street*?" I said in genuine disbelief. "They're performing *that* at my son's *prep school*?"

Clara gave a helpless shrug. "Lily's a bit... alternative. To be honest, it was that or *Chicago* and I'm not quite sure that Molton Prep was ready for those themes just yet."

"And yet they're ready for cannibalism?" I asked.

"They bake people into pies, Daddy. It's bloody brilliant," Ozzie put in. "Margot's Sweeney Todd, and I'm like her *very first* victim."

"Well, there's typecasting for you," I muttered into my pasta. "Margot must be the most bloodthirsty child I've ever encountered."

"She's actually really gentle and empathic, but—" Clara broke off at my raised eyebrow.

"Last month, Margot Harding beat up no fewer than three other children," I told her something she already knew.

"Those boys were bullies!" shouted Ozzie. "They had it coming."

"Ozzie, love," said Clara quietly. "Nobody *has it coming*." She paused. "But those boys *were* twice Margot's size, and they *were* bullying Henry Moretti, so..."

"Ahh, right," I said slowly. "Henry..." I chuckled. "I wonder what Felix thought about his son being defended by a tiny little girl in the year below him."

"I think Mr Moretti is glad that those little sh..." Clara broke off and her face went pink. "I mean, those little scallywags were dealt with."

I tilted my head to the side as I looked at her.

"Is that so? You seem to feel quite strongly on the subject, Clara."

I didn't think it was possible, but Clara's face went even redder.

"I just don't like bullies," she whispered.

There was silence for a moment as the heaviness of her

words seemed to take up physical space in the room. I cleared my throat.

"So, when am I going to be watching this violent extravaganza of, hopefully, *fake* blood and cannibalism?"

The atmosphere lightened, and Clara smiled again. This time, there were actual teeth showing. Her eyes were sparkling, and she went from just pretty to almost breathtakingly beautiful as she explained the bizarre theatrical plans at Molton Prep.

I decided then and there that I was coming home early much more often from then on – and making Clara smile would be my new favourite pastime.

Chapter 12

I'm not scared for me

Clara

"You can't go back there," Lily said as we cleared up the glue and glitter from today's effort at set design. I'm not sure any other production of *Sweeney Todd* had ever involved quite so much glitter, but Molton Prep's version was certainly going to have its own unique vibe.

"Lily, I can't stay with you any longer. It's been well over a month now. House guests are like fish – they stink after three days. I must positively reek now." I chuckled, but then Lily's hand closed over mine, and when I looked up at her face, I could see she wasn't finding anything funny.

"You're welcome to stay as long as you need, Clara," she said, her expression deadly serious.

I sighed. "I know, hun, and I'm seriously grateful, but honestly, I'm pretty sure the flat is okay now."

"Pretty sure isn't good enough," Lily said, giving my hand a squeeze. She swallowed before her next words and I watched in horror as her eyes filled with tears. "I'm scared." She was whispering now and I felt a huge surge of guilt. I

99

was putting Lily in an impossible situation. Of course she was scared.

"That's exactly why I should move out, Lils," I said softly. "I don't want you scared in your own home. I should never have come to stay with you in the first place, but I—"

"I'm not scared for *me*," she snapped. "I'm scared for *you*. I'm scared of what's going to happen next time." Her voice lowered as she looked left and right, checking the coast was clear before speaking again. "Isn't there *any* way we could report what—"

"No," I said sharply, pulling my hand out of hers. "No, Lily. I've told you that is not a possibility. Not in the world I grew up in. You... you don't understand. You could *never* understand." I pushed my glasses up into my hair to rub my eyes. Bloody hell, I was tired. Sleeping on Lily's sofa was taking its toll, but the constant fear was the real problem. "Listen, I'm moving back tomorrow. I've already packed up my stuff. So I can—"

"It's not fucking safe!" she said, her voice rising in anger now and her face reddening.

"What's not fucking safe?" We both jumped in surprise at the low, deep voice from the doorway of the classroom. I dropped an entire open container of glitter which splattered all around my feet. Lord Sterling's large frame filled the doorway to the classroom. As usual, he looked absolutely incredible. When neither of us spoke, he lifted an eyebrow. "Miss Summerfield?" he said in a clipped tone. "I'll ask again. What is not safe?"

"Come along, Lord Sterling," Mrs Clayton said as she bustled into the classroom. "Let's get a move on, shall we? I know the governors are all waiting to—"

"Clara?" he said, ignoring Mrs Clayton as he fixed his intense gaze on me. "Why aren't you safe?"

"Lily's being silly," I said in a shaky voice. "Honestly, it's nothing."

"Miss Summerfield clearly does not think it's nothing. She's on the verge of tears and she was shouting so loudly I could hear her from the corridor. I'll not have my employees unsafe, Clara. I demand to know what's going on immediately."

"Clara's flat's not safe," Lily blurted out and my eyes went wide. What was she doing? "She can't stay there."

"That's all been sorted now, Lily," I said through gritted teeth. "You're being overdramatic."

"I am not being overdramatic," she snapped. Uh oh. Lily was angry, and a pissed-off Lily was not an easy thing to manage. "There've been problems there for *ages*. And nobody is taking it seriously. The area's well dodgy and the outer door's busted, so there's no security. Anyone could walk in." What Lily was saying was all true, but that wasn't why I was unsafe there, and she knew it.

"Lily, shut *up*," I muttered as Lord Sterling narrowed his eyes at us both.

"Well, I happen to agree with Lily," said Mrs Clayton and my mouth dropped open in shock. "I, for one, am tired of your safety being in question, Clara. You cannot continue living in Lily's flat, but I absolutely forbid you from returning to your previous accommodation given the known risks there." She gave me a significant look. "You can stay with me. Mr Clayton and I can make space in the office for you to—"

"I'm sorry, Mrs Clayton, but that is completely out of the question." I would not put Mrs C and her elderly husband on my family's radar. No way. "I'm returning home tonight and that is that."

I felt proud of myself. No stammering, and I was very

firm. I even had my hands on my hips. The effect may have been slightly ruined by the glitter over my shoes and lower legs, but still... *I told them.*

"That's fine, Clara," Lord Sterling put in smoothly. See, even he could tell that I was not to be trifled with. "I'll be ready to take you back to your accommodation in approximately fifteen minutes."

Er... what? Take me where? What the fuck was going on? Ozzie was with his mother currently (something that seemed to be relatively rare) so there was no reason for me to even see Lord Sterling today.

"Miss Summerfield, if you could ensure Clara remains in this classroom for the time it takes me to meet with the governors, that would be appreciated." He turned to me. "Wait here for me, Clara. I won't be happy if I have to waste my time finding you."

"Y-y-you c-c-can't—" Great, I was back to stammering. So much for standing up for myself.

"I think you'll find I *can* and I *will*," he told me. "If the property is safe, then that's fine. I'll feel better making that assessment for myself and in person."

My mouth opened to speak again, but before I could get any words out past my tight throat, he'd turned on his heel and was striding down the corridor.

"He can't take me to the flat," I whispered in horror. The very thought of Lord Sterling seeing where I lived was inconceivable. His house was on another level. My tiny studio would fit in his larder. Also, if he saw where my flat was, my obvious lie about how I was injured would be very exposed. My face felt hot, and when my hands went to my cheeks they were on fire.

"I think this is good, Clara," Mrs C said gently, coming forward so she was in front of me, then patting me on my arm. "Lord Sterling taking you to your flat and checking it is definitely a good thing. He'll make sure everything's okay." It was clear that Mrs C had absolute and complete confidence in Lord Sterling. "He'll make sure you're safe."

It was the hoarseness of her voice as she said those last words that got me. I knew Mrs C had been worried about me, just like Lily, and I knew it was taking a toll on her. She trusted Lord Sterling. If I refused to let him take me home, she'd be more worried and would probably make me stay at hers, putting her in danger.

I swallowed past the lump in my throat. As always, my choices were limited. And, if I was honest with myself, there was a small, dark, fearful part of me that had abandoned pride a long time ago. That part of me liked the idea of big, commanding Lord Sterling coming with me to my flat for the first time since I was hurt. That part of me felt safe with him.

"Is that it?" he asked as I slung my backpack over my shoulder.

"What?"

"Is that all your stuff?"

I shrugged. "Yeah."

"How long were you staying with Lily?"

I bit my lip. "Just a little over six weeks."

His eyebrows went up.

"This bag is actually deceptively large."

"My sister has handbags bigger than that bag," he told me. "She took no fewer than *five* suitcases the last time she went away for a weekend. I doubt her make-up would fit into your backpack."

I grinned. "Well, I don't wear any make-up, so that frees up a fair bit of space."

He scanned my face. "No, you don't, do you?"

Feeling awkward, I looked away from his intense gaze and fixated on his neck. He'd loosened his tie, and some of his throat was showing; it was one of the most subtly sexy things I'd ever seen in my life. I couldn't decide whether he was being critical or not, but I was inclined to believe he wouldn't approve of make-up-less women. His ex-wife certainly didn't swan around with no makeup on. The woman was almost too glamorous to be real.

I swallowed. Poor man having to lug a mousy, awkward woman across London. He probably had better things to be doing. Hopefully, he'd be satisfied with a very brief look at the flat and be on his way without any further inconvenience. I knew why he was doing this. Lord Sterling could not risk me taking any more time off, not with how important I was now to his son. Credit where credit's due – the man would do anything for his son. I was quite sure that was why he'd been making an effort over the last two weeks to come home earlier. I'd given up trying to leave each time he arrived before seven. He seemed very insistent that he get value for money and wouldn't even consider me leaving a minute before I was due. I guess he was paying for my time, and rich people tended to know their way around a pound.

And, well... it wasn't *so* bad. I wasn't scared of him anymore. Yes, he was bossy; yes, he could snap at me if he didn't get his own way; yes, he was a big man, which made him physically intimidating. But he was so kind and caring with his son it was impossible to believe him ever capable of hurting anyone. And the gentle way he put my glasses back on when I'd been struggling to find them; the cashmere coat that magically appeared for me after he'd deemed mine too thin (he said it was his sister's cast-off but it looked brand new to my eyes); the way he made an effort to never block me in or obstruct any exit when he was with me, as if he knew how uncomfortable that made me; how sweet he was with his sister for whom he obviously held great affection, even though she was his complete opposite – these things all spoke volumes about the type of man he was.

Ozzie was starting to let his dad listen to his reading now. He still wouldn't read just to Lord Sterling, but when we curled up on the sofa and he read to me he was okay with his dad sitting next to us. As great as this was for Ozzie, it was playing havoc with my hormones. Especially when Lord Sterling would sit so close that I could feel the heat from his body, and smell his aftershave mixed with his clean male scent. When I allowed myself little peeks at his strong, stubbled jawline and his broad chest under his suit, it actually felt like the desire might be driving me a little insane.

I used to date people years ago, but it never went particularly well. Fear was a real libido killer. But being close to this man over the last two weeks seemed to have woken up my long-lost sex drive.

It was getting ridiculous.

I imagined him doing all sorts of stuff that I'm quite sure in real life would scare the absolute crap out of me. Being pinned down by a large man was my worst nightmare, but being pinned down by Lord Sterling... now *that* (according to my over-active imagination) was a different kettle of fish. And these fantasies were getting dirtier and more creative by the day. He'd called me into his office yesterday to discuss Ozzie's progress whilst Ozzie watched the telly in the living room, and I couldn't concentrate on what he was saying. All I could see was the huge dark-wood desk dominating the room, and all I could think about was Lord Sterling picking me up and laying me down on it, surrounded by all that intense masculine energy.

"You seem a little distracted, Clara," he'd said eventually after I'd had to ask him to repeat himself for the millionth time. I'd bitten my lip and muttered some excuse about sleeping badly (this wasn't a total lie – my sleep was horrendous and had been since I'd been hurt). He'd looked at me for a long time. Long enough for the heat to start rising in my cheeks and then one corner of his mouth had gone up in a sexy smirk. Sometimes it was as if Lord Sterling could see straight through me, right into my depraved, sex-starved mind. It was very disconcerting.

After the make-up comment and the weird stare-down that followed, his jaw clenched in frustration before he clipped, "Right, let's get this over with," and stormed out of the classroom.

I frowned. Why the bloody hell did he offer, or rather *command*, he take me back to my flat if it was such an inconvenience for him? I was out of breath by the time we made it to his car, seeing as my much shorter legs had to practically run to keep up with him. The sleek Aston Martin was parked in the staff car park, but then Lord Sterling likely parked wherever and whenever he wanted with very little consequence. When I drew up next to the passenger seat, he plucked my backpack from my shoulder, gave it a brief, less-than-impressed look before throwing it onto his back seat, then pulled open the passenger door for me to climb inside.

"Oh, thanks," I panted as I lowered myself in. I was so close to him as I squeezed past that my breathing sped up even more.

"You are cardiovascularly unfit," he said when he slid into the driver's seat and started the car.

I bristled and scowled at his unfairly attractive profile, trying to slow my breathing down. "No, I'm not," I said, annoyed that I was still out of breath, which kind of made his point for him. "Some of us just don't have giant, giraffe legs, that's all."

"You can use my gym," he offered. His irritation from before had dissipated with my giraffe legs comment, and now he was smiling, the weirdo. Seriously, the more spiky I was with this guy, the happier he seemed. It was bizarre.

Ugh, gym? No thanks. I opted not to say anything, but he could stick his gym up his arse.

I may have been angry but that didn't stop my eyelids drooping as the car started moving. I'd barely slept last night worrying about going back to the flat, and I'd been in a state of nervous exhaustion all day.

For some reason, sitting in this expensive car with its likely bulletproof glass, next to this strong man who I knew wasn't going to hurt me, made me feel safer than I had felt in a long time. In my fuzzy brain, I didn't think to ask how he knew the way to my flat. I just rested my head back against the leather and closed my eyes.

Just for a moment.

Chapter 13

You don't understand anything

Rafe

"WHAT THE HELL?" I MUTTERED AS I LOOKED UP AT the grimy block of flats beside me. I was loath to cut the engine. In fact, I was loath to stop here at all. This place was a complete dump. Dodgy area aside, the glass in the front door of the building was smashed. What on earth was Clara doing living here? Was Molton Prep really paying its teaching assistants this poorly?

I looked over at Clara and sighed. She'd fallen asleep just a few seconds into the car journey. As she drifted off, she curled into a small ball with her arms around her legs and her head resting against the leather of the seat. Her glasses were askew now, her long eyelashes leaving shadows over her cheekbones. She looked completely at peace, and it was so at odds with her normal expression that it made me realise how much tension she carried in her facial features when she was awake. In sleep, all that drained away, so much so, it was hard to believe the woman next to me was the same person.

Like this, she was breathtakingly beautiful, and I had the mad urge to keep the engine running all night just to watch her. But that would be a bit creepy. I was Rafe Sterling, a highly respected barrister, voted most sexy lawyer in London the last two years in a row and I was *not* bloody well creepy. So I forced myself to cut the engine.

Her eyelids fluttered and then those big brown eyes opened. When she first saw me, before the fear could set in, she blinked a couple of times, and then she smiled. Not one of her small, tense, fake smiles but a real, genuinely pleased one, and, God help me, I smiled right back at her.

As our eyes held, the most bizarre sensation swept over me. A kind of deep acknowledgement passed between us. A recognition. I felt a sense of huge relief, as if I'd found something I hadn't even known I'd been looking for. Everything seemed to shift in that moment.

The universe realigned, leaving Clara and me in the centre.

Together.

But then I watched as the uncertainty crept back into her eyes, and the anxiety settled back over her features. So it was no surprise when she sat up quickly, forcing her glasses to slip even further down her nose. She pushed them back up with jerky movements and tucked her hair behind her ears, a gesture I'd noticed Clara used in moments of discomfort.

"Sorry, sorry," she muttered, and I gritted my teeth. If I never heard another sorry from this woman for the rest of my life, I would be a very happy man.

"Right, well, if we could get this over with, that would be great," I clipped, annoyed by the loss of that smile but even more so by the loss of her trusting, unguarded expression from a moment ago. "As you know, I'm extremely time-poor, and this is a major inconvenience so... Clara? Are you listening?"

She was looking beyond me out of the window at something across the street. I flicked a glance behind me, but I couldn't see anything other than a random teenager loitering outside the pub and a family coming out of the Tesco Express opposite her block of flats. Her face, once rosy from sleep, had now drained of all colour. I frowned.

"Clara?"

"Sorry," she whispered, her gaze still focused out of my window. She blinked a couple of times, then looked back at me. "Of course, you're busy. I-I-I'll just grab my things and be out of your hair." With that, she spun round, grabbed at the door, and tried to open it, but my automatic locks were still on.

"Hey," I said softly, leaning over on instinct and putting my hand over hers on the handle, my body caging her in on the seat. She took a deep, shuddering breath in and let it out slowly. "I'll take you up, okay?"

She shivered. I was close enough to breathe in her lavender scent. I affected her, but I already knew that. I'd seen the way she looked at me. The way her pupils dilated when I was close. The way she tracked my movements. The fact that little mousy Clara had a crush on me shouldn't have made me feel so lightheaded, shouldn't have made my stomach tighten in need, but it did.

For a moment I had a vision of the sleepy Clara from earlier in my bed with her light brown hair splayed across my pillow. I cleared my throat and shook my head as if to clear it. If I pounced on her now, I'd scare her to death.

"Y-you don't have to come in with me," she said in a shaky voice. I pulled back and settled back into my seat.

"Clara, I told you I would go and check the flat with

you, and I meant it. If it's true about the security situation, which from this vantage point seems extremely likely, then we need to contact the landlord."

"Oh, right. Look, Lily might have exaggerated a bit there. It's just a... slight problem I've had... in the past. But it's all resolved now."

"A slight problem?" I said, levelling her with a long look. She shrugged and I sighed.

No amount of digging had turned up the source of what Clara termed a *slight problem*. If it were a violent ex-boyfriend, then he'd covered his tracks well.

"Clara, I'm taking you inside. And that's the end of it."

Her eyes flashed for a moment and the colour came back into her cheeks.

"Fine," she snapped. "I just don't want you to feel *inconvenienced*."

I finally unlocked the car and she yanked the door open to jump out onto the pavement. When she retrieved her sad little backpack from the backseat, she didn't spare me a glance before she jogged up the front steps to her building. I caught up with her easily. She was right – every one of my strides matched two of hers. I frowned in disapproval as she simply pushed open the door. No key code, no security.

The first thing that hit me in the entranceway was the smell of urine. Good God, how did people live like this? Clara turned down the corridor and then we were outside the door to her flat. I looked at the stairs behind us and then back at her door.

"I thought you fell down a flight of stairs... at your home," I said slowly.

"Er... yes, that's right," Clara said in an uncertain voice as she unlocked the door and pushed it open.

I gritted my teeth in frustration. "Clara, you live in a *ground-floor* flat."

"Y-y-yes," she stammered, moving through the doorway into her space. I followed her and almost lost my footing when the scent of lavender and pure Clara hit me. Christ, this obsession with her was getting ridiculous.

"So why, if you live on the ground floor, did you fall down the stairs?"

There was a long pause. We were both standing in the middle of her space now, facing each other. There was a small, bright blue sofa by the window, numerous colourful rugs covering most of the well-worn carpet. A tiny table and chair, an equally tiny kitchen and the bed, all in the same room, all of which could have fitted in my guest bathroom. I mean, Clara was small, but this place was built for a hobbit, and a tiny one at that.

Again, did teachers really earn so little?

"I was exercising," Clara said into the silence, and I focused back on her face which was bright red now.

"You were... exercising?" I said slowly.

"Yes," she explained, focusing on my tie. "I run up and down the stairs to... exercise."

"*That* is bullshit."

"It's really good for you, actually," she said, not willing to back down from her lie. "You should try it sometime. And not all of us have their own bespoke gym set-up."

"Don't lie to me, Clara," my voice dropped lower in warning, and she bit her lip but after a few seconds her shoulders squared and her chin lifted in a defiant expression.

"I'm sorry," she snapped. "But it is none of your business how I choose to exercise, Lord Sterling. Now, as everything seems to be in order here, I think you c-c-can go."

For some reason, I felt a small thrill of pride at her furious rant. She'd gained confidence over the last month. The old Clara wouldn't have *dreamed* of ranting at me. Only the small stutter at the end gave away how stressed this confrontation made her.

She lost a bit of her nerve then and broke eye contact before saying in a smaller voice, "Thank you for helping me. I know you're time-pressured. Honestly, you can *go*."

She glanced out of the window, then back at me. It was a small, fleeting look, but she was definitely searching for something or someone out there, and I could feel her fear from across the room.

Clara was afraid here, in this flat. And there was no bloody way that I was going to tolerate one of Ozzie's favourite people in the world feeling unsafe. At least I told myself that was the only reason for what I did next.

"Right, come on, you're not staying here," I said, grabbing her backpack, swinging it over my shoulder and striding towards the front door.

"What are you doing?" she squeaked, jogging after me. "You can't take my backpack! I'm not going with you. I'm staying here. I'm *perfectly fine* here. Honestly, you are the most insufferable, high-handed, bossy…"

"Yep, I'm all those things," I said, "but you forgot powerful, arrogant, and very used to getting my own way. And I promise you, Clara, I do always get my own way. You *are* coming home with me. Until I can sort out what the fuck has been going on, you *will* be staying with me. Are we clear?"

Due to my job, I routinely witnessed the consequences of domestic violence. Clara was lying. There had been no fall down the stairs. It was the same old story I saw in the courts all the time. Some bloke drinks too much, takes drugs, treats his girlfriend like shit, until one day something terrible happens. In fact, I'd been working in criminal law for long enough to know that the endgame was often much more final than just a trip to hospital, and I wasn't going to let Clara put herself at risk. She'd been beaten up and hadn't gone to the police. Either this bloke was intimidating her, or she hoped to rekindle the relationship, believing he would change – I saw that often enough in the courts as well. The coercive control these manipulative bastards wielded was insane.

"This is ridiculous," she muttered as she followed me out into the corridor, closing the door behind her and locking it. I suppressed a smile. I'd expected her to put up way more of a fight over this, and I was pleased I wasn't going to have to waste my time thinking of ways to force her to come to my house. Physically forcing her wasn't a possibility. She was too easily scared for that.

I felt a flash of anger towards whichever monster had hurt her. Was that who she saw out of the window of my car? Did she see her boyfriend? Was he staking out this flat? I was suddenly completely furious.

"Don't make Ozzie worry about you," I snapped. "Don't be careless with your life. I'm offering you safety. I'm offering you somewhere to stay whilst you sort this out. Women's refuges are few and far between. You'll be better off at mine."

She frowned up at me. "A women's refuge? What are you talking about?"

"A women's refuge for victims of domestic violence, Clara. You're not fooling anyone with the fall down the stairs story, okay?"

She shook her head. "You don't understand anything."

"I understand that the man who did this to you won't stop."

She let out a long breath. "A women's refuge would never have been an option," she said quietly. I had no idea what she meant by that, but when she looked back up at me, her expression was so beaten down, so weary, so exhausted that I felt my chest tighten. "Right," she said. "You're right. I... I'll come with you."

"Good choice," I said, taking her by her elbow and steering her towards the stairs.

She let out a small, slightly hysterical laugh. "Are you pretending that I had a choice in this?" she asked. I could barely make out her next words, they were whispered so quietly. "I never have any choices."

Chapter 14

Were you guys wrestling?

Clara

I was a week into my stay at the Sterling house when it happened.

I'd moved into one of the enormous spare bedrooms, my belongings looking completely incongruous in the large, expensively decorated space. At first, I was desperately uncomfortable. I felt like a stray cat that had been taken in from the street and was having to be house-trained.

Living with the Sterlings was very different to simply working there a few hours every evening for half the week. All sorts of staff came out of the woodwork. I'd already met the indomitable family chef Martha, a warm, smiley Welsh lady in her mid-fifties. And then there was Terry, the ancient gardener who must have been at least a hundred and twenty years old. Apparently, he'd worked for the Sterling family since before Lord Sterling was born. Of course, there was also the *actual* gardener, a young man called Tim in his twenties, who came on Terry's days off to correct the older man's questionable gardening escapades. When I asked Martha about it, she rolled her eyes and told me what a big softy Rafe was. I'd widened my eyes at her in shock, but she just laughed and said that I "didn't know him well enough yet" and that "he's all bark and no bite". Well, seeing as I was *still* having those dirty fantasies about Lord Sterling, some of which involved *actual* biting on his part, that was of little comfort to me.

The physical attraction was getting worse and worse as I realised that, despite this man's size and general scariness, I was actually safer with him than I had been with most of the other men in my life thus far.

It wasn't a very high bar, to be honest, as, excluding my gentle, gangly teenage brother who wouldn't hurt a fly (but who certainly couldn't protect me), the men in my life all had psychopathic tendencies. So, coming across a man with the physicality of Lord Sterling, combined with his gentleness, was a heady combination for me. Any hint of defiance I'd displayed previously had always been met with immediate retribution from the men in my family, but Lord Sterling seemed to love me giving him shit. It was completely bizarre.

And since the flinch incident weeks ago when I exposed myself as a massive scaredy cat, he had, in fact, been very careful with me. More careful, really, than anyone had *ever* bothered to be before. He still barked out orders and blustered around the place as was his way, but I could tell that he was trying to soften his tone around me.

He worked long hours but managed to come home earlier a few nights a week. We always ate together now on those days. In fact, even when Ozzie went to his mum's, Lord Sterling had decreed in that uniquely aristocratic, commanding tone, honed from centuries of commands being issued from the landowners to their serfs, that I would still be dining with him. The first night when I'd backed away, telling him I'd already eaten a cheese and pickle sandwich, he wasn't having any of it.

"You need to eat proper meals," he told me, all Master of the Universe as per usual.

"No, really. It was a *huge* sandwich and I really don't think—"

"Sit. Down." His clipped command, combined with my incessant need to please people, meant I automatically planted my arse in the chair. I resisted the urge to roll my eyes at his smug expression. Then, when I tried to get up from my chair to help serve the casserole Martha had cooked, he gave me another of those stern looks and I sat back down.

"Right," he'd said. "I've had a rubbish day. I could do with a laugh. Tell me more about this *Sweeney Todd* caper."

So I did. It helped that there was a lot of material there, including the fake blood, which Lily had bought two gallons of and was fully planning on using until Mrs Clayton walked into a dress rehearsal that looked like something out of *The Texas Chainsaw Massacre*.

"Seven-year-olds are surprisingly bloodthirsty," I told him when he questioned whether they were traumatised. When his rich, deep, beautiful laughter filled the kitchen completely, I just stared at him. Amused and unguarded, he was so handsome it was almost ridiculous. I made an excuse to leave after that, worried that I would do something mad like jump out of my chair and into his lap. It was bad enough that he'd had to take in a random woman; if that random woman started jumping him in his own home, I doubted he'd be very impressed.

So, yes, a week into my stay and apart from my inappropriate thoughts about my boss which were nothing new, I was settling in well. I'd started eating three meals a day again, mainly because Lord Sterling and his spies (Ozzie and Martha) forced me to, plus Martha bagged up my lunch along with Ozzie's every morning.

There were small things too. Like how when I ran low on Branston Pickle, another jar magically appeared in the cupboard with the exact chunk size I liked. It may have been Martha, but Lord Sterling had caught me eating directly from the jar with a spoon twice now, so I suspected he may have been responsible for that little piece of thoughtfulness. Which was mad, wasn't it? He worked so hard. He didn't have time to make sure I had my small-chunk Branston Pickle available. Surely?

But by far the best thing was that I felt safe. All the time.

Then came *The Incident*.

Ozzie and I had had a particularly good reading session. I'd told him he could go up another level soon and he'd been pleased as punch.

"I think I might be ready to read to Daddy," he told me in a small voice when I was dishing up supper in the kitchen.

"That's great news, Ozzie," I said, trying to keep my voice level and not reveal my extreme excitement. I'd been teaching long enough to know that if you showed children how much something meant and put too much pressure on them, they would invariably back off what you wanted them to do.

When Lord Sterling arrived home shortly after Ozzie's revelation, I took him aside in the corridor to tell him. His smile in response to the news was huge and absolutely beautiful. But his spontaneous hug took me completely by surprise. I was still bouncing on the balls of my feet with excitement when his arms closed around me. I stiffened at first, overwhelmed by the feel of his muscular body against mine, but then as I felt him start to pull away, my brain screamed *no* and that's when I short-circuited. My arms came up to clamp around as much of his large body as I could manage, and I rested my head on the centre of his broad chest, breathing in his glorious scent and revelling in the very feel of him. Mortifyingly, in order for him to separate himself from my spider monkey hug, he had to call my name a couple of times. Eventually, he enclosed my upper arms with his large hands and physically set me away from him.

Once my brain restarted and I realised what I'd done, I took a huge step back, my face burning with humiliation. Luckily, Ozzie appeared at that point to cut through the tension.

"Daddy," he squealed as he flew down the corridor, colliding with his father's legs as was his standard greeting. Lord Sterling dropped down to his knees to give his son a hug, and I tried to slow my breathing back to a normal rate.

The tension between me and Lord Sterling when all three of us settled on the sofa while Ozzie found his place in his book was almost unbearable. I started listing countries in my head where I could move to get away from the acute embarrassment. Maybe Australia needed teaching assistants with chronic shyness and PTSD, who knew?

But then, Ozzie, tentatively at first, but with growing confidence, started to read his book to his father, and the embarrassment dulled as my heart swelled with pride. This was the little boy who, at the start of the school year, when someone suggested he read out loud, would start throwing objects around the classroom. The one who wouldn't even sound out letters with me when I first started working with him.

After a couple of pages, Ozzie paused and looked up at his dad with a cautious expression. I could feel his worry and it broke my heart. His reading was still very hesitant. He skipped words and swapped letters around. With some of the words, even after sounding them out, he still got horribly muddled, and he often made wildly inaccurate guesses, becoming frustrated when they were wrong and he had to try again. Plus, he was obviously nervous with his dad listening, but he'd done so, so well. I prayed that Lord Sterling could see how hard Ozzie had tried, and he wouldn't be dismissive in any way. But, of course, I never should have doubted him.

"That was great, Oz," Lord Sterling said, his voice hoarse with emotion. He swallowed before he spoke again. "I'm so proud of you, you know that, my boy?"

Ozzie shrugged and hid his pleased smile as he turned away from his dad to look back at the book.

"Okay," I murmured, "I'll just be in the other room if you..."

"No, stay!" snapped Ozzie, grabbing my arm before I could stand from the sofa.

I had thought that I needed to give them space to have this special moment together. After all, I was only a paid employee. But both faces, one ultra-masculine and hand-some, and the other so similar but with the softness of youth, frowned up at me in consternation.

"You'll stay," said Lord Sterling, with that imperious Lord of the Manor tone. I smiled at them both. In truth, I wanted to hear Ozzie reading to his dad. It was what I'd worked towards for so long, and I knew how much it meant to both of them. So I settled back down on the sofa and listened. When Ozzie was finished, he did what children tended to do after they'd blown everybody's mind. He simply jumped up from the sofa and asked if he could go watch the telly now.

"Yes, of course," said Lord Sterling, his voice still a little choked. I was shocked when I glanced at him to see a slight sheen of wet over his eyes. I didn't think it was possible to find the man any more attractive. But seeing how much it meant to him to have this connection with his son restored almost made me melt into the sofa.

And then Ozzie raced off to the snug, and it was just me and Lord Sterling sitting on the sofa together. I was about to get up and mumble an excuse, but when I glanced up at him, I couldn't look away. Our eyes held for a long moment, and I felt that intense connection flare again. It was like there was an invisible force flowing between us, anchoring us to each other somehow.

"Clara," he murmured in a low voice. I watched as his pupils dilated, leaving only a thin circle of blue fire around them. His hand reached up and slid across my jawline into my hair at the nape of my neck, and he tilted my head back. My heart was hammering in my chest, my breathing choppy, but I didn't pull away. When his lips brushed mine, I jolted slightly and he pulled back.

"Shit, I'm sorry, Clara," he said, his voice still hoarse but now with an edge of regret. "I shouldn't have—"

I didn't want to hear the brush-off that was coming. This was the culmination of all my fantasies, and I wasn't letting anything stand in my way. So, both my hands flew up into his gorgeous, thick hair to pull his head down so that I could seal my mouth over his in an inexpert, clumsy, overly enthusiastic kiss.

When my mouth opened under his and his tongue slid inside, it felt as though I left my body for a moment. I was burning up from the inside out as I scrambled to move so that I was flush with his hard torso. My glasses got in the way, so I snatched them off my head and threw them onto the floor, not caring what happened to them, which was crazy for me – I always, *always* wanted to know where my glasses were.

"Jesus Christ," he muttered against my mouth as I rocked against him. One of my hands went under his suit jacket to feel his hard, muscular warmth under his shirt.

"Rafe," I breathed, using his first name for the first time ever, but I was too caught up in my lust-induced haze to notice.

He lowered me back onto the sofa, and my head rested on the cushions as he kissed down my throat to my collarbone. His hand slid up under my jumper onto the skin of my stomach above my leggings. I shivered. I could feel him everywhere: his warmth, his strength, his dynamic energy. I was drowning in him.

And then suddenly he was gone...

I blinked in confusion, trying to get my bearings as Lord Sterling jumped up from the sofa. But everything was blurry.

"Were you guys wrestling?" I heard Ozzie say from a few feet away as I scrambled up to sitting, then started to search the floor for my glasses. I knew I should have been horrified, but I was still on a massive high from kissing the man I'd had a crush on for the last six months, and I felt safe in this house. So safe that once I found my glasses and sat back on the sofa to look over at father and son, I almost burst out laughing.

Lord Sterling cleared his throat and shifted uncomfortably on his feet as his son looked at me and then his father expectantly.

"Clara lost her glasses," said Lord Sterling in a hoarse voice. "I was trying to help her find them."

"By lying on top of her?" Ozzie asked.

Chapter 15

Elaborate fantasies

Rafe

I'D HAD MANY ADVERSARIES IN MY LIFE AND, NOT TO BE too arrogant, I'd bested them all. Whether it was the fierce competition within my profession to rise to the top, or the dangerous criminals that I routinely prosecuted, I always came out the winner. With my career, I would stop at nothing to get what I wanted. I *would* be one of the youngest judges ever to be appointed in the UK. Nothing was going to stop me.

So why, then, was a five-foot-nothing, shy little school-teacher managing to best me now?

After the horror of my seven-year-old son interrupting the best kiss of my life, I'd taken Ozzie upstairs to get him ready for bed. This involved an extremely uncomfortable conversation about how I'd tripped and fallen onto Miss Clara, and how she was moaning because of how heavy I was. When that fresh hell was finally over, I came back down to the kitchen, but Clara was gone.

I went to her bedroom feeling like a fucking stalker, but

the door was locked and she didn't respond to my gentle knock. Seeing as her bedroom was right next to Ozzie's, I did not think it appropriate to start banging on the thick oak like a caveman.

After a while I started to feel like a piece of shit for both coming on to an employee and possibly scarring my son. I did want to apologise to Clara, but, really, I just wanted to see her again. Inappropriate as it was, I simply couldn't stay away from this woman any longer. And there were things to be said. I needed to make sure that she knew her job with me was not at risk, whatever happened between us. That I respected her and her bond with my son, that I would never do anything to jeopardise that. That I knew I was in a position of power, and I did not want to be the kind of lowlife who exploited that.

But I'd never be able to say any of this if I couldn't speak to the woman.

The next morning, Clara only emerged just before it was time to take Ozzie to school, and I had to leave for court, so I barely saw her. That evening I got caught up in those two cases that had been dumped on me, both of which were proving to be a fucking nightmare since I'd taken them on, and by the time I was home, Clara was gone, and Martha was babysitting.

"Where's Clara?" I snapped at Martha. "She should be here."

Martha, who didn't take any of my shit, raised her eyebrows at me. "Watch yourself, young man," she said. "That girl is not your indentured servant, you realise. She's gone out."

"Gone out?" I said in surprise.

Clara never went out. She liked my house. I could tell she did, and it gave me a huge sense of satisfaction. Her features always relaxed when she arrived home. Even if she'd just popped out to the corner shop, she was always happy to have come back. And she never went out willingly.

"Yes, she went with her friend Lily," Martha told me. "The girl's allowed to have a social life, Rafe."

When Clara did arrive home later that night, I was too slow to catch her before she could scurry up to her bedroom, clutching her jar of Branston Pickle. She was bloody fast for someone with such short legs.

I felt like I was losing my mind. She was invading all my thoughts. Her soft lips when we kissed, her big brown eyes so unfocused without her glasses and blinking up at me, her lavender and citrus scent, her small, upturned nose that wrinkled when she was deep in thought. It was all driving me insane. And now, smelling her perfume in rooms just after she'd left them as she expertly avoided me was starting to make me angry. Clearly, she wasn't interested in me but didn't have the courage to tell me to my face. I knew I shouldn't have taken advantage of her, and I did want to apologise for that, but I wasn't some sort of monster she had to avoid.

Well, fine, she could have it her way. Any further attempt on my part to approach her could well be categorised as sexual harassment. I was a barrister, soon to be a High Court judge. I could not be sexually harassing my employees.

I was disgusted with myself for having been so willing to chase around after her anyway. There were plenty of women whom I very much did not have to chase — Ophelia Montlake included. Granted, she had low-key annoyed me with how aggressive she was in her approaches, but maybe that was better. Maybe it was easier to be with a more confident woman who knew what she wanted.

I was ready to draw a line under my obsession with Clara. If she could ignore me, then I could ignore her. But Ozzie needed her, and I wasn't going to tolerate her leaving.

These were my not-so-fun thoughts when a knock on my office door later that night interrupted my brooding.

"Yes," I snapped.

Ozzie was with his mum, and the staff had gone home for the night, so there was only one option left for who could be there. After a brief pause that made me roll my eyes, I called out again in irritation. My patience with Clara's goddamn hesitancy was waning now that I was so sexually frustrated.

"For God's sake, Clara. Just open the fucking door."

The door opened then, and Clara popped her head around it, looking across at me with a nervous expression that made me feel like a bloody monster again. Christ, I wasn't going to leap on the woman; she didn't have to be so goddamn worried. I raised my eyebrows. In spite of my annoyance, my heart was hammering in my chest at the sight of her. But I refused to allow her to see how she affected me. If she found me so repulsive that she'd felt the need to hide from me for the last three days, I wasn't going to go around begging.

"Hi," she said, still with just her head poking around the door. "Am I interrupting anything important?"

"Clara, I am always doing important things," I told her, uncaring that I sounded like an arrogant dickhead. "Especially when I'm in this office."

She looked like she wanted to run then, but after closing her eyes for a moment, she seemed to make a decision.

"I'm sorry," she said in a small voice, and I gritted my

teeth. Her relentless apologies weren't as cute now. "This will only take a moment. If I could just really quickly speak to you."

"Fine," I snapped. "But if you want to speak to me, then you can do me the courtesy of coming into the room like a normal human being."

"Oh yes, of course," she said, her face falling. She looked really upset now. To be honest, I felt like a bit of a prick, but I wasn't going to fall for her kicked-puppy routine anymore, not when I knew that she could kiss like that.

She came into the office and sat in the chair in front of my desk, clasping her hands on her lap and looking down at them to avoid eye contact, as per bloody usual.

I sighed.

"Clara, can you please get on with what you want to say?" I told her.

"Yes, of course," she whispered, but her next words were so quiet that they were a struggle to make out.

I frowned. "Clara," I snapped, "for the love of God, drop the shy act. I had my tongue down your throat less than seventy-two hours ago. I'd really rather that we communicate as adults. That involves you actually speaking at a normal volume and maintaining eye contact with the adult that you're addressing. Understand me?"

Her eyes flew to mine. There was that flash of fire that I loved before she quenched it. She cleared her throat to speak again. This time, I could at least make out what she was saying.

"Look, I came to say I'm sorry."

I blinked at her. "You're sorry," I said slowly, then pinched the bridge of my nose in frustration. Good God, what was wrong with her? She was coming to me to apologise for not being interested in me? My God, this had a sexual harassment lawsuit written all over it. If my colleagues in chambers knew what I was up to, they would think I'd lost my bloody mind.

"Clara, I—"

"It doesn't... you don't have to..." she stuttered out, before something flashed across her face and she leapt to her feet. Her hands were trembling before she bunched them into small fists at her sides. "I was totally inappropriate."

She wasn't whispering now, far from it. What the hell was going on?

"It was very, *very* wrong of me to grab you like that. When you hugged me after Ozzie's breakthrough, I'm afraid I..." she broke off, and her face flooded with colour as she sank back into the chair. She briefly looked out of the window before forcing herself to meet my eyes again. "I have a ridiculous crush on you," she told me in a surprisingly firm voice.

My mouth fell open in shock as my mind raced to catch up with what she was saying.

"And *then* I came onto you when you were vulnerable and grabbed you *without your consent*."

Vulnerable?

"Clara," I said slowly, "are you telling me that you think *you* took advantage of *me?*"

"Oh God, this is really embarrassing," whispered Clara, her hands going to her cheeks, which were fire-engine red now. "It's this stupid, stupid crush, you see." She closed her eyes briefly, then focused back on me. "You might as well know everything. I've been watching you. Even before you approached me at the school about Ozzie, I knew who you were. Every Tuesday, I made sure that I was at the classroom window just so that I could..." She broke off, whispering, "Oh, kill me now," before she continued, "...just so that I could... perv over you, okay? Like some weirdo stalker. I mean, it's not totally my fault. You can't really blame me. It's your whole vibe: the three-piece suit, the coat that billows out behind you when you walk, you know, the long fancy one?"

"My overcoat?" I asked, trying to keep the humour out of my voice. Clara looked devastated, and I didn't want her to think I was laughing at her. "You watched me because I wore an overcoat?"

"Oh no. I mean... It's not just the coat. It's the whole package. You must know the effect you have on women? Your body, your face, those piercing blue eyes. Look, I promise I'm not usually like this. I'm not someone who hangs out of the classroom window and pervs over dads. But I'd done it for so long with you and constructed such elaborate fantasies around you that when I had access to your actual physical body, something just tripped in my brain. There you are, giving me an innocent hug, excited for your son, and I practically climbed you like a tree and wouldn't let go. I just couldn't get close enough to you. My monkey brain took over, you know?"

"Your monkey brain," I repeated slowly, trying really hard to suppress my smile now but not quite managing it.

To be honest, I was having a hard time even remaining in my seat since the moment that Clara mentioned her *elaborate fantasies*. Every muscle in my body had strung tight as if I was a predator ready to pounce. I could feel my heart beating in my throat, and there was a strange whooshing sensation in my stomach as if I was free-falling. So much blood went south that I almost felt lightheaded. It was a struggle to focus on her next words.

"You see, my crush was bad before, but when I started working for you, it got even worse."

Clara went on, completely on a roll now. She wasn't looking at me anymore either, which I didn't like at all. She was focusing on the ceiling instead. I looked down at her lap to see that her hands were shaking. That was when I started to feel like a bit of a shit. Whilst this was all music to my ears and entertaining in the extreme, it was clearly distressing for Clara, who had got it into her head that she'd crossed some sort of line.

Her taking advantage of *me*?

Was she mad?

Chapter 16

You'll do as I say

Rafe

"Being here with you and seeing you up close all the time," she carried on, rambling now, "it just ramped everything up and…" She broke off and swallowed, her eyes glazing over with humiliated tears. "Well, you won't believe the… the depraved scenarios I've thought up about you. You've no idea all the dirty, *dirty* things you've done to me in my overactive imagination. Even the kitchen, for God's sake, right there on the granite, which, to be frank, is disgusting from a food hygiene perspective."

I couldn't help but let out a short bark of laughter at that point which I managed to disguise as a cough when she shot a glance at me.

"And this office. Oh my God," she said, tucking her hair behind her ears in another nervous gesture. "Your office and your desk… It's just all so bloody *masculine*. Basically, I'm a total creeper. But don't worry – I'll find somewhere else to live *immediately*. I don't want to make you feel uncomfortable in your own home any longer." That final statement had me standing suddenly from my chair, causing her to finally break off her tirade.

Clara was *not* quitting her job, and she was *not* leaving this fucking house.

Not after that little speech. Not after the relentless, tortured thoughts I'd had of her over the last few weeks. There was no *way* I was letting Clara go anywhere anytime soon.

She was mine.

This confession made her mine.

The fact that I made her feel safe made her mine.

And I wasn't giving her up, not for any reason and certainly not because of her weird, guilty conscience about her *monkey brain* and how she thought she was some sort of dirty pervert when it came to me.

Her mouth fell open, and she shrank back into the chair as I stalked around my desk to get to her. When I was right in front of her, I leaned back against the desk and crossed my arms over my chest. She looked up at me and bit both of her lips between her teeth in an unsure and completely adorable expression.

"Okay, so tell me, Clara," I said in a low voice. "What exactly did your dirty, perverted thoughts about my desk involve?" She followed the movement of my hand as I stroked the grain of the wood surface, eyes flying wide as she swallowed nervously.

"I don't think I should say," she whispered.

I moved suddenly then, causing her to startle in her seat. I leant over her, one hand on each arm of her chair, my face inches from hers.

"In these dirty, depraved, elaborate fantasies," I said, my voice now just above a low whisper, "did we ever do anything like this?" I leaned down and brushed her mouth with mine and she gasped. When I leaned back again, her eyelids had fluttered closed and she was breathing erratically.

"Answer me, Clara," I said. "Did we do anything like that?" My voice was hoarse but still in control.

"M-m-m-maybe?" Clara stuttered as her eyes opened, her brown, uncertain gaze staring up at me.

"How about this?" I asked, as my hands moved from the arms of the chair to her jawline so I could tilt her face to the exact angle I wanted it. My mouth fell on hers again but this time my tongue swept inside. The kiss was long and deep and fucking perfect. When I pulled back slightly to rest my forehead on hers, we were both panting. "Did I kiss you like that, baby?"

Her breath hitched as she nodded and I smiled.

"Did I lift you up like this?" I asked as one hand went to her waist and the other underneath her thigh before lifting her up off the chair and swinging around to put her on top of my desk. Once there, I stepped between her legs as her small hands fell onto my chest. Her eyes were like saucers now.

"Or do this?" I murmured as I kissed from the corner of her mouth to her jawline, then down her neck to her collar-bone, whilst deftly undoing the buttons of her shirt at the same time so that I could get to the smooth, ivory skin beneath. My mouth moved back to hers as her shirt fell open, revealing a white cotton bra with pink flowers on it, containing her small, full breasts. My large hand moved from her waist up to enclose her breast, feeling her nipple stiffen under my palm.

"Did I tease you like this, baby?" I muttered, still cupping her breast over her bra but with my thumb brushing back and forth over her sensitive nipple. She whimpered against my mouth and I smiled again as I pushed her shirt, along with her bra strap, down her shoulder. Then I kissed a path along her collarbone whilst my other hand held her steady at her hip. Once the cup of her bra fell away, she sucked in a shocked breath as I kissed down to her now-exposed breast.

"Did I do anything like this?" I whispered before I licked her nipple, then pulled it into my mouth.

"Oh my God," she breathed, arching her back as one of her hands came up to sink into my hair. After a few moments, I moved to the other side and then lifted my head to go back to kissing her jawline. My hand that had been at her hip came round to the front of her leggings and dipped in.

"Christ," I breathed in a choked voice. "You're soaking for me." I slid one finger inside her, and she let out a low moan. She was so small and tight as she clenched around my finger that the need to push her back, strip her and then slide into her was almost overwhelming. But I wanted to savour this. I didn't want to rush anything with Clara. I had my own dirty, elaborate fantasies to fulfil, after all.

My thumb fell on her clit, putting pressure there. When she started riding my hand, I thought I was going to pass out; my head rush was so intense. My mouth moved to the shell of her ear. "Did I make you come on my fingers, baby?" I said in a low, husky whisper, and that was it – that was enough to set her off. She contracted sharply against me and came with a small, muted scream, which I smothered with my mouth.

I should have stopped there. If I were a better man, I really would have stopped. But witnessing the blissed-out expression on her face as she stared up at me like I was some kind of god pushed me over the edge.

"Wow," she breathed.

"Did I have you on my desk?" I murmured darkly before pulling away slightly to shrug off my suit jacket. She looked unbelievably vulnerable as she sat on the edge of my desk, watching me with glazed eyes. Nervousness was creeping into her dazed expression now, and I couldn't allow that. I didn't want to give her time to have any doubts. So I made quick work of my shirt and then moved back to her, tugging off her leggings and knickers together in one fluid movement. I caught her shocked gasp with my mouth.

"Did I fuck you on my desk?" I whispered against her lips as my hand fell to my belt buckle.

"Yes," she breathed.

"Was I gentle in your dark little fantasies, Clara? Or was it hard and fast?"

She let out a little moan, but when she didn't respond, I licked up her neck and gently bit her earlobe.

"I want an answer, Clara," I said into the shell of her ear. "I wasn't gentle in your dreams, was I?" My hand went up to her breast and I lightly pinched her nipple.

She moaned again and then breathed out, "No."

"How did I do it in your dirty little dreams, darling?"

"Hard. Fast," she whispered, her breathing choppy as I moved my hand to her centre, rubbing small circles. "Blooming heck," she cried, and I almost laughed. Here I was giving her my best dirty talk game, and she came out with phrases like *blooming heck.*

After I'd reached my wallet and rolled on the condom, I leaned her back against the wood of the desk and positioned myself at her entrance. My whole body was shaking in anticipation now and from the effort of holding myself back. I leaned over her again and held her eyes with mine.

"You have to say you want me, Clara," I murmured. "We can stop now if—"

"I want you!" she said on a near shout and I smiled.

"Ask nicely, baby."

Her eyes flared. "Please," she breathed. My control snapped and she let out a small scream as I pushed forward into her. She was so tight, like a vice around me, and for a moment I worried I'd hurt her.

"Clara? You okay?" I asked in a strained voice, my concern for her battling with my need to claim her. "Clara?"

"Y-y-yes," she said in a high-pitched voice. "I think so. It's just you're quite..." she trailed off as I pulled back slightly. When I slid back in slowly, my body still shaking with the effort of the restraint I was showing, her eyes rolled back and she let out a low moan.

"Am I bigger than in your dreams?" I asked, my voice darkening with need.

"Yes," she hissed as I slammed into her again. "Oh God, don't stop, Rafe."

Hearing my name on her lips pushed me over the edge and I began moving faster and deeper.

"That's it, baby," I whispered in her ear. "That's a good girl. That's my good, dirty girl. You'll come again for me, understand?"

She shook her head on the wood of the desk. "I don't think I..." I slid my hand between us, putting pressure there as I continued to thrust into her.

"You'll do as I say," I snapped, and that seemed to be her tipping point. Her body arched against me. Her torso came off the wood of the table, so the back of her head was the only thing resting there and her gorgeous, small breasts thrust up into my chest. My vision clouded and stars sprung before my eyes as I came harder than I'd ever come in my life as she contracted around me.

I collapsed onto her for a moment before leaning up onto my elbows to look down at her face. She was blinking up at me like a deer in the headlights, a sheen of sweat over her forehead and her fringe curling at the ends where it was stuck to her temples. At first, she smiled. Then, gradually, she came down off her high, and the dazed adoration in her eyes faded as real apprehension entered her expression.

I knew she'd be worried now. I knew these weren't ideal circumstances. I knew Mrs Clayton would be furious. But that didn't change the fact that Clara was mine, and *nobody* was standing in my way.

Chapter 17

We have gone way,
way past inappropriate

Clara

At first, I couldn't really process anything. My brain was scrambled from what had just happened. Rafe pulled me up to sitting on the desk and I blinked up at his face, but I couldn't make out his expression. My glasses had fallen off at some point and now everything was blurry.

I felt a little arrow of panic spear through my post-amazing-sex-with-Rafe haze. Did he look disgusted with me now? With himself? I turned to search the desk behind me, looking around for my glasses, but I couldn't find them. My chest tightened. I hated not being able to see.

My older brother Freddie and his friends thought it was funny when we were kids to hide my glasses so that I would have to stumble around the house to find them. He called me Little Mole and would laugh at me and push me around as I tearfully pleaded to have my glasses returned. My other older brother, Ruben, would usually end up putting a stop to it, which would kick off a fight between them. I'd leave them to their violence and sneak away.

Panic rose in my chest the longer I couldn't find my glasses, and the backs of my eyes started to sting. Then I realised that in my panic, I had forgotten that I was still completely exposed.

"Shit, shit," I muttered as I abandoned my search to pull up the cups of my bra and try to get my shirt back on, but it was caught around my elbows.

"Clara?" Rafe's soft voice was full of concern now. "Baby, calm down. You're okay. Everything is okay."

His large hand cupped my jaw on one side as his thumb swept away a tear that had fallen. Then he lifted both sides of my shirt and buttoned it quickly. I was staring down at my hands. Another tear made it down my cheek. He put his knuckle underneath my chin to lift my face to his, but my vision was even more blurry now with tears and I still couldn't make out his expression.

"Deep breaths, darling," he said, his voice still gentle but now firm. Then he slid my glasses back onto my nose. He secured the arms behind my ears, gently pushing the hair that had fallen forwards into my face back over my shoulders, and stroked down my back.

"Sorry, sorry," I whispered, and I heard him sigh. When I looked up at his face, I could see his features clearly now, and he was frowning.

"Clara, why are you apologising?" he asked in a low, gentle voice.

I shook my head and shrugged my shoulders. "I don't know," I said, still whispering.

His frown cleared and he smiled before he gave me a light kiss and stepped back to help me off the desk. Then he grabbed my knickers and my leggings off the floor and helped me back into them. Heat hit my cheeks. I'd forgotten about the whole being naked from the waist down thing.

Once he had completed that task, he sat in the large armchair behind him and pulled me down to sit on his lap. I stiffened. I was still mid-panic attack and not at all sure what was happening. Little Mole Clara did not live out her wild fantasies with men like Lord Sterling.

"I should get up," I whispered as his arms came around me. But the smell of him, the feel of his large body and the need I felt to be close to him won out, and I melted into the warmth of his broad chest. "This isn't appropriate," I muttered half-heartedly. I could feel his smile against me before he burst out laughing into my hair, pulling me even closer to him. His large body shaking with laughter was one of the most wonderful feelings I had ever experienced in my life.

"Clara, we just fucked on my desk," he told me through his amusement. "We have gone way, *way* past inappropriate."

I swallowed. "Ah. Yes. You're right. I'm just not sure what's happening or why it's happening. I'm a bit worried about how I've behaved." I'd been so worried about apologising to Rafe tonight that I'd raided his drinks cabinet and downed a shot of brandy earlier. Being a complete lightweight, it had been enough to decimate my inhibitions.

"How *you've* behaved?" Rafe asked. I looked up at his face; his eyebrows were both raised. He still had his arms around me, and his hands were stroking down my back in soothing movements.

"Well... I sort of cornered you in your office and propositioned you," I said nervously. "I mean, what were you supposed to do when I started talking about all of my dirty fantasies? I basically preyed on your masculine urges."

Rafe stared at me a moment before blinking and then

leaning down to laugh into my neck, even harder than before.

"I don't see what's so funny," I muttered indignantly. When he finally managed to stop laughing, he raised his head from my neck and looked at me with a smile.

"Baby, please never, *ever* say *masculine urges* again. I don't think I can take it," he said in an amused voice.

I shrugged helplessly. "What am I supposed to say?"

He rolled his eyes. "Clara, I've wanted you for weeks. I think I've wanted you since the first moment you looked up at me with those big brown eyes in the classroom that day when I was being a dickhead, and you put me in my place. Now, I just came harder than I have ever come in my entire life. You haven't tricked me into giving in to my *masculine urges*. I'm a man who takes what he wants, and I want you more than I've wanted anything in a very, *very* long time."

"You want me?" I whispered, and his hand came up to my jaw to turn my head gently towards him so that he could look into my eyes.

"You're funny. You're kind. You're intelligent. You're beautiful."

I snorted at the word "beautiful," and his gaze sharpened.

"You don't believe you're beautiful?" he asked, and I broke eye contact to look down at my hands.

"You don't have to say these things to me, you know?" I said in a small voice. "If you want to carry on with..." I waved my hand vaguely in the air, trying to think of a word for it which wouldn't make me blush. I settled on, "...stuff, you don't have to give me any flowery words or tell me what you think I want to hear." I swallowed nervously. "I really, really enjoyed the *stuff*, so you don't have to lie to me."

"Oh, darling," he muttered as he rested his forehead

against mine, his hands coming up to cup both sides of my jaw tenderly. "What happened to you?"

"W-w-what do you mean?"

"What happened to make you believe I'm lying?"

I shrugged, and he wrapped his arms around me again to pull me back into his chest. Feeling overwhelmed and exposed, I decided to just give in at that point. I relaxed against his warm, muscular chest and nuzzled into the base of his neck, loving the feel of his stubble against my cheek and breathing in his clean scent edged with expensive aftershave.

"It's okay," Rafe said softly. "You don't have to tell me yet."

I didn't understand. Not really. But I also didn't have the energy to argue.

"Just listen for a minute, okay?" he said, his voice a low rumble in his chest, pleasant and soothing. I nodded. "So, the situation is a little more complicated than we would like. But let me be clear: if anyone has manipulated anyone here, it's me manipulating you. I am in a position of power. I'm older. I'm your employer. If anyone's in the wrong, it's me. But I have to say, Clara, nothing feels wrong about this. In fact, this feels more right than anything I've felt for a long while. We don't have to work out anything now. For now, I just want to hold you."

"But maybe we should talk about whether——?"

His groan as I attempted to sit up cut off what I was going to say.

"If you wriggle anymore, baby," he told me in a hoarse voice, "I'll give in to some more of those *masculine urges* you went on about. Just keep still, relax and trust me, okay?"

Trust was a difficult one for me. I trusted Lily and Mrs C. I trusted Zach. But that was about it.

I'd made the mistake once of trusting my university boyfriend, who I met whilst I was doing teacher training. Nathan had been a mild-mannered, bespectacled, cardigan-wearing skinny guy. He was gentle, and he was kind. I lost my virginity to him, and I was with him for about three months until he met my family, who apparently "scared the bollocks off" him.

I didn't blame Nathan. My family scared the bollocks off most people. But I thought we'd meant something to each other, so the disappointment of being ghosted completely with no other explanation was crushing.

Worse even than Nathan was Daniel, who had used me as a stepladder into my father's crime syndicate, not even realising what an ineffective stepladder I actually was, seeing as I didn't command the respect of anyone, least of all my father. When he did realise this, Daniel dumped me as quickly as possible. He still worked for Dad, and I saw him occasionally when I had to be at the house. But I never looked directly at him anymore. I never looked directly at any of my father's men anymore.

I was tired. Really, really tired and completely over-whelmed with the strength of my feelings for Rafe. He was so warm and his arms were so strong around me. So, I thought, why not? I would let myself have this moment. I could pretend that he was mine, that he knew who I was, who I *really* was and who my family were, and that he didn't care, that he just wanted me.

I could pretend I was safe.

For now.

Chapter 18

You think about me?

Rafe

"Bloody hell," I muttered as the pounding on the door started again. To my annoyance, Clara, who had been snuggled into my side like a kitten, sat bolt upright on the sofa. "Ignore it," I told her, wrapping my arm around her to encourage her to lie back down against me.

"What?" she squeaked, her eyes flying wide as the banging started again. "You can't just ignore it!"

"Buggering bollocks," I snapped. "Listen, I *can* ignore it if I know exactly who it is. It's nearly midnight on a Saturday night. She can bugger off."

"B-b-b-but—" she stammered, looking between me and the living room exit. The small slither of fear that entered her expression made my chest tighten with anger. The forgot-her-key-again door banger was scaring Clara. "I'm going to kill her," I muttered under my breath as I stood from the sofa, lifting Clara with me and then taking her hand to pull her to the front door. After another string of bangs, which had Clara flinching at my side, I typed in the security code, flipped the lock and yanked open the solid wood all one-handed, keeping Clara's hand securely in mine.

But then I *had* to let go of Clara's hand in order to catch the mad whirlwind of blonde hair and sequined dress that flew at me through the front door.

"Careful, mate," Rory Wallace's deep voice with his distinctive Scottish accent sounded from my front steps behind the whirlwind. "She might vomit again. I've already had to pay the taxi driver off with a hundred quid after she nearly upchucked all over his upholstery. She's a fucking mess."

Poppy's eyes blinked open as she tried to focus on me, then her face went pale. "Oh God!" she muttered.

"Rafe, she's gonna blow!" Rory shouted.

I deftly turned Poppy away from me to face a priceless vase on a shelf next to the door. Rory moved forward automatically to take her from my arms to his and held Poppy's vast amount of blonde hair out of the way as she vomited into the vase.

"Christ alive, what the fuck did you do to her, Wallace?" I asked.

"What did *I* do?" snapped an exhausted-looking Rory. His tie was askew and his suit jacket rumpled. "*You* need to keep her on a tighter leash, Sterling. She's completely out of control. Poppy partied too hard, just like she always does."

"What the fuck are you talking about, mate? Poppy never—"

"Oh, don't bullshit me, Rafe, I'm far too fucking tired. Poppy always parties too hard. You forget I knew her when she was a teenager, and I've seen the articles about her in the years since. Don't make her out to be some sort of teetotal saint."

"She's not teetotal but she certainly doesn't get in this state, *ever*."

"I've held her hair back before when she was in this state."

"That was when she was seventeen, you bastard. People are allowed to be dickheads when they're seventeen. How many times did you vomit at the same age? We all go through it."

Rory snorted. "Don't think I haven't seen her flashing her knickers at the paparazzi."

I knew Rory held a grudge against my sister for an interview he gave her after the Rugby World Cup five years ago. I tried not to let it affect our decades long friendship. But this was beyond the pale.

Before that bloody interview, which I still maintain was Rory's fault anyway, he'd seemed to like Poppy. In fact, she used to be one of the only humans with the ability to make the dour bastard crack a smile. But now, when he did see Poppy (which wasn't often, seeing as she avoided him like the plague), he was cold and dismissive – not an attitude many people adopted with my sister, and certainly not one she was used to.

"You bastard," I hissed. "She was mortified when that happened. You've no idea."

Poppy groaned. "Honestly, Rafe, just leave it. He's not gonna believe you anyway and I am something of a fuckwit. We all know that." She was slurring now but at least she'd managed to stop vomiting.

"Poppy, darling, you're not a fuckwit," I said gently as I scowled at Rory and moved to take Poppy from his arms, but for some reason the stubborn bastard wasn't letting her go.

"If she's such a fucking inconvenience, Wallace, let me look after her and piss off," I told him.

"Sh-sh-she's hurt," I heard Clara's voice from behind me. Rory's gaze shot from Poppy to Clara, and his eyebrows went up in surprise. "Y-y-you hurt her," Clara's voice was rising now, and I could hear the fury in her tone despite her stutter.

"What?" Rory frowned, shaking his head. "I dinnae——"

"She's hurt!" Clara shouted, shocking the absolute shit out of me. I abandoned Poppy to turn to Clara, who was bright red in the face. Her arms were straight down by her sides with her hands clenched into fists so tight her knuckles were white.

"What?" Rory asked in confusion. "She's not... oh Christ!"

I turned back to Rory and Poppy. He was still holding her up with one arm, the other coming up to stroke her hair back from her face. There was a small trickle of blood now seeping from her hairline onto the pale skin of her cheek. It was at that point that I'd had enough. I used the opportunity of his loosened grip around her to pull her away from him, holding her up in my arms instead.

"What are you playing at, Wallace?" I snapped, my voice rising. "You bring my sister home in this state and you didn't even know she was hurt—"

Rory stepped towards us, his face stricken and reached for Poppy again, but Clara leapt in front of me and Poppy, bristling with anger.

"Get away from her!" she shouted, standing toe-to-toe with Rory now, her small fists still clenched at her side. She was shaking, whether it was from anger or fear I couldn't tell. The absurdity of tiny Clara facing off with Rory Wallace, who was six foot four and had played rugby for

Scotland for over ten years, was beyond ridiculous, but she looked fully ready to throw down to protect my sister.

"Clara, it's okay," I said softly. "Rory's not going to hurt Poppy. She's safe."

"You don't know that!" Clara was still shouting as she turned to me, but her voice was shaky and there were unshed tears in her eyes now. She spun back to Rory. "You hurt her," she said louder now.

"I dinnae hurt or touch her, lass," he said. "I *promise* I looked after her. I dinnae know she'd been hurt."

"Out!" she shouted, trying to puff herself up in the face of their size difference, but it was clearly a losing battle. "You shouldn't hurt people! You shouldn't... she's *bleeding!*"

"He didn't hurt me," Poppy slurred. "S'okay, hun."

"Clara, darling, come away from the door," I said, still in a soft, careful voice. "Rory, I think you better leave."

"Her head," Rory said weakly. "I – Rafe, I'm sorry, I dinnae know—"

"I fell and hit a table," Poppy said, "because I'm a fuckwit."

Her voice was weird and slurred. I was beginning to really worry now. This kind of thing hadn't happened with Poppy for years. I hadn't been lying when I said she barely ever drank like this nowadays.

"Poppy, I just—" Rory started but I was done.

"Just fuck *off*, Rory," I said.

"Please let me know she's okay," he pleaded, catching my arm as I went to close the door. "Just text me or something. Let me know she's alright."

I knew full well the disdain Rory held for Poppy. He wasn't going to trick me with his fake concern. He'd already turned up here and bitched about what a burden she'd been, as if she was still just the fuckwitted teenager she once was.

"What do you care? You've made it clear over the last five years that Poppy's the last person you give a shit about. Just *leave* Rory."

I slammed the door in his face then and Poppy's body slumped against me as she let out a small groan. "Rafeeeeey, I feel all squiggly," she sing-songed.

"Oh, Pops," I said as I made my way through to the kitchen, half-carrying my sister with Clara following behind us. "What on earth happened, darling? You can't stand Rory. And you never get drunk nowadays."

"Sorry," Poppy sniffled, as a tear made its way down her cheek. "I was nervous. You know how Rory makes me nervous." I put her down into one of the kitchen chairs and she slumped over the table, then looked up at Clara. "You must think I'm a total loser."

"Of course I don't," Clara said fiercely, squatting down in front of Poppy and taking her hand. "I would never think that."

I crossed my arms over my chest and stared down at my sister. There was a twelve-year age gap between me and Poppy. And at twenty-five, she was still considered the baby of the family. We all loved and indulged Poppy to an almost ridiculous degree. Of course, that meant she could have grown into a spoilt nightmare, but my sister never behaved like that. Yes, she lived her life as if she was the main character and the world revolved around her, but not necessarily in a bad way. Poppy was the kindest girl I knew. She'd had a wild phase in her late teens, but it had all been exaggerated by the papers. The paps always seemed to catch her at bad moments and would make all sorts of stories up about her. But, Poppy being Poppy, she'd turned all that media attention into a vehicle to benefit the Sterling Foundation, our family's charitable trust. There was nobody who could organise a party like Poppy. The more famous she got, the more opportunities came her way. She now split her time between event organising for the foundation, and interviewing celebrities for all the broadcasters that used to pan her.

"Do you have a first aid kit?" said Clara softly as she stood up to face me, still keeping Poppy's hand in hers.

"Yes, of course," I said. "Pops, you're not going to be sick again, are you?"

"I'm fine, Rafey Bafey," muttered Poppy as she rested her head back against the chair. I patted her shoulder a couple of times and then moved away to go and grab the first aid kit, leaving Clara to keep an eye on her.

Bloody hell, this was not how I envisaged this evening going.

After Clara had finally relaxed into me in the office and let me hold her, we'd sat like that for a long while before I heard her stomach grumble. There was no way I was going to let Clara go hungry, not with how underweight she still was. So I lifted her up in my arms and carried her into the kitchen.

"What are you doing?" she'd asked. "I can walk."

I'd grinned down at her. "I know, but this is quicker. Your legs are too short."

She smacked my chest and frowned up at me. "That's bloody rude," she said as I popped her onto one of the kitchen stools.

"I know," I said, kissing her nose. "Now sit here, shorty, while I make you dinner."

"You can cook?" she asked, her eyebrows going up in disbelief.

"I'm a very good cook," I said indignantly. This was a lie. I could heat up Martha's food and I could boil pasta, but that was about it. Luckily, I had pasta and a jar of pesto – a meal even I would struggle to fuck up.

"Lord Sterling," Clara called tentatively, "can I ask you a question?"

I held back a sigh. After what we just did in my study, I had hoped she might be a little less shy. Asking permission to ask a question and not even using my first name was not exactly progress.

"Clara, baby," I said, moving over to where she was sitting on a kitchen stool and then spinning the stool to face me. It was a sudden movement and caused her hands to fly to my chest to steady herself which worked perfectly to my advantage. "I think now you can stop asking permission to speak. And, for the love of God, please, *please* call me Rafe."

She bit her lip. "Okay."

"Okay, what?"

"Okay, Rafe," she whispered at my chest.

"Now, what was your question, sweetheart?"

"Er... right. I just... I'm not sure what this means... between us."

I reached up, cupping her face with both my hands at her jaw to tilt it so her eyes met mine, as my fingers went into her soft hair. "I really, really like you, Clara. That's what this means. Those dirty little fantasies you had about me—"

"Gah! I really shouldn't have told you about—"

"Baby, times those fantasies by a factor of a hundred, add in a lot more creativity and you'll have something approaching the torture I've endured. I think about you *all* the time. It's inappropriate as fuck, but I've gone way beyond caring about that now."

Her eyes were wide as she stared up at me. "You think about me?" she whispered, and I smiled.

"All the time," I whispered back before pressing a soft kiss on her mouth. "Now, stop distracting me, woman, and I'll feed you."

The banging started after I'd fed Clara and convinced her to snuggle into my side on the sofa. Considering all of that took a great deal of effort and persuasion, I was not best pleased to have my peace disturbed. I'd known it was Poppy; she was renowned for forgetting her key and for coming back here to stay if she was on a night out and didn't want to wake up Granny (Poppy lived in a wing of Granny's house and whilst the property was vast, my granny had bat ears). But now, with blood trickling down my sister's forehead, my annoyance was replaced with concern.

"Okay," said Clara quietly as she settled the first aid kit next to Poppy on the kitchen table, took out the surgical spirit and dabbed a sterile cotton pad with it. "This will sting a little bit, Poppy, alright?"

"Hit me, babe," slurred Poppy. "It's fine."

She flinched slightly as Clara gently cleaned the crusted blood away from her scalp.

"This is good," said Clara. "You won't need any stitches for this. It's really small, and the edges are opposed. You'll have to be careful washing your hair, but otherwise you should be fine."

"You a nurse as well as a teacher, babe?" asked Poppy blearily.

Clara laughed. "Not a nurse, I just... well, I've patched up a few people in my time."

That comment got my attention. I gave her a sharp look, but she was too busy cleaning up my sister to notice.

Chapter 19

You and I are happening

Clara

I WATCHED HIM FROM THE ENTRANCE TO THE KITCHEN. He was wearing his full three-piece suit, stubble darkening his jawline despite him having just shaved, and his thick hair curled around his collar, still slightly damp from the shower. Looking at him now, I had a strange sinking feeling, tinged with panic.

I had a habit of thinking three steps ahead to anticipate danger. My whole life had been about anticipating danger, really. It was completely built into my personality now. But Rafe wasn't dangerous to me in the normal way. Rafe wouldn't break me physically; it was my heart that was at risk.

When he caught sight of me, his gorgeous blue eyes lit up, and he smiled. That wide, white, glamorous smile, filling the kitchen with his magnetic energy.

"Hi," I said, feeling lame for my completely inadequate greeting after what had happened the night before. I tucked my hands into my pockets and shifted on my feet, still not moving from the doorway. I wasn't sure how to act around him in the light of day. Last night seemed like some sort of crazy fever dream now. Maybe in my super-stressed, anxious state I'd made all of it up? My instinct was to run, but before I could back away out of the door-way, Rafe put his coffee cup down and strode across the wide space in just a few long strides until he was right there in front of me. I automatically lowered my gaze to the floor, but, just like last night, his hands came to either side of my jaw to tilt my face so that he could look into my eyes.

I'd learned by now that Rafe really did not like when I avoided eye contact. When I was looking straight into his intense blue gaze, his smile widened.

"Hi," he said, before he kissed me briefly, then pulled back to search my face. "You okay?"

I nodded against his hands, which were still in my hair-line. "I think so," I whispered, then glanced behind me before I looked back at him. "Maybe we shouldn't...?" I hadn't slept in Rafe's bed last night, despite him making it clear that's what he wanted. I was still confused about us, and I certainly wasn't going to sleep with him with his sister in the house.

Rafe kissed me again, longer this time. And, of course, because it was him, because he was so glorious, because his clean, expensive smell was invading my senses, because he smelled of shower gel and aftershave and *man,* I slid one of my hands into his hair, my other hand up his back and I melted into him, my mouth opening under his. After a few moments, he broke the kiss to rest his forehead on mine.

"Now that is how I want you to kiss me in the morning, baby, okay?" He was using that tone again, the one that was soft but had a hard edge behind it, the one I knew he expected to be obeyed. I glanced behind me again, slowly coming out of the Rafe Daze.

"Your sister," I whispered.

Rafe shook his head and slid his arms around me fully so that he was hugging me into his chest, his large hands rubbing my back. "Poppy won't be up for hours yet."

"Still, I don't think we should take any chances, Rafe," I said, my voice muffled by his shirt.

Rafe sighed and pulled back from me, but kept hold of my hand.

"Clara, I told you last night," he said in that soft but firm tone, "I don't give a fuck if my sister sees me with you. She knows I'm a grown adult. She knows I'm not celibate and she'll be chuffed to bits that I'm shagging someone who isn't a stuck-up bitch for a change."

I managed a weak smile. "How do you know I'm not a stuck-up bitch?"

He laughed. "Just a hunch."

I dropped my eyes from his and bit my lip. "Rafe, I just don't know if us being open about having a relationship is the best idea for now."

"Clara, I don't—"

"Hear me out, okay?"

Rafe's jaw clenched in obvious frustration, but he gave me a short nod to continue.

"It would confuse Ozzie. It might break some of the trust I've built with him. Most children of divorced parents want them to reconcile. A new girlfriend is not a step towards reconciliation. Ozzie will know that, and it might make him angry. That could affect my progress with him."

Rafe started to shake his head, his mouth opening to interrupt, but I laid my hand over his chest and he closed it with a sigh.

"Trust me, I know kids. I know how they will react to things. Ozzie likes me now because he doesn't think I'm a threat. If he saw me in a different light, it could be very difficult for him to deal with. He's only seven, Rafe."

Rafe sighed but nodded a couple of times. "Okay, okay. I guess you're probably right," he said in a grumpy voice. "I don't want to do anything that might jeopardise how well he's doing."

My chest tightened. He was a good dad. I wished I could be completely honest with him about my reasons for hiding our relationship. My hand moved to Rafe's face to trace his stubble with my fingers, down from his high cheekbones to his strong jawline. I couldn't quite get my head around the concept that I could touch him freely.

"I can't believe that we..." I whispered, then broke off, not knowing how to complete that sentence.

Rafe smiled again, slipped his arms underneath me and lifted me up onto the granite worktop, stepping in between my legs.

"You better believe it, Clara," he said as he kissed the nape of my neck. "You know," he told me, his hands sliding over my jumper up to my breast. "You're very sexy when you're in schoolteacher mode."

"I doubt that, Rafe," I said through a surprised giggle. I was wearing my super soft, but oversized jumper with a pair of leggings. "This outfit is anything but sexy."

"I love this jumper," he murmured against my lips, his hand lightly squeezing my breast. "It's so soft."

"I, uh... the kids like it," I said in a shaky voice, rocking against him, feeling lightheaded. He moved his hand to the apex of my thighs and pressed on exactly the right spot over my leggings, moving in small circles. My breathing started coming in short pants as I felt myself coming closer to the edge.

"And these leggings are very sexy," he said against my ear, his low rumbling voice sending sparks through me. "I can feel everything through them."

"Oh my God," I said, clinging to his neck as my orgasm built.

"That's it, baby," he murmured in my ear. "Right here on the granite, just like in your dirty little dreams." His low, dark voice brought all the memories of last night flooding back and pushed me over the edge. I gave a sharp cry as I came against his hand.

"Well done, darling," he said in my ear, one hand cupping me with firm pressure whilst the other held me up on the granite – otherwise I was sure I'd have melted onto the floor in a boneless heap. After a few moments, he put his hands on my hips again, lifted me off the granite surface and put me safely back onto the kitchen stool. Then he swivelled the stool around to face the kitchen island, reached across and put a mug of coffee in front of me. When I didn't move, he took both my hands and wrapped them around the mug.

"Drink your coffee, Clara," he said, his body caging me in from behind. I could feel his heat and the hardness on my back.

"Right, yes, okay," I said weakly as I managed to raise the coffee up to my mouth. He gently moved my hair back to kiss the side of my neck, then stepped to the side, grabbed his phone off the counter, glanced down and then back at me.

"I'll see you later tonight, okay?" he said.

"Uh, yeah, okay. Um..." I trailed off, glancing down at

his crotch, then back up at his smirking face. I wasn't at all sure of the protocol here. "Are you, I mean...?"

He raised his eyebrows. "No time for that, I'm afraid," he said through a smile. "I've got to get to court, but I wanted you thinking about me all day. I didn't want you to forget what happened or how good it is between us, understand?"

I nodded, taking another shaky sip of my coffee. "Um, so about Ozzie. I—"

"Yes, I agree with you about Ozzie, so we'll wait to tell him."

I breathed a sigh of relief. The reasons I'd given Rafe were true. It *would* be confusing for Ozzie, and I didn't want to upset him or set back the progress I'd made with him, but I had other reasons as well. A public relationship with Lord Sterling would not be in my or his best interests. I had no doubt that eventually my family would come between us. There was nothing in my life that they didn't ruin, after all, but I wanted to wait. I wanted to be selfish for a little while and keep Rafe for myself without my family's interference.

"Hold on," Rafe said as he stalked out of the kitchen. When he came back, he was holding his overcoat, which he shook out, giving me a significant look. "Are you going to be able to control yourself if I put on my coat in here?" he asked, with a twinkle in his eye.

I laughed, feeling my face heat. "I can't believe I told you that! Ugh! Don't tease me," I said as he proceeded to do some sort of ridiculous reverse striptease, by putting his arm slowly in his overcoat, followed by his other arm, and then adjusting it. I was still laughing when he came over to me and closed his mouth over mine.

"I like you laughing," he said softly when he pulled back

from the kiss. I smiled up at him. The truth was, I didn't remember laughing this much in a very long time, if ever. He kissed my nose before he moved away to pick up his bag. "I agree with you about Ozzie for now. But Clara, I'm not going to wait forever to tell him. This is happening. You and I are happening. You understand me?"

I swallowed and then nodded, trying to keep my smile in place, but when Rafe frowned and tilted his head to the side, I knew I hadn't quite managed it.

"You do understand you're mine, don't you, Clara?" Rafe said in that low, commanding voice.

I gave a slight nod. "Yes," I whispered.

"And I'm yours too. Don't forget that either," he said before he turned and strode from the kitchen, his super sexy overcoat billowing out behind him.

Chapter 20

Wrestling?

Clara

"Ozzie!" The scream made everyone's heads in the playground turn towards the beautiful blonde with her arms flung wide, wearing crazy multicoloured leggings and a high-cut hot pink jumper that showed off her flat, toned stomach.

"Auntie Poppy!" Ozzie squealed, breaking away from me to streak off towards her.

She crouched down so that he could run straight into her arms. Once they were hugging, she lifted him up and spun around in circles until she staggered to the side and I was afraid they'd fall. She did look a little green around the gills. I cautiously walked up to them both, not sure of the reception I would get from the now-sober Lady Sterling after I'd seen the state she was in last night.

I really liked Poppy. I'd been intimidated when I first met her at the Sterling house. I'd seen her on the school run before when she'd been picking up Ozzie, but had never spoken to her. We all knew who she was. Everyone in the country knew who Poppy Sterling was. Given my shyness, it should have taken me a while to warm up to her. But I'd never met a less threatening human being in my life. She was like a ball of sunshine, all hugs and smiles and expensive perfume with the most adorable snort-laugh I'd ever heard. She won me over in under a minute, which was good as I'd seen a fair amount of her over the last few weeks. It was clear Poppy was close to her brother and her nephew. Ozzie's mum seemed to be out of the picture more than she was in it, and I suspected Poppy had stepped in after the divorce to support Rafe and his son.

So, yes, I liked Poppy. But I knew better than anyone how badly people can react after you've seen them vulnerable, and I hadn't known her for that long.

"Uh, hi, Lady Sterling," I said quietly, managing a small smile.

"Hey!" she said, Ozzie still in her arms. There was nothing small about her smile and I sighed in relief. Then frowned when she flinched, her hand that wasn't holding Ozzie up going to her head. She must have pulled at her injury. "Clara, you naughty lady. I've told you to call me Poppy." She laugh-snorted. "Or you could call me *total dickhead* after last night if you wanted. It would be deserved. I should have remembered that alcohol and I don't mix."

"You don't usually drink?"

She snorted again as she lowered Ozzie to the ground. "I used to, but I'm too much of a lightweight and it stopped being fun."

I tilted my head to the side. "Then what happened last night?"

"Well, I was nervous for one thing," Poppy said as she straightened and took Ozzie's hand.

"You were nervous?" There was a fair amount of disbelief in my tone. I couldn't actually imagine a nervous Poppy Sterling.

"It was the Sports Personality of the Year awards which was why Rory was there. He has that effect on me. I've never been good with outright contempt directed at me."

"Contempt?" How could anyone hold Poppy in contempt?

"Yeah, it's a whole thing." Poppy waved her hand as if to dismiss it as nothing, but her smile looked forced. "Anyway, I could have *sworn* I only had a few glasses of champagne last night, not enough to get blotto. Not that anyone would believe me. I've a bit of a rep for my lack of restraint. Rafey tells me you cleaned up my head, so thanks."

"It's no problem," I muttered distractedly as we started moving towards the car.

"What's restraint?" asked Ozzie and Poppy giggled.

"Ask Rory Wallace," she said with a derisory snort. "He's the *king* of it."

"He is?" said Ozzie, sounding impressed. "Rory Wallace is a legend."

"Ugh, you would think that, you rugby-loving weirdo," Poppy said. "All Rory's restraint makes for a bloody boring life if you ask me. He's lucky that I liven it up for him occasionally."

He didn't look particularly thrilled last night when he was holding Poppy's hair back while she vomited, but I did what I did best, and kept my mouth shut.

"Listen, Clara, I really am grateful. I thought I'd better come to pick the little guy up and apologise."

I gave her a soft smile. "Honestly, there's nothing to apologise for. I'm a guest with Lord Sterl... I, I mean, I'm a guest with Rafe and Ozzie. I'm very grateful for their hospitality."

"Let's go," said Ozzie impatiently, dragging Poppy along the pavement. "I'm starving."

"You're always starving, kid," she said, ruffling his hair as she let him pull her along. Poppy seemed to know all the mums we passed through the school gate and on the street, greeting them with her natural charm and humour, throwing out compliments as she went, making everyone smile.

When she saw Dave, she kissed the man on the cheek and he went bright red. I'd never seen Dave flustered before. The same happened with the ancient gardener when we arrived back at the house. Poppy might have been the most outgoing person I'd ever met in my life. She seemed to communicate via a combination of affection, flirtation, and genuine warmth. But there was one big problem with Poppy.

She asked a lot of questions.

And her manner was deceptive. Behind the warmth and sunshine energy was a steely determination to rival even her brother's, making it very difficult to get out of answering her.

So far, I'd managed to dodge or redirect a lot of her questions, but that day she seemed to be on some sort of mission.

"You don't have any family?" she said in horror when we had arrived home and were in the kitchen, having a cup of tea and getting Ozzie his after-school snack.

"Um, n-n-no." I stuttered, feeling guilty for lying to Poppy, but I really needed to shut down the family conversation early.

To my horror, her eyes filled with tears. "That's dreadful," she said in a wobbly voice. "I'm so, so sorry. I couldn't *bear* the idea of not having my family."

I cleared my throat. "Uh, really, it's... It's fine."

"But how did they die? What happened?"

"Um, well..." I was feeling more and more guilty by the second. "I don't really want to talk about it, Poppy, if that's okay."

"Oh God, right, of course. I'm a total dick," she said, wiping away one of her tears before stepping forward to me and grabbing me into a massive bear hug.

"Uh, Miss Clara's actually *my* friend," said Ozzie, sounding a little put out as he looked up from his cookies. "You and Daddy shouldn't really be hugging her all the time. I haven't given permission to share her yet."

Poppy let out a surprised giggle as she pulled back from me to look at Ozzie.

"Oh, she's yours, is she?" she said, raising an eyebrow. "And she's been hugging Daddy, has she?"

Ozzie shrugged. "Well, yeah. But that one time was 'cause Daddy was looking for her glasses."

"What?" asked Poppy, a knowing smile on her lips. "Your daddy hugged Miss Clara because he was looking for her glasses?"

"Yeah, yeah," said Ozzie, not picking up on his aunt's amusement. "He was looking for her glasses, and he tripped and fell on her on the sofa. I thought they were wrestling because that's sometimes what I do with my friend Josh. But Daddy said it was 'cause he fell. I've never really seen grown-ups do wrestling before."

Poppy's eyes were dancing, and her lips were pressed firmly together.

"Wrestling?" she managed to get out in a slightly choked voice as she lost the battle with her laughter. "Yes, you're right, Ozzie, it *is* a bit weird for adults to wrestle... but I bet it's fun."

"Right, come on then, Oz," I said in a fake bright tone, deciding to skirt around the whole wrestling issue. "Let's get some reading done before dinner, love."

I had thought that Poppy wouldn't be that interested in hanging around for Ozzie's reading book, but she sat down on the sofa with both of us, listening intently as Ozzie stumbled through his current book, which was the next level up from what he was used to.

"That's amazing, little man," Poppy said, her voice shaking slightly. When I glanced at her I was surprised to see a sheen of tears in her eyes. "You've come on loads in the last month."

I blinked at her. "Ozzie was reading to you?" I asked.

"Oh bugger," she mumbled.

"That was supposed to be our secret," Ozzie put in.

Poppy made an eek face. "Yeah, we didn't want to hurt your dad's feelings, did we, Oz?"

"That's okay," I said reassuringly. "You're reading with Daddy now so I'm sure he won't be upset, and I wouldn't tell him if you didn't want me to. But, Ozzie, why could you read with your auntie and not with Daddy?"

I looked at Poppy and she bit her lip. "Well, I think it's because Ozzie knows I'm not... Well, I find reading a bit of a bugger if I'm honest."

"Auntie Poppy can't read very good," Ozzie put in.

"Can't read very well, short stuff," Poppy corrected automatically.

"That too," Ozzie said. "So I didn't have to be worried when I read to her, because I knew she's not gonna think I'm stupid. And anyway, sometimes Auntie Poppy can't read the words either."

Poppy shifted on the sofa, her face flushing red. It was the first time I'd seen her even slightly embarrassed. "Yeah, well. I've *no* chance now, have I? You're getting so good you've shot up above *my* reading level now."

"Ah, okay," I said, giving Poppy a soft look. "Oz, lovie, why don't you go and get vegetables out of the fridge? You know, you can choose the ones you like." I'd found this was the best tactic with Ozzie. If he thought he was *choosing* to eat broccoli, he would normally partake in more than just a cursory nibble. With kids, it was all about choice and autonomy. Ironically, something I'd never had as a child. Ozzie grinned and shot to his feet to run to the kitchen. I suppressed a sigh. The last time I asked Ozzie to do this, he'd told me there were no vegetables, and I later found a cauliflower in the airing cupboard. But at least it bought me a few moments alone with Poppy.

"Hey, um, Poppy, you know there are some resources I could show you if you were keen?" I turned to her. She was the one to break eye contact this time.

"I won't waste your time, Clara," she said in a small voice, so far from her normal self that it was almost jarring. "I'm a bit of a lost cause."

I frowned. "I'm sure that's not the case, hun," I said carefully, but Poppy just shrugged and fiddled with the hem of her jumper. "Does Rafe know?" I'd found that a lot of people with severe dyslexia managed to hide it quite successfully. Even close family members could be unaware.

"He knows I'm thick as two short planks if that's what you mean," said Poppy defensively, her normal sunny expression clouding over with pain.

"Poppy, you—"

"He knows I'm dyslexic, but he also knows I'm a lost cause."

"I could help, you know?" I said very quietly.

Poppy rolled her eyes. "I've had tutors before, Clara."

"Not like me, you haven't," I told her. I wasn't a confident person in general, but knew down to my bones that I was a good teacher. And when it came to helping people to make sense of the muddle dyslexia made of letters and numbers, I was fucking amazing.

Poppy's eyes flickered with interest for a moment, but then her expression blanked as she looked away.

"Dyslexia doesn't make you stupid, Poppy," I said.

"Of course it doesn't," shouted Ozzie from the doorway. He was scowling over at us with his arms crossed over his little chest, looking very much like his father. "You don't think I'm stupid, do you, Auntie Poppy?" he said accusingly.

She looked horrified. "Of course I don't think you're stupid, Oz. You're the cleverest little shi... I mean sugar-lump I know. But I'm not like you."

Ozzie stamped his foot. "Who says? Just because you find your letters hard doesn't mean you're not clever. Isn't that right, Miss Clara?"

"Yes, that's quite right, Ozzie," I said with a firm nod.

"It's just that our brains work different," Ozzie went on. "It gives us super brains."

"Super brains?" Poppy asked, her eyebrows going up.

"Sometimes dyslexic people can have more creative flair," I told Poppy softly. "And they can be more spatially aware, more likely to be visual thinkers. It can give them advantages in all sorts of fields."

Poppy looked between me and Ozzie, a little of that sunniness leaking back into her expression as she tilted her head to the side.

"Okay," she said softly. "I guess if my brother and Oz trust you, I can try it too."

My chest tightened as I looked back at her, feeling that twinge of guilt deep in the pit of my stomach.

Trust.

They were trusting me, the Sterlings.

And they shouldn't, not really.

Chapter 21

Very incompetent minions

Rafe

"I don't know, Rafe. I've never cooked a roast in my life," Poppy said, throwing her hands up.

"I thought you were coming over to help, you numpty," I shot back at her as I glared at the massive beef joint that was sitting on my granite work surface.

"Brother of mine, I bring the vibes. You know this. I do not bring culinary expertise. I can't even remember the last time I turned an oven on if I'm honest with you. Even the microwave confuses me slightly."

"Great, we're buggered then."

I heard the door creak and looked over to see Clara's face peeking around it into the kitchen and I smiled. "Hi, Clara."

She gave me a small, tentative smile in return and a low wave. We'd been together now for two weeks, but Clara still wasn't happy for my family, or anyone else for that matter, knowing about us. It was beyond frustrating to have her in my arms most nights but have to keep my distance in front of anyone else. And right then all I wanted to do was just take her in my arms, kiss her and hug her to me.

But, as always, my sister had no such qualms about embarrassing anyone in any given situation.

"Clara, darling!" she shouted, dancing over to where Clara was standing, throwing her arms around her. "You're always so bloody gorgeous in the morning. I'm literally green with envy."

Clara was stiff for a moment in my sister's arms before she hugged her back. I did catch a small eye roll as she said, "Poppy, you know perfectly well that you're the most beautiful girl in any room, you daft article."

My eyebrows went up. Clara was gradually getting braver. I knew my sister had won her over and the shyness was retreating. I suspected that deep down, Clara wasn't actually that shy. We still weren't at the stage where she would tell me everything, so I couldn't know what exactly she'd been through. But somehow life had made Clara feel like she needed to make herself smaller, quieter, lesser than she should be. And that shit was ending very soon if I had my way.

But the first step of the plan was to integrate her just that little bit more into my world, hence Sunday roast at my house. Normally, we all went to Mum and Dad's, considering it was a bloody huge country mansion and staffed twenty-four-seven. However, I knew there was very little chance of me persuading Clara to come with us to meet my entire family. And this way, if they came here, then she was a captive audience. The only fly in the ointment was my inability to cook.

I'd attempted to solve this by roping in Martha, who had

prepared a roast for me, including batter for Yorkshire puddings, roast potatoes, a beef joint and vegetables, all of which apparently I just had to "bung in the oven." What Martha failed to do was leave me very specific instructions on exactly which oven, what temperature and how long, or in fact how to switch the oven on. So, I was somewhat at a loss.

"Save us!" Poppy cried dramatically as she rocked Clara from side to side in a tight hug. Clara was giggling now, which I took as a very good sign. Clara's giggles were few and far between, but they remained, other than my son's laughter, my very favourite sound in the world.

"Help!" Poppy cried again as she pushed Clara over towards where I was standing by the granite. When she was within reach, I risked a short side hug and a very soft kiss on her temple. She flushed bright pink but didn't actively push me away – another encouraging sign.

Clara looked at the beef joint and all the other prepared trays and then blinked. "It looks like you've done every-thing," she said in confusion. "What do you need my help with?"

"*Martha* did everything," I told her.

"We are merely her minions and, unfortunately, very incompetent minions," said Poppy.

"Well, just turn the oven on to one-eighty, and, well, the beef will take the longest so put that in first."

"Right," I said, looking at the oven, then back at Clara. "Turn on the oven, you say?"

"Uh, yes."

I scratched the back of my head. "But the problem is, I've got three of the blighters and zero clue which one cooks beef."

Clara let out another small giggle. This time she even snorted, very softly, but it was there. I'd embarrass myself with my shit kitchen skills all day if it could invoke this kind of reaction.

"Well, there's not a specific oven for beef, Rafe." Her casual use of my first name was another step forward, especially in front of Poppy. "Most people just have one oven total. Not meat ovens and vegetable ovens."

"Right, yes." I paused. "As for actually switching the confounded thing on? Is there a specific...?"

Clara let out another little snort-laugh and moved to brush past me to get to the largest oven, turning it on then moving the inner trays around to make room for the beef which she put in. "We can cook the roasties in the same one."

"What about the Yorkshire puddings?" Poppy asked. "I bloody love Yorkshire puddings. I don't want to miss out on Yorkshire puddings."

She smiled at Poppy. "They only take around twenty minutes, so two hours might be overkill."

"Oh wow, I'd have bunged everything in at the same time and called the job a good 'un."

"Right, well," Clara said in an unsure voice after she'd turned the oven on and put the meat inside. "I'll just get a cup of tea, and then I guess I should..." She glanced nervously at the door to the kitchen, then back at us, and then straightened her shoulders. "I guess I'll be popping out."

I frowned at her. "Clara, you're not going anywhere."

Her eyes went wide, and when she took a small step back, I realised I might have come on a bit strong. I gentled my tone when I spoke again. "I just meant, it's Sunday, and you don't want to traipse all around London on a Sunday. Stay and have lunch."

She pulled her lips between her teeth to bite them as she looked between me and the roast potatoes, clearly tempted. "Um, it's just I think I said to Lily that I, um..."

"Oh, Lily's coming," Poppy said, and Clara's head jerked in her direction.

"Lily's coming *here?*"

"Oh yes and she's bringing someone called George?"

"George the goldfish?"

Poppy laughed. "Ah! That makes more sense. She said she was tired of feeding him and cleaning him out. I *thought* it was a bit of a bizarre intro. Anyway, it'll be a laugh. Mum and Dad will get a kick out of her."

"What? Your mum and dad?"

"Yeah, of course. They should be here after the wicked witch brings Ozzie back."

"Poppy," I said in a warning tone.

"Ugh, calm down, Rafe. Clara must know what a mega-bitch your ex is."

"You know I try to keep it civilised for Ozzie," I gritted out.

"Well, Oz isn't here yet, so I can say what I like. You met her yet, Clara? As Ozzie's teacher, I mean."

Clara shook her head in sharp jerks. "N-no, I don't meet the parents."

"Oh? You met my brother though?"

"Er... well, Rafe sort of..."

"I bulldozed my way into meeting Clara," I told Poppy.

"Standard," she replied with an eye roll.

Clara's smile was strained now. "Listen," she said as she looked at me. "Rafe, I really don't think it's appropriate for me to meet your parents or your ex-wife."

I stepped closer to Clara, wanting to take her in my arms but very aware that she wasn't comfortable with PDA in front of my sister.

"It's just Sunday lunch, darling," I said softly. At the endearment, Clara's eyes flew wide, and she glanced at Poppy, then back at me. Poppy, always intuitive, winked at me and took this as her cue to leave.

"Oh, just remembered we don't have any mint sauce," she said in mock horror.

"You don't eat mint sauce with beef," Clara replied.

"*I* eat mint sauce with everything. Back soon." Poppy skipped out of the kitchen, and we heard the front door open and shut.

I moved to Clara then and did what I had wanted to do since she poked her head around the kitchen door – took her in my arms and kissed her mouth very softly. After I was done, she blinked up at me with the look of wonder in her eyes that I didn't think I would ever get used to seeing.

"Honestly, I really think that—"

"Mum and Dad want to meet you, darling," I said gently as I lifted my hand to brush her hair behind her ear. "They know what you've done for Ozzie, and they want to meet the amazing teacher who's helped him. They feel like they let Poppy down, and they're so grateful that history's not repeating itself with Ozzie."

"Yes, but it's not—"

"Appropriate?" I cut her off with another soft kiss. It took a few seconds, but eventually her mouth opened under mine, and she was melting against me. When I pulled back, her eyes were glazed as she blinked up at me. After a moment, she cleared her throat, the glazed look melting away into a frown.

"Don't think that you can just kiss me and get your way, Rafe Sterling," she said in an attempt at a stern tone.

I grinned down at her. "I don't," I said before pressing my lips to hers again. Then my mouth moved from the corner of her lips, across her delicate jawline to her ear. "I wouldn't dream of it," I said with mock affront. "Now let me make your tea. *That* I can do."

Chapter 22

The one Mrs Clayton hides from everyone

Clara

"What even *is* gravy?" asked Rafe.

Poppy put her hands on her hips and tilted her head to the side. "Oh, I've never really thought about it. I've only ever seen it in the gravy boat. Never considered how it was actually made. Isn't it just sort of meat juice?"

Lily snorted. "Meat juice? Holy crap! Save me from spoiled aristocrats who've never had to lift a finger for themselves their entire lives. No, Lord and Lady Sterling, it is not *just* meat juice." Lily sighed. "Where's your flour? I'm a shit cook but I'm better than you two numpties."

"Lily, let me do it," I said, stepping forward and taking the flour out of her hands.

Lily gave a sigh of relief. "Thank God for that. Clara is a brilliant cook."

"Yes, I know," said Rafe, through a smile.

Lily lifted an eyebrow. She looked between Rafe and me. "So you're cooking for Lord of the Manor on the reg, are you, Clara?" she asked.

I attempted a casual shrug which was not casual in the slightest. "Well, I'm living here. It's the least I can do. I mean, Ozzie likes my meatballs, so…"

"Yeah, I love Clara's meatballs," shouted Ozzie as he sprinted into the kitchen, straight to me, colliding with my legs and sending me back onto one foot. I just about managed to keep hold of the flour, but some of it puffed up from the open top, settling in a cloud over me and Ozzie, so we were covered in a light dusting of white.

"You're here!" shouted Ozzie as he looked up from his tight hug around my middle.

I smiled down at him, my heart tugging painfully. "Of course I'm here, Oz."

"And George is here!" He ran to the small fish tank on the granite surface and pressed his nose up against the glass. "Hi George. I'm gonna feed you every day until you're massive!"

"Careful, you don't make that fish explode, Oscar Sterling," said Lily.

Ozzie's gaze shot to her and his eyes flew wide. "Miss Summerfield," he breathed as he took a step away from me and pointed straight at Lily. "Miss Summerfield is here." He was staring and pointing at her as if she were a lion that had escaped from the zoo.

Poppy laughed and came over to scoop him up, ruffle his hair, and give him sloppy kisses on his cheek, which he reluctantly accepted. "Don't be rude, you little squishball," she told him.

"Auntie Poppy," he said under his breath, "you can't call me *squishball* in front of my teachers."

"Oh, come on, everyone can see how squishy you are," she said, tickling him until he laughed.

"Hey, Oz," said Lily, "I hope it's all right that I—"

"For Christ's sake, Rafe!" A cut-glass posh accent cut through what Lily was going to say and I heard high heels clicking across the tiles of the kitchen. "Your fucking guard dogs tried to oust me from my own bloody house again."

Ozzie moved back into my side and I automatically reached to brush some of the flour out of his hair.

The most glamorous woman I'd ever seen in my life stopped a few feet from the kitchen island, thrust out her hip and put her hand on it. She had a tall, willowy frame, her hair perfectly styled in blonde waves. I suddenly felt distinctly underdressed in my baggy jeans and sweatshirt combo. This woman was wearing a beautiful, what looked like cashmere jumper, combined with a mid-length silk cream skirt and a structured blazer, and was carrying an Hermès bag. She could have walked straight off a Paris catwalk and not have looked out of place.

"Sophia," Rafe said through gritted teeth.

Of course, this was Rafe's ex-wife. I'd seen photos of her in various magazines. To be honest, in real life, she was even more glamorous and intimidating than she looked in the society pages.

"Hi, Soph, always a pleasure," Poppy muttered. It was the first time I'd ever heard Poppy less than her one hundred and ten percent enthusiastic self. If I were honest, I didn't think it was possible for her to sound like that.

"Yes, quite," Sophia said through a fake smile. Then her eyes snapped to me.

I realised that my hand was still in Ozzie's hair. I quickly let it drop to my side.

"Who are you, and what are you doing in my husband's house?" she said, taking a couple of steps towards me.

I automatically took a step back and saw a flash of

triumph in her eyes. This woman was a bully. I could recognise bullies easily. I'd been around them all my life, after all.

"*Ex*-husband, Sophia, remember," Rafe said again through gritted teeth.

"Semantics," she said with a wave of her hand.

Rafe shook his head. "Not semantics. Very legal, Sophia. Very, *very* legal." He sighed. "Sophia, this is Clara and Lily, Ozzie's teachers from school."

"And they're in your house. Why?" she said, narrowing her eyes at both of us.

"Because I invited them, Sophia."

"Hey, Oz," Poppy put in as she took Ozzie's hand. "Why don't you show me your new Lego set? Daddy said you'd built a bat cave or something."

Ozzie snorted and rolled his eyes. "Not a bat cave, Auntie Poppy. It's an Avengers Assemble Age of Ultron Base."

"Sorry, my mistake, squishball. Come on then, show me this masterpiece."

Sophia turned her attention from me and Lily to look at her son and the transformation was instant. Her face warmed and her expression softened.

"Come give Mama a hug before you run off, darling," she said in a tone so gentle and loving that she seemed like a completely different woman.

Ozzie ran to her as she squatted down and she folded him into her arms. "Don't be mean to Miss Clara and Miss Lily, Mama," I heard Ozzie whisper. "Miss Clara's the one what helped me read good."

She stroked his hair as she pulled back to look into his eyes. "I won't be mean, baby boy."

"'K. I'll miss you."

"Miss you too, gorgeous little man."

As Poppy led Ozzie out of the kitchen and Sophia straightened, I could see a sheen of tears over her eyes, but she blinked them away rapidly.

"Hello," Lily said bravely, stepping forward and holding out her hand to Sophia. "I'm Lily – Miss Summerfield. I don't think we've met. I think you might have been away for parents' evening." Sophia looked at Lily's hand for a long moment. I thought she was going to leave Lily hanging but in the end she did deign to touch her fingers to hers very briefly.

"Sophia doesn't tend to go to parents' evenings, do you, Sophia?" said Rafe.

Sophia rolled her eyes, her cold mask slipping back into place. "Some of us have to travel for work, actually." Her eyes shot back to me and narrowed. "Oh, you're the teaching assistant, aren't you? The one Mrs Clayton hides from everyone. My son talks about you all the time. He tells me that you're staying here. Is that true?"

"It seemed expedient for Clara to stay here, Sophia, as that nanny you recommended was a complete bitch. I needed childcare. Plus, Clara is helping Ozzie. You know that."

Sophia's lip curled and I could see she was gearing up for a fight. But Rafe and Sophia fighting wasn't productive. It was the last thing Ozzie needed.

"Oz talks about you as well," I told her quietly. She tore her gaze away from Rafe and blinked at me.

"W-what?" she asked, totally thrown.

"He tells me about his beautiful, kind mummy. About how you give the best hugs in the world." I smiled at her. All of this was true. Whatever Sophia was like to everyone else she was definitely loving with her son. "He also told me that you got very cross with him when he said he thought he was stupid. That you think he's the smartest little boy in London."

"Oh..." She turned away and smoothed her hair back over her shoulders, clearly trying to gather herself. "I..." she cleared her throat. "I'm sorry. I was rude just now."

"Not at all," I told her. "If living arrangements change, it's important for everyone to be aware."

"Yes," she agreed.

"You should have told Sophia I was living here," I told Rafe.

Rafe looked between me and Sophia and then gave a stiff nod. "Yes. I should have done. I apologise, Sophia."

She nodded back, then turned to me again. "Miss Clara, I... thank you."

"What—?"

"For what you're doing for Ozzie. He read with me last week so... thank you." That sheen was over her eyes again but she blinked rapidly to clear it. "And I'm sorry I was rude before. I just... I'm finding it difficult after the divorce." She turned to Rafe. "If you'd just talk to me about *us*, I—"

"Sophia, we've been over this," Rafe said firmly. "There's nothing to talk about."

Sophia shook her head. "Rafe, please. I—"

"Sophia, darling," a posh voice sounded from the doorway of the kitchen and we all turned that way to see the Earl and Countess of Dorset standing there with an elderly lady that must have been Rafe and Poppy's Granny. "I think it's time to run along now," the countess continued.

"Yes, sod off," put in the elderly lady. "Bloody Knightsbridge riff-raff. Honestly Rafe, you should have known better."

Neither the countess nor the dowager were wearing the kind of red-soled, high-fashion heels as Sophia. Their shoes were far sturdier and the countess had teamed hers with perfectly fitted trousers, a twin set and pearls, whilst the dowager wore a headscarf and, bizarrely, a wax jacket. Rafe's father had streaks of grey in his hair and the same lordly air as Rafe, but was wearing a tweed coat which on anyone else would have looked ridiculous. On him, it only enhanced his old-money aura.

"This is my home," Sophia said, her face flushing and her expression twisting with anger.

"It hasn't been your home since you decided to shag that actor fellow, darling," said the earl and I blinked in shock. These people were clearly the level of posh where zero fucks were given. "Run along and do give your father my regards. I understand his estate has been faltering of late."

Sophia's eyes snapped to the earl and her face paled.

His voice changed subtly with his next words, dropping just that little bit lower with a hint of menace threading through the words. "It would be a shame if the estate went under completely, don't you think, Sophia? It can be difficult to protect these old legacies. Such a shame."

A shiver went down my spine. I was very attuned to sensing danger. There was something about this man, behind the gentlemanly exterior, that was almost scary.

"So important for everything to be pleasant after a divorce, isn't it?" put in the countess, her smile more like a baring of teeth now. "For Ozzie. It would be terrible if that *weren't* the case."

Sophia looked afraid now. The way the earl and the countess were looking at her was almost sinister, more like members of *my* family would look at people they were intimidating.

I swallowed nervously. The comparisons were making me feel unsettled.

"Right, I'll just be going," Sophia muttered as she hurried to leave, bobbing a curtsy as she went past the earl and the countess.

Oh shit, was I supposed to be curtsying as well? I grabbed onto Lily's arm and she gave me a confused look, clearly not understanding what I was panicking about.

But then the front door slammed and it was too late. The earl and countess were descending on Lily and me. The sinister look in the earl's eyes was completely gone now. He looked just like an affable older gentleman should on a Sunday. Kind smile on his lips, one hand in his pocket, totally relaxed.

"The amazing Clara. I've heard so much about you," he said as he crossed the kitchen towards me. "And Miss Summerfield, I presume."

"Lord Sterling," I stuttered out as I performed an inexpert curtsy complete with comical wobble.

"Oh, darling," said the countess as she moved to me, took me by my shoulders and then air-kissed either side of my head, before giving Lily the same treatment. "You don't have to bother with all that. Sophia only does it because my husband scares the bollocks off her. She's a good mum when she's actually here, but she can be a raving bitch otherwise and it's best to keep her reined in. Now, no Lord or Lady bollocks. We're George and Eleanor."

"And you can call me Granny Sterling, dear," put in the dowager as she gave me her own air kisses. "Every other bugger does."

Lily let out a high-pitched, squeaky laugh. Her hand flew to her face, which went red.

"So you're the dynamic duo who've been sorting out my

grandson," the earl said. "We owe you a debt of gratitude, I understand."

"I—well, we—it's Ozzie who's done all the work. We just—"

"Clara, honestly," Lily cut me off. "Don't listen to her. Clara's an absolute wonder when it comes to working with the kids with dyslexia and bringing them out of themselves. And Oz is a great kid to have in class. He's so bright."

"Yes, he really is bright," I managed to get out in a quiet voice.

"Well, of course," the countess said. "I've always known that. Jolly good show, smoothing things over with my ex-daughter-in-law, by the way."

"Rafe," the earl said. "If Sophia is giving you trouble again, we could consider——"

"Dad, not now," said Rafe.

I had no idea what Lord Sterling was about to say, but I did notice that sinister quality come back into his eyes.

If I were honest with myself, I would admit that this family scared the bollocks off me as well.

Chapter 23

Slipping through my fingers

Clara

"Your dad wants a word with you."

I startled at Pete's voice and spun around on the pavement to face him, fear stealing my breath for a moment. Pete might look scrawny, but he was just as dangerous as the rest of them.

"Fuck off, Pete," I snapped, skittering away from him. It didn't matter that we were on a busy pavement and it was broad daylight; I wasn't safe near any of my father's men. I turned to walk away, but strong fingers closed around my upper arm, bringing me to an abrupt stop.

"You can't ignore him, Clara," Pete hissed, squeezing harder and then giving me a small shake. "You know what happens when you ignore him."

I yanked my arm out of his grip and took a few steps back, nearly colliding with a suited businessman walking in the other direction. Pete jerked his head towards an alcove next to a shop, and I gritted my teeth but followed him there.

"Like I said, he wants a word," said Pete.

I crossed my arms over my chest, swallowing down the bile that had risen into the back of my throat.

"The last time I spoke to my father, it didn't go well for me, Pete," I said, levelling him with a steady look. Pete looked away and shifted uncomfortably on his feet. I was surprised when colour crept up his neck, staining his cheeks. He knew what had gone down, and clearly, he hadn't been working for my father for long enough to lose his humanity completely.

"It'll be worse for you if he has to have you brought in," Pete said stiffly.

My eyes widened. "How much worse could it possibly be?"

"What happened was an accident," he said, his voice lacking conviction.

"An accident?" I said, my voice rising with my panic. "My father's fists *accidentally* slipped, did they? Pete, he was teaching me a lesson. I've learnt the lesson. I won't go near him ever again."

"You know it doesn't work like that, Clara," Pete said, losing his patience. "You know you can't just walk away from your family. No one walks away."

I huffed. "That's bloody ridiculous. We're not the Mafia."

Pete's gaze sharpened on me. He didn't reply. I had a sinking feeling in the pit of my stomach as I went over the facts of my situation.

Shit.

The term *mafia* basically just describes an organised crime network. My father and brothers did control a large portion of east London. Bloody hell. They basically *were* a mafia operation. Just a slightly crap, unattractive version who drank beer, wore England shirts and conducted their crime deals in the local pub. I knew my father's organisation had grown since I left home, but he was clearly more powerful than even I'd realised.

"I-I-I am not going back there," I whispered. "He can't expect me to."

"Listen, you stupid little bitch," snarled Pete. "You *will* go back to that house and you *will* speak to him."

I straightened my shoulders, reaching for the backbone I knew was in there somewhere. "I can't, I—"

"You know you will, and you know why," he said, shifting again in discomfort.

It took me a moment but when I realised what he was saying I rocked back as if he'd physically struck me. My shoulders slumped as the spine I'd been reaching for disintegrated again.

Zach.

That's what Pete meant. That's why he knew I'd fall into line. If I were honest with myself, I knew that I'd buried my head in the sand over the last three months. Living in a world where I travelled in a bulletproof car and stayed in a house complete with a high-level security system had shielded me from my worst fears for a while, had allowed me to hide from the shitshow that my life actually was. Because, in reality, I didn't exist in a world with handsome men wearing billowy cashmere overcoats, who held me at night and gave me multiple orgasms. But this new reality had been too good for me to resist.

We'd fallen into a comfortable daily routine which involved me eating with Rafe and Ozzie, listening to Ozzie read to Rafe, then curling up with Rafe on the sofa after Ozzie had gone to bed. Rafe would play with my hair, stroke my back, hold my hand, either watching the telly with me and making derisive but often hilarious commentary on the crap reality programmes I favoured, or working quietly on his laptop balanced on his knee but keeping me plastered to his side.

I was no longer on edge all the time. My BMI was no longer in a dangerously low range and I felt safer than I had in years. I was getting a full night's sleep, mostly in Rafe's arms, although I insisted on retreating to the guest room before Ozzie woke up (something Rafe was becoming more and more frustrated with, especially as he was ready to be open about our relationship).

I'd never known the level of endorphins I was currently experiencing. Only this morning Rafe had accomplished the logistical feat of shagging me up against the tiled wall of his ensuite bathroom whilst his multiple shower heads blasted us from all angles. As if that wasn't enough, the man then cooked me bacon. He gave me two orgasms before nine o'clock in the morning *and* bacon. How was anyone supposed to resist that? Those regular endorphin rushes were now addling my mind. This unadulterated happiness was like a drug, and I was an addict not wanting reality to invade our bubble.

That was the real reason why I still insisted on secrecy. If I let Rafe tell Ozzie, I knew the next step would be going public with our relationship. Something I had actually been wavering about over the last few days, given how safe I was feeling. But this conversation with Pete was proving how right I'd been. Rafe was a high-profile man. He was an aristocrat, had a famous sister and he was set to be one of the youngest high court judges appointed in over a hundred years. There was no way that my relationship with him could remain under any sort of wraps – and I needed to fly under the radar of my family as much as possible.

The only other person who knew about me and Rafe was Poppy. Given how frequently she was at the house and her rampant curiosity, it really wasn't feasible to hide it from her. Also, if Ozzie was at his mum's or after he'd gone to bed, Rafe would happily hug me in front of her, kiss the nape of my neck when he brought me tea and even pull me down onto his lap in the living room. Poppy was certainly not unaware of what was going on. And now that she was at the house even more regularly to work with me on her literacy, it was even more difficult to hide.

But I had a geeky, six-foot-tall, skinny reason why I couldn't stay in this bubble forever. The same reason why I hadn't left London years ago, or more recently when Grant offered to set me up out of harm's way.

I'd thought this time I was justified in staying away from my family. To be fair, Zach had been so shaken by what happened after I'd come over to help him revise that he didn't want me anywhere near the house either. He'd told me he'd be fine, and that he needed me for when he was actually able to leave, and until then I should stay safe.

"I don't know why they hate you so much, Clara," he'd said when he'd come to see me in the hospital. "I just don't understand it. It's as if they resent you for what you represent, or what you're trying to represent to me. But you've never hurt them, you've never hurt *anyone*. It's not fair."

"Life's not fair," I'd croaked, trying to give him a small smile despite the swelling in my face. "We know that better than most. Just keep your head down, Zach. Try to stay out of their way. Maybe spend a bit more time at the library."

I knew that Zach was now shielding me from what was going on at home. My texts were answered briefly. He was always "fine". The same went with phone calls: brief, to the point and leaving so much unsaid between us.

He wasn't fine, but I had been scared to find out just how bad things were.

And in the back of my mind I knew that these last three months were only a brief reprieve. It was the same pattern in our childhood when most of the attacks were on Mum. Dad would regret it afterwards, and he'd back off for a while. But then things would start slipping, and his behaviour would begin to deteriorate again.

I re-adjusted my glasses on my face and forced myself to make eye contact with Skinny Pete.

"Okay," I agreed, that one word heavy with defeat. "When and where?"

Skinny Pete's tense stance relaxed slightly. I didn't feel sorry for him. He was a violent son of a bitch, just like the rest of them, but I knew there would have been repercussions for him had I completely refused to meet with the family. And to be honest, I didn't want any more violence on my behalf.

"Tomorrow, six pm, at the house."

I shuddered at the thought of returning to that house and felt bile rise in the back of my throat but swallowed it down.

Rafe

Clara was hiding something from me. Well, no, that wasn't strictly accurate. Clara was hiding *everything* from me. Until now, I hadn't quite appreciated how much she deflected questions about herself. She was quiet in general, yes, but about herself she was *silent*.

Now, Clara was a relatively good liar – her friend Lily, however, was not. I'd wanted Clara to feel settled here, for her to feel like this was her home now, so I told Clara to invite Lily over again last week. It was one of the evenings that Poppy was here which was perfect. Last Sunday, after the initial intimidation of meeting someone so famous, Lily had taken to Poppy immediately. They were actually both pretty similar. Poppy loved that Lily had chosen *Sweeney Todd* as an appropriate play for seven-year-olds, and she had all sorts of ideas to make some scenes even gorier.

It was when Lily was here and the conversation turned towards families that I realised something was amiss. Poppy, curious as ever, had asked Lily about hers, and they'd chatted for a while, comparing mad family antics. But then my sister's eyes had softened when she looked at Clara, and she'd apologised for bringing the subject up.

"Sorry, Clara, darling," Poppy said softly. "I'm an insensitive clod."

"Er... what exactly are you sorry for?" Lily asked, and Poppy's eyebrows went up.

"Well, I just thought Clara might be a bit sensitive about family chat. She told me the other night about how her parents died, and she doesn't have any other family. I really am sorry for banging on about mine like a complete ninny."

Lily's eyes widened at this, and her mouth dropped open, but before she could speak, Clara sent her a sharp look, and she snapped her mouth shut. I knew Clara didn't have any family. She'd already told me she was an only child and her parents had died a few years ago, one of cancer, the other a heart attack. What was there to hide about that? Something was not right here.

And I just couldn't shake the nagging suspicion I had in the back of my mind that Clara was slipping through my fingers.

Intent on knowing Clara's full story, I'd even tried

cornering Mrs Clayton last week to pump her for information. Mrs Clayton was just as tight-lipped as Lily and just as bad a liar. But the most interesting thing about that one-sided conversation with Mrs Clayton was the flash of fear in her expression when I mentioned Clara's background and parents. That startled me. What on earth was there to be frightened of?

Now, for some reason, in the last few days, Clara had lost her openness from before. Her shields had gone back up with me, and it was pissing me off. I'd worked hard to gain her trust and I'd done nothing to warrant losing it. When I asked her what the matter was, she said she was *fine* and gave me one of those small, tight smiles that I hated. Gone were her giggles, gone were her wide grins that lit up her entire face and, in turn, the room.

To compound my frustration, her complete refusal to talk to Ozzie about the fact we were together now, and her absolutely adamant avoidance of being seen in public with me was starting to *really* piss me off. Most of the women I dated in the past couldn't *wait* to be seen with me, all of them happy to be featured in papers and magazines as a potential future Lady Sterling.

Clara was the complete opposite. In fact, when I'd mentioned taking her out for dinner last night, her face had lost all colour and she'd swayed on her feet for a moment like she might actually pass out. I'd been so shocked at the time that I just steadied her, before hugging her to me and telling her I would get fish and chips instead. She'd melted into me like she always did, kissed me like she always did, and even made love to me later that night like she always did, but I knew her shields were still up. There seemed to be no way of getting through to her.

And now, the woman who had consistently refused to

go anywhere with me over the last few days was telling me that she had to go out.

"That's fine," I said in a measured tone, crossing my arms over my chest. "But where are you going?"

Clara bit her lip and then tucked her hair behind her ears before she answered, one of her tells for when she was anxious.

"Just to meet an old friend from teacher training," she said.

Okay, so I wasn't happy about it, and not just because I was a possessive arsehole – I still had the memory of her bruised face after her "fall" down her non-existent stairs. And I could tell that she didn't actually like being out in the open. She didn't even really seem to like the walk from the school to the car. Her shoulders were always tense and her posture stiff until she was in the backseat with the door slammed behind her. Same went for the walk from the car to my house. I could feel her relief once I shut the front door. I'd wanted to ask her about it, maybe even suggest some therapy about what I was starting to suspect was some form of agoraphobia triggered by past trauma. But now she was going out alone on a whim? It didn't make sense.

I gave her a small smile. "How about I come too?" I suggested.

Panic crossed her expression for a moment before she blanked it. What the fuck?

"Uh... you'll be at work. I'm meeting her early."

"I can try and get out of work in time," I said, knowing that would be incredibly difficult. The two interlinked cases I was working on were taking up a huge amount of our time. The first one was proving relatively simple: a charge of GBH with intent, two witnesses willing to come forward and the whole thing captured on CCTV – open and shut case, in my opinion. But the second case being brought against the family-run East End crime organisation... it was beyond complicated, with so much evidence streaming in from the encrypted messaging network that the police had managed to gain access to; it was going to require an entire team of barristers once the arrests were made.

But at this point, Clara was my priority, which, for someone as obsessed with work as I was, was saying something.

"No," she snapped, a hint of that fire that I usually liked in her expression now, but when it came to her being stubborn about something that worried me, it only served to piss me off. "You *can't* come."

I held my hands up in surrender. "Okay, okay." I pushed my hand into my hair and shoved my other hand into my pocket to stop myself from reaching for her. "Just be safe, Clara. Understand me?"

Clara nodded and then tried to pull away from me in a sharp jerk. But I kept my arm wrapped around her waist to hold her in place for a moment. My other hand came up to her jaw to tilt her head back.

"I'll see you later, yeah?" I whispered low in her ear. "Tonight?"

"Yes," she said in a shaky voice. I could have sworn she was on the verge of tears, but when I pulled back, her eyes were dry.

Chapter 24

It's time for you to step up

Clara

I took a deep breath and pushed open the front door to my family's house. The first thing I saw as I walked in was Mum standing in the middle of the hallway, facing the entrance.

"Hi, Mum," I said softly. Her vacant expression cleared for a moment as she met my eyes. We were both small women, just a touch over five feet, and delicate – *too* delicate. It had been the same for generations – the women of the family were tiny, the men all tall and well-built. Zach was really the only skinny aberration, but I suspected that if he wasn't under so much stress and didn't have to avoid the common areas of the house so much, he'd fill out quickly.

"Mum?" I pressed when she didn't respond. Mum wasn't really there anymore to be honest. She was present in body, and she functioned... Well, most of the time, she functioned. Sometimes she just sat at the kitchen table and stared into space. She still wore make-up. Concealer was a must, as it was a rarity for her face to be totally clear of bruising, but she wasn't the beauty that she once was. Her nose had been broken a couple too many times, and she had a cauliflower ear on one side. I doubted that she cared though. I doubted she felt much of anything now.

"Clara," she breathed, moving to me and giving me a weak hug. I hugged her back more fiercely but mindful of her fragility. "You're late," she whispered as she pulled away. "You know your dad doesn't like it when you're late, love."

"Okay, Mum. How are you?"

She looked confused for a moment. For Mum, direct questions, let alone those asking her about herself, were a rarity.

"I'm fine. Don't keep your dad waiting."

I swallowed down my bitter response. This had been the pattern of my childhood.

Don't keep your dad waiting.

Don't run. Don't make too much noise, your dad doesn't like it.

Put those toys away, your dad likes a clean house.

Everything had centered around what my father liked or didn't like. Nothing had been for us; nothing had been for Mum. It was all to please a cruel man who didn't deserve to have a family.

I sighed. "Okay, let's go through."

Nobody acknowledged me when I entered the kitchen. Dad, Ruben and a man I knew as Pinky (so named because he had a penchant for chopping off people's pinky fingers if they pissed him or my father off) were sitting at the large table.

"If they've lost the product," Dad snapped, "then that's *their* fucking problem. They still have to pay, understand?"

"Yeah, yeah," Pinky replied. "We'll get it sorted."

They talked business for a couple more minutes, and I stood stock still in the middle of the kitchen, hands clasped in front of me, waiting. I knew better than to interrupt my father or do anything that might piss him off. My mother, for her part, drifted into the kitchen, removing the empty beers from in front of the men and replacing them with new ones.

I hated this house, but I especially hated the kitchen. For some reason this seemed to be my father's preferred area to conduct business, especially if he was "sending a message." I'd accidentally walked in a few times as a child to those types of scenarios. Frank Mason liked people to kneel in front of him; he liked total submission before he did whatever sick, violent thing he was going to do to those he considered had "fucked him over." More than once, I'd walked in on men kneeling in front of my father, shaking in fear. If I'd been lucky, I would escape before Dad saw me.

"Right, off you fuck, Pinky," Dad finally said. "I've got to speak to the runt here."

Pinky nodded to my dad and grabbed his beer, barely glancing at me as he strode out of the kitchen. I still didn't move. It was better if I waited. Nobody took a seat in Frank Mason's house without his express permission, not even his children.

"Little Mole," Ruben said in a grumpy voice. "What the fuck are you doing here?" His tone was annoyed, but there was an edge of worry there too.

I wasn't scared of Ruben. He'd never hurt me physically. Yes, he'd been cruel and dismissive, but, in a way, I felt sorry for him. He'd been groomed from a young age to be just like my father. But when Dad had caught me revising with Zach and punched me before throwing me down the stairs three months ago, it was Ruben who'd told him to back off. It was Ruben who'd driven me to hospital.

"I'm sorry, Little Mole," he'd muttered when we pulled up outside the emergency department. "But you shouldn't have come to the fucking house. Dad's proper mental at the moment. The police are all over us after everything with Freddie. Just stay away, right?"

My father scowled at Ruben. "She's here because I bloody well told her to be here," he told him. "So you can fuck off an' all, son."

Ruben looked between me and Dad.

"You heard me, boy," Dad said in a low, menacing voice. Pinky appeared in the doorway then, jerking his head to the side to indicate for Ruben to follow.

"We don't need no more trouble, Dad," Ruben said. "Not with Freddie banged up and his trial round the corner."

Dad's eyes flashed. "*I'll* say what we need. Now piss off."

Ruben's jaw clenched before he let out a deep sigh, grabbed his beer and stalked out of the kitchen.

I flinched when Dad kicked out a chair from the other side of the table.

"Sit," he barked. I moved then, darting to the chair and sitting down, my hands in fists on my lap to stop them from shaking. Dad, as usual, got right down to business. "Skinny Pete tells me you're now fucking that barrister. Is that right, Clara?"

Cold fear trickled down the back of my spine as my eyes flew wide.

"N-n-no," I forced myself to say, and saw a flash of annoyance in my father's eyes at my stutter. He hated my stutter. Never mind that he was the most likely culprit behind its development.

"Don't lie to me, Runt," Dad said in a low, dangerous voice.

Runt had been his favourite name for me for as long as I could remember.

"You're living with the guy. There's no other reason for him to move you in there."

"I'm a teacher, Dad," I told him, something he already knew. "His son has dyslexia. You know that I teach additional needs and I..."

Dad's snort cut me off. "Even if his kid is a total no-hoper, he's not going to move you into his house without fucking you."

"Dad, it's not like that. I—"

"Shut the fuck up," he snapped. "Listen to me. You're a part of this family, Clara. You owe us loyalty. You know that. So far, you've been a useless piece of shit in terms of helping us. But you fucking that barrister changes things. I have to say, when we engineered to have your Mr High-and-Mighty Law Maker prosecute Freddie, we didn't realise just how good a play that would turn out to be. I mean, we knew you taught the bloke's kid and hoped you might be able to pull some info for us, but I would never have believed you had it in you to fuck the guy."

I blinked at him, my whole body going cold now, no longer able to control the shaking in my hands despite them being still clenched into fists under the table. I knew that my father had a number of corrupt police officers (or grasshoppers as they were known in Dad's circles – coppers who liked to grass) in his pocket, but I had no idea the corruption went high up enough for him to be able to influence the choice of prosecuting barrister for his son.

"It's time for you to step up," Dad said, a sly grin forming on his lips. "It's time for you to do something useful for the family for a change. Your brother's going to need the prosecution to go easy on him, and maybe your Lord Sterling needs a bit of... persuasion."

I had no idea what sort of "persuasion" my father was talking about, but I felt like I was going to vomit. Somehow even me just being near Rafe had infected him with my family's bullshit.

"He d-doesn't discuss his work with me, Dad," I said in a rush. "There's no way of me being useful to any of you. He doesn't allow me that k-kind of access."

Dad smirked, sitting back in his chair and crossing his arms over his barrel chest, causing the muscles in his biceps to flex. I eyed his fisted hands warily; flashbacks of one of them driving into the side of my head ran through my mind. I had to swallow down another lot of bile at the sudden surge of fear.

"Don't worry," he said. "You don't have to steal any information. Just stay in that house for now and keep fucking him. We'll let you know when you can be useful."

I swallowed again and forced myself to speak past the lump that had formed in my throat.

"I'm not going to help you with this, Dad," I said, just above a whisper. "I can't. You'll have to think of another angle."

I let out a small squeak when anger flashed through my father's eyes and his fist crashed down on the table. "You'll do as I fucking well say!" he shouted. My eyes stung with tears but I held them back. Crying only made Dad angrier. He leaned forward on the table towards me, and I leaned back in my chair in response.

When he spoke again, he was no longer shouting, but

the danger in his voice was even more evident. "It would be a shame if Zach decided to drop out of school," he said softly and my heart dropped. Dad shrugged. "Happens though. Happens all the time. You know, kids like that, they get in with a bad crowd. Drugs, alcohol."

My brother had never taken even a sip of alcohol before in his life. And the idea of him taking drugs was completely laughable.

"They go off the rails," Dad continued. "Run away from home. Disappear. You know, there's never really any questions asked, is there?"

I felt the blood drain out of my face, and for the second time that week, my shoulders slumped in defeat. I looked down at my hands for a moment, acknowledging that, yet again, I didn't have any choices. I was powerless. Eventually, I managed to look up and meet my father's steady gaze to whisper, "What do you want me to do?"

Chapter 25

I'm here. I'm yours

Rafe

IT WAS BEYOND A JOKE NOW. CLARA HAD COMPLETELY withdrawn from me. Since the night she went to meet her friend, who she still wouldn't tell me about, she'd retreated right back into her shell, barely speaking or eating, flinching away every time I reached for her. She didn't sleep in my bed any longer, and she was even muttering about returning to her dilapidated flat. Her interactions with Ozzie were the only glimpses I had of the old Clara. She put on a good show for him, but I guessed this was ingrained in her due to her career as a teacher. And I knew first-hand how important it was to her that children weren't let down by the adults in their lives.

I had this awful sinking feeling that something bad was going to happen. The only explanation I could think of was that she was planning to go back to whatever arsehole beat her up. After a week of Silent Clara, I begged her to tell me what was happening, but all she'd say was that she "didn't think this was working for her".

"Please, baby," I'd begged. "Please just talk to me. Tell me what's wrong. Of course you don't have to be with me if you've changed your mind about us, but please, tell me what's going on. You're scaring me, Clara." Even when my voice cracked and I was near tears with worry, she wouldn't make eye contact. And when she did, her expression was completely blank.

So tonight, I was going to shock her out of it. It was the Sterling charity gala that Poppy had organised. The one I'd asked Clara repeatedly if she'd go to with me. Even before Clara had retreated completely, she had been adamant that she wouldn't come, citing Ozzie as an excuse, which was total bullshit. Ozzie wasn't a stupid child; he knew that I was with Clara. He'd even asked me the other night if she was going to live with us forever, and I told him if I could convince her, then yes. And even though Clara put on a good show for him this week, Ozzie could tell something had changed.

Last night, he had been about to drop off when he'd said sleepily, "Okay, Dad, she likes Branston Pickle and she likes reading and she likes *me,* so maybe you could, you know, use that stuff to get her to stay."

Ozzie giving me tips on how to keep my girlfriend was a new low, but her withdrawal was making him anxious. If Clara's aim was to protect Ozzie, then her pulling away from both of us was not going to achieve it. But for some reason, she just couldn't see that, and I'd had enough.

I *knew* Clara cared about me, and I was going to show her what would happen if she continued to withdraw from me. Ozzie was at Sophia's and, seeing as Clara wouldn't accompany me to the gala, I'd found someone else who was only too happy to.

But now that Ophelia had arrived, I was realising I

might have made an error of judgement. The glamorous blonde swept into the kitchen in her designer dress, totally ignoring Poppy and Clara to drape herself over me. She even went in for a kiss, which I only managed to partially duck at the last second, but she still caught the corner of my mouth, her cloying perfume making me feel a little ill.

Clara had frozen in her task of pulling one of Martha's lasagnes out of the oven. For a moment, as she looked between me and Ophelia, the blankness in her expression faded away, and I could see complete and utter devastation left in its wake. I blinked in confusion at her. Why was she devastated? She'd been openly planning to leave me for the last two weeks. Why was she showing this emotion now? I hadn't expected complete devastation, to be honest. I'd expected anger, maybe a bit of her fire back again – that I could work with. That would have been better than the relentless nothingness. But I didn't want to hurt her.

"Clara," I breathed, pushing Ophelia away to move to her. Her eyes glassed over as she stared at me across the kitchen. She was still standing stock still, holding the lasagne but using only a couple of flimsy teatowels. She flinched, looking down at her hands and arms as if forgetting where she was. Then I saw a different pain flash across her features as she winced. I looked down at the pan she was holding, realising part of it was in direct contact with her skin.

"Clara!" I shouted and she dragged her eyes from the lasagne pan to me as I flew across the space, grabbing a towel, then taking the pan from her, and throwing it onto the chopping block. When I turned back to Clara, she was still frozen in place. "What the hell are you doing?" I snapped as I grasped both her hands, turning them so that they were palm up. There were red marks up her arms, some of which were starting to blister. "Shit, shit!" I hustled Clara's stiff body across the kitchen to the sink, turned the tap on to cold and enclosed her from behind to hold her hands and arms under the stream of water. "Baby, you've hurt yourself," I said, panic threaded through my voice.

"Step back," Clara spoke for the first time that evening and I clenched my jaw in frustration.

"I will not step back. Not if you're going to hurt yourself. You need to keep the burns under water, or they'll—"

"Step back!" she shouted, and the kitchen went deathly silent.

"Clara," I said softly, not letting her go. "You need to—"

She laughed then, but it wasn't like any of the other times I'd heard her laugh. No, this was a hollow, bitter and utterly sad sound, full of pain.

"You've no bloody idea what I need, Rafe. Now, step back."

"Rafey," said Poppy carefully from behind us, her hand settling on my shoulder. "Maybe you should go. I'll look after Clara and follow you there."

Fucking hell, what was happening? How had I lost control of this situation so utterly? A wave of helplessness swept through me, quickly followed by anger. I wasn't used to feeling out of control, and it was pissing me off.

"Fine," I snapped, lifting my hands off Clara, holding them high up in the air above my head and stepping back. "I'll leave if that'll make you happy. Nevermind this is *my* fucking house, but fine. Have at it, Poppy."

Poppy moved forward to Clara, gently guiding her back to the sink when she tried to step away.

"But you keep those fucking hands and arms under the water and I'm calling a fucking doctor to look at them. Understand me, Clara?"

She was still looking down and the wave of frustration that crashed over me was so strong that I felt like my head was exploding.

"Goddamn it, Clara! Look at me when I speak to you." I slammed my hand down on the granite surface, and Clara flinched away so violently that it took her almost into a crouch on the floor. She was shaking. Christ, I'd made her shake.

"Baby, please—" I said in a broken whisper, but it was Poppy who cut me off.

"Just bloody leave, Rafe," she snapped. "You're only making her worse."

Ophelia was looking completely baffled at the unfolding scene.

"Er, hi," she said to Clara. "Sorry about your arms, babe."

"Hi," said Clara softly. "Sorry about the drama."

Ophelia shrugged. "I *live* for drama."

"Fi, you go on with Rafe," Poppy said, smiling at her friend. "I'll see you guys there, okay?"

THE GALA WAS A COMPLETE SHIT SHOW, AND I ALMOST didn't make it past the champagne reception.

Ophelia was all over me from the moment we exited the car, and the press ate it up. It would be front-page news by tomorrow, with Ophelia being pegged as the next Lady Sterling, along with my ranking as the second sexiest aristocrat in the UK (the Duke of Fuckingham beat me last year, the bastard – but I was convinced that his very public love story with his gorgeous now wife playing out in the media a few years ago helped. I'd get him next year.)

All I'd wanted to do was go home and check on Clara. I felt sick at the devastated expression on her face, and then at the fear in her eyes when I'd made her flinch. I'd scared her, something I *promised* myself I'd never do again. But although my mind was completely on Clara, I knew that for Poppy's sake I had to at least stay for the dinner. As soon as that was over, however, I made my excuses and left, Ophelia still in tow. Thankfully, Dave agreed to drive her home as soon as he'd dropped me off.

Once I made it home and shut the door, I looked up to see Clara on the stairs only feet away as if she'd been waiting for me.

"Rafe," she said, her voice full of that same longing it had held before all the blankness crept in.

"Clara," I breathed, holding out my hand to her. But I hadn't locked the bloody door behind me and Ophelia used the opportunity to push her way in and fling her arms around my neck. Clara froze on the stairs, her eyes going wide with shock and that same devastation from earlier.

By the time I pushed Ophelia away and instructed a sheepish Dave, who'd run after Ophelia when she'd given him the slip, to "take her bloody well home this time," Clara had turned and run back up the stairs. Once the door was safely shut and locked behind me, I ran after her and started pounding on her door.

"Clara, I'm not leaving until you let me in," I snapped.

"I'm fine, go back to her," she called through the door in a shaky voice.

I leaned my head against the wood. "Clara, please let me in." My voice had changed from demanding to cajoling now. "Baby, open the door."

It worked. When she pulled the door open, I felt my chest tighten at her red-rimmed eyes behind her glasses.

"I'm sorry," I said.

She shook her head. "You have nothing to apologise for."

"Clara, I only took Ophelia to the gala because—"

She reached up and pressed her fingers over my mouth. "It doesn't matter," she said, her tone so sad it gutted me.

"Of course it matters," I tried to say, but her fingers were still over my lips.

"Rafe, I love you," she told me. "You've got to remember I love you, okay?"

She sounded so final.

I frowned, reaching up to pull her hand away from my mouth and hold it in mine.

"Clara, I love you too, darling. What do you mean by 'I've got to remember'? *Please* talk to me, tell me what's going on."

She smiled a sad smile and went on as if she hadn't even heard me. "You made me so happy," she said in just above a whisper. "I felt so safe with you. I didn't know that life could be this good. I didn't know I could love anyone this much."

A warm feeling spread through me and I smiled. "Sweetheart, that's wonderful. I love you too. I'm so glad that we're resolving this now. I'm sorry I took Ophelia out, but—"

She shook her head. "You looked right together. I can see that now."

I frowned, searching her face. "I'm not interested in Ophelia," I said slowly. "You understand that, right?"

Her hand came up to trace my jawline as she stared at me as if cataloguing every detail of my face. I caught her hand in mine. "Clara? I fucked up, but I want you. Not her. Yes?"

"Sometimes I think I'm dreaming," she whispered, a lone tear falling down her cheek. "That I've finally snapped, and my mind's taken me to an alternate reality where I'm yours and you're mine."

A trickle of unease went down my spine as I swiped her tear away. "You're not dreaming, baby. I'm here. I'm yours." Jesus Christ, something was really wrong with Clara. What the hell was I thinking pulling that stunt with Ophelia? "Clara, you're scaring me. Please, can't you tell me why you're so sad? Why did you retreat from me this week? I'd rather you got angry with me about Ophelia. I can't bear this sadness, darling."

Clara shook her head. "I'm not angry with you. I—"

There was a beat of silence, and then she moved, coming up onto her toes to close her mouth over mine.

Chapter 26

Stay with me

Clara

RAFE GROWLED LOW IN HIS THROAT, AND I LET THE feelings I'd been repressing rush in as he kissed me back. His arms clamped around me like a vice, as if he was worried I'd slip out of his grip. After a moment he pulled back to scan my face, still holding me tight. When I tried to kiss him again, his hand came up to my jaw to hold me steady.

"What... what's happening?" he asked in a hoarse voice. "Is this what you want?"

I stared straight into his gorgeous blue eyes and told him the truest thing that I had ever said.

"Rafe, all I want is you."

He hesitated, holding my gaze as his pupils dilated and he kissed me again. We fell back onto the bed, the reassuring weight of his solid body settling on top of me. The feel of him, the smell of him, everything about him calmed the anxiety-riddled, whirling thoughts in my brain. I allowed the endorphins to flood my system, basking in the glow of him. It was a heady feeling after two weeks of shutting down all my emotions.

Since I'd gone to see Dad, all the happiness I'd been reaching for seemed to have drained through my fingers like water. I was back to not eating, losing all the weight I'd managed to put on. And really, it was worse in a way. There was a sense of hopelessness now that hadn't been there before, like I was in a deep, dark hole with no way out.

Months ago, when I'd taken the risk and done the Big Terrible Thing, I'd believed that eventually I'd be free of my family. But as time went on, my faith in that gradually eroded. Until I moved in here with Rafe, and then I thought that maybe my luck was changing. I should have known it was too good to be true.

So I'd decided to take one last moment of happiness before everything went black. I tore at his clothes, desperate to feel his skin on mine, but my hands were clumsy and shaking as I tried to unbutton his shirt.

"Hey," he said in a hoarse voice, catching my hand in his at his shirt front. "It's okay, baby. We've got time. Deep breaths, Clara."

I wanted to scream at him that, *no*, we did not have any bloody time. That I needed him *now*. I needed him to shut out all the noise for me. I closed my eyes to try and get myself under some sort of control.

"I just need you," I said in a shaky whisper.

"I've got you, baby," he said in that soft but firm voice. "I'm right here with you."

I nodded, and he put his hand behind his back to pull his shirt off in one smooth motion, revealing his muscular torso. I made a low sound in the back of my throat as I traced his chest down to the ridges of his abdomen lightly with my fingers. His pupils were huge when I looked back up at his eyes.

"I missed you so much," he growled, covering me again with his weight as he pulled off my shirt and then my bra. When we were finally skin on skin, I let out a sharp breath. Cocooned under his large, warm body, feeling him surround me completely, I felt an arrow of need pierce through me, but also some sort of acute relief, as if holding back from him physically had been inflicting a kind of unacknowledged pain on my body which was only now finding its resolution. I could feel him hard against me now, and I knew I needed to be connected with him.

"Please, Rafe," I said, my voice choked as I pushed down his trousers. "I need you now. I can't wait."

And then we were both naked and finally, finally he was pushing inside, stretching me and filling me as I cried out and clenched around him. The sheer rightness of it, of having him moving with me, taking the emptiness away was so beautiful I felt my eyes start to sting.

"Baby," he murmured, slowing to kiss one of the tears at my temple away. "Clara, are you okay?"

"Yes, yes," I said in a half-sob, "please, Rafe. It's just that I need you so much."

"Okay, okay," he said, a flash of concern crossing his features at the desperation in my tone. "I told you; I've got you."

My arms came up around him to hold him to me, my hands feeling the muscles moving under his skin as he thrust inside. I wrapped my legs around his back, more tears falling and my cries intensifying as I fell over the edge. Rafe's movements became uncontrolled as I contracted around him, and then he followed me there with a hoarse cry. He let me take his weight for a moment with me still wrapped around him, not wanting to let him go, and then he leaned up on his elbows to search my expression. His hands came up to swipe at the tears that continued to fall.

He kissed me lightly before he pulled away to lie back on the bed, gathering me into his arms so that I was tucked into his side as he stroked my hair and pulled the duvet over us. More tears fell onto his chest where my head was resting and his arms gave me a squeeze.

"Darling, why are you crying?" he asked softly. "I didn't do anything to hurt you, did I? I don't—"

"No, of course not," I said. How could he think that he'd hurt me? I cleared my throat. "I'm sorry I'm crying. I just feel a bit... overwhelmed."

"You don't have to apologise for crying, Clara," he said softly. "I just want to understand why. Something's wrong. You've avoided me all week, and believe me, I'm beyond happy that you're back, but this feels like it's edged with some sort of... grief? I still feel like you're slipping through my fingers. I'm getting a horrible sense that in some way you're saying goodbye, or that you're gone even though you're right here in my arms. Like I said before, you're scaring me. Just tell me what's going on. There's nothing I can't fix."

I almost smiled. Wasn't that just like Rafe? Nothing he can't fix.

I imagined that in most other areas this was true. God knows he kept his free-wheeling, crazy sister out of harm's way. He was wired to protect, to be relied upon, to provide safety. But nobody could keep me safe now, not even Rafe.

For one mad moment, I considered telling him everything. Confessing all my lies about my background so that he could fix all my problems. But once he knew the truth, would I still be held in his arms like this? Would he still look at me the same way? How would he feel when he realised that there was no simple solution to my family? That they would always taint everything about my life with the black horror of their reality?

Even pulling the trigger on the Big Terrible Thing hadn't sorted them out. All it had done was gradually make me more and more anxious, waiting for the other shoe to drop.

"I'm with you now," I told him, not willing to spout any more lies. "I'm with you tonight."

He sighed, holding me even closer against him as if the tighter he held on, the less likely I was to slip away.

We woke up in each other's arms in the middle of the night and made love again, slower this time, after exploring each other for what felt like hours. He made me come with his fingers and his mouth before finally slamming back into me, not letting up until I came a third time.

"You're perfect," he'd said over and over again, then, "I love you. Stay with me."

It was as if he was edging into desperation now too. As if he could sense he was losing me and trying to use our physical connection to keep us together.

I wanted to tell him again I loved him too. Holding the words back was causing actual pain to build in my chest. But the pain of what I had to do would be more acute somehow if I kept acknowledging out loud how far I'd fallen. If I said out loud how much I needed this man. How much I loved him.

That morning, he hugged me before he left for work, and I held on, burrowing inside his overcoat, feeling small and safe and protected. Revelling in that feeling whilst knowing that it might be the last time I ever had it.

"I'll see you tonight," Rafe said firmly as he looked

down at me once he'd finally pulled back. It wasn't a question; it was a command. His eyes were troubled as they held mine. When I broke eye contact, his hands came up to my face to tilt my head back so I was looking at him again.

"You'll be here tonight." His voice was laced with steel now. "I mean it, Clara. You run away, and I'll come looking for you."

No, he wouldn't.

After today Rafe Sterling wouldn't want anything to do with me.

Chapter 27

Clarabelle Mason

Rafe

I WENT OVER THE DOCUMENTS IN FRONT OF ME ONE last time, trying my hardest to concentrate, but I couldn't shake my worry over Clara. Last night and this morning there was still that desperate quality about her that scared me, and I still had this weird feeling that she was saying goodbye.

I shook my head. That was ridiculous. Of course she wasn't saying goodbye. She was bringing Ozzie home today like she did every Monday. I gritted my teeth in frustration. The secrecy was going to end today. No more lying to Ozzie. No more hiding. I was taking Clara out on a goddamn date, and then I was introducing her to all my family and friends as my goddamn girlfriend.

I ground my teeth together. I was the most eligible bloody bachelor in London, according to the *Guardian*. There were women vying for a chance to be my girlfriend all the time. Why, then, did I have to fall hopelessly in love with one who'd rather bonk me in secret and not tell a soul?

Wasn't that what the billionaire lord was supposed to be doing to his staff, not the other way around? How had everything got so out of my control that now *I* was the dirty secret?

Bollocks to *that*.

"Lord Sterling?" the court attendant said as he poked his head around my door.

I huffed. "I've told you lot to call me Rafe," I snapped, and the poor man looked like he was going to soil himself. Worry had frayed my patience and temper so much that now I was snapping at innocent, if slightly wet, court staff.

"Yes of course, Lor... I mean Rafe."

I sighed. "Let's just get this over with."

"Er... I just wanted to warn you that... well..." the court attendant trailed off, and I raised my eyebrows as I waited for him to finish. Luckily, I was saved from snapping at him again by Willow.

"It's an absolute shitshow in there, Your Lordship," she said as she pushed my door wide open and strutted past the court attendant, giving him only a cursory look. Willow was an absolute shark of a barrister, and I was glad to have her on this case with me. We'd been working on it together for months and it was airtight.

"Stop with the bloody lordship stuff. You know it pisses me off. And what are you on about?" I hoped nothing was going to jeopardise our hard work. If anyone deserved to be taken down it was the pond scum on trial today. Putting that violent shitbag behind bars today would ensure the larger, more complex case would go to trial – and then the rest of his family would be going down with him. Successfully prosecuting these two cases would make my career, and my pathway to being a high court judge would be assured.

"The courtroom is absolutely rammed," she told me.

I shrugged. "Well, it's a high-profile case."

She shook her head. "It's not just reporters. There's all sorts out there. I've never seen such a circus."

"Well, we can't let any of their fuckery put us off," I told her. "This is too bloody important."

Willow's jaw set with determination. She wanted this conviction as much as I did. "Fine. Let's go."

I adjusted my wig as we stood outside Court Number Three, the horsehair irritating my neck. To be honest, I just wanted this first court day done and dusted so that I could get home and check on Clara. As I stared at the heavy oak door in front of me, I had the most bizarre feeling of impending doom. The hairs on the back of my neck stood up. Willow glanced up at me with a frown.

"Ready?" she whispered.

"Always," I said, clenching my jaw and willing myself to get my head in the game as we pushed open the courtroom double doors.

Willow was right – the court was packed, with the public gallery completely full. Nothing like a violent crime to draw spectators. I noticed the plaintiff's family sitting immediately on the left side, their faces tense. The plaintiff himself, Dawson, was among them, the scar under his left eye visible even from this distance. The poor man had been a bouncer at a central London nightclub when a drunk Freddie Mason had attempted to cut the line and stumble into the club holding a bottle of vodka. Dawson unwisely tried to bar entry, which led to Freddie screaming, "Do you know who the fuck I am?!" in his face, smashing his bottle and then using the broken glass in a sustained and frenzied attack on Dawson, only stopping when two of his cronies eventually pulled him off.

Freddie Mason was a fucking animal, and I was going to enjoy nailing him to the wall. The Masons likely had assumed that Dawson would not testify against them; they'd certainly got away with much more serious crimes routinely in the past, but what they did not anticipate was that Dawson's son had been a drug addict who was supplied by the Masons' network. Unfortunately, the twenty-year-old had died earlier that year from an overdose. Dawson told me he had nothing left to lose and that if taking the Masons down was his last act on this earth, then so be it.

As I walked to the prosecution table, my gown billowing slightly with each step, I glanced up at the rest of the gallery out of habit. The right side would likely have the Masons and their associates, unsavoury as they were.

That's when I saw her.

Clara.

She was seated directly behind where the defendant would sit. My stride faltered. For a moment, I thought I was mistaken – some trick of the light, perhaps, or a woman who merely resembled her. But then she looked up, meeting my eyes. There was no surprise in her expression, only a guarded watchfulness that confirmed everything in an instant.

I glanced at the people surrounding her: all Masons, all people I had seen in various police descriptions, along with another woman who looked like an older version of Clara and who I knew to be Frank Mason's wife. The two women looked tiny amongst the huge thugs on either side of them.

My mouth went dry as I stared at the woman I'd held in my arms all night, the woman I declared my love to this morning. She stared back. That nothingness was back in her eyes again. My grip loosened on the file I was carrying and some of the papers slid out of it, fluttering to the floor.

My mind flashed back to all the information I'd researched on the Masons. There was very little information on the daughter, but unlike most of the Masons, she wasn't considered a person of interest.

Her name was Clarabelle Mason.

My blood ran cold and I froze, right there in the middle of the courtroom.

"Rafe?" Willow whispered from behind me, jerking me out of my shock. I blinked, then bent to retrieve the papers that had escaped before I continued over to the prosecutor's bench, setting down my papers in a controlled move that belied the chaos erupting inside me. My mind raced as I methodically arranged my papers. Clara. Here. Sitting on the defendant's side. Sitting with her... family.

"Prosecution," the court usher approached, "the defendant is being brought up now. Right Honourable Lady Chief Justice Harris will be in shortly after."

I nodded, barely registering his words. How long ago was it that I was assigned this case? Everything clicked into place. Of course. The Masons had more reach than even I realised. To influence the allocation of cases at the CPS requires some high-level corruption. Who even was Clara? Was it all an act? The shy teacher helping my kid when nobody else could.

Ozzie.

Icy fury shot through me at the thought of my son. My own flesh and blood had been manipulated and used to get to me. Here I was, accusing Sophia of being a shit parent whilst I'd actually allowed a gang member's sister into my home. Left her alone with my son.

The side door opened, and Frederick "Freddie" Mason was led in by court officials. He took his place in the dock. He had the same light brown hair as Clara, the same chocolate brown eyes, but that was where the similarities ended. Freddie Mason was well over six foot and looked as though he'd been on the roids for some time. He was in a suit and tie but pulling at his collar, clearly uncomfortable and pissed off.

I forced myself to breathe steadily, to organise my thoughts. What had I told Clara about this case? Had I named names? Mentioned evidence? I'd been careful, I was always careful, but we'd talked about work. General terms, hypotheticals... but had I slipped?

"Are you alright?" Willow whispered, frowning at me. "You've gone quite pale."

"I need to—" I began, but was interrupted by the court clerk's announcement.

"All rise!"

The entire courtroom stood as Judge Katherine Harris entered in her robes and wig, her expression stern as always. I rose mechanically, my body following years of training while my mind continued to race.

"Be seated," Judge Harris said, taking her place. "Court is now in session. The Crown versus Frederick Mason. Are both counsels ready to proceed?"

Mason's defence barrister, Priya Sharma, rose smoothly. "Ready, My Lady."

All eyes turned to me. I stood, straightening my shoulders.

"Lord Sterling? Is the prosecution ready?" Judge Harris prompted when I didn't immediately respond.

"My Lady, before we proceed, I must request an urgent matter be addressed in chambers," I said, my voice remarkably steady despite the hammer of my pulse in my ears.

The judge's eyebrows rose slightly. "Without even commencing the trial, Lord Sterling?"

"It is a matter of some urgency regarding my ability to represent the Crown in this case, My Lady."

Judge Harris studied me for a moment, then nodded. "Very well. Court will recess briefly while I speak with counsel in my chambers. The jury will remain in the waiting room until called."

As the judge rose, I gathered my papers, still avoiding looking at Clara though I could feel her eyes on me. The anger was building now, replacing the initial shock. Four months of preparation. A solid case. A dangerous offender who deserved to be convicted. The other case linked to this, a career-making case. All potentially compromised because I'd let my guard down with a woman I clearly barely knew.

"Rafe, what are you doing?" Willow said in a harsh whisper, her eyes flashing with anger. I didn't blame her. We'd worked for months on this case, and now I was flushing it down the bog because I was a weak, gullible idiot.

I shook my head before I glanced back at Clara again. She was sitting there with that same blank expression on her face. It felt like she'd detonated a bomb in the courtroom but was totally unaffected by the back blow of the explosion.

"Conflict of interest," I muttered, nodding discreetly toward Clara in the public gallery. "I know her. Personally."

Willow's eyes widened in understanding. "Oh, God. Is she—?"

"Family of the defendant, it seems. I had no idea until just now."

In the privacy of the judge's chambers, with Priya Sharma present as required, I stood rigidly before Judge Harris's desk.

"My Lady, I must recuse myself from this case, effective immediately," I stated, fighting to keep my tone formal despite the humiliation burning inside me. "I have just become aware of a personal connection that constitutes a significant conflict of interest. I have been... socially acquainted with a woman who appears to be a member of the defendant's family. This relationship was not disclosed to me, and I had no knowledge of her connection to the defendant until I saw her in court today."

Judge Harris's eyes narrowed. "I see. How long has this acquaintance existed, Lord Sterling?"

"Approximately four months, My Lady. She is a teaching assistant at my son's school. We met to discuss my son and formed a relationship. She was..." I broke off to clear my throat. Fuck, this was degrading. "She *is* living with me and my son at this current time and has been for the last three months."

Judge Harris's eyebrows were in her hairline now. "Living with you?"

"Yes, My Lady."

"And you've had no indication of this connection until now?"

"None whatsoever, My Lady. Nevertheless, the Crown Prosecution Service's ethical guidelines are clear. I cannot continue to represent the Crown in this case."

Priya Sharma looked both surprised and calculating. I could practically see her mind working, wondering if this could benefit her client.

"My Lady, the defence will need to consider whether this warrants further investigation. If sensitive case information has been compromised—"

"That is a separate matter," the judge interrupted. "For now, we must address the immediate procedural issue. Lord Sterling, I accept your recusal. I'll contact the CPS immediately to arrange a replacement prosecutor. Court will be suspended in this case for the present time."

"Thank you, My Lady," I said, holding my professional mask firmly in place. "I apologise for the disruption to the court's schedule."

"These things happen, Lord Sterling, though rarely so dramatically," Judge Harris said with a hint of sympathy. "I trust you'll brief your replacement thoroughly."

"Of course, My Lady."

Judge Harris turned to Priya and her team. "Counsel for the defence, please go and brief your client. I want to speak to the prosecution alone for a moment."

Priya seemed like she was going to object, but Judge Harris gave her a stern look and she thought better of it. After they left, Judge Harris sank back into her large leather chair and pulled her wig off to slam it down on her desk.

"Rafe, what the hell are you playing at?" she said in a disappointed tone.

Katherine Harris was one of the most well-respected judges in the country and something of a mentor to me. I hated disappointing her.

"I'm sorry, Katherine."

"What a bloody waste of time! Honestly, Rafe, do you have to go around shagging the criminal underbelly of London? Aren't there enough nice girls around to satisfy you?" She shook her head and I looked down at my shoes, not wanting to meet anyone's eyes. But for some weird reason, when Katherine called Clara the "criminal underbelly", I had the insane urge to defend her. I was officially losing my mind. She threw her hands up in exasperation.

"Right," she snapped. "I'd better go back in and tell that circus out there what a fuck-up you've made. In all my years trying cases, I've never come across anyone being recused over something so ridiculous."

With that, she swept out of the office, leaving Willow and me alone. When her door slammed behind her, I sat down heavily in the solid oak chair next to me and slumped forward with my head in my hands. Bile rose in the back of my throat and I swallowed it down.

"Rafe?" Willow said tentatively, and after a few moments, I felt her hand on my shoulder. "Hey there, Your Lordship. You doing okay?"

I started laughing then and she sunk down in the chair next to mine, her hand remaining on my shoulder. "Well, I've been fucking the accused's sister for the last three months. She's made a complete spectacle out of me. I've just likely tanked my bloody career, which I've been dreaming about since I was five years old, and the girl I thought I was in love with is an absolute back-stabbing bitch. I'm very fucking far from okay."

"I didn't know you were seeing anyone," she said softly.

"She wanted to keep it low-profile. Said it was so we didn't upset Ozzie." I sat up then and rubbed my hands down my face. "Christ, Ozzie. She's his teacher. I need to talk to the school. She's given them a false name and God knows what other bullshit she's pulled. The last thing they'll want is the likes of her around all the kids. I'm certainly not going to have her teach Ozzie anymore. If she even is a teacher? Maybe it was a front? Maybe her degree is as fake as her name?"

"She was the skinny one with the glasses, right?" Willow asked. "Brown hair?"

I nodded and she frowned.

"She looked tiny sitting there with her mum in among that lot," she muttered.

I shrugged. "She's small, but she can certainly do some damage of her own. Because of her, the whole case will be suspended until they can appoint alternative counsel."

Willow was frowning as she tilted her head to the side. "Did you see any of the police interviews with the mum?"

I nodded. "Yes, of course." The interviews were pretty irrelevant, really, but we'd wanted to be thorough with our research. Make sure no stone was left unturned. What a joke that was now.

"She looked tiny then as well. It was weird, remember? Sort of like the lights were on but nobody was home. And she seemed to flinch at everything. Even the scraping back of the chairs seemed to startle her."

I shook my head. "What are you trying to say, Willow?"

"I just... maybe you shouldn't jump to conclusions about—"

"Jump to conclusions? Willow, I've been fucking this woman for over *three months*. She had every opportunity to tell me who her family was, but instead, she lied repeatedly, going as far as telling me her parents were *dead*. She fooled me, my sister, my parents, but worst of all, my son. She's a lying, manipulative bitch, and I wouldn't touch her again with a barge pole. So, no, I'm not interested in how some gangster's wife reacted in an interview weeks ago. What I do know is that Marie Mason gave absolutely no useful information about her husband's criminal activities to the police, despite the fact she has clearly witnessed those activities repeatedly. As, presumably, has her daughter. Both of those women want to protect that family, and as far as I'm concerned, the lot of them can jog on."

Chapter 28

I was a product of them, wasn't I?

Clara

"WHAT A PIOUS TWAT," MY FATHER SPAT.

I glanced up at his scowling face, which was flushed an angry red colour.

"Recusing himself because he's fucked you. Honestly, these legal wankers have sticks rammed so far up their arses it's a wonder they can sit down."

I didn't reply, keeping my head down as we walked down the corridor from the court. The judge had dismissed us until new counsel for the prosecution could be appointed. Freddie had been taken back into custody, so my father and his vast entourage had wasted no time getting out of there. Courtrooms were not their favourite places.

"At least we don't have a fucking shark prosecuting him now," Pinky said to my father. "That's something. If he's not in our pocket, the bastard's conviction rate would be a big fucking problem."

Dad rolled his eyes. "Would have been better if Runt here had done her fucking job properly." He tightened his grip on my elbow and gave me a small shake. "Why didn't you prime him before the hearing? Did you even ask him for a favour? He looked like he had no idea you'd be there. You were supposed to butter him up. Make sure he went easy on Freddie."

"I did ask, but he refused, Dad," I lied in a small voice. "I told you that last week. Rafe would never have thrown the case." I was feeling lightheaded now with the stress of the situation and the pain of my dad's iron grip on my elbow.

If my father found out that I hadn't even asked Rafe to throw the case, he would beat me.

But Freddie's case was child's play compared to the case I'd probably triggered with the Big Terrible Thing. If Dad *ever* found out about the Big Terrible Thing, I knew without a doubt he would kill me.

I did not want to be beaten or killed, so I kept my mouth shut.

"Where the fuck has that scrawny bastard gone?" Dad muttered, pausing to turn us around to look for Skinny Pete. "Fuck's sake," he snapped. "He can catch us up."

But when Dad tried to haul me along to keep moving, I stayed frozen in place, my gaze still fixed back down the corridor. I couldn't look away. Striding towards us was Rafe with his redheaded assistant counsel. They had both removed their wigs but they were still wearing those long black robes over their suits. It made Rafe seem even more intimidating and larger than life.

As I stared at him, for one mad moment my feet itched to start running towards him. I wondered what would happen if I ran straight into his arms and told him everything.

I winced as my father's fingers tightened around my elbow and he gave me a rough shake.

"Let's get a fucking move on, girl," he snapped.

But I was too fixated on Rafe's face to move. I opened my mouth to speak, but no sound came out. Then Rafe's gaze moved to me and I flinched again. I'd expected anger, but not quite the level of absolute hatred burning like blue fire in his eyes. He had a right to that fury. A stupid little girl like me had wrecked his case, his *career-building* case. For a powerful man like Rafe that had to be galling.

And he *was* powerful. I'd always known that. But seeing him here in the majestic surroundings of this court-room, wielding his power and influence in the legal system, seeing how he fitted here, how he ruled this place, I understood exactly how powerful Rafe Sterling was.

More powerful than my family?

For a moment, it was like the fog of my anxiety cleared, and I was struck with a realisation. Rafe Sterling was powerful enough to help me. Why hadn't I just told him what was happening? Why hadn't I confided in him about the Big Terrible Thing? I'd been ready to tell him the day he brought Ophelia to the house, but then seeing him with her had changed my mind. But so what if a woman like her was a better match for him? So what if he didn't love me after what happened today? He had enough moral fibre to still help me, and he was powerful enough to do so.

Christ, I'd been really, really stupid. I was so used to being let down by people – from corrupt police officers who'd turned a blind eye to my father's activities, to everyone around me who had always been powerless in the face of my family. But Rafe wasn't corrupt and he certainly wasn't powerless. He could protect me and he could protect Zach. Watching him stride through this courthouse corridor

I knew that now, down to my bones. My father started tugging me along, but I found a surge of strength from somewhere and wrenched myself out of his grip to run to Rafe and the redhead. When I stopped in front of them, I was out of breath and my pulse was pounding in my ears with the stress of what I was going to do.

"Rafe," I said as I blocked his path. He came to an abrupt stop and stared down at me like I was a lower form of life. But I was too desperate now to be put off by the hatred radiating from him. So I took a chance and stepped into his space, my hand going to the middle of his broad chest.

"Rafe, I—"

"I have nothing to say to you, *Clarabelle*," he snapped. "I don't want to hear any pathetic apologies or excuses."

I shook my head. "No, I—"

He barked out a laugh. "So you're not even going to try to apologise? Why am I not surprised? Tell me, Clara. How long were you stalking me? The shy little schoolteacher act – was that your father's idea? Fuck's sake, you lied to my *son*." His voice broke on that last word, and I felt like I was going to throw up.

"Please," I begged, my eyes filling with tears. I had to make him understand. "I need your help, Rafe."

My fingers on his chest curled in to grab onto his shirt. He froze for a few seconds, then disgust swept over his features.

"Let me be very clear," he said in a low, dark voice. "I wouldn't spit on you if you were on fire. You're sorely mistaken if you think for a minute I'm going to help you and your disgusting family." He let out a bitter laugh. "But don't worry, you've managed to get me recused. I'm sure you'll all land on your feet. Your kind always do."

My kind.

He was lumping me in with my family. Of course he was. I was a product of them, wasn't I? I'd seen enough over the years to be complicit. It was fear that had held me back from doing anything about their descent into violence and tyranny. I'd known what was going on in that house when I lived there, and I didn't say a word to anyone. Shame washed over me as I blinked up at him. Okay, so maybe I was one of them in a way. But I didn't *ask* to be born into that family. And I knew Zach and I deserved a life outside of it. So I had to take this chance, and I wasn't above begging.

"Please, Rafe," I whispered, my hand tightening on his shirt to fist the expensive material. "Help me, you don't under—"

"Get the fuck *off* me," he clipped, grabbing my hand in a painful grip and literally throwing it away from his body.

I stumbled back a couple of steps towards my *disgusting* family.

As soon as he was free of me, Rafe strode off down the corridor without even a backward glance, looking even more like the lord he was, still the most beautiful man I'd ever seen in my life. Time stopped as I watched him walk away. When I came back to myself, that redhead from before was right in front of me. But instead of the fury that had been in Rafe's eyes, hers held curiosity and maybe even a hint of concern.

"Clarabelle?" she said softly as she took a step towards me.

I stutter-stepped away from her and straight into what felt like a solid wall behind me.

"Watch where you're going, Runt," snapped Pinky before he grabbed my arm and yanked me back towards my dad. I flinched at the pressure on the bruises already there from Dad's previous punishing grip, and the redhead's eyes flared. Her mouth opened, and she took a step towards me, but before she could say anything I was dragged along behind my dad and his entourage to the waiting cars.

Chapter 29

Oh my God, you are such a dick!

Rafe

MY FIRST INSTINCT WAS TO PROTECT MY SON. LUCKILY, thanks to Clara, my schedule was clear for the foreseeable future. I had all the time in the world to go to the school. There was to be an investigation into the reasons behind my recusal, which I had encouraged. I had nothing to hide apart from the shame and humiliation of my poor judgement. So, at school drop-off that morning I was determined to speak to the teachers.

Ozzie had asked after Clara last night, and I hadn't had the heart to tell him that she wasn't coming back, or that he would never see her again. It was going to devastate Ozzie, and I was devastated enough for the both of us. I didn't think I could cope with a crying Ozzie on top of that. So I just told him that she wasn't well and that I wasn't sure when she'd be back.

"Wasn't well like last time?" Ozzie had asked in his worried little voice, and I hated Clara even more. How dare she worry my son?

"I'm not sure, buddy," I muttered. But then my mind flashed back to when Clara had been "ill" before, to the bruising and the cast on her arm. For a moment my blood went cold before I shook my head to clear it. Clara was with her family now. I doubted the Masons would let some dickhead ex-boyfriend near the precious daughter of the family.

"Miss Summerfield," I snapped as I strode into her classroom. Fuck the diktat about parents not being able to invade their sacred domain. I was done playing by an arbitrary set of rules that, quite frankly, made absolutely no sense to me.

"Lord Sterling," Lily said, frowning across at me. "I'm terribly sorry, but I think you'll have to return later. As you can see, I'm incredibly—"

"No," I cut her off and her eyebrows flew up into her hairline. "I will *not* speak to you later. I'll speak to you *now*. Have someone else take your class." All the kids were staring up at me then. Ozzie looked furious.

"Well, I don't think that this is—"

"It's about Clara."

Her face fell. "Oh," she breathed out. "Right. Is she—?"

"I need to talk to you about Clara privately," I told her.

Lily took in the seriousness of my stance and my unwavering glare and took action. Within five minutes, the teaching assistant from the class next door was supervising hers.

When we were outside the classroom, Lily turned to me. I could see the worry in her expression clearly now. "What about Clara?" she asked. "Rafe, where is she?"

"I do not wish to conduct this discussion in the middle of a corridor, and due to the seriousness of the situation, Mrs Clayton should be present."

"The seriousness of the..." Lily muttered, her eyes going wide. "Oh my God, has something happened to Clara?"

I blinked at her. "What? No. Clara's fine."

She let out a huge breath, her shoulders sagging in relief and I started to have an uneasy feeling in the pit of my stomach. "Thank Christ," she said, with real feeling. "Okay, let's go and see Mrs C."

Once we were in Mrs Clayton's office, with both of them looking at me expectantly, I let rip with my misgivings.

"You have a Clarabelle *Mason* in your employ," I said. Miss Clayton's head tipped to the side. She glanced at Lily and then back at me. The woman knew Clara's full name, that much was clear. This was not a surprise to her. I frowned down at her. "Are you in the habit of employing people who have to go by false names?" I said in a stern voice. "I would have thought that in order for there to be a correct DBS check, you would need to be using the person's full and correct name."

"We've done all the relevant checks on Clara," Mrs Clayton snapped. "Yes, we knew that Morris was not her real surname, but there were exceptional circumstances that we—"

"Do those exceptional circumstances include your employee being part of a criminal network so horrific that it has been the source of nearly thirty percent of all violent crime in east London for the last two years?"

Mrs Clayton frowned at me then. "Part of?" she whispered.

"What the hell are you talking about?" Lily put in. "Clara is not part of their criminal network."

"I'm sorry, did you not just admit that her surname was Mason?"

"Just because that's her bloody surname doesn't mean that she has anything to do with those animals," said Lily, her voice rising now.

"Let me be clear," I said, having had enough of this nonsense. Why on earth these women felt they needed to cover up for Clara's ongoing association with her family was a complete mystery. "I will not have my son attend a school that employs someone like Clarabelle Mason. Her employment will be terminated with immediate effect, or I will be withdrawing my funding from the current plans for the new performing arts studio. I will also be withdrawing my son from this school and encouraging my friends to do the same. I saw Clarabelle with her family yesterday in court. She very much *does* have everything to do with them."

I was quite pleased with my rant. I felt it conveyed all the threats and disappointment in a dignified manner. However, it was as if Mrs Clayton and Lily hadn't heard me. They weren't even looking at me. They were staring at each other.

"Oh God," said Lily in a shaky voice.

Mrs Clayton's gaze snapped back to me then. "Listen to me, Rafe. You tell us right this minute where Clara is."

I raised my eyebrows. "Did you not hear me? I do not want Clara employed at the school here anymore, and furthermore—"

"For fuck's sake, Rafe!" shouted Mrs Clayton, and my mouth fell open in shock. I had never heard her utter anything that could even vaguely be classed as a swear word, let alone imagine that she could actually pull out the F-bomb. "Have your little temper tantrum another time. Tell us where Clara is *now*."

I threw my hands up in frustration. "With her fucking family, I imagine," I said. "She seemed pretty cosy with them yesterday in court, where she was sitting directly behind the defendant in an extremely high-profile criminal case."

Mrs Clayton sat back down heavily in her chair, her face draining of all colour as her hand went to her throat.

"I am sorry that I had to inform you of this," I said stiffly. I didn't want to give the poor woman a heart attack after all. "And I am sorry that you trusted someone like Clarabelle Mason, but quite frankly, I—"

"Shut up, Rafe," snapped Lily.

"How dare you speak to me in that manner? I—"

"I'm afraid I'm going to need you to rein in the arsehole long enough to tell us where the fuck Clara is," Lily continued as she glared at me across the room. "You may not give one single shit about her well-being, but I assure you *we do*."

"Why should I give a shit about Clarabelle Mason's well-being?" I said, losing my grip on my temper now.

"Oh, I don't know," Lily said, "maybe because you're in love with her? But then I wouldn't expect a stone-cold fuck-waffle like you to take something petty like that into consideration."

"Did you hear what I told you? She was sitting with her family *in the courtroom*."

"Yes, I heard what you told me, you wanker. Why do you think I'm so fucking stressed out? Do you know where she is now or not?"

"I have no idea and no interest in the whereabouts of Clarabelle Mason. I'm merely here to establish—"

"Oh, do bugger off, Rafe," Mrs Clayton put in, and I gaped at her in disbelief. What was wrong with these women?

"Listen," I said in one last attempt to get them to see

reason. "She's been stringing you all along as well. Aren't you pissed off?"

"Clara has done nothing but *protect* herself," Mrs Clayton said, her voice steady now with that thread of steel I'd heard many times before as a child. "Everyone has a right to protect themselves, Rafe. I'm sorry she didn't tell you more, but it's obvious that she didn't trust you enough. And to be honest, from your behaviour here today, I think that was a good call, don't you?"

"*My* behaviour? What the...?" I spluttered. "I don't think you understand. I had to recuse myself from a case that I'd been working on for *months*. Clarabelle Mason has completely fucked up my career. I'm under investigation. You can't imagine the amount of hassle this is going to cause me."

"Oh, I'm sorry," said Lily, not sounding sorry at all. "This is going to cause you some hassle, is it?" She rolled her eyes. "Give me a break. Take your self-important, pompous arse out of here. We've got to start looking for Clara."

"I cannot understand this attitude," I snapped. "Quite honestly, it's ridiculous that you—"

"Oh my God, you are *such* a *dick!*" shouted Lily. My head ticked to the side in surprise, and my eyes narrowed, but Lily continued undeterred. "If you saw Clara with her family, then *she is not safe.*"

"Why wouldn't she be safe with her family? She's one of them, for God's sake! Believe me, I saw her; she was right there with them in full support."

Mrs Clayton stood up from her chair, patting her hair down. Her previous slip with her emotions forgotten, back to the stoic headmistress that I knew.

"Rafe Sterling," she said, that thread of steel still there. "You've made your threats. You've done what you came here to do. I'm sorry if you think that Clara has messed with your precious career. But I would really like you to leave now."

"Did you have any contact with her at the court?" Lily asked suddenly. "Did she say anything to you? Did she at least try to...?" She broke off and swallowed before going on. "Did she try to speak to you? It's really important."

I shifted uncomfortably on my feet. "She did make an approach after I'd recused myself and been bloody well thrown out of my own courtroom. But I wasn't in the mood to speak to the architect of my downfall. I'd been humiliated enough."

"Oh my God," Lily whispered, her eyes filling with tears. "She tried to stop you. She tried to speak to you, and you brushed her off? Are you serious?"

"What the fuck is going on?" I shouted at them, losing my temper then.

"Just go away, Rafe," Mrs Clayton said, sounding weary now.

Well fuck it. I wasn't wasting any more time on some career-ruining bitch and two teachers who weren't making any bloody sense. Anyway, seeing as Clara hadn't had the gall to return to work, I didn't need to throw my weight around to get her fired. I told myself that was a good thing. It meant I wouldn't have to see her again, and that was the last thing I wanted... wasn't it? I ignored the deep ache in my chest at the thought of never being near Clara again, and the twist in my gut when my brain conjured up the image of her small face, looking up at me in that corridor yesterday, the desperation I had seen in her eyes. How she'd asked me for help.

I was quite sure her family *were* desperate, and they would only become more so once the next case came to fruition. The evidence against Freddie Mason was overwhelming, and as for the rest of the Mason network... they were fucked.

Even with me out of the picture, the prosecution was solid. Clara probably would do anything to help her brother get off, but I wasn't going to help her. I wasn't having her manipulate me any more than she already had. Apart from anything, it could be a career-ending mistake. So I stormed out of the school without looking back.

But as the day went on, I had this nagging feeling in the back of my mind that something was very wrong. That's why after Ozzie read to me, having been placated with more lies about Clara's whereabouts, and I put him to bed, I decided to ring Grant.

Grant Mitchell was the main coordinating detective inspector for both Freddie Mason's case and the case being built against the Mason family. And he was the one who knew the most about the dynamics of the organisation. He picked up after two rings, and I wasted no time telling him why I was calling.

"Clarabelle Mason," I said simply, and he sighed.

"Where are you going with this, Rafe? I heard what happened in the courthouse. There's no point in talking to you about Clara."

I frowned. "Clara? How do you know to call her Clara?"

There was silence on the other end of the line.

"Listen," I went on, "why wasn't Clarabelle Mason mentioned in any of the investigating paperwork for the Mason case? You talk about the mum, you talk about every single member of that family, but you don't mention Clarabelle at all, except in passing."

"There was no reason to talk about Clarabelle Mason,"

he said firmly, having reverted to her longer name, but the slip-up had already been made, and noted by me.

"You know her," I whispered. "You know Clara, don't you?"

"Listen, Rafe. All the relevant information to convict Freddie was in that file. We only interviewed the family to see if we could expand the case to any of their other activities, but nobody talked. It's irrelevant now because, for the upcoming case, we have everything that we need to take down the Masons anyway, thanks to our access to the messaging network."

"Why would you keep Clara's name out of the file?" I pushed. "You had extensive reports on each member of that family. The mum hasn't hurt a fly, but there were two pages dedicated to her. Why not the same for Clarabelle?"

"This is pointless old ground," said Grant.

"Don't lie to me," I snapped. "What aren't you telling me? For fuck's sake, Grant, can you just—"

"Look, why do you even care?" Grant snapped. "First Willow, and now you giving me hassle."

"Willow rang you?"

"I told her the same as I'm telling you: I can't compromise my sources. Got me?"

"Your *sources*? What does that have to do with Clara?"

"Drop it, Rafe."

And that was when I realised.

I sat down heavily on my office chair and felt the blood drain out of my face.

Christ. I had been so goddamn blind.

"Grant, I'm going to need your help."

Chapter 30

You'll get her back?

Rafe

"Are you going to explain to me why you're here in your house at two pm on a Tuesday afternoon with the gate wide open, and not in your chambers beavering away to make the country a safer place?" Poppy said. "I've pretty much never known you to take a weekday off in my entire life."

"Pops, I'm sorry," I muttered, tearing my hands through my hair for what felt like the hundredth time that day. "But I don't have time to explain. I just need you here and I need you to pick Ozzie up from school. Listen, are you sure you haven't heard anything from Clara? Text? Call? Anything?"

"No, Rafe," Poppy said, her voice softening as she watched me pace the kitchen. "I already told you. She cut off all contact with me way before you instructed me to block her."

After all that shit that went down at court, hurt pride and frustration meant I'd told Poppy to cut Clara off completely. Thank God my little sister didn't ever listen to a word I said, because not only had she *not* blocked Clara, but she'd immediately tried to ring her after bollocking me over the phone for believing that Clara could ever deliberately set me up.

"Listen, Rafe," Poppy went on in a placatory tone. "I'm sorry, but I really doubt Clara's gonna take you back anyway, not after the way you behaved."

"It's not just about getting her back," I snapped. "It's about making sure she's safe."

"W-w-what?" Poppy's face paled, and I immediately regretted my words. The last thing I wanted to do was scare my little sister. I was scared enough myself and I needed her to keep her shit together for Ozzie. "She's not safe?" Poppy whispered.

I let out a deep sigh, the weariness and worry dragging me under for a moment. I'd barely slept last night, and had spent all morning gathering resources to track Clara down. I was coming up against brick wall after brick wall. Grant was willing to help, but there was only so much he was able to provide me with, given that I hadn't been able to come up with a solid reason for extracting Clara from her family. In order for the police to initiate any kind of intervention, there had to be evidence of a credible threat to Clara's life.

If I had let her actually speak to me in the courthouse corridor and not brushed her off like the prideful bastard I was, we likely wouldn't be in this position. But now all we had to go on was my bad feeling and the memory of Clara's frightened face. It was too weak to action what I wanted, which was a full-on armed response team invading the Mason family home right now, not for them to wait until they were bloody well ready.

What I did know was that Clara hadn't been back to her flat. The courtroom appearance was the only time she'd been spotted in public.

"You're going to find her, right?" Poppy's words were trembling now. She wanted her big brother to reassure her that everything was going to be okay and that her friend was fine. I pulled her into a hug. More for myself than for her.

"It's fine," I muttered. "She's coming back. She'll be home soon."

Because this was Clara's home now. Her home was with me and Ozzie. I may have forgotten that for a while, but it didn't make it any less true.

I pulled away from Poppy when I heard banging on the front door and walked to yank it open, only to be confronted by a tall, lanky teenager with familiar chocolate-brown eyes and a thunderous expression. I opened my mouth to speak, but before I could say anything, both his hands came up to my chest and he shoved me back, hard. It was more surprise than anything that made me go back onto one foot. The kid didn't exactly pack the kind of muscle required to floor me, which had clearly been his intention.

"You bastard wanker!" he shouted.

I held my hands up in surrender to try and diffuse his anger.

"Hey, kid, calm the fuck down, okay?" In any other circumstance, if a six-foot teenager had come to my door and shoved me, you can bet your arse I was shoving him back, and it wouldn't be gentle. But something familiar about this teenager stopped me in my tracks. Not to mention the fact he was shaking. Underneath the bravado, he was terrified.

"Clara said that you were a good guy," he snapped. "She

said that you were keeping her safe. But she was wrong. You're a proper *dick*."

"Okay, okay," I said slowly. "I'm a dick. We've established that. Now, I want you to tell me how you know Clara."

"She tried to talk to you in the court, you twat," he went on. "She tried to get help and you just shoved her away like she was nothing. You looked at her like she was one of them. She's not one of them. She's not like them at all. *You* are though. You might think you're way above all the criminals you bang up, but you're just as much of a wanker as they are."

"You were there in the court?" I asked.

I didn't remember seeing him, but then I'd been so focused on Clara, and my vision had been so clouded by the red mist of my anger that I hadn't been able to see anything past it.

"Do you work for the Masons?" I asked in confusion.

The kid's eyes went wide as his lip curled in disgust. "Work for those animals? You've got to be kidding me? I *had* to go to the bloody court. We have to put up this bullshit *united front*, whatever the fuck that means. If I don't go to the sodding courtroom to see my psycho brother get convicted, I get the shit kicked out of me. Enough information for you? And *Clara's* my family, not the fucking Masons. They've never been my family. Blood or no."

I let out a long breath.

"Zachary," I said. "You're Zachary Mason. Jesus Christ, you're tall for fifteen."

"Oh well, the birds in our family get all the short genes, don't they?" he said in a grumpy tone, shifting on his feet on my porch and looking a little lost as he realised I wasn't going to fight back. "The blokes are all big, broad bastards, all the better for beating the shit out of people, I suppose."

Zachary Mason had certainly inherited the tall side of things, as for the broad, I'd say that gene may have passed him over. My eyebrows went up.

"Yeah, yeah, just because I'm not built like a brick shit house like you, gym bro, doesn't mean I can't handle myself."

Given the strength of his push just now, I would dispute the veracity of that statement. But again, I kept my mouth shut. It would not do to piss off Clara's brother, likely the only source of information I currently had as to her whereabouts.

"Zachary, calm down and come inside," I said in a soft but firm tone, not unlike the one I would use with Oz when he was playing up. "I was wrong when I pushed your sister away, but we're not going to solve anything like this."

"Don't tell me to calm down, you fucking prick," Zachary muttered, but the heat had left his voice now, leaving just fear and uncertainty.

"I'm not doing this outside, kid," I muttered, grabbing him firmly by both upper arms to pull him through the front door easily, and then slamming it behind us. He looked startled for a moment and another flash of fear crossed his expression before he cleared it. I let him go as soon as he was inside, holding my hands up to show him I wasn't a threat. "Okay, maybe we can start again. You know about me and Clara? She talked about me?"

Zachary opened his mouth to speak but then his eyes flew wide as his gaze went over my shoulder.

"Rafe? What's going on?" Poppy said as she walked towards us, giving Zachary a wary look.

"You're Poppy Sterling," Zachary breathed, and I

managed not to roll my eyes. At least the appearance of Poppy had taken some of the wind out of his angry sails.

"That's right," said Poppy carefully, looking between me and Zachary.

"Pops, this is Zachary Mason, Clara's younger brother."

"Oh," Poppy said, then after a beat of shocked silence she smiled at him. "Hi."

Zachary blinked a couple of times under the force of that smile. My sister could be an annoying little shit but she had her uses. I took a step forward.

"Poppy cares about Clara just like *I* care about Clara," I told him firmly. "We both want to know that she's okay, and we both want to find her. We're worried, mate. I'm betting you're worried too, or you wouldn't have come here, right?"

I watched as his anger built again when he turned from Poppy to me. "You didn't want to help her in the courthouse," he snapped. "You— you threw her away like she was trash. You didn't help her then. She practically begged you, and you wouldn't even listen to her."

"I was a fucking prick in that courthouse," I admitted. "I completely agree with you, and I'm sorry. Maybe you won't ever forgive me. Maybe your sister won't ever forgive me. But for now, we've got to focus on making sure that Clara is safe. So if you want to pull your head out of your arse, *maybe* we can move forward and you can tell me what you know. Right?"

Zachary was blinking at me in surprise. Clearly, he didn't expect me to admit that I was a fucking prick. His shoulders sagged and he seemed to deflate before my eyes. The anger just draining away.

"Then why did you recuse yourself?" he asked, and I could just about detect a small shake to his voice. The kid was losing it.

"I had to recuse myself, Zachary," I said, my harsh tone softening. "I didn't have a choice. Clara would have known that."

Zachary tore his hands through his hair and looked up at the ceiling before looking back at me and Poppy.

"Couldn't you have just pretended you didn't know her? Couldn't you have played along to keep her safe?"

"Zachary, I'm sorry but I had no idea she wasn't safe. Clara did not tell me who she was. She didn't warn me what was going to happen in that courtroom. And honestly, I don't think she *wanted* me to play along. I bet you know that too."

He deflated even more then. "No, no, she wouldn't," he muttered. He blew out a long breath. "I don't know what to do," he said, his voice small now and the shake in it much more obvious. "I snuck out of my window to come here. They'll lose their minds when they know I'm gone." His eyes had reddened slightly and his lower lip was trembling. In that moment he looked much more like the child he was than before.

"I don't have anyone else but Clara." His voice cracked on her name. When a rogue tear fell down his cheek, he swiped it away furiously, his face reddening in embarrassment. "Mum checked out years ago. You know what Dad and my brothers are. Clara's the only one who cares about me. I can't lose her."

That last sentence was like a shot of ice through my veins. For a moment, the sheer panic made my chest too tight to speak, but I managed to force out the next.

"Zachary, why are you talking about losing Clara?" I gritted out.

He paced away from us and then back again, his hands still ripping through his hair. "She thought when she did the

Big Terrible Thing that it would happen quickly. But then it was months of hearing nothing. Freddie was arrested for his dumbfuckery but the rest of them were fine, still free to do whatever fucked up shit they wanted, including dragging Clara and me to that stupid trial. But it's all fucked because they're still free, and they can still hurt her. And now... something's wrong. Dad's been twitched since Freddie's arrest, but it's been worse since the trial." Zachary swallowed as panic lit his eyes. "If the Big Terrible Thing comes out then..." he trailed off. His face was almost unnaturally pale now.

"What's the Big Terrible Thing?" Poppy asked.

Zachary swallowed again and I decided to reply for him.

"Clara is an informant for the police," I told her. "She told them how to access the encrypted messaging network that the Masons communicate through on the dark web. There's a huge case being built now against her family that all hinges on the information Clara gave to them by allowing them to access that network."

"She snitched," Zachary whispered, as if someone might overhear him. He sounded terrified now. "In our world, you never *ever* snitch. But it was the only way out we could see."

His shoulders sagged more and another tear slipped down his cheek, making him look even younger.

"My dad's not a good man. He... he hurts Mum. Like really hurts her. He's broken her, I think. It's like the lights are on, but no one's home most of the time, but that doesn't seem to stop Dad. And Clara..." He trailed off. The tears were coming thick and fast now. "She's always been so bloody brave. B-b-but he hurt her too. He hurt her loads and I couldn't stop it. I'm not strong enough to stop him. Clara had to leave, but she comes back for me when I ask her. A few months ago she came over to help with my revision. I'd begged her to come. I'm such a selfish shit, but I begged her. And then Dad... it wasn't good."

"Here you go, mate," I said, handing Zachary a handkerchief as one of my hands landed on his shoulder, giving it a squeeze. He wiped his face with it, sniffing back the rest of his tears. "That's why Clara was hurt at the start of term, wasn't it?"

He nodded, avoiding eye contact and shuffling his feet, but what he didn't do was shrug my hand off his shoulder.

"Yeah," he said in a hoarse voice. "And it was my fault."

"Hey," I said firmly, taking hold of both his shoulders now. "It wasn't your fault. *You* didn't hurt her."

"I should've been able to protect her," he whispered. "But I've never cared about all that muscle-building crap, and I've never been a good fighter. I—"

"It's not your job to protect her, Zachary. You're a child, and even if you weren't, there was nothing you could have done."

He shook his head, still avoiding eye contact. Poppy came up next to him to lay her hand on his back.

"I should have stopped her doing the Big Terrible Thing," he whispered. "But I was scared. I didn't want to live there anymore, and we thought this could be a way out. Plus, we thought maybe we could protect Mum. They needed to be put away, and this time it needed to be done properly."

"What Clara did was brave," I told him. "You and Clara have been brave for a long, long time. I know you're used to having to deal with everything by yourself. I know you think it's just you and your sister against your family but that's not true now, understand me?"

"Y-y-you mean it?" he whispered, meeting my gaze then, his big brown eyes so much like his sister's that my chest felt tight.

"I love your sister, mate," I told him. "I made a mistake in that courthouse. A really fucking stupid mistake, but I won't do that again. I won't let either of you down ever again. I promise. You need to start trusting me so I can help get her back. I know you don't know me very well, but I *am* powerful. My family is powerful. *Very* powerful, Zachary. I won't let them hurt Clara and I'm going to make sure they either go to prison or something else happens to them. I have the power to do either. Understand me?"

"Something else...?" he started to say then swallowed thickly. I gave him a firm nod.

"Yes, something else, Zachary. Something else which would render them unable to hurt you or your sister ever again. I have resources neither of you can even imagine."

"You'll get her back?" he whispered.

"I promise."

He stared at me for a beat, searching my expression, and I stared right back.

Clara was mine, and that made her brother my responsibility too. They would both be moving in with me once I extracted Clara from wherever she was now. After a few more seconds Zachary's face crumpled and he started sobbing in earnest. I pulled him in for a hug, wrapping him in my arms and giving him firm pats on the back.

"I can't lose her," he sobbed into my shoulder. "She's everything. She's always looked out for me. Taken the abuse for me. And I let her. I always let her because I was scared. I'm not brave or strong like Clara. But they won't just beat her this time. S-s-snitching isn't something they forgive. They'll kill her."

I pulled back so I could look at his tear-streaked face.

"I'll get her back, Zachary. If you help me, I can make her safe. You aren't alone anymore."

"But he *knows*. This time I really think he knows and—"

"It's okay, Zachary. *I'm* going to deal with it. Understand me? All I need is an address."

Chapter 31

Nobody leaves

Clara

"There you go, Mum. Nice cup of tea." I put the steaming mug in front of my mother. When she glanced up at me, for a moment, the vacant clouds cleared as if she was noticing me there for the first time, and a flash of terror shot through her expression.

"Clara," she said in an urgent voice, her hand coming up to grip my wrist so tightly I could feel the bones grinding together.

"Mum, what are you doing?"

"Tell me you didn't do it," she begged in a hoarse whisper, and I froze.

"Mum, I don't know what you're talking about."

Mum glanced at Pinky who was just outside the kitchen door, then back at me.

"Tell me you didn't snitch. Tell me it wasn't you."

"Of course not, Mum," I said, shooting Pinky a nervous glance, but he was thankfully facing away from us. "I don't understand what's happening to be honest.

You know I never get involved in any of Dad's business."

Relief had her slumping back in the chair, a shaky hand coming up to push her hair off her face.

"Okay, love," she whispered. "Okay."

"Mum, listen," I said tentatively, hoping that this moment of clarity might mean I could get through to her. "I'm really going to have to go to work. I can't keep calling in sick like this." I gave a nervous laugh. "Lily can't manage all of those sprogs without me in the mix."

Mum waved her hand before she picked up her tea. "Dad needs you here, love," she said vaguely, back to her normal checked-out self.

I gritted my teeth in frustration. "Dad doesn't need me here, Mum. I should get back to the school."

"You're not bloody well going anywhere," my father's gruff voice cut through the air of the kitchen. Mum shrank back into herself like she always did, her eyes clouding over and her expression becoming even more vague. I pushed her tea towards her, took her hand in mine and wrapped it around the handle.

"Drink your tea, Mum," I whispered.

"Did you hear me, Runt?" Dad shouted.

"Yes, Dad," I said quietly, knowing better than to make eye contact with him, something my father often saw as a direct challenge. I took a deep breath and let it out slowly before I gathered the courage to go on. "Dad, I c-can't stay here forever," I said, my voice trembling as I turned to face him, still keeping my gaze lowered.

It was risky, but I had to get out of this house. We'd been in lockdown since yesterday. I overheard Skinny Pete saying something about a police investigation. There was talk of a snitch. An insider who gave them away.

They knew.

In some ways, I was relieved. I'd been carrying the burden of this secret for months, waiting for the other shoe to drop. I knew what I was doing when I did the Big Terrible Thing. I knew what I was risking. I had just hoped that I could hide in plain sight, that I could keep my head down like I always did and blend into the background as usual.

But, because of Rafe, the spotlight had fallen on me, and now blending into the background was no longer an option.

"Nobody leaves until we find the snitch," Dad said slowly, his head tilting to the side. The steadiness of his words was scarier really. With my father, controlled violence when he was in his right mind, when he was sober, was actually worse than the spontaneous violence that erupted from his drinking. "Tell me, Clara, have I not provided a good life for you and your little shit of a brother?"

I cleared my throat and glanced at Mum, who was still staring vacantly into space. Dad took a step closer, and my gaze flew back to him.

"Of course you have, Dad," I said in a small voice.

"You think you're better than us, don't you?" he returned. "You swan off, go to uni, like you're a big shot, just to earn a fucking pittance as a teacher. No, scrap that, not even a proper teacher, are you? Just an assistant, just a grunt. I pay our cleaner more than you get."

"Yes, Dad," I whispered.

"Putting ideas into Zach's head so that he's put off joining the family business."

I nearly snorted at that. Family business? Dad was talking like we owned a chain of department stores or something. Not sold drugs, blackmailed people and terrorised a large portion of East London. Some business.

I shook my head slowly. "I didn't mean to——"

"Don't contradict me, you little bitch!" he shouted, slamming his hand down on the table and making both me and Mum jump.

I took a small step back, and his gaze shot to my feet before his lip curled in disgust.

"I've had some information today from one of my grasshoppers. Now this guy, he tells me that the snitch is a member of my own family. I says to him, 'Mate, none of my family are gonna be that bloody stupid,' but this fucking guy *insists*. When I press him, the bastard shows me a photo."

Dad pulled his phone from his back pocket and my heart sank as my blood ran cold. Everything moved very fast then. He advanced on me, and I lurched back. But I came up against the kitchen sideboard and I didn't duck fast enough. He grabbed me by my hair and held the phone up in front of my face.

"Do you see what I see?" he said in that low, dangerous voice again. My eyes stung with tears as he yanked on my hair. His phone screen blurred in front of me but not before I'd seen an image of me sitting in an interview room, talking to Grant – Superintendent Mitchell.

"It's not what it looks like, Dad," I whispered and he barked out a laugh.

"Oh really? Because it looks like a skinny, four-eyed, disloyal runt selling out her entire family to the pigs. That's what it looks like to me."

"Dad, I—"

"You've fucked up everything. Do you even realise what you've done? They have so much shit on us now it'll take a fucking miracle to dig our way out. The whole fucking organisation is going to go down for this, you stupid bitch!" He screamed the last part, yanking my head even further back until my neck was bent at an unnatural angle.

"Frank, please," Mum's voice came from behind Dad. She was standing behind him now, wringing her hands in front of her as she looked between us.

"Sit the fuck down, Marie," Dad snarled.

"Please, Frank. Clara's sorry, aren't you, love? Don't hurt her anymore. She just—"

Dad dropped my hair as he spun around to face Mum, his face red with fury. His hand was a blur as it went whistling through the air to backhand her. I cried out as she was sent flying onto her hands and knees on the floor.

"Maybe now you'll shut..." he aimed a kick at Mum which connected with her side and she crumbled in a small heap, "...the fuck..." another kick, "...up."

He turned back to me, ignoring Mum's whimpers on the floor as she attempted to crawl away from him. "See what you've made me do to your mother?" he asked.

I stared at him, not shying away from eye contact this time. The terror was still there, but after watching him attack Mum there was something else building in my chest, like a small spark of fury had been lit and was gradually catching fire.

So yes, I made eye contact with the bastard, and for once, I didn't look away.

"You cowardly piece of shit," I said through my teeth and shock crossed his expression, quickly replaced by anger.

"What the fuck did you say to me?"

"You heard me, old man," I taunted. "You're a fucking coward."

"Why you little—"

He made a grab for me, but I darted around to the other side of the table.

"You know what? I did snitch. I'm *glad* I snitched. I hope you and your team of violent, disgusting bastards are put away for a good long fucking time."

His face was nearly purple with rage now as he ran around the table to try and grab me, but I darted away out of his reach to the opposite side.

"I'm going to testify against you for that beating you gave me four months ago, as well as all the others. I wonder what they do to men in prison who beat women? You're the big man out here, beating your wife and daughter who are both half your size, but what happens when you're up against other hardened criminals who don't like massive, cowardly bullies much?"

In the back of my mind, I was aware that this wasn't the best idea. If I pushed Dad hard enough, I had no doubt he would kill me. But years of hatred were spilling out, and weirdly, now that he knew I was a snitch, I felt like I had nothing left to lose. I glanced behind Dad to the back door, then over at Mum who was huddled in the corner with her arms wrapped around her knees, trying to make herself as small as possible.

That's what we did, Mum and I, we tried to make ourselves small. That's what this man had done to us, and I'd had enough of it. Dad feinted left and I saw my chance. I sprinted across the space between me and the back door. My hand closed over the handle, but just as I was about to pull it open, searing pain went through my scalp again as I was yanked back practically off my feet by my hair.

"Where the fuck do you think you're going?" Dad shouted, throwing me against the side of the table like a rag doll. I saw stars when my face connected with the wood and I would have fallen to the floor, but Dad grabbed me by my hair again and hauled me upright. "You won't be testifying about fucking anything," he growled before his fist connected with the other side of my face.

He was going to kill me.

I'd pushed him over the edge and now he was going to finish the job he'd started countless times before. His other fist connected with my stomach, and I bent over, clutching my sides and trying to breathe through the pain. I could hear Mum sobbing on the floor. I imagined Zach crying at my funeral, all alone, and my vision flooded with red.

How fucking dare he?

How dare he make us live in fear our whole lives? How dare he force us to be complicit in his life of crime? How dare he beat me? He had no bloody right. My body flooded with an unnatural strength as my anger built and my hands balled into tight fists. I managed to straighten despite the pain in my stomach. Surprise crossed my dad's face for a moment, and I used the opportunity to strike.

One of my fists shot out and punched him square in the throat. His eyes went wide as he started gasping for breath, clutching at his neck. I brought my knee up and connected with his groin in a sharp blow that took him to his knees. I knew it wouldn't take him long to recover, so I hobbled over to the sink and pulled out a frying pan, lugging it back over to where my father was still wheezing. Holding it with both hands, I lifted it up and brought it down onto the back of his head with a dull thud. Dad slumped forward face-first onto the floor. I watched him for a few seconds. When he didn't move I dropped the pan which clattered at my feet, and I ran over to Mum.

"Mum," I croaked, glancing up at the door to the

corridor then back at her crumpled form on the floor. "Can you walk? Get up and come with me."

Mum's head emerged from being buried in her legs, and her wide eyes shot to me, then to my father's prone form on the floor.

"Clara, what have you done?" she whispered.

I shook my head in disbelief. That motherfucker was going to kill me.

I grabbed her shoulder and gave her a small shake. "We've got to go now, Mum," I hissed. "Get up."

She shook her head, her eyes flying wide. "I c-c-can't leave," she said.

"Yes, you can," I told her, pulling on her arm now in an attempt to get her moving.

"You've killed him." Her voice was horrified. She couldn't take her eyes off Dad. I glanced over at him, registering that his chest was still moving.

"No such luck, Mum," I snapped, pulling on her arm again.

"How can you say that? He's your father."

That rage flooded through my system again and I dropped her arm to take a step back.

"Look at my face," I snapped at her. I knew it was bad, as blood was dripping down into one of my eyes, and the other's vision was restricted now from the swelling. "That man is *not* my father."

She totally ignored me and started crawling over to the man in question.

"Frank?" she called to him when she made it over to sit next to his body, gently shaking his shoulder. "Oh, Frank, love."

I blinked down at her. This woman genuinely seemed to want her husband to wake up. She must have known he was going to kill me, but she still wanted him. Needed him. The choice she was making had never been so stark. Marie Mason chose Frank Mason over everything, even her own daughter's life.

And to think I'd done the Big Terrible Thing partly for her, so that she could be free of him and his abuse. To get her back to the happy, loving woman she'd been when I was little.

But the mum I knew then was gone. This woman wasn't my mother, just like the man lying face down on the floor wasn't my father.

"Bye, Mum," I whispered before I spun on my heel and ran for the side door. I could feel my head spinning and the dark closing in, and I knew I had to escape now before it was too late. I hesitated after I pulled the door open and looked back at Mum, but she was still fussing over Dad. So, I decided to make a decision for me for once. I had to save my own life. In truth, there was nothing left of my mother to save.

Chapter 32

Now that will be
quite enough of that

Rafe

"Ladies, what in the fuck are you doing here?" I growled as I leaned into the open window of Mrs Clayton's old Ford Focus. Neither Mrs C nor Lily had heard my approach and both of them jumped in their seats at my sharp voice.

"Good Christ, Rafe!" squeaked Mrs Clayton, her hand clutching her chest as she spun to face me with wide eyes. "You can't sneak up on a middle-aged woman with questionable bladder control like that. Are you crazy?"

I stared them both down as I leaned against my hands on the open window.

"Am *I* crazy?" I asked, raising my eyebrows in disbelief. "My question is, what is a middle-aged schoolteacher with questionable bladder control and her fuckwit sidekick who's more used to wrangling primary school children than dealing with London's hardened criminals doing sitting in a clapped-out Ford Focus outside this address?"

"Shit, Rafe, keep your voice down!" hissed Lily, looking furtively up at the house. I rolled my eyes.

"Why in the fuck would I keep my voice down?"

Lily's wide eyes blinked up at me in disbelief.

"Because of the bloody Masons, of course. We're here to case the joint."

"Tell me, ladies, what were you planning to do after you'd, in your own words, 'cased the joint'?"

Mrs Clayton bit her lip, and Lily crossed her arms over her chest, her chin tilting to a stubborn angle.

"Well, we've not got that far yet," she said irritably. "We haven't had a chance to bloody well case the joint, because some big stupid *lord* has arrived and has likely blown our cover."

"Don't be absurd. You *have* no cover. You both stick out like sore thumbs. You are totally out of your depth. Stick to teaching my child and putting on dodgy plays, rather than dabbling in dubious rescue attempts from the criminal underworld."

"Oh, right, and what are you gonna do then?" Lily said in a grumpy voice.

My eyebrows went up. "What do you think I'm going to do? I'm going to walk up to the front door, demand to see Clara and I'm not going to leave without her."

"You can't just do that," Lily breathed.

"Why not?"

"Well, well... they'll kill you, that's why."

"In broad daylight they're going to kill a barrister, right out here in public? We're not in Sicily and this isn't the Italian Mafia. They may have a couple of bent coppers on their payroll, but they don't own the judicial system. This is the United Kingdom, and this is London. If they are keeping a woman imprisoned against her will, a woman who, by the way, is *mine,* then they are going to give her back immediately, and they will pay in a court of law.

"I'm the only one who seems to be able to see the situation here clearly. These people are *fucked.* There is an absolute avalanche of evidence against them. They will not come out of this free men – and, prior to that, they will not harm a hair on *my* woman's head. If either of you or, indeed, Clara herself had come to me *months ago,* we could have avoided all this bullshit. As it is, I'm dealing with it now, and I'm *not* leaving without her."

"Thank goodness," breathed Mrs Clayton, her shoulders slumping in relief.

Lily wasn't quite as quick to yield under my superior judgement. She narrowed her eyes at me and her arms stayed crossed over her chest.

"What happened to your opinion about Clara being *part* of the criminal element? What happened to you wanting us to sack her? What happened to you hating her?"

"I was wrong," I said immediately, and her combative stance relaxed just slightly, "and I'm a fucking prick."

"Rafe, language," admonished Mrs Clayton half-heartedly, still not quite on telling-off form after the wind had been knocked out of her.

"I'm not used to being wrong," I told both of them, "but in this instance, I was. And, unfortunately, it was about one of the most important people in my life. I'll have to live with that, but I'll be damned if I let my mistake mean that I lose her. Now, if you'll excuse me, I'm going to get my woman and take her home to her brother."

"Zach's with you?" asked Lily, and I nodded.

"Yes, Zachary did what nobody else seemed to be capable of doing, which was coming to me and actually telling me what was going on."

"Is he okay?" said Lily. When her eyes filled with tears, I suddenly regretted my abrasive tone. She clearly cared for the boy.

"He's fine, Lily, no physical injuries that I could see. He told me about the Big Terrible Thing. I'm sure you two know about it as well, but he's terrified for his sister. Now, I'm going to go and get Clara. You two can watch from the safe distance of your car. Do not approach the door. Am I understood?"

"What if—?" Lily started to speak, but I cut her off.

"Do not approach the Mason house. Not under any circumstances. I can't have you two thrown into the mix and have to worry about you as well."

Both women deflated at that and sat back in their chairs. Not wanting to waste any more time, I jogged across the road, through the luckily open gate, across the big front garden and up the steps up to the massive wooden door. This was one of the Masons' nicer properties and was situated in Hampstead, away from the hub of their east London crime network. They had another five houses like this, but Zach was sure that Clara was here, and he was also sure that she couldn't leave.

Zach and Poppy had wanted to come with me, but I'd strictly forbidden it. Zach was a child, and Poppy attracted *way* too much attention. Plus, she was about as much use as a chocolate teapot. So I'd left them together, her making him a cup of tea and coaxing him to tell her about his plans for veterinary training. On the way to the Mason house, I'd rung Grant to let him know what I was doing. Grant wasn't *totally* on board; he told me in no uncertain terms I should wait, rather than going in based on the say-so of a fifteen-year-old boy, but I was done waiting. I felt like I'd been waiting for Clara my whole life. I'd be damned if I was going to wait any longer.

So I pounded on the solid door until a massive beast of a guy with a bald head yanked it open, flanked by two other equally unsavoury-looking individuals.

"Good day, gentlemen," I said. "I gather this is the Mason residence."

"Who wants to know?" grunted the bald man.

"I'm Lord Sterling. I believe you may recognise me from the courtroom last week. I had to recuse myself during the trial of Frederick Mason. I'm here to collect Clarabelle Mason. She lives with me, and she's been missing for the last seventy-two hours. I'm reliably informed that she is at this address."

Bald Man snorted. "There's no fucking Clarabelle here. You can do one, mate."

"I assure you I will not be *doing one*," I told him. "I will be leaving with Clarabelle."

"Like hell you will," he said, pushing his large body through the door to invade my personal space. The smell of cigarettes and beer almost made me gag.

I tensed, ready to get around this guy if I had to, but then I heard movement from the side of the house. When I whipped round in the direction of the noise, I saw Clara staggering out onto the front lawn. Her face was swollen. There was blood dripping from her temple into her eye, and she looked seconds from collapse.

"Clara!" I shouted, running down the steps towards her. She spun to face me, frowned in confusion, then blinked a couple of times before she sank to the ground like a stone. "Clara, shit, Clara!"

I ran to her with my heart in my throat and skidded onto

my knees next to her. My relief when I felt her chest moving under my hand was so acute I almost couldn't breathe. I gently moved her onto her side, pulling her arm across her body and tucking her hand under the side of her face, so that she was in the recovery position. Footsteps came thundering from the same side entrance Clara had collapsed through and I looked up to see Frank Mason glaring at me across the lawn. He too had a blood trail, this one running from somewhere around the back of his neck down his chest onto his shirt.

"Stay back," I growled at him, leaping to my feet to stand in front of Clara. "Stay away from her."

"Don't tell me what to do with my own daughter, you lawyer cunt!" Frank Mason spat out.

"She's not your daughter. Fathers don't do this to their daughters."

"The little bitch punched me in the throat, kneed me in the balls and slammed my head with a frying pan."

"Good," I said. "Sadly, you're still alive. Now fuck off. I'm taking Clara to hospital."

"This is family business; you're not taking her anywhere." Frank took a step towards me, then staggered on his feet, looking slightly dazed, clearly still suffering from the blow to the back of his head. He looked over at his men at the door and jerked his head in my direction.

The big bald one came at me first. He threw a slow, lumbering punch at my head which I easily ducked.

I punched him in the jaw just like I'd been taught in the gym at the private school I'd gone to, and he went down like a sack of shit. You didn't go to the boarding school I went to without learning how to fight.

When the other two came at me, I had a flash of panic. I needed to protect Clara and get her out of this situation, and I was terrified she could be caught in the crossfire. But as they started to move, a sharp, commanding voice cut through the air, and everyone froze.

"Now that will be quite enough of that," Mrs Clayton said in her best headteacher take-no-shit voice. "I have never witnessed such appalling behaviour. We will be taking Clara to hospital where she will be seen to by medical professionals. Get back inside that house *this instant* and await the relevant authorities."

The men blinked at her. Having a short, slightly over-weight, grey-haired lady give them a bollocking as though they were still in primary school was likely unexpected, but I was guessing they'd all had enough experience of their own grandparents, mums and teachers of the same ilk to stop them in their tracks.

"And I'm filming this, motherfuckers, so you better watch yourselves. No more getting away with being violent fuckwaffles with impunity anymore. Not on our watch." Lily was less intimidating than Mrs Clayton, but the men did flinch when they glanced at her phone.

"You're in enough trouble already, aren't you, lads?" I said to them. "Frank here's going down for a long time, and likely so are you. Now you can choose what kind of time you'll serve. If you want to contribute to killing his daugh-ter, I'd say you'll be in prison a damn sight longer. Do you know what they do in jail to people who hurt women? *I* know, and it's not pretty."

"You fucking useless twats," Frank shouted when they didn't move. "Get that stupid bastard. Don't listen to him. I've never gone down before. I'm not going down this time either."

But I'd planted the seed of doubt now. These men weren't going to help him get Clara back into the house. Then I noticed one of them behind the bald guy, much skinnier and younger than the other two. I recognised him from the street outside Clara's school. He'd clearly been watching her for a while.

"Let her go with him, guys," the skinny guy said. He was sweating and looking increasingly nervous. "Let Clara go. Listen, if they've got into the network like we think, we're all fucked. Let Clara go, or it'll be even worse."

Then I heard footsteps running on the pavement. Ruben Mason came into view and screeched to a halt outside the house.

"Clara!" he cried, taking a step towards her but I blocked his way.

"That's close enough," I told him. "I'm taking her to hospital."

"Is she okay?" Ruben asked in a hoarse voice.

"She's alive, but I need to get her out of here."

Ruben looked between me and Clara for a moment, then focused on his father who was staggering towards us. "Get the fuck away from her, Dad," he said through gritted teeth. "All of you get away from my sister." He was shouting now and seemed to have a damn sight more authority than the skinny guy from before. All Frank's men started moving back despite Frank screaming at them.

I wasted no time in spinning around to pick Clara up. I knew it wasn't ideal. I knew she needed an ambulance, but I had to get her out of there before these men changed their minds. She let out a soft groan as I held her up against my chest. There was blood on her temple, her glasses had a crack through one of the lenses and one of the arms was broken.

"It's okay, baby," I said. "Everything's going to be okay now."

Chapter 33

I'll be keeping you safe

Clara

I BIT MY LIP, TRYING TO CONTAIN MY CLAUSTROPHOBIA and lie perfectly still as I was moved through the CT scanner. Everything from the last hour was fuzzy: the sound of the frying pan and the dull thunk as it connected to my father's head, the dizziness as I ran out onto the front lawn, Rafe appearing as if my fevered imagination had conjured him to life. All of it was a jumbled mishmash in my mind.

I had a cracking headache and my temple was still throbbing from my father's fist and the wood of the table. I knew that there was a cut there. I could still feel the dried blood around my eye, but I didn't know the extent of the damage. No one had given me a mirror yet. I'd lost consciousness after the head injury and, although it had only been brief, I'd then become disoriented once we reached the emergency department, so I had been immediately rushed for a scan.

The last place I wanted to be was inside this horrid,

noisy tube. I wasn't convinced it was necessary, to be honest.

I'd been knocked out once before when I was a teenager. That time I'd woken up on the kitchen floor, with Zach crying next to me; he'd helped me into bed afterwards. There was no hospital assessment involved then.

Finally, the noise was over, and I closed my eyes in relief. They'd asked me if I wanted to listen to music, but I'd turned them down. In the back of my mind I think I was worried that music would make me *feel* something. I didn't want to feel anything. I just wanted to be numb; to not be scared all the time.

"Alright, love?" the porter asked me as he wheeled me back down the corridor to the ward.

"I'm fine." I whispered the lie easily, then turned my head to the side to look at the walls and doors of the wards as we whisked past.

I'd expected to be wheeled back to the overcrowded emergency department, but instead the trolley turned into a different wing of the hospital and then finally into a private room containing Rafe, Mrs Clayton and Lily.

"The results?" snapped Rafe at the porter, expecting instant feedback on a scan I'd had only minutes before.

"Don't look at me, guv'nor," the porter said. "Expect they'll let you know in a bit. I just move the patients."

Rafe huffed out an annoyed breath and then turned to me.

The fuzzy memories of Rafe holding me in the back of Mrs Clayton's car filtered through my mind: his strong arms around me, his deep voice telling me how everything was going to be fine, how he had me now, how he wasn't going to let anything hurt me. The thread of fear in his tone had thrown me. I'd never heard Rafe scared before. Was he scared of my father? Of what my family could do? He was right to be. I knew that better than anyone.

I couldn't deal with Rafe at the moment, so I closed my eyes to shut him out and turned to Lily and Mrs Clayton instead.

"I told you not to come to any of Dad's houses," I said, my voice hoarse. Mrs C's face was pale, and Lily's eyes were red-rimmed as if she'd been crying.

"Young lady, I will not follow illogical orders," said Mrs Clayton in her no-nonsense tone.

"We were terrified, hun," said Lily, her voice trembling. "I didn't know what else to do."

"I didn't want you involved." My voice was weaker now. *I* was weak. "I didn't want you exposed like that. You're all I have and..." My throat seized up, and I had to swallow against the tightness there, but when I opened my mouth to speak again, Rafe cut me off.

"They are *not* all you have," he said in that firm, authoritative tone. Even though it hurt to look at him, I still made myself do it. He was frowning at me from across the room. Was he still angry with me about my family? Now that he could see I was going to be okay, were we back to him judging me for shit I couldn't control? Was he implying that I had my family, so not just Mrs C and Lily? I knew he was angry that I'd lied about that. But I was simply too exhausted to deal with an angry Rafe at that moment, so I turned away from him again to look at Lily.

"Did you go to him?" I whispered. "Y-you shouldn't have done that. I—"

"I can understand why you'd say that, darling," Rafe cut me off again, but this time his voice was soft. Darling? What was going on here? "I was a complete bastard at the courthouse."

I blinked at him. I wasn't wearing my glasses, so I couldn't make out the expression on his face clearly. "W-what?"

"I was humiliated when I had to recuse myself. Instead of taking a second to actually think, I pushed you away when you needed my help." His voice cracked at the end of that sentence and surprise shot through me. He sounded wretched.

"In my defence, despite the fact I pride myself on my high IQ, I simply couldn't reconcile everything quickly enough. So I will add stupid sod to total bastard."

"Agreed," muttered Lily, but Rafe ignored her.

"You were asking me for help in that courthouse corridor, weren't you, Clara? Not help for your family, but help for you and your brother."

"My brother?" I said weakly. Rafe knew about Zach?

He moved quickly then, striding over to the side of my bed. When he was close enough, his large hand came up to cup my face gently.

"You were hurt," he said in a broken whisper. "You were hurt, and I'll *never* forgive myself." To my complete shock, his eyes filled with tears.

I shook my head, my cheek and then hair sliding through his fingers. "I'm not your responsib—"

"Don't say it," he cut in, his voice still hoarse. "Please don't say you're not mine. I've fucked up. I admit that but—"

"I was never yours," I whispered. "Everything we had was built on secrets and lies. You wouldn't have gone near me if you knew where I came from. And now this is just pity and guilt. You're a good man and you feel bad. But I'm not your problem. I—"

"Stop. Talking." Rafe's eyes flashed as he leaned into

me, his gorgeous face so close now that if I leaned forward just an inch, my mouth would be on his. "I don't know where you've got this whole good, self-sacrificing man idea from about me. I'm ruthless, I'm ambitious, I will step over people to get what I want, and I do take what I want. I think you may be under the false impression that I'm a man who would be with a woman out of guilt, which couldn't be further from the truth. Guilt or no, you're *mine*, Clara. You were mine before I even laid eyes on you, and you know it."

I shook my head again, and his jaw clenched as a frustrated expression settled over his features.

"Well, we can sort this out later after you've come home and you've recovered."

My eyes flew wide, flinching away from his hand so hard that pain shot through my temple, and I winced.

"Rafe," Lily said cautiously from behind him. "I think you should step back from her now."

A muscle ticked in his jaw as he scanned my face, then eventually he dropped his hand and took a step back from the bed, crossing his arms over his chest.

"I'm not coming home with you," I whispered.

"Don't be absurd," Rafe said dismissively as he stared across at me. "Of course you are. I've told Poppy that—"

"Don't involve Poppy," I said, my voice rising in horror. Poppy was the most vibrant person I'd ever met, but there was a thread of vulnerability there. This situation would terrify her. I'd done enough damage already.

Rafe's eyebrows went up. "Of course Poppy's involved. She cares about you too, Clara."

I shook my head again, then winced when the sharp pain came back.

"Shit," Rafe muttered as his face paled. "You need some

more analgesia." He moved forward and pressed the call bell on the side of my bed before I could stop him.

"I'm fine," I said. "And this is the NHS, you can't just ring and expect to be..."

"Lord Sterling?" A nurse had appeared in the doorway. "How can I help, sir?"

"Clara needs some analgesia, please. Now."

"Yes, of course. Right away." The nurse practically ran out of there to do his bidding. What the hell was going on? Then I started looking around at my surroundings and my heart skipped a few beats.

"What did you do?" I asked in a low whisper. "Why did that nurse come so quickly? Why do I have my own room?"

"I was not having you stay on a goddamn trolley in the emergency department when you'd been knocked unconscious," Rafe said, his voice ringing with that authoritative tone again, which was starting to piss me off.

"I can't afford a private room," I said through my teeth.

His brows lowered. "You're not paying for the room. I am. Obviously."

"You've got to stop," I said, my voice rising. I felt for the side table and blew out a relieved breath when my fingers closed over my glasses. My hands were shaking as I put them on. I blinked through the large crack in the centre of one of the lenses, but at least I could see clearly now.

"This has got to stop." My eyes started to sting, and Rafe's expression went from annoyed frustration to concern in an instant. I closed my eyes to shut him out and summoned up the way he'd looked at me in that courthouse corridor. He hadn't been concerned then. I would never forget the disgust on his face as he looked down on me and then looked away. Never forget the pain of that rejection. I couldn't go through that again.

"Clara, darling," he started to say as he took a couple of steps back towards the bed, but I held up my hand to ward him off and he came to an abrupt halt. He uncrossed his arms and reached back with one hand to grip the back of his neck, the muscles of his chest and arms flexing under his suit. Suddenly, I was wishing that I didn't have my full vision back again. Rafe in all his gloriousness was enough to short-circuit any woman's brain into making poor choices. I'd made enough poor choices already. Number one of those was the Big Terrible Thing.

"Let me take care of you." His voice now had an almost pleading quality to it which was so un-Rafe-like it took me a few seconds to answer.

"I'm going back to ED," I told him, trying to keep my voice steady. "Then I'm going back to my flat." I looked around at all of them standing around the bed with various expressions of concern on their faces. "You should all distance yourselves from me."

"Clara," Lily snapped. "What the hell are you—?"

"I've put you in enough danger as it is. I won't continue to risk other people's safety." I swallowed, and when I spoke again, my voice had dropped like it always did when I discussed the Big Terrible Thing. "I shouldn't have done it. They can't protect me. It wasn't worth it. But I've learnt my lesson. I'm going to take Zach and we'll go somewhere. Maybe even out of the country. It's not safe here. I can't—"

"You will do no such bloody thing," Rafe said. The concern from before had been replaced with near fury now. "You're not going anywhere."

"It's not safe for me here," I said, my voice cracking over the words. How could he not understand this? "They won't stop now that they know. I'm a sitting duck and I—"

"Of course you'll be safe." His voice now was full of complete masculine affront. "*I'll* be keeping you safe."

"No, you will not. I'm leaving and you can't—"

"That's enough!" His voice cracked through the room like a whip. If it had just been the shout, then maybe I could have managed not to react, but he accompanied it with his hand slashing through the air to make his point. The combination brought out my deep-seated survival instincts. My hands went up to cover my face, I cringed back into the bed and I let out a frightened whimper which seemed to suck all the energy from the room. "Shit," Rafe muttered in horror. "Shit, Clara, baby, I—"

"Stay back, Rafe," Lily said, her voice shaking as she moved to me and took me in her arms. "It's okay, love. You're safe here."

I burrowed into her, and that's when the floodgates opened. "I thought I was d-d-doing the right thing," I said through my sobs as I soaked Lily's jumper with my tears. "I c-c-couldn't see another way. I thought they'd keep us safe, b-b-but I just made things worse. We'll never be safe. I d-d-don't even know where Zach is."

"Zach's fine, hun," Lily said, her voice shaking with tears as well now. "He's fine. And what you did was incredibly brave."

"I'm not b-b-brave," I said in a broken whisper. "I'm scared all the time. I'm so tired, Lily. I'm so tired of this fear."

Chapter 34

Oh, you want the police here now?

Rafe

"Listen, Sterling," Grant said as we all disembarked from the cars. "This isn't exactly your scene. Why don't you let us handle things and you get back to your cosy courtroom?"

I glared at Grant. "Ah yes, because you've been *handling things* so well up until now? The ten stitches in the side of my girlfriend's head tell me everything I need to know about how you were handling things."

"Fuck you," Grant spat. "I didn't see you protecting your fucking girlfriend either, mate. Not by the way you shook her off at the courthouse like she was shit on the sole of your aristocratic shoe. So don't go blaming me for not protecting her."

"I didn't have all the information," I said through gritted teeth. "Had I known that Clara was an informant, then I   "

"You didn't bloody well listen to her!" Grant snapped. "I know I fucked up. We should have moved against the Masons earlier, but we wanted to be sure. We wanted to build the best case possible, and that meant giving them the opportunity to incriminate themselves even more whilst we were listening. But I *never* wanted Clara to get hurt. And if she'd have come to *me, I* wouldn't have ignored her and walked away. So fuck you and your judgement."

I tamped down my anger. Grant was right, but the fact remained that he'd had all the facts and he still hadn't protected Clara when he should have. "Fine, but this is getting sorted today. That's why I'm here. And remember what you promised?"

Grant gave me a strong bit of side-eye. "That might be a tricky one, Sterling."

"I don't care how difficult it is. Let me and my family smooth over the optics after the fact. Understand?" I'd phoned Dad yesterday and he'd mobilised the full force of the Sterlings' influence. Just like me, Dad was a ruthless bastard when it came to getting what he wanted, and he hated injustice. If the Masons thought they had police officers in their pockets, they were nothing compared to us. We'd been manipulating this country's legal system for hundreds of years. I'd told Dad everything and he'd been just as appalled as I was. It was rare we used our influence to intervene in any real way, but the power was still there for us to wield. And wield it we would if it was to protect the woman I loved, even if I'd already failed once on that score.

The memory of Clara sobbing into her friend's jumper yesterday floated through my mind.

I'm not b-b-brave. I'm scared all the time.

Bullshit was that woman not brave. She was a damn sight braver than half of east London, in my opinion. Nobody had ever dared go up against the Masons. That small woman was taking down an entire crime syndicate, and she didn't think she was brave?

And bollocks to her being scared all the time. Bollocks to her being scared *ever again*. I wasn't having it. Hence my presence at the Mason house today, to make damn fucking sure Frank Mason knew that.

"Fine," Grant clipped before raising his fist and banging on the front door.

I'd done my research on the Masons over the last few days, so I knew that the massive bloke who opened the door to us was called Pinky, and I knew why. My lip curled as I scanned his beer-bellied body filling the doorway.

"What the fuck do you want?" he asked.

"Good morning, Mr Gibbons," Grant said in a conversational tone. "We're here today to arrest all of you and seize all the goods in this property. So if you could kindly move aside, then we—"

"The fuck you are!" shouted Tony Pinky Gibbons. He moved to slam the door in our faces, but my foot shot out to block it from closing.

"We thought you might say that," I said through a smile before leaning back and hurling my body at the door, using all my weight to shoulder it open. The solid wood slammed into Pinky's face with a satisfying *thwack*, and he staggered back before falling onto his arse in the corridor. I straightened up, readjusted the cuffs of my suit and then strolled into the house, stepping over the prone form of Pinky to walk down the corridor. As I walked in, the armed response unit poured in behind me with their riot gear and weapons, fanning out into the house to swiftly secure all the other rooms.

By the time I'd made it into the kitchen, they had everyone there either at gunpoint or in handcuffs. Except that was, for Mrs Mason, who was sitting at the kitchen table in shock.

Grant had offered me the riot gear as well but I'd declined, preferring instead to wear my own kind of armour: a tailored Savile Row three-piece suit.

"What the fuck is going on?" spat Frank Mason as he pushed the officer who was attempting to handcuff him. "You pigs have no bloody right to barge in here! This is private property."

"Oh, I assure you we have every right," I told him as various scuffles and arrests were made around us.

"You?" he shouted, his face going red as he pointed at me. "What the fuck are *you* doing here?"

"I wanted to make sure that the dismantlement of your organisation was carried out to my satisfaction."

"Fuck off back to that snitch cunt," he spat out as he pulled away from the officer attempting to arrest him.

"Rafe?" I turned towards Grant's voice and he lifted his visor up to make eye contact with me. "Five minutes, right?"

I nodded. "Five minutes will be sufficient."

"Mrs Mason," Grant said in a softer voice to Clara's mother, who was still frozen in shock at the kitchen table. "If you'd like to come with me into the other room until we've cleared the entire house."

"The entire house?" Marie Mason breathed. "You're taking... everyone?"

"Yes, everyone."

"But my son, Zach," her voice rose in panic. "He's not—"

"Zach has not been at this house for over forty-eight hours, Mrs Mason," I told her, not taking my eyes off Frank. "Don't worry. He's safe."

"Oh, right," she muttered, and a wave of disgust swept

through me. What kind of mother was this woman? "But I don't... Frank? What should I—?"

"Your husband is going to be indisposed for quite some time, Mrs Mason," I told her, still keeping my eyes on Frank. "I suggest you get used to living a life where you do not defer to his instructions, as he will not be there to dispense them."

"Mum." We all looked over to the door of the kitchen where Ruben Mason was standing, staring at his father. "It's over. You've got to listen to the police now, not Dad." He rubbed his hand down his face, looking utterly defeated. "We should never have listened to that psycho in the first place. Come on."

Ruben held out his hand and Marie stood up slowly from the table to make her way to him. As they were leaving the kitchen, Ruben looked back at me, meeting my steady gaze before looking away. Two flags of colour appeared high on his cheekbones as his expression flooded with shame.

"Look after her," he said, just above a whisper, then he was gone, followed out by the other police officers.

The kitchen door swung shut, leaving Frank and me alone.

Frank looked left and right in confusion. "Where the fuck have they all gone?"

I tilted my head to the side. "I thought you wanted everyone to 'fuck off out of your house'? Seems they took you at your word."

Frank frowned. "What's your game, mate?"

I shrugged. "I requested five minutes alone with you before you were arrested."

"What's a poncy git like you want with me?"

"This *poncy git* is quite unhappy, Frank." There was an edge to my voice now. "This poncy git didn't appreciate his girlfriend being admitted to hospital with a head injury yesterday."

He rolled his eyes. "Didn't look like she was your girlfriend when you shook her off."

"That was a mistake I won't be making again." My voice lowered as I spoke the next words. "Clara is mine, and *nobody* hurts what's mine."

"Stupid bitch clocked me with a fucking saucepan! She could have killed me!"

"And yet, unfortunately, here you stand."

"You don't know who you're fucking with," Frank spat out. "I *own* this fucking city. *Nobody* fucks with Frank Mason."

It was at this point that I decided I had had enough of this irritating conversation. I needed to get back to Clara, and I'd have to stop off on the way to get more Branston Pickle as we were running low. I did not need to be conversing with this low-life piece of shit for any longer than was strictly necessary.

Frank's eyes flew wide as I covered the distance between us in a couple of long strides. I put one of my hands to his neck as the other grabbed his coat, and I pinned him to the wall.

"You think *you* run London, do you?" I said in a low, dangerous voice.

"Get the fuck off me," he shouted, struggling against my hold. I wasn't having that, and he clearly wasn't listening to me, so I pulled him away from the wall to slam him back against it. The force of the impact rattled the door next to us. "You'll pay for this," Frank said in between his winded gasping breaths. "I'm the fucking gaffer around here."

"Don't be absurd," I told him, my voice still low and controlled. "Families like mine have been in charge of this country for *centuries*. Do you think we came by that level of power lightly? Do you think for a moment we aren't many times more ruthless than you? There's a bridge in Bath that, in order to cross, you have to pay one pound to my family. People have been paying to cross that bridge since the sixteen hundreds. When it comes to extortion, you're light-years behind us. I have the support of the police, the judiciary, the government and the very people I extort. You should have thought twice before you decided to yank the chain of a member of the aristocracy, you stupid fuck. Before you fucked with me and my girlfriend, I was willing to simply prosecute you to the full extent of the law. Now it's not just the law I'll be utilising. I have influence *everywhere*. Your family's gangster activities are child's play compared to mine."

I released him suddenly and he fell forward a couple of steps, rubbing his neck and gasping for breath.

"Where are the fucking police?" Frank asked as he staggered away from me.

I pulled my cuffs down and adjusted my watch as I stalked him casually. The man was not very light on his feet and clearly a stranger to cardio, given how loudly he was still gasping for breath.

"Oh, you want the police here now?" I asked. "I thought you weren't overly keen on the police?"

He made a lumbering dash for the exit, and I cut him off easily.

"Now, now, Frank," I said, stepping to block his way when he tried to duck around me. "You're being unconscionably rude. We haven't finished our conversation yet."

"F-fuck off," he said, real fear in his tone now.

"It might interest you to know that I had access to your daughter's medical records yesterday."

He blinked at me in confusion. "What do you—?"

"Unfortunately, we don't have time to match the full extent of her injuries. But I feel it's sufficient for now to simply go through the ones inflicted this calendar year. Let's start with the most obvious."

Frank's eyes flew even wider when he realised my intention. He swung a clumsy fist at my head, which I dodged easily before driving my own fist into the side of his chest.

"Holy shit," he gasped as he nearly went down. "You've broken my fucking ribs!"

"I do hope so," I told him. "That was, after all, the intention. Two of Clara's were broken, so I'm hoping to at least match that. Now, where was I? Ah yes. I believe this is, in fact, your signature move." I drew my hand back, and it flew through the air to connect with the side of Frank's face with a satisfying crack. "You didn't actually break the orbital bone with this blow, and I'm quite sure your bone structure is not as delicate as your daughter's, given she is half your size, but hopefully we'll get lucky and you'll sustain at least a hairline fracture... Oh, do get up."

The blow had taken Frank down onto one knee. He staggered to his feet and away from me, but I wasn't done. Not yet.

"Now, on to the wrist."

Chapter 35

You both deserve some peace

Clara

I STARTED TO GATHER MY HAIR UP INTO A PONYTAIL, but then winced when I pulled on the stitches.

"Fuck it," I muttered under my breath as I threw the hairband into my small backpack and tucked my hair behind my ears. I took in a deep breath and let it out slowly before slinging my backpack over my shoulder and turning away from the bedside table.

"Miss Mason?" a nurse called to me from the doorway and my eyes closed in frustration. "You're not leaving, are you?"

"I've seen the doctor this morning. I've had twenty-four hours of observation. There was nothing to find on the scan. I'm going home."

She darted a nervous look behind her, then back at me. "Listen, I don't think you should—"

"I cannot afford private care," I said through gritted teeth.

"But that's not a problem," the nurse said through a wide smile. "Lord Sterling is—"

"Lord Sterling has nothing to do with me. I'll pay my own bill, and I'm leaving right now."

"Thank you so much, but please don't worry, nurse," Rafe's deep voice came from the doorway, and the nurse's shoulders dropped with relief. "I'll take it from here."

"Of course, Lord Sterling," the nurse said in full deferential mode, just like everyone slipped into around Rafe. She smiled at me before sweeping past Rafe to leave the room. I gritted my teeth.

"Oh, this is good," he said, holding eye contact with me as he stepped into the room. "You're all packed. That'll save us some time."

I blinked at him. "There's no *us*, Rafe." My voice was neutral. To be honest, I felt completely drained. I couldn't take on the unstoppable force that was Rafe Sterling at the best of times, but now, in my physically and emotionally exhausted state, I didn't stand a chance. "You are not responsible for me."

His eyes flashed, but he didn't snap back. Instead, he clenched his jaw and shoved his hands into his pockets, but not before I saw the scrapes and bruising over his knuckles. I dropped my bag and flew over to him without any conscious thought as if it was just an instinct I had to follow.

"What happened to your hands?" I asked, reaching to pull one out from his pocket, then holding it in both of mine. When I turned it over, I gasped at the injuries on the knuckles and down to the wrist.

He shrugged, watching me carefully as I stroked the skin next to the scratches.

"I'm okay, darling," he said softly, and my eyes flew to his.

Being this close to him again was a total sensory over-load. It cut through the numbness I'd been mired in, taking me completely off guard. His other hand slowly reached up to my face and so, so gently swept some of my fringe back from my forehead. The contact was electric and the look on his face was almost savage in its intensity.

Lost in the moment and overwhelmed at having him this close, my body swayed towards him like it was on autopilot. His pupils dilated and he leaned down a fraction, but before my mouth could make contact with his, I dropped his hand and took two rapid steps back.

Frustration crossed Rafe's expression for a moment, but he clenched his jaw again and reined it in. Somehow, I could tell that his instinct was to not allow me any form of retreat, but he was holding himself back. I remembered my flinch from the day before and I felt my face heat.

This was yet another reason Rafe and I would not work. I was simply... broken. Like a clock that still ticked but never told the right time. If I were ever to consider another rela-tionship, it would need to be with a quiet, short guy with very little musculature and an extremely patient disposi-tion. Not someone like Rafe: someone alpha, ultra-mascu-line, entirely too tall and too built, with innate arrogance and the kind of terrifying presence that dominated every room no matter who might be there.

I wrapped my arms around my middle and broke eye contact with him to look out of the window.

"H-how did you hurt your hands?" I repeated.

There was a long pause. "I had to deal with something... unpleasant, but that's over now. Clara, I've come to take you home."

"Back to my flat?"

"No." He didn't snap the word at me or shout, but that

one syllable rang with absolute authority. "You're coming back to *our* home."

I shook my head. "I'm going back to my flat, Rafe. I—"

"Darling, I'm sorry. I want to give you whatever you need, but I can't let you go back to your flat."

"*Let* me?"

"If you don't want to be with me anymore, I understand, but you're *not* putting yourself in danger while your family and their associates are being prosecuted. It will be too risky for the next few weeks until I can tidy it all away."

My gaze shot from the window to him and I blinked. "Tidy it all away? You're tidying all *what* away?"

He shrugged. "Your family and their bullshit."

"M-my family? What do you have to do with my family? You *hate* my family."

"Well, I don't hate *all* your family. Your brother Zach seems like a reasonable chap, and certainly not of the criminal persuasion."

I stiffened. "When did you meet Zach?"

"Oh, you know. When he came over to shove me and shout at me for being a total arsehole."

"He *what?*" My voice was pitched high now as I started to panic. "He-he wouldn't... Zach wouldn't do that. He's gentle and—"

"Yeah, well, the boy does need to work on his attack skills. Being good at science is one thing, but a man's got to be able to defend himself too. But there'll be time for that in due course. Certainly, he needs feeding up, an endeavour which Martha is likely embarking on as we speak. He and Ozzie should be home from school now having been collected by Dave before he came here."

"Home from school?" I said weakly, still a little dazed.

"My brother's home from school, and he's at *your* home? But you don't even know Zach. How could he possibly—?"

"Oh, Clara, darling, do keep up," he said softly as he moved to me, gently took my backpack, slung it over his shoulder and then put his hand on my lower back to guide me towards the exit. "I know you've been through a lot in the last three days, but I'm afraid I'm going to need you to focus.

"Your brother is staying with me. As are you for the foreseeable future. Your mother has been offered alternative accommodation but would prefer to stay in her own home. Seeing as she now has the run of the place after your father, brother and all their associates were arrested – and as the large majority of your father's money is in her name, so she does not lack funds – I considered this arrangement acceptable.

"Zachary is a different matter. He is *not* staying with your mother. I cannot guarantee his safety there, plus it's not a supportive enough environment. Zach needs to focus on his upcoming exams. The GCSE board will not make exceptions for the recent turmoil. He needs a safe, quiet home in which to study, and he needs to be with you so he doesn't worry.

"Now, we need to get a move on because Poppy unfortunately purchased the *large chunk* Branston Pickle from Waitrose earlier, and I know that is unacceptable to you. So we need to make a pit stop on the way, and they'll worry if we're not home in time for Martha's lasagne."

My mind was turning all this new information over and over as I allowed Rafe to steer me out of the room. We walked down the corridor, past the nurses' station where Rafe was his normal charming self, and out of the glass double doors at the front where, of course, Dave was waiting for us, completely oblivious to any parking regulations whatsoever.

"Hello, love," Dave said softly as he held the door open for me, and I slipped into the back, followed by Rafe.

"Er... hey," I whispered, giving his kind face a half-smile.

"My brother really shoved you and shouted at you?" I asked Rafe once we were settled in the back. I felt the familiar cocoon of the plush bulletproof environment wash over me.

"Yes, as he bloody well should have," Rafe said, completely casually. "To be honest, I was on the verge of punching myself in the face at that stage, so it wasn't altogether unwelcome."

I shook my head slowly. "I'm not sure I understand what's happening here," I whispered, looking down at my hands that were twisting in my lap and feeling my eyes sting. Very slowly, Rafe reached over to me. His large hands covered mine and then gently held them between us so I was turned to face him.

"All you have to understand now is that you're safe," he said in a soft but firm tone. "Let that sink in before we try to address anything else. You and your brother have been very brave for a very long time. You both deserve some peace whilst you recover."

I looked up from our joined hands to his face, and one of my tears spilt over down my cheek. His jaw tightened as he tracked its progress.

"Safe," I whispered.

"Yes, darling," he said softly, lifting one of his hands from mine so his fingers could very gently swipe away the tear.

"O-okay."

Rafe wanted me safe. This I could understand. He'd found out I was responsible for the downfall of the Masons, and he felt guilty. Zach and I were obligations now. If I were braver, I would refuse his help – I didn't want to be an obligation or a burden to Rafe. But my head was hurting, and I wasn't that brave, not really. So that was why I nodded. Why I let Rafe gather me into his arms and hold me close the rest of the car ride home. If Rafe's guilt meant that I could breathe in his expensive aftershave and innate Rafe smell, feel his strong arms around me and hear the steady beat of his heart under my ear, then I decided I could live with it.

For now.

Chapter 36

Now eat your bloody sandwich

Clara

"WELL, THERE'S THE MAKINGS OF A SANDWICH, LOVE," said Martha. "But I know you can be a wee bit of a fusspot about how it all goes together. Rafe said you'd prefer if I let you spread the pickle."

Zach laughed. "Fusspot? More like obsessional."

I managed a weak smile for them as I took the kitchen stool and sat down. After a few minutes, I realised Zach was still watching me as he made his cup of tea.

"Zach, you don't have to hover. I'm fine."

"Can you just eat the sandwich?" he whispered, shooting a furtive look at Martha who was pretending she couldn't hear us. I could always tell when Zach was stressed. His face would get tight, and he would start rapidly blinking in a nervous tick left over from childhood.

"I'm eating fine," I told him. "You don't need to worry about—"

"Rafe said that—"

"Oh my God," I snapped. "Can you please *not* keep quoting Rafe all the time? It's like he's your new Yoda or something."

Zach huffed. "It's not my fault if the man knows what he's talking about when it comes to you."

"Yes, Cla-Cla," put in Ozzie as he ran into the kitchen, kicking the football that technically wasn't allowed in the house in front of him. Despite the fact he'd only met Zach two weeks ago, they were already fast friends – and he'd immediately picked up Zach's nickname for me. "I mean, if *Daddy* said that you should eat a cheese and pickle sand-wich, then you should really eat it. He can be a bit grumpy if you don't do what he says. He's quite bossy."

I smiled at Ozzie. "You're right there, your father is bossy."

"What's that now?" Rafe's deep voice sounded from across the kitchen, and I looked up to see him filling the doorway. He was still wearing his long overcoat, as was his habit now. He tended not to take it off until he'd made sure I'd seen him in it. The sneaky bastard.

"Bossy, Daddy," said Ozzie helpfully. "*Super* bossy. Sometimes super grumpy if you don't get your own way."

Rafe's eyebrows went up as he strode into the kitchen, scooping Ozzie up for a hug before letting him get back to his football and giving Zach a quick back slap as he walked past to get to me. Then, as was also becoming his habit, he swept my hair away from my face, over my shoulder and kissed me on my temple. "There's nothing wrong with wanting my own way," he said against my hair in a low voice, and I suppressed a shiver.

I felt that voice everywhere, from the ends of my hair right down through to the pit of my stomach. Memories flooded back of how *very* bossy Rafe could be and how *very* much he did want his own way, leaving me lightheaded. But then the fog of anxiety settled over me again and those feelings disappeared like smoke.

"Eat your sandwich, darling," he said close to my ear in that same low voice.

A direct command from Rafe seemed to be almost impossible to resist. When I started slicing the cheese, he gave me a brief side hug as a reward before moving back.

Rafe wasn't pushing things with me. It was all light kisses and side hugs and unending patience. As big and abrasive as Rafe could be, the mind-bending gentleness and patience he demonstrated with me were so unbelievably attractive I almost couldn't breathe.

"You'll feel better once you eat," he said.

I knew he was right. I'd been losing weight that I really couldn't afford to lose again. But as Zach put a cup of tea in front of me, my stomach was churning. In order for my appetite to return, I needed to feel safe and, unfortunately, that was still not the case.

Logically, I knew that Rafe's house was a safe place, but I still had trouble convincing my mind and body of that. To be honest, it was nearly impossible to adjust to the new reality. None of my father's network were free men. The only ones with even the prospect of freedom were Skinny Pete and Ruben as they'd agreed to testify against the family. The three of us were all snitches now. The irony of Skinny Pete's threats a few weeks ago was not lost on me.

If my father were ever released, he would be well into his eighties.

It was impossible for me to reconcile this new reality where everything that had terrified me since childhood had simply been removed. Even if my father hadn't been immediately detained that day, there wasn't much chance of him being a threat to me, seeing as he had a broken wrist, a number of fractured ribs and some facial fractures.

It wasn't clear how he had obtained these injuries either. The explanation so far was that he'd "resisted arrest".

I knew exactly how painful a broken wrist and fractured ribs were.

Exactly.

I blinked down at my plate. That was true, wasn't it? I *did* know exactly what it was like to break ribs and a wrist and recover from a blow to the head. I looked up slowly to lock eyes with Rafe who tilted his head to the side. I glanced at Zach, but he was busy kicking the football back and forth with Ozzie, something definitely not allowed in the house, but something which Martha seemed to be turning a blind eye to.

"Were you there when Dad was arrested?" I asked Rafe.

He gave me one of those careful, assessing looks. A look that told me that he was weighing what he said next with his typical precision.

"I'm not going to answer that, Clara," he said in a measured tone. I felt a shiver of fear run down my spine but, as if he knew, Rafe's large hand covered my lower back and rubbed a circle gently there. "I'm not ever going to tolerate you being hurt, darling. Do you understand me? It's a message I'm willing to deliver in whichever way is most effective."

"I am arrived!" trilled Poppy from the door to the kitchen, distracting me from my racing thoughts about Rafe *sending messages* on my behalf. The flash of something in his eyes when he said that was not the cool, urbane aristocrat persona I knew. Not even close.

"About bloody time," Rafe grumbled. "We're cutting it fine as it is, Pops."

"Oh shut your grumpy cake hole, you big oaf," she said, dismissing him with a wave of her hand. She skipped over to where Ozzie was dribbling the ball to kiss his head. Not an easy task seeing as he wouldn't keep still. She smiled a big smile at Zach, who proceeded to blush then miss Ozzie's pass, causing the ball to crash into the kitchen cupboards for what must have been the hundredth time.

"You've still got plenty of time," Poppy told Rafe as she gave his cheeks a couple of smacks before going up on her tiptoes to give him a kiss on the cheek. "And anyway, Clara's got to eat her sandwich before you go." She gave me a big, loud kiss on the cheek and then repositioned my glasses when they went askew.

I sighed. Everyone was so obsessed with me eating. Annoying as it was, I had to admit that I actually did feel better, not that I had drunk any tea or eaten any of my sandwich yet. No, it was the Poppy effect. I'd noticed that about her. She had this way of lightening the atmosphere. It was almost uncanny, as if she could control the mood in any room.

I smiled a small smile at her and looked at Rafe again.

"What are you going to be late for?" I asked.

"*We're* going to Zach's sixth form open evening," he returned.

"Oh bugger. I'm so sorry, Zach," I said in a horrified tone. "I completely forgot." This numbness that had settled over me was making me forget everything important. The swelling on my face had gone down but the bruising was still evident, as were the headaches and brain fog from the concussion. That combined with the pervasive fear I couldn't seem to shake was making me sluggish, as if I was only ever half there.

"Cla-Cla, I'm not a baby anymore," Zach told me. "You don't have to remind me about everything. You guys don't even have to come with me. I can navigate a stupid open evening on my own."

"Of course I'm going to come with you, love," I said, trying to stop my voice from shaking. This would be the first time leaving the house since I came home from the hospital. The thought made me feel a little ill.

But I knew Zach would hate to go on his own. He had been really worried about his A-level choices, and he absolutely hated interacting with any figures of authority. Zach was so shy that he tended to go into himself and mumble. It was frustrating as I knew he'd struggle with interviews if he carried on like this. But facing sixth form open evening alone, talking to the teachers about which subjects he should take without any backup was well out of Zach's comfort zone.

"We'd better get a move on, though," I said. "The school must be a couple of bus rides away from here." I pushed back my sandwich, about to stand from my stool, but Rafe blocked my way.

"Eat your fucking sandwich," he said sharply, his patience slipping.

"Daddy!" Ozzie shouted. "Miss Clara will put you on the thunder cloud for bad words!"

"Sorry, mate," Rafe said, keeping his gaze fixed on me.

"And use your indoor voice with her," Ozzie continued to boss, and I found myself suppressing a smile.

Rafe looked briefly up at the ceiling before focusing

back on me. "Noted," he threw back to his son. "Eat your sandwich, Clara. *Please.*"

"That's better, Daddy."

"We've got plenty of time. Dave will take us. I'm not getting on a bus, Clara. I haven't used public transport since... Christ, Poppy, have we *ever* used public transport?"

"I don't think so, Rafey," Poppy said as she leaned up on tiptoes to grab the biscuit tin off the top shelf. "Can't say I've ever been tempted. The tube at rush hour maybe, as it's hellish traffic crossing Piccadilly at that time, but otherwise no."

"B-but you're not coming with us," I whispered.

"Why the hell not?" Rafe said.

I threw my hands up in confusion. "Because it's a sixth form open evening. Why would you come? Zach's not your—"

"Goddamn it, Clara," Rafe snapped, and I flinched. He closed his eyes slowly and clenched his jaw, taking a deep breath in through his mouth and out through his nose. When he spoke again, he deliberately softened his tone. "I'm sorry, I didn't mean to snap at you. But will you *please* stop saying what you and Zach are *not*. You *are* living here—"

"For now," I interrupted. "We're living here *for now.*"

His jaw clenched again and a flash of frustration crossed his face. When he spoke again, it was clear he was trying to still be gentle, but it was through gritted teeth.

"You are living here now. And I *like* Zach. I'm coming to his open evening. I've already researched A-level options."

I blinked at him. "You've what?"

"His A-level options, Clara," he said in a patient tone. "You know he doesn't have to be restricted to only the sciences just because he wants to study veterinary medicine. He could still take English literature. It's not completely out of the question. I mean, there are lots of unis that—"

"You've researched Zach's A-level options?" I asked in shock.

It was clear at this point that Rafe had had enough. He closed the distance between us to spin me on my stool to face him, his hands landing on either side of the arms of my stool, boxing me in.

"Pops," he called, keeping eye contact with me. "Take Ozzie into the sitting room to start his reading. Zach, get your stuff together, mate, and meet us by the door, yeah? Martha, thank you for tonight, but you can go."

As was the way when Rafe issued a command, everyone did his bidding until it was just the two of us.

"Clara," he said softly, leaning closer now. So close I could smell his expensive aftershave and the clean, manly scent of pure Rafe. So close I could see the flecks of green in his blue eyes. "I'm going slowly. I'll go at your pace for as long as it takes. I'm not going to push you, baby. But when it comes to Zach, you have got to let me help. It's too important for him to choose the right options at this stage. I can't let you stand in the way of that. I know you're not sure of me, and you've damn good reason to doubt me. I completely understand your reticence. But his future has to be decided *now,* and I'm here to help. You and Zach are going to be in my life. I know you don't believe that. I know it's going to take time for you to accept that. But you have to get with the programme today. Because, baby, this is happening now."

"O-okay," I whispered, still in shock from his calling me baby. Twice.

He huffed out a sigh of relief and then reached up to my

face very slowly. When I managed to not flinch, he smiled, his teeth white against his tanned skin and stubble.

"Okay," he whispered back before brushing his lips against mine in the barest hint of a kiss. Before I could react to that shocking development, he pulled back and looked down at me with a satisfied expression. "Now eat your bloody sandwich."

Chapter 37

Closure

Rafe

"Your older brother's asked to see you," I told her, watching her face carefully to gauge her reaction. The blankness was gradually receding, but the fear in her eyes was always evident.

It was the day after the sixth form open evening, which had gone surprisingly well. To be honest, I was glad of the open evening as an excuse to get Clara out of the house for once. She had retreated too much into herself over the last two weeks since her discharge from hospital, and I was starting to worry.

It helped that her brother, Poppy and Ozzie were all here to coax her out of herself, but I could tell that she really wasn't with it. Her clothes were often on the wrong way round. She only wore leggings and huge jumpers, all in her standard black or grey and she hid under her fringe, which was long overdue a cut.

I became almost desperate to see her pretty eyes. Sometimes I even gave in to the urge to gently push her hair back from her face, just to look into them. Other times, I even risked a light kiss. And when I did, often I'd see a flash of Clara through the blankness. A spark of recognition. Then she'd settle back into the nothingness.

I gave her space, but didn't let her retreat completely. If we all watched a film together in the evening, I'd make sure she sat next to me on the sofa and would pull her into my side.

The first time I did it, she stiffened for a moment, but I muttered, "Settle," into her hair and kept my arms tight around her and eventually she melted into me. Within a few minutes she'd fallen asleep, and I gently took off her glasses. I didn't think she got much sleep otherwise, so at the end of the film I made everyone, including Ozzie, be very quiet so they wouldn't wake her, and I arranged us so that I was lying on the sofa and Clara was sleeping alongside me.

I didn't sleep much myself that night. Instead, I watched the peaceful expression on Clara's face, so at odds with the troubled one she wore in the daytime.

When we'd arrived at the open evening yesterday, it was clear Zach's teachers all knew Clara well. Even though Zach had mentioned that Clara was the one who went to his parent-teacher conferences, it still took me by surprise. But then I'd come to understand that Marie Mason had tapped out of parenting in any real way when Zach was small. How Clara and Zach weren't totally fucked up was a minor miracle.

Zach had started counselling already, but whilst Clara would agree to me organising and paying for her brother, she was still resistant to me doing the same for her, which was frustrating me no end. With her level of PTSD, there was no other choice but to seek professional help. I'd already found the perfect psychologist on Harley Street, but so far Clara had completely refused. She was still talking about paying me back for that bloody hospital room, for God's sake.

"Which brother?" she whispered, and I cursed myself for being such a complete dickhead.

"Ruben," I reassured her. "If Freddie wanted to talk to you, I wouldn't have even brought it up."

She'd confided in me about her brothers, her father, and her childhood. If I could beat the shit out of Frank Mason again, I would have. As for the brothers, Freddie was clearly cut from the same cloth as Frank, but Ruben, although violent and enmeshed in the Mason criminal activities, seemed to be surprisingly protective when it came to Clara and Zach.

"What does he want?" she asked. She was sitting huddled in a small ball on the sofa. Her troubled eyes blinked up at me from behind her glasses. I glanced at the pot of Branston Pickle that was on the coffee table and I almost smiled. This was a good sign. Eating Branston Pickle straight out of the jar in my living room while she watched mindless telly was a damn good sign.

There were a few days when I checked on Clara in her room, and she was just staring out of the window at nothing. I'd had to remind her to eat and I wasn't sure how much she was sleeping. She flinched at every loud noise and still always seemed like she was trying to hide in plain sight, although today there was something different about her. I tilted my head to the side as I realised that she was wearing a pink T shirt.

I didn't think I'd ever seen Clara in anything but dark colours. But I knew that Poppy had brought a load of clothes over the other day for Clara. She claimed her wardrobe "needed a clear out" and that she just "couldn't be bothered to lug these old things to the charity shop". I knew my sister, and a lot of that stuff still had labels on. She picked out all that stuff for Clara specifically. If there's one thing Poppy was competent at, it was shopping. And Clara did need more clothes here. She was still refusing to move anything out of her flat, other than George the goldfish, who'd stayed here throughout all the drama, diligently cared for by Ozzie.

Clara pulled both her lips in between her teeth and bit them. I waited until she was ready to speak. It was getting better, but Clara's responses were still sometimes slow, as if she was weighed down too heavily with her fears to process the world around her.

"I don't want Zach to see him," she said, as always thinking of anyone but herself. "It might upset him."

I held back a sigh. Zach was engaging with counselling, he was eating like a horse, he got on well with Ozzie and the rest of my family, and he was chuffed to bits to live somewhere he could revise in peace. She was worried about Zach, but in my mind the real concern was Clara.

"No, he only asked to see you."

She nodded. "Okay."

"Okay, you want to go?"

"I'm the reason he's in there. I owe him a visit if it's what he wants."

"You don't owe anyone anything," I said through gritted teeth. When the request from Ruben had come through, I'd debated even telling Clara. But the PTSD counsellor I consulted told me that as long as Clara felt safe, seeing him might actually offer her some closure.

"Will you…" she broke off, looking down at her lap and fiddling with the sleeves of her cardigan. When she spoke again, it was just above a whisper. "Will you come with me?"

I sighed and moved to sit next to her on the sofa carefully, keeping my movements steady and slow as she tracked me with her brown eyes. Before, I would simply have jumped over the coffee table, snatched her into my arms and held her against me, but now that was not a good idea. A wave of frustration and self-loathing swept over me again. If I'd just been a touch less of an arrogant, self-righteous dickhead, Clara would not have been hurt again by her father, and she would likely not now be flinching at sudden movements. She wouldn't startle at the loud sounds of the bin men in the morning.

"Clara," I said to her softly once I was sitting next to her, my leg just brushing against hers. She reluctantly looked up from her lap to meet my gaze, that fucking wariness that I hated still lingering in her eyes. "There's no way in hell I would let you go to HMP Wandsworth on your own. Understand me?"

"*Let* me?" she said, a little of the fire back as her eyes flashed. I almost smiled.

Come on, Clara, I begged in my head. *That's it, baby. Tell me I'm a bossy know-it-all prick.*

I must have been the only man in history mentally begging a woman to snap at him. But then the fire died and the blankness returned as she shrank back into herself again, and I suppressed a sigh. Then Clara surprised the fuck out of me.

"I want to see my father as well," she said, her quiet voice now edged with steel.

I frowned. "Clara, I don't think that—"

"I'm going to see him, Rafe," she told me, using my name for the first time since before the courtroom. The colour in her cheeks was heightened now. I looked down to see that her hands were clenched into small fists so tight that her knuckles were white. This was costing her. Speaking up like this was terrifying Clara. Great, the very first thing she asks of me is something I desperately don't want to give her.

"Clara, you're traumatised. Seeing that fucking..." I broke off and rubbed a hand down my face. My voice was rising, and the last thing I wanted was to shout at Clara. But the thought of her breathing the same air as that sadistic bastard was untenable. I took a deep breath in before I spoke again, trying to keep the rage out of my tone. "It's not a good idea, darling."

She met my eyes again, that fire back in hers. I would have been thrilled if she wasn't fighting me on seeing her fucking father.

"This wouldn't be the first time I've seen my father after he's hurt me," she said, and my chest felt so tight it was almost too hard to take a breath in. "But this time, you'll be there. And you won't let anything hurt me."

I let out a long breath as I rubbed my hand down my face.

But then a plan formed in my mind and something clicked into place.

Closure, the therapist told me, was good.

That I could deliver.

Chapter 38

Now we're done

Clara

I STARTLED WHEN RAFE'S LARGE, WARM HAND CLOSED over mine as we sat in the waiting area of HMP Wandsworth, then gritted my teeth in frustration. I was so bloody jumpy. He noticed me flinch and I felt his hand start to move, but I grabbed it in mine before he could lift it away. I knew I shouldn't be using Rafe like this, leaning on him. I knew I was taking advantage of his guilty conscience.

"You don't have to do this," he said in a low voice close to my ear. "We can leave right now."

I took in a shuddering breath, trying to calm my racing heart. The prison was exactly as oppressive as I'd imagined it would be: high brick walls, metal detectors, sullen-faced guards and the distinct smell of industrial cleaner failing to mask the underlying scent of hundreds of men living in close quarters.

When we'd arrived, Rafe had moved through the security process with the kind of confidence only aristocrats possessed, as if submitting to having his pockets emptied and his body scanned was a choice he was graciously allowing rather than a requirement. Even here, in a place specifically designed to restrain and control, Rafe Sterling somehow managed to look like he owned the building.

The same could not be said for me. My hands had trembled so badly during the biometric verification that the officer had been forced to scan my fingerprints three times. The whole experience was almost too much – the clanging of heavy doors, the echo of voices in cavernous spaces, the watchful eyes of the guards. It felt too oppressive.

"I'm fine," I whispered back to Rafe, my eyes fixed on the institutional green wall opposite us.

Rafe's jaw clenched, a muscle ticking at the side. "I'm getting really fucking tired of you telling me you're fine when you're not."

I bit my lips between my teeth to stop my instinctive apology. Rafe sighed.

"Sorry," he muttered and I blinked at him in shock. "I'm being a pillock."

Then, despite the intimidating environment, despite my rampant nerves, I let out a small snort of laughter. Rafe's head whipped round to stare down at me in surprise and then his face lit with a pleased smile as he squeezed my hand. He opened his mouth to speak but a buzzer sounded, and I flinched again. The overhead speakers crackled to life, "Visiting session starting in ten minutes. All visitors to the main hall."

"Last chance to change your mind," Rafe said, but he was already standing, helping me to my feet with a gentle tug on my hand.

"You'll be there the whole time?" I asked, hating the desperate edge to my voice.

Rafe's expression softened as he looked down at me.

"I'm not letting you out of my sight, darling. The second you've had enough, we're gone."

I nodded, swallowing around the lump in my throat.

We followed the other visitors through a series of security doors into a large room filled with small tables, each with a chair on either side. Guards stood at regular intervals along the walls, arms crossed, expressions blank. Prisoners in identical grey tracksuits were being led in from another entrance, their eyes scanning the room for their visitors.

I spotted Ruben immediately. At six foot three with broad shoulders and our father's intimidating presence, he was difficult to miss. When his eyes found mine, I was shocked to see relief flood his features.

Rafe's hand settled at the small of my back as we approached the table, a silent reminder of his presence. When we reached Ruben, my brother stood awkwardly, his expression now uncertain. It was jarring. I'd so rarely seen my older brothers or father look anything less than supremely confident.

"Hey, Little Mole," he said softly, no accusation in his tone. I blinked at him in surprise.

"Hi," I replied, my voice barely above a whisper as I sat down. Rafe took the chair next to mine, angling it slightly so his body partly shielded me from my brother. His hand found mine under the table.

Ruben's eyes flicked to Rafe. "Alright, mate," he muttered. Was I in an alternate universe? Where was Ruben's animosity towards me and Rafe?

"Mason," Rafe said in a tight voice.

"I know what you did," Ruben said, still looking at Rafe. "And I want you to know I've got no beef with you for it. Should have done it myself years ago."

I frowned, not understanding the subtext. Rafe merely

inclined his head slightly, neither confirming nor denying whatever Ruben was implying.

"How are you?" I asked, changing the subject. It was a ridiculous question under the circumstances, but I didn't know what else to say.

Ruben let out a short, humourless laugh. "As well as you'd expect." He gestured around. "This is Wandsworth, not a holiday camp. But I'll manage." He paused, scanning my face. "You've lost more weight."

I shrugged. "I'm fine."

Rafe gave my hand a squeeze but he didn't say anything.

"Is Zach okay?"

"He's safe," Rafe answered before I could. "He's living with us."

Ruben's eyes widened slightly. "You've got Zach at yours?" When I nodded, he visibly relaxed. "That's... good. That's good."

An awkward silence fell between us. I broke it, finally asking the question that had been plaguing me since we received his request. "Why did you want to see me, Ruben?"

He looked away for a moment, then cleared his throat before he looked back at me. "I want you to know, I tried," he told me, a broken quality to his voice now. "I tried to protect you and Zach. I—"

"You failed," Rafe said, cutting him off. Ruben's eyes flashed and I got a glimpse of the old Ruben. The one who wouldn't tolerate disrespect. The scary motherfucker who could make men piss themselves with just a look. Then he rubbed his hands down his face and the look was wiped clean, leaving an unfamiliar, defeated expression.

"It wasn't that easy," he growled out. "I was born into

that shit. I lived and breathed it from the moment I could process. I had a mother that never protected me and—"

"I was born into it too," I snapped. "I was there too."

"But you had me." His voice was raised now and he'd lifted up slightly from his chair. A guard took a couple of steps towards us, but Ruben settled back down and Rafe waved the guard away. "You had me," he said again. His voice now was quieter but firm.

"I don't under—"

"When you were born you were so tiny." His voice was hoarse now. "So, so small. So vulnerable. Same with Zach. I couldn't let the same happen to you as it did me. I know I didn't always manage it, but I deflected Dad and Freddie. I distracted them, redirected them and their violence, at least I tried to."

He glanced at the yet-to-fade bruise on my cheek and flinched. "I could have tried harder," he whispered.

There was a long silence then, during which some memories filtered back into my mind: Ruben buying presents for me and Zach at Christmas, Ruben helping me change Zach's nappies when he was a baby, Ruben barring my entry to the house more than once after I'd left home, sometimes with that wild look in his eyes, telling me to fuck off. It was his way of shielding me; keeping me separate from the family was his only way of protecting me.

Then other fuzzier memories came through: me at five years old, having fallen and scraped my knee, Ruben picking me up and cuddling me, straightening my glasses and then putting a plaster on the small scrape, calling me his brave little mole. Then Dad's angry voice:

"*Stop fussing her. She needs to toughen up.*"

"*Keep that brat away from the gear for fuck's sake, Ruben.*"

I leaned forward and placed my hand over my brother's on the table. He flinched and his eyes flew to mine. To my shock, they were glassy with tears. "You did the best you could," I told him in a hoarse voice. "You tried."

"I should have been braver," he pushed out. "What you did..." He shook his head once. "Now that's bravery. You, Little Mole, you're braver than all of us fucking thugs."

"Ruben I—"

"You'll look after her," Ruben cut me off, looking at Rafe now. It wasn't a question; it was a command, but I could hear the thread of desperation running through it. Ruben was worried and he was powerless. "And Zach. You'll protect them."

"Always," said Rafe firmly.

Rafe

Ruben Mason hadn't deserved my reassurance. Maybe he had tried to protect his younger siblings, but he could have done more. I almost told him to fuck off when he barked his command at me, but the broken look in his eyes stopped me. Frank Mason had damaged all of his children in different ways.

As we walked out with the other visitors, I took Clara's hand again and she gripped it like a lifeline. A wave of apprehension swept over me. Maybe this wasn't such a good idea.

"Clara," I said softly, pulling her gently to a stop and letting the other visitors stream past us. "Don't you think that's enough for today? If you want to come back in a few months, then we can—"

She shook her head, that fire back in her eyes. "No. I need to do this, Rafe."

By God, she was brave. I could feel the nervous tremors running through her, see how pale her face was, but her jaw was tilted at a stubborn angle, her mouth set in a grim, determined line. Clara Mason was not leaving here without seeing her father. I sighed.

"Lord Sterling?" a guard said as he approached us.

"Is the room ready?" I asked, resigned that this was going to happen, but relieved that it would be my way.

He nodded. "As requested."

"Lead the way," I clipped, and we followed him as he led us in the opposite direction to the crowd. We emerged into a long corridor and then stopped in front of a non-descript door.

The officer unlocked the door, revealing a small, austere room with a table and three chairs.

"He's being brought in now," he said. "The systems are offline for the next fifteen minutes. I'll be outside. Knock when you're finished."

"Offline?" Clara whispered. I grabbed her other hand as the officer left the room and turned her to face me.

"Are you sure?" I asked. Uncertainty flickered across her expression before that fire was back.

"I'm sure."

I felt a sinking sense of foreboding, but before I could drag Clara away from this bloody place, the door on the opposite side of the room opened. Two guards entered, escorting Frank Mason between them.

His eyes widened when he saw Clara, then narrowed when they shifted to me. The bruises on his face had faded to sickly yellow-green, but his left arm was still in a cast. He looked smaller somehow, diminished in his prison-issue clothes, without his expensive watch and signet ring.

"What's this?" he demanded, glaring at the guards. "I was told this was about my case."

"Leave us," I told them. They hesitated only briefly before exiting, closing the door behind them.

Frank's face twisted into a sneer. "Playing Lord of the Manor even in here? Must be nice to have the system in your pocket."

"Sit down, Frank," I said, my voice cold as ice.

"I don't take orders from—"

I moved too quickly for Frank to have time to react, darting forward, grabbing him by the collar and shoving him into the chair with enough force that it skidded back several inches.

"I said," I repeated, leaning down until my face was inches from his, "sit down."

Real fear flickered across his expression as his eyes darted between me and Clara. I let go of his collar and moved back to her side.

"What's the snitch doing here?" he asked, jerking his chin towards me.

"Frank, you piece of—"

"I came to tell you, I won," Clara said, cutting me off and shocking the absolute shit out of me.

"Proud of yourself, are you?" Frank sneered. "You and your pathetic brother. You've always been weak; the pair of you are an embarrassment."

"And yet we're not the ones in prison."

"I wouldn't bloody well be here if it wasn't for you, you fucking snitch cunt!" he yelled. "You happy now? Your father and brothers banged up. Your mother alone. When I get out of here I'm gonna—"

"That's enough!" screamed Clara, her hand slamming down on the table in front of her. Frank flinched as the noise cracked through the room. His face paled as he stared up at his furious daughter. "You are *never* getting out of here. Not ever. You will rot in this place or you'll be killed, either is fine with me, but you will never be a free man again. So, I won. I brought you down. I snitched and, yes, I *am* fucking proud of myself."

Frank blinked at her, his face flushed and his nostrils flaring.

"I'm done here," Clara said after a few moments had passed. "I've said what I needed to say."

"We're not done," I said, focusing on Frank. "We still have five minutes."

Frank's red face drained of colour as he swallowed, his eyes darting to the door the guards left through. "What are you on about, five minutes?" he snapped.

"There have been some power outages at Wandsworth in the last few weeks, Frank," I told him almost conversationally. "Unfortunately, an outage is currently affecting the legal consultation rooms. To be more specific, *this* legal consultation room." I checked my watch. "For the next four minutes."

Frank stood suddenly, his expression now panicked. "Stay away from me, you posh psycho."

"Kneel, Frank," I said softly.

"Fuck off," he spat. "I'm not..."

"I could break your neck right now, and the official report would say you tripped and fell. Or maybe you'll have an accident in prison. Fall down the stairs. Slip in the shower. Happens all the time."

Real fear flashed in his eyes then.

"You can't be——"

"On. Your. Knees. *Now!*"

I had thought I would have to force him down, but

Frank had seen the stone-cold determination in my eyes. Clara gasped as he dropped down awkwardly onto the floor.

"Now, apologise to your daughter." I took a step towards him and he shrank back slightly. "I'm waiting, Frank."

"I'm sorry," he said in a low, almost inaudible voice.

I raised an eyebrow. "Again," I snapped. "But this time you say: I'm sorry for being an abusive piece of shit. I'm a pathetic coward who picks on people half my size to make myself feel like a big man."

I made him say it three times, each time a little louder than before. Then I looked at Clara.

"Enough?" I asked.

"Not quite," she muttered, staring at her father. Before I could stop her, she took a step forward and spat in his face. I pulled her back out of his reach as he surged forward. The timer on my phone went off at that moment, and the guards burst into the room to grab Frank who was seemingly trying to attack his daughter.

Clara looked up at me and smiled. "Now we're done."

Chapter 39

You died magnificently

Clara

"Margot," I said with no small amount of horror, "where did you get all that fake blood from?"

Margot looked down at her outfit then back up at me with a satisfied smirk. "It's bloody brilliant, isn't it?"

"You haven't actually killed anyone at the start of the play, love."

She shrugged. "How do you know?"

I rubbed my temples as I straightened up from my crouch. "It's too late to find you a clean apron now," I muttered. "Okay, go to Miss Summerfield and we'll—"

"Going well, I see," Rafe's deep voice sounded in my ear, and I whipped round to face him. He was smiling down at me, looking impossibly handsome amidst the chaos of Year 3's performance preparation.

"Rafe, you can't come back here," I told him. "This is a parent-free zone. Lily says that the kids need to get into character before they go on. No distractions."

Rafe glanced over at Margot Harding, who was now

wielding a plastic straight razor with alarming enthusiasm, practising her slashing motion with such vigor that Lily had to grab her wrist.

"Ease up on the enthusiasm, Sweeney," I heard Lily tell her. "Save it for the performance, yeah?"

Beside them, Ozzie was in the barber's chair (aka Mrs Clayton's office chair), gurgling and jerking in the throes of his mock death.

Rafe looked back at me and raised one of his eyebrows. "The children being in character does not appear to be the most pressing problem at the moment, darling," he said dryly, and I let out a short laugh. His eyes warmed as he stared down at me and he reached up to brush my fringe back from my eyes.

"I was just checking you were okay," he said softly. "This is... a lot."

It was my first week back at Molton Prep. All the bruising had faded now and the headaches had largely settled, plus Lily really needed my help with the play. None of the teaching assistants who had stood in for me could really handle Margot. Mrs Clayton had insisted I take as much time as I needed, but I knew I had to reclaim some part of my normal life, even if "normal" now meant helping Lily stage a gory musical with inappropriately young children.

"I'm fine," I muttered, then winced. Rafe hated me telling him I was fine, but it was a reflex now. A loud crash echoed across the stage and I flinched, instinctively flying into the safety of Rafe's body. His arms closed around me as we both looked over to see the barber's chair tipped on its side with a red-faced Ozzie next to it.

"Sorry!" he shouted.

"It's okay," Rafe whispered in my ear. "You're safe."

Gah! Why did I *still* have to be so bloody jumpy?

"Ozzie!" snapped Lily. "Honestly, calm the death throes down a bit. You'll do yourself a damage."

"It's gotta be realistic!" he said in a grumpy tone, going to climb back up into the chair, but before he could mount it fully, Zach hooked him round his middle and lifted him up in the air to carry him over to the side of the stage. I'd roped Zach in to help tonight – after he heard the title of the play, he was all in.

"Curtain's going up, little man," he said as he set a disgruntled Ozzie on his feet.

"Wow," Zach said as his attention turned to us, still wrapped around each other. "Rafe, bit much for a Tuesday afternoon at a primary school, mate." He was attempting a disgruntled tone, but he couldn't suppress his smile. Zach was still Rafe's biggest fan.

"Daddy!" shouted Ozzie. "You can't be back here! You can cuddle Miss Clara *later*."

Rafe did a lot of that. Cuddling. Some of my haze had lifted since I'd seen my father, and I could see even more how very *very* careful Rafe was being with me. It was still all light touches, cuddles, no sudden movements, keeping his tone level and soft, even when I was frustrating him. It was like I was a bowl that he'd broken, and he felt like he had to hold me carefully in case I fell apart again.

"Okay, buddy," Rafe said as I pulled away from him under the curious stares of the kids around us. He ruffled Ozzie's hair and told him to break a leg before he sauntered off to find his seat as the lights dimmed.

"Showtime!" Lily whispered excitedly next to me, practically bouncing on the soles of her feet.

A spotlight clicked on, illuminating Mrs Clayton standing centre stage in a surprisingly elegant black dress.

"Good evening, ladies and gentlemen," she began, her crisp voice cutting through the murmurs. "Welcome to Molton Prep's production of *Sweeney Todd*." She paused, clearly struggling to maintain her professional demeanour. "I feel I should warn those of a sensitive disposition that this production contains scenes of... enthusiastic violence." A ripple of laughter went through the audience. "Before we begin, I'd like to thank Miss Summerfield for her, er, creative vision, and Miss Clara for her invaluable assistance with the children."

Lily gave me a light shove and we both stepped out onto the side of the stage, giving the audience a small wave. I looked out into the audience and saw the Sterlings sitting near the front. The earl, the countess and Granny Sterling beamed at me, and Poppy blew me an enthusiastic kiss.

I'd been worried about seeing the Sterlings for the first time after everything happened. What would a family as posh as theirs think about having such a close association with a criminal's daughter? But the first time they came over, when I was still bruised and swollen, Lady Sterling had hugged me for over a minute. It was one of the few times I cried. A maternal hug like that cut through the numbness, warming me from the inside out. Even the ultra-posh, reserved Granny Sterling had patted my arm, which was a level above her usual affectionate limit. Rafe's dad had found me later when I was getting some water in the kitchen, staring out into the garden.

"Brave thing you did," he said, and I nearly dropped the glass I was holding. "Sorry, I didn't mean to startle you."

"I-it's okay. I'm a bit jumpy, is all."

"I mean it, though. You're a brave woman."

"People keep saying that," I mumbled.

"You don't agree?"

"All I did was snitch. It's not exactly—"

"Don't be absurd!" he snapped. "You're braver than most of the women and men of my acquaintance, and I know some extremely questionable fellows in the military. Without you, your family's network couldn't have been dealt with... via the legal route, that is."

Before I could ask the earl what the other route would have been, he'd gone.

A wave of applause broke out, but Mrs Clayton wasn't having any of it.

"I'd hold that thought if I were you," she said ominously. "Let's see how you all feel *after* the performance. So, without further ado, Molton Prep proudly presents *Sweeney Todd: The Demon Barber of Fleet Street!*"

Mrs Clayton walked off the stage as the lights came on to reveal the elaborate, if a little bizarre, set of old London, constructed entirely of cardboard, glitter and what appeared to be an excessive amount of aluminium foil. The parents burst into another round of applause and, despite my nerves, I found myself smiling.

When Margot finally made her entrance as Sweeney Todd, the audience's reaction was a mixture of laughter and genuine alarm. The tiny girl, dressed in a miniature barber's outfit complete with fake bloody apron, had a manic gleam in her eye that seemed far too authentic for comfort. I glanced out into the audience again to see the Duke of Buckingham grinning from ear to ear, whilst his wife, Lottie, gripped his arm, focusing on her daughter with a horrified expression.

Ozzie's moment came at the end of the first act. Playing Sweeney's first victim, he was positioned in the barber's chair which was up on the higher part of the stage as

Margot circled him dramatically, plastic razor gleaming under the stage lights.

"You're cooked, Pirelli!" Margot declared, going completely off-script in a moment of inspired improvisation.

Then, with a dramatic flourish, she drew the plastic razor across Ozzie's throat. Hugo Knightsbridge, one of the smaller year threes, was positioned behind Ozzie and let off a party popper with red streamers (something Lily had come up with when Mrs C banned a device that would spurt fake blood across the stage). Ozzie then began his dramatic death, complete with gargling and clutching at his neck. Margot handed him something from the depths of her apron and he fumbled with it at his neck until red blossomed from it and soaked his shirt.

A collective "Ewww!" rose from the audience, followed by uncertain applause as Ozzie's "body" slipped off the chair and down the slide Lily had nabbed from her neighbour's garden, onto the table on the lower part of the stage to be met by two other children dressed as equally bloodthirsty barber's assistants, who were preparing to chop Ozzie up and turn him into a pie.

I looked out at the audience again, all now gaping in shock at the scene. Some camera phones were being slowly lowered.

Poor Lottie Harding looked like she might throw up.

Bloody Margot.

The interval was a blessed relief, until of course Zach dragged me out from backstage to join the Sterlings. Rafe wasn't the only Sterling Zach worshipped. The earl had arrived last week for a Sunday roast with a black Labrador puppy.

"Heard you want to be a vet, my boy," he blustered as he handed the squirming puppy to my open-mouthed brother. "Can't train to be a vet if you don't have a dog. Bloody ridiculous."

"Dad, don't you think you should have checked with me first?" asked Rafe in annoyance.

"Now see here, Rafe—" the earl started to say, but Zach cut him off.

"Thank you," he said in a choked voice; the puppy was licking the underside of his jaw then. "I-I-I just... thank you." His eyes filled with tears, his face reddening with the effort it must have taken to hold them back.

Rafe huffed out a breath, but his annoyance evaporated. I bit my lip to stop myself saying anything. I'd wanted Zach to have that moment, but there was no way we could keep a puppy at my flat when we moved back there. Maybe Zach could visit?

The last thing I wanted was to outstay my welcome with the Sterlings. They'd been very kind, but I knew Rafe's guilt was consuming him. That was why he'd taken us in. He felt responsible for what happened.

Yes, he still called me darling, he held my hand, he even kissed me lightly, but I knew he was just helping me to heal. Over the last two weeks my libido had come back with a vengeance and I really didn't want light touches anymore. I wanted Rafe to do *very* filthy things to me again, and that did not seem to be on his agenda at all. So no, my brother and I were not going to be imposing on the Sterlings any longer than we needed to. Once I was brave enough to go back to the flat, we would move out.

"Did you see me die, Gran?" Ozzie shouted as he ran towards the countess and flung his arms around her for a hug, likely ruining the expensive outfit she was wearing.

"Wonderful performance, darling," she said, smiling

down at his upturned face as she brushed some blood-soaked hair from his forehead. "Absolutely gruesome."

"You died magnificently, young man," put in Granny Sterling.

"Yes, bloody brilliant, squishball," said Poppy, grinning as she bounced over to him. "You smashed it. Best death I've seen in ages."

"Hugo didn't pop the party popper when he was supposed to," Ozzie grumbled.

"I don't think that matters, Oz," I told him, smiling at the Sterlings as I approached.

"Margot sliced an artery, Clara," Ozzie said in a patient tone. "It's supposed to start spurting straight away."

The earl, the countess, Granny Sterling and Poppy all moved to hug me and Zach (the earl's hug for Zach being more a manly back slap), and then Rafe claimed me, pulling me into his side.

"Fab cardy, Clara," said Poppy, and I smiled. The soft wool cardigan I was wearing wasn't actually one of the ones Poppy had bought me (she might claim they were cast-offs, but I knew better); it was one I'd bought a few years ago when I qualified as a teacher. Bright orange with purple edging and so, so soft. I'd bought it but never worn it. But tonight it just felt... right.

Like it was okay to be noticed.

Like it was safe.

Chapter 40

Th-the woman you love?

Rafe

Sꜱᴇ sᴛᴏʀᴍᴇᴅ ɪɴᴛᴏ ᴛʜᴇ ᴋɪᴛᴄʜᴇɴ ʟɪᴋᴇ ᴀ sᴍᴀʟʟ, ɴᴇᴏɴ pink ball of fury and I had to hold back a smile. Smiling in the face of her anger would not be a good idea. But I loved angry Clara. Well, I loved Clara however she came really, but angry Clara was particularly fascinating.

It also felt like a massive achievement that she felt safe enough to be angry with me, and a huge contrast from those early days of total blankness with the occasional fear reaction after she was discharged from hospital. But now, a few weeks in, she was slowly coming out of herself and I bloody loved it.

I was not by nature a gentle or patient man, but with Clara I was learning how. I had to. For a start, she was traumatised. She had finally started counselling last week, after her initial flat refusal. It was only after I'd asked Mrs C to help me convince her that Clara agreed to it. Bending the truth slightly (at my behest), Mrs C told Clara that Molton Prep had a fund for staff counselling services and that they happened to have a specialist trauma counsellor on their books. Mrs C was a surprisingly good liar. Clara had already had two sessions with Mary Tandent, the very best counsellor for PTSD that I could find. I knew it was helping. I could see Clara improving. But she still had a long way to go, and me forcing her into a relationship would probably not be the most sensible move at the moment.

The other, not insignificant, reason for my patience was that I had been a complete and total arsehole. The longer I had to stew on it, the more I tortured myself with what I'd done in that courthouse corridor.

I had nightmares where I woke up sweating after replaying the sight of Clara's pale face and her desperate expression when she stopped me that day. In my dreams, I could feel her grip on my arm, hear her whispered "please" as she begged me for help. I shook her off, just like I had in real life, even though my mind was screaming at me that I was making a mistake, that what I needed to do was hold her, scoop her up and carry her out of that fucking place, away from her family. I'd allowed the woman I loved to be hurt, and the guilt was eating me alive. So, if she came to me, it had to be on her own terms. I wouldn't push her... well, not much anyway.

However, on the issue she was currently revving herself up to rant at me about, I was *not* going to relent. The puppy stirred from his nap in his dog bed in front of the Aga and he bounced over to us. Clara paused to lean down and tickle his tummy before continuing her rant.

"Rafe, what are all my worldly belongings doing here?" she snapped.

"I like your jumper," I said through a smile.

"My...?" she trailed off as heat hit her cheeks and she

stamped her foot in frustration. My smile grew even wider. "What has my jumper got to do with anything?"

"That's a beautiful colour on you," I told her the truth, and her blush deepened.

I was hoping that the clothes were another sign of recovery. In the last two weeks, Clara had gradually abandoned the unrelenting black and grey. Yesterday she wore a bright yellow t-shirt with leggings that had tiny daisies all over them. Granted, she had a grey cardigan over the top, but still, it was brighter than any of her old clothes.

The pink jumper she was in now, paired with light blue jeans, was a real leap forward. Poppy was still keeping up the steady stream of clothing into Clara's wardrobe.

"Right... well, thanks but that's not the point," Clara said in frustration.

"I'm sorry, darling. What exactly was the point again?" I asked, feigning confusion.

"Rafe Sterling, you know exactly what I'm talking about. All my stuff is here now, including George the goldfish."

"Well, technically George never left. He's a Sterling now."

Her lips twitched but her eyes narrowed at me. "Don't think I haven't noticed my mugs have made their way into your cupboard and my grandma's throw is on the sofa. You've moved me in! Is there anything left in my flat?"

I paused for a moment, then, "No."

"Ugh! Rafe, I'm not staying here."

"Why not?"

"Because it's... it's inappropriate."

I tilted my head to the side. "How so?"

Clara threw her hands up in the air. "I'm just some random teacher with a dodgy background that you barely even know. And I've disrupted your whole life, r-r-ruined your career..." she broke off as tears filled her eyes.

"Clara," I said in a firm tone as I stood from my stool, ready to go to her, but when I took a step towards her, she took a corresponding one back and I froze. I'd promised myself not to stalk her or corner her like I wanted to. Only a total dickhead would crowd and bulldoze his way in with a traumatised woman. I had to be careful, even if all my instincts were screaming at me to close the distance between us and take her in my arms.

"No, Rafe, let me finish," she said in a shaky voice. "I need to say this. Zach and I should move out. You c-can be free of us. I'm like a millstone around your neck now. I've barely been functioning, and I can't just hide here forever. I should have been stronger and left sooner. It's just this house feels so safe, and I think I needed that." She broke off to pick up the puppy who was scrabbling at her feet, lifting him up so he could snuggle into the soft wool over her chest. Lucky dog. "But I'm getting better. I'm not as scared anymore. I'm back at work part-time, and last week I even went out. Okay, it was with Poppy and Lily, and okay, we had close protection shadowing us, but it was a big step for me, and I think it shows I'm ready to be on my own."

"Clara, do you *want* to be on your own?" I said softly as I stared straight into those deep brown eyes.

"It doesn't matter what I want," she whispered, one of her tears falling down her cheek and then onto the puppy's fur. My chest tightened and I had to expend a considerable amount of effort not to stride over there and take her in my arms.

"Yes, it does, darling. It's the *only* thing that matters. Why do you think you ruined my career?"

She blinked across at me. "You had to recuse yourself

because of me. I know that hurt your career, Rafe. If I'd been honest with you from the start, then it could have all been avoided."

"How do you *know* it hurt my career?"

She threw her hands up. "All you've ever wanted was to be a high court judge, and I ruined that for you. And now you're here way more than you ever were before. You used to work long hours, but you've cut right back. I'm not an idiot. *I* did that. I know I did. You might not resent me for it now because your judgement is clouded with some warped sense of guilt about what happened at the courthouse. But you can't just keep letting Zach and me stay here out of guilt. *I* can't let you do it."

"Guilt?" I stared at her as everything about the last month rearranged in my mind. "You think you're here because I feel guilty?"

She frowned at me. "Well, yes, of course." Her voice dropped again to a whisper. "And I love being here so much, being near you so much that I let you do it even though I knew it was wrong. I'm taking advantage of you, and you're letting me because you're a good man."

That was when my control snapped. I simply could not listen to any more of her nonsense. Of course I felt guilty. I *was* guilty. But guilt being the reason behind me wanting her to stay with me? What was she on about?

Fuck giving her space. Fuck not crowding her. I'd had enough.

"I think you may have the wrong impression of me, Clara," I said in a low voice as I stalked towards her, "I'm *not* a good man."

Her eyes flew wide and she took a couple of steps back, the hand that wasn't holding the puppy coming up to ward me off, but I didn't stop until I'd backed her and the puppy up against the kitchen counter, caging them in with my hands resting on the granite either side of them.

"Yes, I've felt guilt over walking away from you in the courthouse. I will regret that for the rest of my life. But that is not why you and Zach are here."

"It's not?" she whispered as she stared up at me, her eyes still wide but the tears now had thankfully receded.

"No, baby," I said softly as my hand came up to gently stroke her hair back behind her ear. "And my career is fine."

"B-but why aren't you at work?"

"Why do you think?" I asked as I searched her face.

She frowned in confusion.

"Clara, I took a leave of absence from work so I could be here with you. And now I'm only back a few days a week, and then only when you're at the school."

Her mouth dropped open in shock. "You're here for me? W-why?"

The puppy wriggled between us and I chuckled. "Right, mate," I said to the ball of black fluff, stroking his head as he licked my hand. "You jog on for a minute." I took him from Clara and set him down on the tiles. He dashed off in the direction of the living room. "And don't you dare piss on that carpet again!" I called after him. Bloody Dad inflicting a dog on me. Although I had to admit that the look on Zach's face when he came home every day to that beast did make it worth it. That boy had been through enough. He deserved some joy.

I moved back to Clara, caging her in again and resting my forehead on hers.

"I'm here because the woman I love was scared. Because I knew that, even if she didn't feel the same way about me anymore, she felt safer if I was there. And because

I simply couldn't tear myself away from her, not after she was hurt."

"Th-the woman you love?" she said in a tentative voice, her small hands resting on my chest now but not to push me away. "B-but you've barely been touching me."

"I touch you all the time."

I did risk a fair bit of physical contact with Clara. Hugs, holding her on the sofa, kissing her temple, stroking her hair back from her face. Of course I wasn't allowing myself to touch her like I wanted. After what she'd been through, I didn't think that fucking her on every available surface of my house, which is what my fevered imagination would frequently come up with, was the best plan.

"Not like you did before," she said in a small voice, and my hand that had moved into her hair at the nape of her neck automatically tightened. Her eyes flared at that, and a shot of pure hot desire flooded through me. "I thought that you didn't want me anymore... like that, I mean."

"Jesus Christ." My voice was rough with desire. "Not want you?"

I didn't often make an error of judgement, but clearly, not fucking Clara during her recovery was a massive one that I would be *very* happy to rectify. And I certainly wasn't wasting any more time.

Chapter 41

Get used to that, darling

Rafe

She let out a small squeak as I reached down and lifted her up onto the granite surface, then stood in between her legs, letting her feel how hard I'd been for the entirety of this conversation, how hard I was most of the time around her.

"Does that feel like I don't want you?" I growled, moving against her now as she let out a small moan.

"Rafe," she said in a needy voice. "Oh God, I-I..."

"Have you been as frustrated as me?" I asked, still with that growl in my voice. "Being around you and having to hold myself back from touching you like I want has been the worst form of torture." My mouth moved to hers, but not for the usual light kisses I gave her. No, I took her in a deep, hard, demanding kiss which she returned, her hands gripping onto my shirt and her hips moving against mine in needy, desperate little jerks. "God, I missed you so much, baby."

"Rafe, please." Her voice was breathy and had a pleading quality which matched my own desperation.

"Please what, darling?" I murmured as I kissed from the corner of her mouth to her ear, taking the soft lobe in my teeth.

"Ugh, I can't..." she broke off in a long moan as I rocked against her centre.

"Use your words, Clara," I teased. "Tell me what you need."

"I need you inside me," she choked out. "Please, Rafe. I can't wait. I feel like I'm burning from the inside out."

"Good girl," I muttered. "Let me take the edge off first, though."

"Rafe, I—"

She broke off as I pulled her leggings and knickers down until they were on the floor. Her jumper and t-shirt were the next to go until she was just in her bra.

"What are you... Oh!" I gently pushed her back so she was leaning up on her elbows as I pressed her legs open wider and kissed down from her jawline to her breasts, pulling down the cups so that I could close my mouth over her nipples, then continuing down the flat of her stomach. "Rafe, I need you to... ah!" Her hands gripped into my hair as I used my tongue to cover her in one broad lick. "Holy shit," she breathed when I used the flat of my tongue to focus on her clit whilst my fingers entered her in one smooth motion and she contracted around me.

"Fuck, you're so tight," I muttered against her before focusing back on her clit, my finger pumping into her in controlled movements.

"Oh God, Rafe. I can't... ah!" She flew over the edge with a scream as the pulses of pleasure shot through her onto my tongue and fingers. I stayed there, milking the last of the contractions out of her until she was practically bone-less, then I moved up her body to cover her mouth with mine, the taste of her still on my tongue.

"Oh my God, you're good at that," she breathed, and I smiled against her mouth. The glazed look in her eyes started to clear and she stiffened. "Rafe! It's the middle of the day! What if Martha comes in?"

"You're right," I said, scooping her up so that she was straddling me and then carrying her out of the kitchen.

"What are you doing?" she said through a laugh which went right through my chest, flooding me with warmth. "We can't..."

"We can do whatever the fuck we like," I told her as I jogged up the stairs, kicked the door of my bedroom open and then slammed it behind me with my foot.

"Rafe, I... oh!" I dropped her on the bed and followed her down so that my body was covering hers.

"We've got about an hour until we have to leave to pick Ozzie up," I said in between kisses, moving to the side so that the heel of my hand could press against her core again and she let out another moan. "So we don't have much time to spare if I'm going to make you come twice more."

"Twice?" she breathed.

"Yes, baby. At least."

"Holy shit." She arched against me as I increased the pressure on her core and my mouth fell down to her breast. "Rafe, y-you... I need you—"

"I know what you need, baby."

"Clothes. Off." Some bossiness was leaking into her tone now and I loved it. She then shocked the shit out of me by slapping her hand on my shoulder. "Now, Rafe."

I raised my head from her chest and grinned up at her

before reaching back to pull my t-shirt over my head and throw it to the side.

"You're so beautiful," Clara said in a reverent whisper as her fingers traced over my pecs and then down over the ridges of my abdomen. I managed to unbutton my jeans and throw them on the floor, then I covered her body again and kissed her. The feel of her skin on mine was beyond amazing. My cock was pressing against her now and she moaned.

"You are so stunning that sometimes I feel like I can't breathe," I told her against her lips before I pulled back to scan her face, both my hands coming up to push her hair back. "Being around you and not having you has been torture, Clara. I haven't been able to take a full breath in over a month. I love you. Do you understand me?"

"Rafe, I—"

"And you're mine, understand?"

"Yours."

"Too fucking right," I snapped as I pushed forward, filling her in one smooth thrust. She let out a muted scream and arched against me.

"God, yes!" she semi-shouted. "Like that. Please, Rafe. Harder."

"Fuck, you feel so good," I gritted out as I powered into her, unable to hold anything back. "I missed you so fucking much. Tell me again that you're mine."

"I'm yours, Rafe."

"Tell me that you'll stop talking about leaving."

"Christ, yes, anything, please."

"Say it, Clara." I thrust deep inside and then pulled nearly all the way out. "Tell me you'll stay."

She clawed at my back, her legs tightening around me. "Rafe!"

"Tell me, Clara."

"I'll stay! Of course I'll stay. Please Rafe... ah!" I started my rhythm again, my thrusts so brutal they shook Clara on the bed, but she moved with me, begging me for more until she fell over the edge, letting out another scream as she contracted around me. The feel of her coming pushed me higher until my thrusts became uncoordinated and I came with a deep shout. Pleasure I'd never known before flooded through my system. Everything I had was focused on making her mine. Nothing else mattered but Clara.

I kissed her as we both came down, letting her take my weight for a moment but then pushing up to look at her face.

"You okay?" I asked softly.

"Wow," was her only reply and I let out a relieved chuckle.

"That doesn't exactly answer my question, darling. I was rough. Are you okay? I didn't hurt you?"

She frowned up at me. "That was perfect, Rafe Sterling. I'm not made of glass."

I grinned then levered up to push off the bed. "Wait there," I told her, not fully trusting this Clara that had promised to stay with me. I stalked to the bathroom to grab a flannel and wet it with warm water. When I came back, Clara was in the bed with the covers hiked up to her chin. She was flushed and some embarrassment had crept into her expression.

"You didn't stay," I accused as I stalked towards her.

She rolled her eyes. "I'm not staying splayed out on the bed naked in the cold light of day."

I pulled the covers back and reached to part her legs. She squeaked.

"What are you doing?"

"I didn't use a condom," I said as I cleaned her with the

flannel before throwing it onto the side table and moving fully into the bed to take her in my arms.

"Oh," she replied, stiffening in my arms as I rested back against the pillows, pulling her onto my chest so that her head was resting under my chin and her leg was thrown over mine. "I'm sorry."

I chuckled again. "One day you'll learn not to apologise for shit that's not your fault. Clara, the condom is *my* fuck up. I'm clean. I was tested a couple of months before we met, and I haven't slept with anyone since then."

"You haven't?" she asked in surprise.

I frowned. "Of course not."

"Didn't you and Ophelia? I mean, I assumed..."

"There's been nobody but you, Clara."

"Oh."

"So we don't have to worry about that. But I'm sorry I didn't protect you pregnancy-wise."

"Pregnancy?"

"Yes, Clara. Contraception. The possibility of a pregnancy doesn't bother me, but..."

"Oh, I... I'm on the pill. I started it back when we... I mean... when we started, er... and I thought I'd carry it on. Just in case."

"Okay," I said, kissing the top of her head.

"It wouldn't bother you if I were to get pregnant?"

I paused, not wanting to say the wrong thing and also really not wanting to sound like too much of a caveman. "No, Clara. I love you. I'd be bloody ecstatic if you were pregnant. But of course, I wouldn't want you to be upset. And it was irresponsible of me to—"

"You love me?" The tentative quality in her voice broke my heart. How this amazing woman had ever been made to feel unlovable made me furious. I tamped down the familiar flash of anger towards her useless fucking family. Those bastards never deserved to breathe the same air as Clara. How dare they ever make her feel she had to hide, make her feel like she had to be small? And how fucking dare they lay a finger on her? How could anyone hurt anything so precious?

"I love everything about you, Clara," I told her as I shifted us and then flipped her onto her back, hovering over her to search her uncertain expression. "I love the way you feel, the way you smell, the way your nose crinkles when you disagree with me but don't want to say, the way you nurture the kids in your class, the way you love my son, the way you eat Branston Pickle straight out of the jar, the way you bite both of your lips when you've done something you know will piss me off." She rolled her eyes but there was a smile on her face. I grinned back at her, then my smile faded as I held her gaze. "I love your quiet humour, your kindness, the way you stand up for what you believe even if doing it terrifies you, your strength—"

"I'm not st—"

"Darling, you're the strongest person I know," I told her firmly. "What you did to save your brother and your mother will have saved other people too. The ripples will be felt throughout London. *You* did that. And you've protected your brother his whole life. There are very few people with that level of resilience, with that strength."

She shook her head. "I don't think you see me clearly."

"It's you who doesn't see yourself clearly," I told her firmly. "But we'll have plenty of time to turn that around. You've agreed to stay here with me, remember?"

"Rafe, that was under duress!"

"You promised."

"You cheated to get your way."

I grinned. "Get used to that, darling."

She opened her mouth and then closed it again. I waited, knowing that I had to let Clara say what she needed to say in her own time. She looked away for a moment, then swallowed before her jaw set at a determined angle and she turned back to me.

"I love you too," she said, her voice just as determined as the set of her jaw but still with that slight shaky quality. I smiled down at her.

"That's my brave girl," I praised, lowering my head to kiss her, softly at first then deeper. I flipped us back in a sudden movement so that Clara was straddling me, her hands braced against my chest as I hardened again underneath her. "Right, we've got about twenty minutes left for you to show me just how much you love me."

Clara let out another laugh that I felt straight down to my soul. I would never get tired of that sound.

Then she showed me how much she loved me before we both left to pick up Ozzie.

And again after he went to bed that night.

Epilogue

You gave me colour back

Clara

"Wowsers, Clara!" Poppy cried as she rushed towards me across the room, abandoning her large circle of admirers. I smiled at her as she gathered both my hands in hers and started jumping on the spot. "You look incredible! I knew you'd go for the pink."

We hadn't gone dress shopping like normal people. No, standard shopping was not Poppy Sterling's vibe at all. She invited me and Lily back to her house, where she had about a million dresses delivered for us to try on after we'd all drunk some champagne.

"This is better," Poppy had told me. "I can't get sloshed properly when I'm out and about anyway, but it's safe here."

For someone as effervescent and social as Poppy, she was incredibly cautious now. The press had taken advantage of her openness too many times before, and, given everything that had happened this year, she only ever drank in her own home with people she trusted, and even then very rarely.

The champagne had worked its magic. Before my second glass, I had only considered black or navy dresses, but after it started to kick in I gravitated way more towards colour. That was the thing now. I wasn't afraid of colour anymore. My life before had been all about blending into the background, avoiding being noticed at all costs. But now that I felt safe, I was starting to think about what I *wanted* to wear and not what I needed to in order to avoid being seen. And it turned out I liked colour. Hence the bright pink, floor-length, strapless dress I had on now.

Make-up I was still getting used to, but there was no other option than bright pink lipstick to go with the dress. To be honest, I left all of those decisions to the army of people Poppy had sent to my house earlier that day. When they'd finished with me, I barely recognised the woman looking back at me in the mirror. I'd actually teared up until the make-up artist scolded me for potentially ruining my smoky eyes.

"My brother is going to lose his shit when he sees you!" Poppy was still bouncing. She was a very bouncy human being. Tonight was another Sterling charity gala – the first one I had agreed to attend. I just hadn't had the confidence before now, but Rafe had been patient with me. When I chickened out of the previous one, I'd asked him in a small voice if he was disappointed in me.

"I could never be disappointed in you, Clara," he told me in a fierce voice. "Of course I want you there, but if you never want to come to one of these dog and pony shows, that's okay. Not everyone has to love this shit like my sister does. My ex-wife lived for coming with me to these things and resented that there weren't more opportunities to parade around on my arm in front of the paps – and look how that turned out. I love you, gala or no gala, it doesn't matter."

It wasn't like I never went out with Rafe. After that day at his house, when I finally accepted that he loved me and agreed to stay, he'd ramped up the romance, much to Ozzie and my brother's disgust.

"Ugh, Dad!" Ozzie had shouted at him when he'd kissed me in the kitchen after I agreed to go out on an official date with him. "You can't kiss in front of me! I'm a child!"

"I'm actually still technically a child as well. And I agree with Ozzie. You're basically scarring us both," Zach had complained into his cup of tea, but there was a smile on his face that told another story.

To be honest, in Zach's eyes, Rafe still could do no wrong. He'd settled into the Sterling house with surprising speed, and I knew he loved the sense of family we had here. The Sunday roasts with Rafe's family, the interest everyone showed in Zach's education, the unconditional support he received from Rafe. And, of course, his beloved dog Mungo, who slept in Zach's bed every night, much to the earl's horror:

"That's a working breed, boy!" he'd tell my brother. *"Needs to be out shooting."*

Zach got on well with the Sterlings, but he drew the line at hunting.

"Sometimes I think they're more bloodthirsty than our family, Cla-Cla," he'd confided in me one day. He wasn't exactly wrong either.

"Get used to it, kid," Rafe said as his arms closed around

me and he kissed me again. "There's way more where that's coming from."

So, I'd agreed to the date. I did tell him it was a little weird, seeing as I was already living with him, but he insisted that we weren't going to miss any of the steps.

It wasn't always easy. I still had a touch of agoraphobia, and I'd never be fully comfortable leaving the house on my own, but I'd made massive progress.

Tonight was a big part of that. It was also a big fuck you to my father. His sentencing had been last week, and he'd gone down for the maximum possible time: three life sentences to be served consecutively.

Everyone in my father's organisation was totally fucked. Cracking the code to their messaging network had been the key to a slew of evidence, the like of which the police said they'd never seen before. The stupid bastards had shared everything over that messenger: photographs of their violence to use as deterrents, details of drug deals, all their protection rackets, everything.

I'd wanted to look that bastard in the eye when he went down. Everyone tried to dissuade me, but Rafe seemed to know that it was what I needed. Direct eye contact with my father had always been risky. He often saw it as a challenge, and I'd learned to avoid it. But that day in court I stood up as he was led away, and when he turned towards the sound of my chair scraping back, I looked straight into his eyes and held his gaze. There was hatred in his expression and resentment, but also just a flicker of defeat. In the end, I won, and he knew it.

From what I heard, he wasn't having an easy time in prison, and I gave exactly zero fucks.

Now the trial was over, I didn't want to think about my

family. Yes, I had to work through the trauma they'd caused me in therapy, but other than that, they were best forgotten. That went for my mother too. She'd only made vague attempts to contact Zach and never pushed for him to return home. I had more patience with her than he did, and would at least visit her in that mausoleum of a house, but she was still drinking, still checked out, more so now than ever before. I offered to help, to go with her to see the GP, to help find her a therapist, but she refused that too. The final straw was when she asked me, "When do you think I can visit your dad?" I left after that, and I hadn't contacted her since.

"Do I really look okay?" I asked Poppy, feeling nervous as I scanned her outfit. As always, she shone brighter than anyone in the room. There were film stars, politicians, all sorts of celebrities, but Poppy outshone them all easily.

"Of course you do, you numpty," Poppy told me, and I just couldn't help myself. I moved to her and gave her a grateful hug. Her hug in return was surprisingly fierce, and when I drew back and scanned her face, I realised that despite her normal effervescence, there was something very wrong with Poppy tonight: lines of tension around her mouth that weren't normally there and this close up, I could see her eyes were very slightly red-rimmed as if she'd been crying. I frowned. I had a feeling I knew exactly who was to blame. That grumpy Scottish bastard!

"Pops? Is everything—?"

"You guys hug *way* too much," Zach said to me as he drew up alongside us. "It's like a disease."

"Dr Zach!" Poppy cried and he rolled his eyes. She then proved his point by giving him a firm hug as well.

"Again, Poppy, not a doctor. Not even a vet student

yet," Zach muttered as he patted Poppy on the back and disengaged himself as quickly as possible. He couldn't manage these hugs without turning tomato red.

"Details, details. And animal doctors are just as important. Christ, you're even taller. What's Martha feeding you?" The height difference between them was almost comical. "And look at these muscles!" she squeezed his biceps. His cheeks darkened even more.

"Give over, Pops," he complained, but he was clearly chuffed with the compliment. Zach had filled out in the last year. Being in a stress-free environment where he wasn't scared to leave his room, and having three square meals a day was likely a big factor in that, as was Rafe's home gym and the personal trainer he insisted work with Zach when Zach had asked to use it.

"Cla-Cla!" I turned sharply at Ozzie's voice, squatting down just in time to intercept an eight-year-old-little-boy-shaped hug-seeking missile as he flew into my arms. "You've got pink lips!"

I laughed as I kissed the side of his head, then pulled back to look at his little face. "That I do, love." His hair had already broken out of the hairstyle it had been brushed into earlier, sticking up in all directions, and there was a leaf on his jacket. I plucked it off and held it up in front of him, raising one eyebrow. "What have you been up to, Oscar Sterling?"

"Oh! Me and Margot found a—"

"Ozzie!" Margot herself cut him off and we both turned towards her. "Don't tell the adults anything," she hissed. "Come on, before you land us in the shit."

"Language, Margot!" I called as I straightened from my crouch, but they'd already darted off into the crowd.

"Poppy, Zach, have you seen Clara? Rory said——" Rafe's deep voice sounded from behind me. I turned around to face him and he froze. When he showed no signs of movement, I smiled at him and took a few steps forward to close the distance between us. "Clara?" he breathed, scanning me from head to toe. "What the fuck?"

Poppy punched him in the arm. "Incorrect response, you absolute twatwaffle."

"Hi," I said softly as my hands landed on his chest and I gazed up at him. "Rafe? You okay?"

"You look different," he said in a choked voice.

"Oh my God!" Poppy cried. "Where has my smooth operator brother gone? 'What the fuck' and 'you look different' are the best you can come up with? Are you serious?"

"Yeah, Rafe," Zach put in. "Where's your rizz, mate?"

But Rafe just ignored them. He was too busy scanning my face. His jaw was clenched so tight that a muscle was ticking at the side. "How soon can we leave?" he asked me and I frowned.

"You want to leave already? Rafe, we only just got here, and you're giving a speech."

The gala tonight was to raise money for domestic violence charities and women's refuges in London. Poppy had organized the expansion of the Sterling Foundation to support these causes over the last year under my guidance, and that of Mia Hardcastle and Lady Clare Harding, friends of the Sterling family and themselves both victims and survivors of domestic violence. Mia and Clare were giving a speech together with other survivors, but I wasn't ready to do that. Not yet. Rafe would introduce them on behalf of the foundation. He'd recently been appointed as a High Court judge. So he had enough background knowledge of crimes against women to talk for hours, but he was going to keep his speech short. The main event, he said, should be the survivors and their stories.

He moved suddenly then, but I didn't flinch. My flinching days around Rafe were over. His hand shot out around my waist and the other came up to cup my face. He pulled my body flush with his and his head lowered so our lips were almost touching.

"Remind me again why I'm even here?" he muttered and I smiled.

"Rafe Mungo Bartholomew Sterling!" Poppy cried. "If you kiss her, I will kill you. Her lipstick is not to be ruined, you bloody caveman."

"Also, I'm standing right here," Zach said in amused disgust. "Your guys' PDA is well out of hand."

"I think we have to stay," I whispered as I watched his pupils dilate. "Your speech, remember?"

"I barely remember my own name," he whispered back.

"Honestly, Rafe." The posh accent cut into our bubble and I turned my head to see Rafe's mum frowning at us from next to Poppy. "Unhand poor Clara before you dishevel her completely."

"Oh, let the young people have their fun," Granny Sterling said as she approached on the arm of the earl who was looking almost as handsome as his son, both in their black tie.

The earl chuckled. "I think letting them have their fun might cause a bit of stir, Mum," he said. "If it's the kind of fun I think my son has in mind."

"Daddy! Ew!" Poppy objected.

"Lord Sterling," Mia Hardcastle interrupted, and we both turned to her and Lady Clare Harding, who were both smiling at us from a few feet away. "We've got the speeches now." She turned to me. "Hi, Clara," she said softly.

"Yes, do hurry up, Rafe," Clare Harding said through her smile. "I'm sure you can ruin Clara's make-up quite thoroughly after we've finished." She winked at me and my face flooded with heat.

Mia, Claire and I had grown closer since working together on the Sterling Foundation. I knew that Mia used to be even more withdrawn than me, but sometimes that was difficult to believe. "Mind if I borrow your Rafe? We've got the speeches now."

"Of course," I said to her, smiling back. I would have moved to hug her, but Rafe's arms were still locked around me.

I looked up at him. "You might have to let me go," I whispered.

"Never," he whispered back and my eyes started to sting.

"Oh balls," Poppy said when she looked back at us after hugging Mia. "Not the eyeliner!"

"Honestly, Rafe," Lady Sterling said. "Do bugger off. You're keeping Mia and Clare waiting." She turned to Mia and Clare. "I'm so sorry, darlings."

"It's fine," Mia said in an amused voice.

Rafe sighed, eyes still locked with mine as if there was nobody else in the room. "I have to go."

"Okay," I whispered.

"Okay," he whispered back, then kissed the corner of my mouth before he let me go.

"Don't let her out of your sight," he said to his dad, who walked over to me and took my arm.

"Of course not," the earl replied as if affronted that there was even a small possibility he might leave me. I suppressed an eye roll. All the Sterling men were incredibly overprotective; however, after a lifetime of the men in my family being anything but protective, I admit it didn't annoy me as much as it should have.

"Come on, darling," Lady Sterling said warmly after giving me the required cheek kisses. "Let's find our table. Your friend Lily is there already, talking to the prime minister about educational reform. I'm not overly sure she's safe to be left."

"Oh balls," I muttered as we hurried across the room. Lily was a goddamn liability. I was distracted as we walked through the crowd, but the earl's voice was enough to refocus me back on him.

"My son loves you, you know," he said, slowing us slightly so that we were out of earshot of the others. I looked up at him. He was staring across the room at the podium where Rafe was preparing to speak.

"I-I love him too." I cleared my throat. Ugh, that bloody stutter creeping in again. It was rarer now, but there was an edge to the earl that brought it out.

He brought us to a stop a few feet from the table and looked down at me with his head tilted to the side. "I intimidate you, don't I?"

I bit my lip. I didn't want to insult him, but somehow I knew he would be able to tell if I lied. "Yes," I whispered.

"You're cautious. You've had to be."

I nodded slowly.

"You're right to be cautious."

I blinked. I hadn't expected him to admit that.

"But you know that, don't you?"

I nodded again.

"My family can be dangerous in lots of different ways, Clara. We've been that way for hundreds of years. But we will *never* be dangerous for you. I know it will take time for you to believe it, but we will never hurt you. We protect our own. Understand me? You and Zach are under our protection. You're a Sterling now. And nobody fucks with a Sterling."

"Lord of the Manor!" Lily's excited voice drew our attention as she hip-bumped the earl. Actually hip-bumped the man! I may have been wary around this man, but Lily had no such reservations. To her, he was just the posh grandpa of one of her kids who lived in a big house and who provided great Sunday roasts – well, at least his staff did. But the earl was good at that *good old boy* front. I was an exception in being able to see past that persona, but I'd had years of practice when it came to sensing dangerous people. The Sterlings might be at the other end of the class spectrum, but in many ways they were *much* scarier than my family.

"Lily," the earl said warmly. "Frightfully good to see you, young lady. Any more plays for us on the horizon?" The earl had bloody loved *Sweeney Todd*.

"Oh, I'm working on Mrs C to let me do either *Animal Farm* or *1984* but she's being a bit stubborn. I guess the complaints we had after last year might have something to do with it."

"I loved your play. Watching the Harding child slit my grandson's throat was highly entertaining."

"Thanks, Lordie S! I told Mrs C that not everyone thought it was 'completely inappropriate'. Honestly, some parents are so sensitive. What's a bit of cannibalism between friends? Bore off, poshos."

He laughed. "Bore off indeed."

Everyone started laughing around us then and I got the giggles as well. I was still laughing when I looked up at the stage and my eyes locked with Rafe's. There was a small smile on his mouth as he watched me. Clare Harding was talking to him, but he clearly wasn't listening. All his attention was on me. And his expression was fierce.

Rafe

The urge to drag Clara home had been stronger than usual since I saw her in that goddamn pink dress. I'd had to arrive at the venue early, which I realised on seeing her may have been a mistake. We definitely shouldn't have been in public when I saw Clara in that dress for the first time. My reaction was not for public consumption, especially among the "poshos," as Lily so aptly called my friends and family. English aristocratic restraint was legendary and did not generally include taking your girlfriend in your arms in the middle of a packed ballroom and looking like you wanted to eat her alive.

But now, finally, I could leave this stupid event.

I was trying my best not to be selfish with Clara. For a long time, she would barely leave the house, so it was bloody brilliant that she felt comfortable enough to come out to one of these things. But I had to admit that I didn't like sharing her. Of course, I'd hated the anxiety that had kept Clara housebound, but in the not-for-public-consumption, deep dark possessive part of my monkey brain, I had enjoyed having agoraphobic Clara all to myself. However, now she was very much out. And beautiful. So, so unbelievably beautiful. Of course, my Clara was always beautiful, but in that dress and with that lipstick, it was almost otherworldly. Hence the need to take her home at the first available opportunity.

"What on earth is the hurry, Rafe?" Clara said breathlessly as I led her down the corridor towards the exit. "And where is Ozzie?"

"Ozzie is going for a sleepover with Margot Harding, God help him. We are going home before I kill any of my stupid fucking ex-friends for bloody well hugging you and kissing you and doing all manner of inappropriate things right in front of my face."

Clara laughed and gave my hand a tug. "Slow down, you big idiot. I can barely walk in these heels, let alone run."

"I'm not running," I grumbled, reluctantly slowing my pace.

"Maybe not by your standards, daddy long legs. But us normals can't cover ten feet in one stride."

"Did you just call me *daddy long legs?*" I smirked down at her but did slow my strides somewhat. I wished it was socially acceptable to simply pick her up and then walk as fast as I damn well wanted, but I doubted English high society was ready for that and I'd already embarrassed her enough for one night.

I would have just left our coats, but Clara's dress was strapless, and it was freezing outside, so that wasn't an option. Plus, there was another very good reason for me to put my coat on, which was evident when I shook out the long, black wool overcoat and threw it on in one smooth movement, and Clara's eyes flared as she watched me.

"You love doing that to me," she complained, but that didn't stop her from spinning around after I'd helped her into her own coat and slipping her hands through the folds of my suit to my chest, her head tipped up to stare into my eyes and a small smile formed on her lips.

"Doing what?" I asked innocently as I scanned her beautiful face.

"Putting your coat on all sexy like that."

I raised an eyebrow. "I was merely attiring myself

appropriately for this time of year, young lady. If that gets you going, then it's down to your dirty mind."

She laughed at that. The kind of laugh I fucking loved to hear from her, and I was fucking thrilled to be close enough to hear it. All evening, Clara had been too bloody far away, and I'd had to endure seeing her laugh without actually hearing it clearly. Her eyes were twinkling behind her glasses, her cheeks were pink and her fringe messy from me marching her across the ballroom. For a moment, I couldn't breathe. She was just that beautiful. All my romantic plans went out of my head and I simply blurted out what I'd wanted to say for months.

"Marry me."

Her laughter cut off abruptly. "W-what?"

"You'll marry me." Wow. I was the least romantic bloke in England. I'd asked my girlfriend to marry me outside a cloakroom in a corridor. No, actually I hadn't even asked, had I? I'd bloody well told her to. "Ah, bollocks," I muttered. "I'm buggering this up. I meant to do this somewhere special. I was going to take you to Paris next week. But I've been carrying this around and..."

I reached in my pocket and my fingers closed over the ring box. Clara watched with wide eyes as I fumbled, then eventually opened it, took out the ring and then grabbed her hand to put it on her finger. The large pink diamond glittered in the light.

"It's your favourite colour," I told her as she blinked down at the ring in shock.

"Only now it is," she whispered.

"What, darling?"

"It's only my favourite *now*. Only since you made it safe for me to like it again." When she looked up at me, there were tears in her eyes. "You gave me colour back."

"All I did was love you."

"That's all it took."

I dropped her hand to cup her face and kissed her then, right in the middle of the bloody corridor. When I pulled back to scan her face, she smiled up at me.

"I've ruined your lipstick."

"I don't care."

"Are you going to marry me or not?" I asked in a grumpy tone. I mean, she was wearing the ring, but I was a man of legalities. I wanted a verbal contract, goddamn it.

"I didn't think you were asking. It seemed like more of a command. Something you're good at."

"Well, yes, it was."

"And Lord Sterling expects his commands to be followed without question."

"Yes, he bloody well does."

"Well, I'd better marry you then."

It was my turn to smile before I kissed her again.

For a free bonus epilogue to *Law Maker*, giving you a snapshot of Clara and Rafe with their family and friends in the future, follow this link:

https://dl.bookfunnel.com/6gz7gdyor8

Thank you so much for reading *Law Maker*.

Poppy and Rory's book, *Deal Breaker*,
is available for pre-order now.
Read on for an excerpt:

Deal Breaker

Chapter 1

Poppy

"How do I look?" I spun around, my skirt flying out around me in a shimmering mass of tulle and sequins.

"Like a sexy if slightly demented Tinkerbell," Josh said, and I beamed at him.

"Nailed it! Exactly what I was going for."

Josh rolled his eyes and smoothed down the front of his suit. There was nothing demented about Josh's outfit. As always, he looked utterly perfect, not a stitch of Armani out of place.

"At least it's better than Granny's description," I went on as I gave him a shoulder bump to ruffle his feathers. "I think it was 'mad prostitute with a penchant for glitter'."

Josh's serious expression cracked then, and I even managed to score a chuckle to go with his eye roll.

If Josh had his way, we'd be arch-rivals. We both frequented the red carpet, stalking the same celebs. We were both considered to be firmly in the fluff category of journalists, interviewing actresses and pop stars rather than politicians and world leaders. We both made people laugh, Josh with his desert-dry sense of humour and subtle but cutting put-downs, and me with my *obnoxiously bubbly personality,* as Josh would put it. But bitter rivalry just wasn't my vibe. Life was too short for that nonsense. And from the first eye roll I managed to eke out of him at the Cannes Film Festival five years ago (after irritating the shit out of him for the entire hour we'd had to wait on the carpet) I knew we'd be mates. He'd told me I was more persistent than impetigo and more annoying than a Powerpuff Girl. I was lucky that he settled on Powerpuff as my nickname and not Impetigo, to be honest.

I bit my lip. "Honestly, Grumpyface, do I look okay?"

Josh frowned. "What the fuck is this? Where's your misplaced, overblown confidence? Oh God, please don't tell me your celebrity is turning you into one of those oversensitive little bitches we interview? I enjoy insulting you, Powerpuff. Don't take away one of my few pleasures in life."

I forced a laugh. "Of course not, you twatwaffle." He turned to me then as his eyebrows went up.

"That was a *fake laugh*," he said in horror. "You never laugh like that. Where was the obnoxious snort? What the *hell* is going on?"

I shrugged and rolled my eyes. "Jesus Christ, can't a girl ask if she looks okay without making your head explode?"

"You know perfectly well that you look absolutely off

the charts, mouth-wateringly gorgeous. If I were into vaginas, I would have already had my way with you behind the screens over there, so what's the problem?"

I looked down at my feet and bit my lip. "Do you think my shoes are ridiculous?" They'd seemed fun and sexy when I bought them, but since my mind had flashed to Rory's serious disapproving face, my confidence had faltered. I doubted he would view my towering heels covered in sequined butterflies as anything other than totally insane.

"Oh. My. God. What on earth is going on? Where is my best friend? Who is this insecure weirdo who's taken over her smoking hot little body?"

I forced another laugh, and his expression slipped into alarmed territory.

"Holy shit. What is *wrong*, Powerpuff?"

I shifted on my feet and tightened my grip on my microphone. "You remember I told you about Rory Wallace?"

"The hot rugby player who hates you because he's an insecure manbaby?"

Ugh, I really wished I wasn't such an oversharer. Josh was the least discreet man in England.

"Yeah, that's the one. Well, he'll be here tonight. They're honouring him with a Contribution to Rugby Youth award."

"You're nervous because that twunt's coming? Babe, forget about him. He's the start of an angsty romance novel. Grumpy brother's best friend who hates you for '*reasons*.' He needs a kick in the balls, *not* you worrying if you look okay."

I managed a small grin. "He's not a twunt," I muttered. "It's not a capital offence to dislike me, you know."

"Everybody loves you, Powerpuff," Josh's voice had

gentled now. "Even *I* love you, and I'm a grumpy git who hates literally every other human being on the planet. He's lucky I've softened the c-word with a *tw*. I reserve the right to change my mind if I observe any questionable behaviour."

The first of the limos pulled up then, and Josh turned towards the road.

"Right, Powerpuff. Woman up. Tits out and let's bloody well do this. You are Lady motherfucking Poppy Sterling. Some over-jacked rugger bugger's not going to make you doubt yourself. Game face on now, okay? I don't want to have to steal all your interviews from you again."

"You never steal my interviews, you arrogant twunt."

"Hey! No using my personal swears against me. Game time."

The red carpet filled up surprisingly quickly. As this was the award ceremony for the UK Sporting Excellence Awards, most of the celebrities were sportsmen and women, so they were more nervous and way less camera-ready than our normal fare. But Josh and I were the type of extreme extroverts who thrived on winkling introverts from their little shells and sucking the banter right out of them. Sort of like the opposite of fun sponges. I guess we were like fun sprinklers or maybe even fun tsunamis; we just swept awkward, shy people right along with us for the ride.

"We must stop meeting like this," I said to Alex Costas, the billionaire tech company owner who was sponsoring this entire event.

He grinned down at me. Alex and I had my standard red-carpet relationship – teasing, non-threatening flirting, with me making regular suggestions that he sweep me away to his billionaire batcave and him pretending that this was an imminent plan.

"It's true. I'm stalking you. Feel free to report me to your union."

"Ooh great idea! Hey, Grumpyface," I poked Josh in the ribs, interrupting his interview with a football player who was definitely *not* of the shy variety.

"I'm in the middle of a conversation with this strapping young man, Powerpuff," he said with fake annoyance. I knew for a fact that he thought the particular football player he was talking to was an out-and-out c-word with no *tw* in the mix.

"What's our union called?"

"How should I know? Useless, overpaid, overdressed fuckwits 'r us?"

I smiled. "Ah yes. That's the one. You may go about your business." I turned back to a smiling Alex. "You can expect a very severe reprimand, young man."

"I shall look forward to it," Alex said with a wink as his handlers moved him on.

"Bloody typical." That low, deep, rumbling Scottish voice went right through me like it always did, and I turned to see Rory Wallace standing feet away from me and looking supremely uncomfortable in a tailored suit. Of course, with his massive frame, he'd *have* to have a suit tailored. There was no way he'd be able to buy anything off the rack that could cope with those shoulders and that musculature.

I searched my memories. Other than when he won the Rugby World Cup for Scotland five years ago, I hadn't seen Rory in a suit before, and the one he wore back then had been an ill-fitting nightmare, nothing like the well-cut, expensive gloriousness he was wearing today, along with his scowl.

Rory Wallace did not like me. It didn't matter how

many smiles I directed his way, how many conversations I tried to start with him, or how many compliments I threw at him. He was the one human completely resistant to my charm.

My mind blanked as I stared at him, and for the first time in my life, I was lost for words – and I was *never* lost for words.

"What? Ye're no gonna do your fake flirting thing with me like you did with the jumped-up tech bro? Only reserve that bollocks for the billionaires?"

I swallowed and attempted a shaky smile. "Rory!" I exclaimed like he was one of my favourite people, and I didn't feel completely rattled as he stared down at me with that disapproving expression. I didn't cope well with disapproval. It made my stomach clench and threw me off balance. So off balance that one of my heels wobbled out from under me and I nearly fell. I would have done if his large hands hadn't shot out and enclosed my upper arms, keeping me on my feet.

"Christ, Poppy," he swore, letting me go as if I'd burnt him once he'd established I wasn't in danger of falling at his feet anymore. "Don't wear ridiculous shoes like that if you cannae walk in them. Ye're a goddamn liability."

I felt heat spread up from my neck to my face. Rory had the uniquely effective ability to make me feel small. It hadn't always been that way. As my brother's best friend, he'd known me since I was eight. And back then, he'd seemed to like me just fine. He'd always been a bit dour, but my antics made him smile, even laugh out loud, which my brother told me was super rare.

As a child, I idolised him, but as a teenager, I'd fancied him something rotten and been fairly obvious about it. Then, five years ago, I finally got my way, and even if it was only a kiss, it had been *glorious*. Rory Wallace was a talented man on the rugby field but, if that kiss was anything to go by, he was gifted in other areas too.

Then came that bloody interview after Scotland won the World Cup, and everything blew up. Rory unceremoniously dumped me, and his entire attitude towards me flipped; no longer charmed by my eccentricity, but irritated. The man who'd patiently sat with me to help me revise for my A-levels, never once making me feel stupid for my crippling dyslexia, was now dismissive and cruel.

So yes, my favourite horror film is me declaring my undying love for Rory Wallace after he kissed me, agreeing to wait for him whilst he trained to represent his country and hiding the fact I was head over heels for him from my family on his instruction (this should have clued me in right there to be honest) only to have him ghost me after he won the match. *Ghost me.* It was humiliating, and I couldn't even complain to my family as they were totally in the dark about it all. My brother was still mates with the man.

"Thank you, Gok Wan, for that wonderful fashion advice," I said through a forced smile. "I shall look into flats for my next event, but I fear eye contact may be a problem with most people if I eschew the heels completely. How's the weather up there, by the way?"

Rory *didn't* crack a smile, forced or otherwise. I decided to soldier on. We were being filmed, and I had a job to do. Steve, my cameraman, gave me an encouraging pat on the back, and I straightened my spine. For some reason, Rory transferred his scowl to Steve after he laid his hand on me, and his expression darkened, which was impressive as I didn't think it could get any darker.

It seemed his hatred extended to my entire team. Good to know.

"So, Contribution to Rugby Youth Award, you talented man. Excited to be here?"

Rory grunted and pulled on his collar, clearly not comfortable in his formal wear. "Excited? To be in this monkey suit and have to talk to you lot? No likely."

I flinched at those verbal blows. What was wrong with him? We were on the red carpet at an event which was supposed to be fun. It was in aid of the charity he supported. I was doing my bloody job. There was a camera pointed at him right now, recording an interview that I would no doubt have to dump.

Honestly, when would he let his resentment go? I didn't even do anything wrong. And it was him who broke my heart. If anyone had the right to be a grumpy bitch in this situation, it was me.

"Right, Incredible Hulk," snapped Josh as his latest interviewee moved on and he turned to Rory. "Off you fuck. Nobody but me speaks to Powerpuff like that."

"Powerpuff?" Rory said in confusion, staring at Josh like he was a creature from outer space.

"You don't deserve to breathe her air, big man," Josh told him. "You should be begging to walk through hellfire to drink her bath water, not behaving like you've got a stick lodged up your arse. I may not be built like a brick shit-house, but I bitch-slapped my way out of a fight with a six-foot queen in a gay bar in Vauxhall yesterday, and queens in Vauxhall are *way* scarier than you could ever be. So off you go to hang out with your little rugby dickheads and leave *Lady* Sterling alone."

Rory was staring at Josh throughout this little speech. At first, he'd bristled, especially when Josh had put his arm around me halfway through, but for some reason, at the mention of gay bars, his scowl softened and the corners of his mouth turned up in something that may have almost passed for a smile.

"Okay, chief," he said through his almost-smile, holding his hands up as he backed away. "Ye can stand down."

"Stand down from what?" A tall brunette in a stunning floor-length black dress came up next to him and took his arm. My chest tightened. Her effortlessly understated style was the total opposite of mine: soft make-up, chic up-do, only a hint of cleavage showing – *nothing vulgar*, as Granny would say.

Now *my* girls were hard to miss, and I'd long since given up trying to minimise them. I was the Dolly Parton to her Princess Catherine. Don't get me wrong, I *loved* Dolly, but after the withering looks from Rory, I was for once wishing I could manage a more regal vibe.

Still having a crush on Rory Wallace was ridiculous. The man hated me.

I shook my head to clear it and reached for my game face.

"Thanks, Josh," I said through gritted teeth. "I've got it from here."

Josh gave my shoulder a squeeze and Rory another scowl before moving to his own mark. Bless him. By leaping to my defence, he'd probably missed a couple of interviews already.

"Miss Hawthorne," I put in, and when Rory's plus one turned to me, I was proud that I managed a smile. It wasn't her fault that she could channel royalty and bag a man that my demented brain fantasised about running off the rugby field covered in mud and shagging me before I gave him the chance to shower. That was *my* dysfunction. "You're here to support Mr Wallace?"

"You don't have to answer her," Rory muttered to Maggie Hawthorne, who frowned at him.

"Why wouldn't I answer her?" she asked, seeming bewildered, then turned to me with a smile.

"Poppy Sterling," she gushed. "I watch your interviews."

"Oh dear. Bad luck," I said my standard reply with a mock grimace. Aside from interviewing celebs at red carpet events, I also booked them for one-on-one interviews which were conducted in one of the pods of the London Eye. It was perfect really, if a bit high pressure due to the thirty-minute time constraint. We called it *Pod Dates with Poppy* and posted the interviews on my YouTube channel. It was way more successful than I could ever have predicted, and over the last few years my Pod Dates had branched out from UK-based celebs to international stars. But however famous the celebs were, they all got the same pod and the same thirty minutes.

She laughed. "No! You're so funny and really insightful." She stepped closer then, ignoring Rory, who clearly wanted to move on. "I actually think you're terribly clever." She tilted her head to the side as she studied me. "The way you use humour to help people open up. And you make all of your subjects feel special. That's a real talent."

I blinked up at her, thrown for a moment, but as I always did, I recovered quickly. "Wow. Please don't tell me you're a beautiful, intelligent, famous political correspondent who's also really nice. Give us something to hate, for God's sake."

Maggie laughed. Even that was understated and beautiful. When I laughed, there was invariably actual snorting involved.

"Good luck tomorrow, by the way." The whole country

knew about Maggie's upcoming interview with the Prime Minister.

Maggie smiled. "Thanks. Maybe you should come along with me? I'd probably get a lot more out of him that way."

Rory grumbled something next to her, and she shot him an irritated look.

"Yes, yes, okay, Rory. I'm coming. Lovely to meet you, Poppy."

I breathed a sigh of relief as they moved on, but unfortunately, that relief was short-lived.

"Oh bugger," I murmured as I spotted Alastair Roxburg through the crowd, headed towards us. He was another Scottish rugby player, but the type of Scotsman who didn't have a broad accent like Rory. His family owned a castle near Edinburgh but spent most of their time in London. Alastair went to boarding school in England, and his accent was as posh as mine.

The Sterlings and the Roxburgs knew each other (just as most aristocratic families did in the UK) and attended a lot of the same events. Alastair had always given me a creepy vibe. He was objectively handsome, but quite frankly an arse. He made cruel jokes at other people's expense. He'd made my cousin Lola cry at her debutante ball after wondering out loud why they didn't "apply a weight limit to the posh birds they truss up in white for these things." And he was so arrogant that my repeated rejections over the years had gone down like a tonne of bricks each time, with him even asking me once how long I was going to be a "tedious cock tease" when I knew he was the most logical choice, seeing as he was in his own words, "practically Scottish royalty."

Unfortunately, as loathsome as he was, the man was talented on the rugby field and was part of the squad for the

Scottish team in the World Cup (although Alastair was actually on the bench as a sub for Rory's position). After my disastrous interview with Rory, Alastair had cornered me in the chaos and told me I was better off without "that low-life, Braveheart-wannabe peasant" and asked if I wanted to fuck him instead. I certainly did *not*, and I made that clear by kneeing him in the balls so that he would let go of my arms.

I'd managed to successfully avoid the man over the last five years, and I had no idea what he was doing here now. I doubted Alastair was in the running for any accolades unless there was a Biggest Bellend in Rugby award I didn't know about.

"Ah, my old friend, the lovely Poppy," Alastair drawled as he stopped in front of me, his gaze sweeping me from head to toe, making me feel a little bit sick.

I held back an eye roll and forced myself to smile as I looked up at his arrogant face.

"Mr Roxburg," I said through gritted teeth, holding my microphone so tightly that my knuckles turned white, and shuffling back as far as I could with the banners and Steve behind me.

"Mr Roxburg?" he said, his eyes wide with mock surprise. "Come on, Poppy darling. We've known each other since we were kids. Let's not dwell on formalities."

Before I could dodge away from him, he leaned right in, kissed my cheek and grabbed me around the waist so that my body was flush with his. Then, out of view of the passing celebrities and my cameraman, his other hand came up under my short skirt and grabbed my arse.

I let out a muted scream and pulled away to take a couple of shaky steps back, running into Steve, who had to catch me before I stumbled.

Now, I was usually a fairly good advocate for myself,

but in that moment, I simply didn't know what to do. We were in the middle of the red carpet. Interviewing and flirting with celebrities was my career, and there were hundreds of people around us. I wasn't in any danger, but my heart was still hammering, and my face felt like it was on fire.

Alastair was smiling his shark's smile down at me as he tilted his head to the side.

"Oh, come on now, Poppy. We're all friends here, aren't we? I *know* how friendly you can be."

What was the slimy git talking about? I'd never even kissed him.

He chuckled and lifted a hand up towards my face. I flinched back from him, wobbling on my heels again. When I opened my mouth to call out to Steve, suddenly Alastair's hand was gone.

"What the fuck do you think you're doing, mate?" snapped Rory, who seemed to expend very little effort grabbing Alastair's arm and pulling him back several feet away from me.

Deal Breaker **is available for pre-order now.**

About Domestic Abuse

As a GP I worked with victims of domestic abuse and those in a women's refuge. I'm so sorry if anyone reading this does not feel safe in their own home. You are not alone. There is help available. This should **not** be happening to you.

For UK readers: The Gov.uk website lists all the information and helpline numbers: https://www.gov.uk/guidance/domestic-abuse-how-to-get-help

For US readers: The National Domestic Violence Hotline provides 24/7 support: 1-800-799-7233 or visit thehotline.org

For Canadian readers: Canada's national hotline is available 24/7: 1-866-863-0511 or visit endingviolence-canada.org

For Australian readers: 1800RESPECT provides 24/7 counselling and support: 1800 737 732 or visit 1800respect.org.au

For readers in other countries: Search online for your country's domestic violence hotline to find support services.

Acknowledgments

I will start by thanking the brilliant Jenny Walker, whose expertise and advice about dyslexia were invaluable.

To my fabulous and talented friends, Elodie Hart and Rosa Lucas, who were kind enough to be very early beta readers and put up with an inordinate number of typos! I am so grateful to you both for believing in Law Maker so strongly.

To Jo Edwards, my brilliant editor and dear friend – thank you, thank you, and I do so enjoy our little arguments in the comments (Jo is a stickler for everything making sense, which I am not—yes, Jo, I realize it's still Tuesday and has been for five chapters, whatever!)

My fantastic audiobook narrators, Shane and Zara, thank you for bringing all my characters to life so brilliantly.

Of course, thanks also to all my readers. I never dreamt that people would take the time to read the stories I have thought up in my quirky brain, and I am honoured beyond words. I am eternally grateful to the reviewers who have taken a chance on me – your feedback has made all the difference to the books and is the reason I've been able to make writing not just a passion, but a career.

Susie's Book Badgers - you are wonderful humans, and your support means the world.

Last but not least, thanks to my very own romantic hero. I love you and the boys times infinity.

PHOTO COURTESY OF THE AUTHOR

Susie Tate is a *USA Today* and #1 Amazon bestselling author of addictive, feel-good but heart-wrenching contemporary romance. The real and raw themes that underpin Susie's stories are often inspired by her experiences working as a doctor for the last twenty years, most recently as a GP, during which time she looked after a women's refuge for victims of domestic violence and was child safeguarding lead for her practice. Susie's medical career gives her unique insight and understanding of the social, psychological, and physical issues some of her characters face. One of the most common problems Susie came across among her patients was loneliness. This inspired her to include the theme of found family across all her books. Susie lives in beautiful Dorset, England, with her wonderful husband, three gorgeous boys, and even more wonderful dog. She is addicted to happy-ever-afters, strong coffee, long walks by the sea, and warm blankets, and is never happier than when she has a book in her hand and a dog on her feet.

Join her Facebook group for fun book chats and the latest on all things Susie Tate: Susie's Book Badgers

Visit Susie Tate Online

susietate.com

SusieTateAuthor

SusieTateAuthor

SusieTateAuthor

Susie's Book Badgers

uin Random House LLC
Broadway
Y, 10019

://www.penguinrandomhouse.com
)-733-3000

authorized representative in the EU for product safety and compliance is

uin Random House Ireland
son Chambers, 32 Nassau Street
YH68

://eu-contact.penguin.ie

9798217436149
se ID: 156275337